PUSHOVER

Also by Dianne Pugh

Cold Call
Slow Squeeze
Body Blow
Foolproof

PUSHOVER

Dianne Pugh

HEADLINE
FEATURE

Copyright © 1999 Dianne Pugh

The right of Dianne Pugh to be identified as the Author of
the Work has been asserted by her in accordance with
the Copyright, Designs and Patents Act 1988.

First published in the UK in 1999
by HEADLINE BOOK PUBLISHING

A HEADLINE FEATURE hardback

10 9 8 7 6 5 4 3 2 1

All characters in this publication are fictitious and any
resemblance to real persons, living or dead, is purely coincidental.

British Library Cataloguing in Publication Data

Pugh, Dianne
Pushover
I. Title
813.5'4[F]

ISBN 0 7472 2171 5

Typeset by Avon Dataset Ltd, Bidford-on-Avon, Warks

Printed and bound in Great Britain by
Mackays of Chatham PLC, Chatham, Kent

HEADLINE BOOK PUBLISHING
A division of Hodder Headline PLC
338 Euston Road
London NW1 3BH

Special thanks to Headline editors Anne Williams and Victoria Routledge. I am grateful for your continued enthusiasm and support.

To Nicholas Ellison, agent and ally, for standing with me.

To Ann Escue, Mary Goss, and Dean Schonfeld, good friends who are brave enough to tell me what they really think.

To Gerald Petievich, fellow sojourner, for giving me a different point of view.

To my family, for all the large and small things.

And to Charles Emley, for love and other immeasurable feats.

For Rowland and Pearl Barber
Friends and fans from the start.

Prologue

Iris Thorne opened her eyes and squinted at the bright sun, low in the sky. She touched her lips. 'Did you kiss me?'

Garland Hughes leaned down, bracing his arms against the back of the Adirondack chair and lightly brushed her lips with his. 'Yes.'

She ran her hand through his hair, holding his face close to hers, then let him go, only then noticing that he was dressed to leave. 'What time is it? I must have dozed off.' She yawned and stretched, wriggling her toes in the grass of her backyard.

It was a warm September afternoon. The air was still and the Pacific Ocean, down the cliff and across Pacific Coast Highway, was calm and glassy.

'Time for me to leave. You must have had a nightmare.'

'Why?'

'You were moaning.'

'I was?' The dream, as ethereal as a residue of perfume on a long-closeted garment, had nearly dissipated, but his comment brought it back vividly to her.

She was in Paris. It was night, a light rain was falling, and she was running down the street, wearing only a slip. Her bare feet were unsteady against the slick cobblestones, and the thin slip, damp from the rain, clung to her skin. She either wasn't aware of her state of undress or didn't care, feeling neither cold nor shame.

She stopped in front of *Le Café des Quatre Vents* and peered through its double doors, past the daily menu written on the glass panes in black wax pencil. The café was thick with smoke and crowded with workers having a drink before heading home. She looked this way and that and finally saw him sitting at the back table. She saw Todd Fillinger and was happy.

She pushed down on the tarnished brass door handle, rubbed shiny in spots, and opened the door. A rush of warm air billowed the hem of her garment and her hair. Across the room, Todd stood to meet her. Suddenly, without having walked there, she was next to him. They kissed. No one paid any attention to them. He pressed her against the table, sending a demitasse, spoon, and saucer of sugar cubes clattering to the floor. Still no one noticed them. He raised the slip above her head and pulled it off as she unbuckled his belt, his pants dropping to his ankles. They made love.

1

A ceiling lamp bathed them in a harsh light and images danced behind her closed eyelids.

Iris blushed as she recalled the dream, the heat ascending her neck to her face. She cupped her hand to her forehead, shielding her eyes against the bright setting sun that had migrated into her subconscious. The gesture also hid her eyes from Garland. 'I did have sort of a funny dream.'

He was too rushed to ask about it. For once, Iris was glad instead of irritated. He jerked his arm forward to uncover his watch underneath the cuff of his shirt. 'I have to go. I have to drop off the rental car before my flight.'

She took the hand he offered and let him pull her up from the deep chair. Cinching the belt of her terrycloth bathrobe more tightly around her, she walked hand-in-hand with him across the small yard, taking the steps to the redwood deck and moving past the sliding glass door that led to the bedroom of her 1920s bungalow. 'Garland, I wish you'd change your mind and come with me. It's only for a week.'

'I have a slew of meetings I can't change. Plus, you don't want me to go with you.'

She didn't respond.

His rubber-soled casual shoes squeaked against the polished hardwood floor as they walked down the hallway and into the living room. At the front door of the small house, he turned to face her, running his thumb across the backs of her fingers. 'Iris, I trust you, in Moscow or anywhere. You know I don't mean that. I just have a . . .' He sighed as he carefully chose his words. 'I'm uncomfortable with this. Something about it seems strange.'

'I agree with you.' She stood with one bare foot on top of the other. 'But if you knew Todd Fillinger, it wouldn't seem strange. Turning up in Moscow, sending me a letter out of the blue after not being in touch for years, asking if I want to get in on the ground floor of his latest business venture is very Todd.'

'He was very Todd when you left him standing at the altar in Paris five years ago. How do you know he's not carrying a grudge and this isn't some sort of a setup?'

She angled her mouth with amusement. 'A setup? Pretty elaborate, wouldn't you say? Especially when he asked me to bring a boyfriend, husband or whomever with me.' She slipped her arms around his waist. 'It's a chance to see Todd and clear the air. I'm not proud of how I treated him.'

'I have to admit it made me a little nervous when you told me about it.'

'It was a weird time in my life. It was a stupid, impulsive, nutty thing to do. I've always wanted to tell Todd I was sorry. I wrote him a letter some years ago, but I guess he never got it. And it has nothing to do with us.'

Garland checked his inside jacket pocket for his airline tickets. He was flying home to New York City. 'Maybe he wants to see if he still has a chance with you.'

'*Garland*, I told him about us.' She frowned. 'If you don't want me to go, I won't go.'

'*I'm* not going to be the man who tries to stand in your way.' He rested his hands on top of her shoulders. 'Look, it's a good business move for you. The Russian Federation is an emerging market. It couldn't hurt politically at your firm to have first-hand knowledge of the region.' He gently shook her shoulders. 'But *please* be careful.'

'I've lived in Los Angeles my entire life. How much worse could Moscow be?'

'Don't go anywhere alone—'

'I won't.'

'And try to blend in. Don't look like an American.'

She sniggered. 'Yeah, right.'

'I'm just a phone call and an airplane flight away.'

They kissed. He opened the door and picked up his suitcase. 'I've had enough of this bicoastal romance. We need to talk about a more permanent arrangement.'

'I'll line up some negotiators,' she joked.

They kissed again.

'But I'm not living year-round anyplace where snow falls from the sky.'

'She's stated her opening position. Love you.'

'Love you, too.'

He gathered his belongings and she followed him out the door, standing on her front lawn and waving until his car disappeared around the curve at the bottom of Casa Marina Drive. She wrapped her arms around herself and looked at the empty street that matched the hollowness she felt inside. From her pocket, she took Todd Fillinger's letter. Tucked inside the envelope was the snapshot he'd sent of her and him in front of *Le Café des Quatre Vents*. Through the windows, she could glimpse the corner table from her dream.

Chapter 1

When Iris awoke after the jet engines had finally lulled her into a fitful sleep, her first thought was that she was thirsty. Her next was, *What the hell am I doing*? But it was too late to turn back.

Her tendency to act first and think second had usually served her well. If she'd thought too hard about some of the steps she'd taken in her life, she'd probably have talked herself out of them. Her blue collar background and dicey family life provided little guidance for navigating the hard-scrabble world of high finance where she'd desperately wanted to be a player. Without a mentor's firm hand to guide her, she'd had to rely on her gut instincts.

Now, as the jet flew through heavy clouds as it made its descent to Sheremetevo International Airport over a landscape of forests broken by farmland and towns, that little internal voice was coming through loud and clear. Swept away by the promise of adventure, she'd ignored it until now. *Coming to Moscow was a bad idea, Iris*, it chided.

She defiantly shook her head and whispered aloud, 'It's going to be great.' Since she'd already broken her first rule about following her instincts, she'd follow her second: never look back.

Sheremetevo Airport was ragged around the edges and too small for the traffic that passed through it. Iris waited in a long line to retrieve her luggage from a scant number of carousels then stood in another line queuing to too few passport control kiosks.

The official there wore the same stern, skeptical expression that she'd seen at ports of entry from Los Angeles to the Virgin Islands. Iris couldn't take her eyes off this one though – he bore an uncanny resemblance to a young Jack Nicholson. He scowled at her papers, which she knew were in order, and barked a few questions at her in broken English. She responded with a silly smile on her lips, which didn't improve his demeanor, but she was unable to keep from picturing him wearing Ray Ban Wayfarers. He stamped her passport and slid it across the counter.

She entered the crowded terminal, pulling her wheeled suitcase and searching for Todd Fillinger. People surged around her with no regard for personal space. She was accustomed to the relative standoffish attitude of Los Angelenos, except when driving, of course. To have strangers so close always made her feel wooden and suspicious, adding to her distress when she didn't immediately see Todd.

The crowd was comprised of the same cultural cross-section that passes through any major airport, but here she'd seen more fur coats in ten minutes than she'd see in twenty years in LA. Everyone seemed pallid, but that's how Iris saw most of the rest of the world. Living a lifetime in LA had permanently skewed her perceptions. There was one constant – the teenagers here also wore urban gangsta outfits of grossly oversized clothing and backward baseball caps.

She held her suitcase close and clutched more tightly the strap of her shoulder bag as she pressed through the crowd, suppressing a wave of panic. She exhaled in relief when she saw an outstretched hand above the sea of heads and glimpsed Todd's face behind it. Pushing and shoving with the best of them, she finally reached him.

Todd squeezed her in a bear hug that lifted her feet off the ground.

'Hi, you!' she exclaimed.

'You're here!' he enthused.

'Yes!' was the only response that came to her mind.

He put his hands on her shoulders, held her at arm's length, and looked her over. She was vividly reminded of why she'd fallen in love with him.

'You look great,' he said.

'You don't look too shabby yourself.'

He took the pull-handle of her suitcase and put his other arm around her waist. She put hers around his in a long-unused gesture that seemed completely natural.

'You grew a beard,' she said.

'It's cold in Russia.' He grinned and scratched his cheek. 'I need all the fur I can get.'

'I like it. I never imagined you with a beard.'

'You look great. Just like I imagined you.' He hugged her tighter.

She felt his ribs through his cashmere sweater. 'You've lost weight.' She ran her fingers down his side. 'You're a lot thinner than you were in Paris.'

'Been busy.'

'Look!' Iris touched a ring that he wore on his left pinky finger. 'My class ring. You're still wearing it.'

He self-consciously closed his fist. 'I told you I'd never take it off.'

Iris gleaned the unspoken message: *And I follow through on my promises.* She let the topic drop.

They walked through the concourse past the usual conglomeration of airport concessions. Todd pushed open the outside door and Iris stepped outside into a chilly, gray day.

'Brrrr,' she said.

He helped her put on her coat. 'It's been in the fifties. We had a little rain, but it's supposed to have passed through.'

'It's been in the nineties in LA. Typical hot and dry Indian summer.'

6

'I haven't been in LA in . . . probably fifteen years. How is it?'

'Always changing and always the same.'

Walking again, they passed tour directors counting heads and herding their charges on to buses, businessmen filing into a stream of waiting taxis, and college students with backpacks studying maps.

'Everything looks fairly normal so far,' Iris commented. 'If you go by what's on the news, Russia's going to pieces.'

'There's definitely instability, but she's gonna make it. There's still plenty of money to be made.'

A slender man in jeans and a black leather jacket who had been leaning against a large Mercedes sedan moved toward them, a lit cigarette between his fingers.

'There's Sasha,' Todd explained. 'My driver.'

With his buzz cut hair and fresh complexion, Sasha looked like a boy scout, which made the handgun that Iris spotted stuck in his waistband at the small of his back even more discordant.

He muttered, 'Hello. Welcome to Moscow,' and shook Iris's hand, then stuck the cigarette between his lips to better fumble with the release on the suitcase handle.

Seeing Iris's eyes widen at the sight of the gun, Todd explained, 'He's also my bodyguard.'

'Part of doing business in Moscow?'

He smiled wryly as if she'd guessed correctly.

While Sasha stowed Iris's coat and suitcase in the trunk, Todd held the Mercedes' rear door for her. Walking around to the opposite side, he reached in to remove a tan camelhair coat from the back seat, then climbed in after her.

'We have about a half hour ride to the city. You hungry?'

'Starving.'

He smiled fondly at her. 'That's my Iris. I thought I'd take you to a little bistro I know for a snack. For dinner, we'll get dressed up and do the town.'

'Sounds great.' Iris ran her hand across the black leather seat. 'Nice steel.'

'Like I wrote in my letter, Moscow has been very good to me.'

Iris was glad to see Sasha toss his cigarette on the ground after one last, long drag. He climbed into the driver's seat with a squeal of leather on leather. He turned the key in the ignition and unnecessarily gunned the car's big engine.

'Mercedes six hundred,' Iris observed. 'The car of choice for Moscow's wealthy businessmen and mobsters. I read that Mercedes six hundreds are such frequent targets of car bombings, mothers warn their children not to play around them.'

Todd laughed. 'If you're afraid of Moscow, why did you come?'

She smiled. 'It's more a fascination with the sensational.'

7

'So why *did* you come?'

'To look at investing in your art galleries, primarily for myself but also for my clients.'

'Come on, Iris.' He cocked his head at her. 'I want you to invest in my business, but I'm surprised you came halfway around the world just for that.'

She looked at him coyly. 'What other reason could there be?'

'From what you said on the phone, it sounds like things between you and your boyfriend are getting serious.'

'Yeah. So?'

'So maybe you came for one last fling with your favorite bad boy. Your rogue across the waters.' He smiled crookedly and drew his fingertips across the back of her hand. The atmosphere grew prickly. 'We hit that clear, singing high note, didn't we?'

She blushed, moved her hand to her lap, and tried to make light of it. 'That's what you thought, huh? Sorry to disappoint you, but . . . No dice.'

He crossed his arms over his chest and sighed. 'Well, like my sister used to say, live in hope and die in despair.'

She had to grin. 'Isn't just being friends OK?'

'Oh *sure*. I *love* being friends,' he replied sarcastically.

She pointedly glowered at him.

'Then my guess is you came to see if you still have feelings for me before you wander into the sunset with whatsisname . . . Herb, Beowulf . . .'

'*Garland*,' she corrected him, laughing.

'Garland. How could I forget?'

She jabbed him with her index finger. 'You think you know all about me, don't you?'

'Sure.'

'You're still a smug son of a bitch.'

He slid his arm around her waist and pulled her close. 'That's what you love most about me.'

As his eyes traveled over her face, she looked at his thick, dark brown hair, expressive lips, and deeply set sable eyes that gleamed with devilishness. In the cool light provided by time and distance, the depth of her attraction to him had come to seem irrational. Now, she had to agree – there was nothing rational about it. She removed his arm and slid to the opposite side of the car. 'Look, Todd, I hope I didn't say anything to mislead you. I'm in love with Garland. But I am happy to see you again.'

'You didn't. Just thought I'd try. All fooling around aside, I'm sincerely glad you've found someone.' He looked at her affectionately. 'However, I do have a brilliant investment opportunity for you.'

'I *hope* so. How else am I going to deduct this trip on my taxes?'

He chuckled and she looked out the window. The broad highway cut a path through a landscape of dry fields and low forests broken by clusters of boxy, run-down buildings.

'So tell me about your business,' she said.

His eyes were bright with enthusiasm. 'Fillinger and Lazare, dealers in fine art. I've known Enrico Lazare for years. Actually, he was around when we were in Paris, but I don't think you ever met him.'

Iris replayed the name in her mind and shook her head.

'He's this crazy Corsican, always wheeling and dealing. Anyway, in his travels, he started picking up pieces of art. In my travels, I came across people who wanted to buy art. A year ago, I came to Moscow on a whim and discovered that the *novie bogatie*, the new rich, have an insatiable appetite for Western art to decorate their homes . . .'

Two men on a motorcycle sped past the Mercedes, then slowed again until they were level with it.

A look of concern flitted across Todd's face. 'And offices.' He touched the driver's shoulder; the man nodded once in response and floored the Mercedes, quickly leaving the motorcycle behind.

'The *novie bogatie* are very big on keeping up with the Godunovs . . .' Todd glanced out the back window. He relaxed only when the motorcycle was a dot in the distance. 'The logical next step is to open a chain of mid-priced galleries like you see in some of the better shopping malls in the US. It's a completely untapped market. Iris, whoever gets in on the ground floor will make a ton of money.'

'I'm impressed by this entrepreneurial side of you that I've never seen before.'

'Who would have thought that a small-time freelance photographer would become one of Moscow's top art dealers?' Confidentially, he leaned closer to her. 'Lazare and I are about to close our biggest deal yet on a very rare piece of art. Worth megabucks.'

'Really?'

'It'll set me up big time.' He jerked his chin toward the window. 'We're entering the city limits. That wooded area is called the Sparrow Hills and that skyscraper is Moscow State University. I'll show you around tomorrow.'

The traffic and buildings grew denser the farther they drove into the city. Clutches of people, both young and old, were selling vegetables, bread, vodka, and cigarettes from impromptu shops set up on blankets on the sidewalks.

'Sasha, go to Mziuri.' Todd glanced at a gold, antique watch that had a large, curved face.

Iris admired it. 'Nice watch.'

'Thanks.'

'Are you doing any photography?'

'A lot, actually. Built up a good business here. Moscow's wealthy like to do everything Western-style, so they're into the lavish weddings, big birthday parties for kids, and so on. I've hired a couple of guys to do videos. It's growing. I've also done a little magazine work. Life is good.'

9

'I'm happy for you, Todd.'

'You haven't done too poorly yourself. That job that you left Paris to start has turned out OK.'

'I'm branch manager now, running the whole office. Hard to believe I only started working for McKinney Alitzer five years ago.'

'A lot can happen in five years.'

'Indeed.'

Sasha wove the big car through the busy streets with little regard for lane markings. Iris had no idea where they were going, but sensed the driver was forced to take a circuitous route to avoid huge sink holes, building construction, and streets closed for no apparent reason. The air rang with the din from car horns and power drills. Shabby Soviet-era gray-block structures stood next to McDonalds and Pizza Huts. Aging babushkas and gangs of children panhandled near exclusive members-only clubs. Gold leaf was everywhere.

Sasha stopped the car in front of an elegant but faded building where laborers were working to melt grime from the façade. He cut the engine and started to open the car door when Todd touched his shoulder and said, 'Wait.' They both watched as two men dressed in dark suits walked toward them on the sidewalk.

Sasha turned his head slightly and raised an eyebrow at Todd, then watched the men ascend the steps and enter the building.

'Let's go to the King's Head,' Todd said to Sasha who sped away from the curb. 'You mind, Iris? It's a British-style pub, few Russians go there. You'll have ample opportunity to sample the real Moscow before you go home.' His expression suddenly became bitter. 'You'll be gagging on it.'

'Todd, what's up?' Iris asked. 'Is somebody after you?'

He pursed his lips and hesitated, then reluctantly admitted, 'Yeah. I got cross-wise with the Russian Mafia.' He shook his head. 'Every time Lazare and I did a deal, a henchman for the local boss came calling, wanting a cut. I finally refused to pay. It wasn't too smart, but I just got fed up.'

Iris glanced at Sasha. 'At least you've hired protection.'

'It's something, but I can't fool myself. If they want you, they'll get you.'

'What are you going to do?'

'Go about my business,' he replied, a bit cavalierly in Iris's view.

They got out of the car in front of a plain building and descended a set of stairs that led to a basement entrance. The smoke-filled pub was dark, loud, and lively, full of Brits and Americans. Several dartboards were seeing heavy use. Iris and Todd sat at a corner table and ordered Cornish pasties, fish and chips, and draft Guinness.

Todd laughed at Iris's grave expression. 'Come on. I've been in worse fixes. If it gets too hot, I'll just leave. Won't be the first time I've blown a town.' Changing the subject, too quickly, he asked, 'Tell me about this boyfriend, Garland.'

10

'He's a partner in a small venture capital firm. Been married before, has two kids that are almost grown, and he lives in New York.' Speaking of Garland made Iris realize how much she already missed him.

'New York? She likes distance between her and her men.'

She didn't respond to his all too accurate observation. He seemed to enjoy skewering her.

'Does he know about us?' Todd asked. 'I mean our history?'

'More or less.'

'I'm surprised he let you come here by yourself.'

'He would have joined me, but he had meetings he couldn't change. I don't mind. I wanted to see you alone.'

'You do?' He was glib. 'A few minutes ago, you firmly reminded me that we're just friends.'

'We are. But you're right about what you said earlier. I didn't come here only for business. You're a loose end in my life, the source of many what ifs, regrets, and above all, shame. I want closure on our relationship.'

'Ahh, *closure*. Psychobabble from a genuine Californian.' He surveyed the crowd and drummed his fingers on the table.

'Todd, I came to apologize to you.'

When he looked at her again, he was smiling but it seemed forced. 'Iris, what's past is past. No hard feelings. Closure has been achieved.' His rigid posture belied his flippant comment. He quickly tipped back the glass of beer, leaving a foamy residue on his moustache, which he blotted with a square paper cocktail napkin. He carefully smoothed the napkin against the table top, folded a narrow pleat down one side then folded another next to it.

Iris took a breath, steeling herself, determined to say what she had traveled here to say. 'I'm sorry I ran out on you.' She paused and he didn't look up, absorbed in folding the napkin. She went on, 'The three months we spent together in Paris, they . . .' She blinked at the memory, gazing at the smoke-filled room as if it were a window into the past. 'I don't have a good reason for why I left. All I can say is that it was too intense, too unreal. It seemed to be something that couldn't go on, that was bound to self-destruct.'

He methodically folded pleat after pleat into the napkin, creasing each one with his thumbnail. She continued unreeling her limp explanation, knowing it didn't make any sense as soon as the words hit the air. She kept putting them out there anyway.

'I could have handled it much differently. Should have.'

The napkin now completely folded, he released it on the table, the accordion folds bursting open. He closed it again, held the folds together at one end, letting the other end open in a fan. Now tired of it, he flicked the napkin across the table where it rested against the glass salt and pepper shakers.

11

She opened her hands toward him in a gesture of supplication. 'I'm sorry.'

When he didn't respond, she went on. 'A few weeks after I left, I tried to explain in a letter. Did you get it?'

He met her eyes. 'No.'

'That's odd. I sent it to your Paris apartment. When it came back, I sent it to your sister's house in Bakersfield.'

'I didn't get it.' He smiled stiffly. 'Iris, like I already said, no need to explain. If I was still angry with you, I wouldn't have invited you here, would I? Let's just enjoy the next few days and live for the moment. That is my specialty, you know.' He winked at her.

A waitress brought their food and Iris dug in, relieved to have voiced the regret that she'd held in for five years. She couldn't predict Todd's response. He'd been a little strange, but she thought it had turned out fine.

Iris took her time dressing for dinner in the room Todd had reserved for her at the elegant, Art Nouveau Metropolis Hotel. The ceiling was twelve feet high and decorated with elaborately carved molding brushed with gold paint. A crystal-and-brass chandelier hung from the center. Thickly looped wall-to-wall carpeting covered the floor. The furniture was heavy, made of dark wood, upholstered in rich fabric. Carved wood trim outlined in gold divided the walls into panels. It was refined and old-world, a style, Iris recalled, that Todd appreciated.

She gave Garland a call, surprised at the speed of the connection. Sipping Russian champagne and nibbling crackers thickly spread with caviar, she told him the events of her day, leaving out Todd's situation with the Russian Mafia, not wanting to give him anything more to worry about.

'I'm glad I finally smoothed things over with Todd.'

'I'm glad you're glad.'

'You wish I'd come home.'

'Well, as a matter of fact, I do.'

'I changed my flight. I'll be home Thursday instead of Saturday.'

'Iris, that's only three nights in Moscow. Don't change your plans on my account.'

'It's plenty of time to have a look at what Todd has in mind for these art galleries and to see some of the sights. It's a little weird here.'

'Is it Todd? Is he treating you all right?'

'No, he's great.'

'How do you mean, weird?'

She back-pedaled. 'I just mean . . . I'd rather be here with you.'

'Have a good time, sweets. Make the most of it.'

They said their goodbyes. She threw her coat over her arm and grabbed her unusually light purse. She'd stored her money, passport, and wallet in the hotel safe, carrying only a lipstick, California driver's license, two credit cards, one hundred dollars in small bills, and enough roubles for any small expenses.

At the end of the hallway, she gave her room key to the *dezhurnaya*, a sort of concierge stationed on each floor of the hotel. She had long, dark hair and wore a pink dress that reminded Iris of a waitress in a US diner. But this girl was very tall and had the bone structure of a fashion model.

Iris descended in the highly polished wood-paneled elevator to the lobby where she was to meet Todd in the bar. The elevator stopped several times until it was full of businessmen and tourists of many nationalities.

She walked through the plush lobby, attracting stares from both men and women. She at first thought the stares were because she looked fetching in her black cocktail dress, which she did, but then realized the larger reason – she was a woman alone. She pulled herself taller and kept walking.

Entering the bar through beveled glass and brass doors, she looked for Todd and didn't see him. She went to a corner table by a window and slid into a banquette.

A waiter wearing a short, red jacket and a stiff apron asked her something in Russian.

She assumed he wanted to know what she'd like to drink. 'Champagne,' she said, hoping it was part of the international language. She'd liked the Russian champagne she'd had in her room.

Just then, Todd breezed into the bar, looking handsome in a dark suit and tie, his tan camelhair overcoat draped rakishly over his shoulders. 'Sorry I'm late, Iris.' He didn't move to sit down.

'You're not late. I barely got here myself.'

'And I have to leave again. I need to make a quick phone call.' He shrugged apologetically. 'It never ends.'

'Take your time. I'm not on a schedule.'

'I'll be ten minutes, then I'll be yours for the entire evening.' He smiled and turned, the hem of his coat swirling out, and left the bar.

Several minutes later, the waiter brought Iris's champagne. She sipped it appreciatively and entertained herself by eavesdropping on a group of American tourists at a nearby table.

Suddenly, there was a flurry of popping noises outside the hotel. The din in the bar decreased slightly as the patrons cast worried glances at one another. Someone started screaming.

Iris turned to look out the window and saw a crowd gathering on the hotel's front steps. Panic shot through her when she spied a tan overcoat draped haphazardly there. She kneeled on the banquette and pressed both hands against the glass. A man with a beard was crumpled next to the coat.

'Todd!' she screamed. She clambered from behind the table, knocking over the glass of champagne and forgetting about her purse and coat. Whimpering, she pushed through the people gathering in the lobby and made her way out the front door. She clasped both hands over her mouth at the sight of Todd sprawled across the hotel's front steps, his blood running down the worn marble.

The crowd maintained a safe distance from the fallen man, no one offering assistance.

'Oh my God!' Iris rushed to kneel next to him. His body was riddled with bullets, his face covered in blood. His labored breathing made small bubbles in the blood trailing from his lips. She took his hand and tried to remain calm.

'It's going to be okay, Todd. Hang on.' She lost her composure and started to sob. 'Hang on, Todd,' she cried. Through her tears, she saw his eyes flutter. He exhaled a long breath. His chest didn't rise to take another.

'Todd!' She watched and waited, praying for him to breathe. He didn't. She laid his hand, which still bore her class ring, against his chest and sat back on her heels, keening. She became aware of someone behind her pulling her arm. She jerked away. Then strong hands slid underneath her armpits and raised her to her feet.

'Wait a second!' She turned to see two men in blue–gray uniforms with red lapels and red bands around their hats.

One of them said to her, '*Edyomtye samnoy.*'

She tried to struggle from their grasp. 'I don't understand. I don't speak Russian.'

They began pulling her away from the scene.

'Wait!' she protested, dragging her heels and thrashing back and forth. 'Where are you taking me? My purse—'

They lifted her off the ground and carried her into a waiting Jeep.

Chapter 2

'For the third time, I met Todd Fillinger five years ago in Paris.' Iris massaged her temples. 'I was between jobs and took an extended vacation in Europe. We were friends. I came home to Los Angeles and we lost touch until last month.'

'Why were you between jobs?' Detective Anatoly Davidovsky sat behind a large desk with a fake teak finish that was peeling at the corners. A black rotary telephone was on the corner. Next to it was an ashtray of gold pressed glass that was overflowing with cigarette butts.

A tall, scrawny man leaning against a fingerprint-smudged metal filing cabinet in the corner pressed a fresh butt out in the ashtray. From his conversation with Davidovsky, Iris figured out that his name was Dmitri. He was wearing the blue-gray wool pants of a *Militsiya* uniform and a black turtleneck sweater. Iris hadn't been introduced to him and suspected his knowledge of English was scant by the way he cocked his ear toward her and frowned, nodding and appearing pleased when he caught a scrap of what she was saying.

'I'd received my Master's degree in Business Administration that June. In September, I was starting the broker training program at the firm where I'd accepted a position. I quit my job teaching grade school a few months early so I could travel.'

Davidovsky leaned back in a rickety wooden desk chair. His thinning dark hair was rumpled on top. A double chin obscured his short, thick neck above his barrel chest. Behind him, rain pattered against a dirty window over which lime-green curtains of fraying nylon were pulled closed, but didn't meet in the center. 'Where did you travel in Europe?' His accented English was perfect.

'I mostly stayed in Paris. I fell in love with it.'

'And with Todd Fillinger,' Davidovsky added.

Iris sighed and let her eyes roll toward the ceiling. She was sitting in a straight-back, armless wooden chair. 'I don't see the point of this interrogation. I told you Todd was afraid of the Russian Mafia. He said they were demanding protection money from him. Find Todd's bodyguard, this Sasha. He'll tell you.'

Davidovsky sniffed and pressed his thin lips together. 'You said you hadn't heard from Fillinger for five years. Why did you come all the way

15

to Moscow to see this man after such a long time?'

'He'd seen an interview with me in the *Wall Street Journal* and found out I'm an investment counselor. He needed investment capital to start a chain of art galleries in Moscow. I had my hands on people looking for places to invest their money. He contacted me. It happens every day.'

'People don't travel so far for such a thing.'

'Some people do.'

'Tell me again about this big art deal and Enrico Lazare.'

Iris pounded her knee with her clenched fist. 'Why do you persist in asking me these same questions over and over? The Russian Mafia wanted protection money from Todd. Why don't you go after them? Or can't you? I heard the Moscow police are in their back pocket.' She immediately regretted the comment. It was tough talk coming from a woman wearing a skimpy cocktail dress who had no money, identification, or even a coat to cover her bare arms, having left everything in the hotel bar when she ran out to investigate the shooting.

Davidovsky looked at her evenly, his eyes obscured behind his fleshy lids. 'Miss Thorne, I had not heard of Todd Fillinger before today and I resent your suggestion. If Fillinger was afraid of the Mafia, he was running with the wrong crowd. You say he was the middleman in some art deals. In Russia it can be dangerous to be a middleman.'

Iris abruptly stood in a show of bravado. 'I've had enough. I'm an American citizen. You can't hold me like this for no reason. I demand that you call the American Embassy. I'm hungry, I'm cold, and I have to go to the bathroom.'

Davidovsky gave Iris a long, steady look, his face expressionless as if he were trying to decide if she were lying, or telling the truth but holding something back. Or maybe he was just trying to make her uncomfortable.

So much had happened so quickly, Iris hadn't had time to feel scared. It now occurred to her that the situation was grave. She met Davidovsky's stare, engaging him in his game of chicken. Suddenly she felt shaky, light-headed and sick to her stomach. Part of it was caused by lack of food. Still meeting the detective's eyes behind his drooping lids, she shivered and rubbed her hands up and down her bare arms. She thought of Garland. Since she'd arrived at the police station, she hadn't felt like crying until then. The tears welled up and she swallowed hard to keep them down. She managed it, but not, she realized, before Davidovsky had seen her distress. She looked at the dingy, buckled linoleum floor, regained her composure, and faced Davidovsky again. 'I demand to speak to the American Embassy.'

Davidovsky, still keeping an eye on her, spoke to Dmitri in Russian. They shot unnerving glances at her as they spoke.

'Miss Thorne,' Davidovsky leaned back in his chair and folded his hands across his belly. 'Please sit down. The more cooperative you are in answering our questions, the sooner you can leave.'

Iris dropped back into the chair, tugging on the hem of her dress.

There was a quick knock on the door and then it opened. A diminutive man wearing a well-cut navy blue suit and a tidy fringe of hair around his shiny, bald pate entered the room. He had a neat, narrow face with sharply angled features, like a fox. He nodded without speaking to Davidovsky who nodded back a bit stiffly. He didn't seem happy to see the visitor.

After a small bow to Iris, the man walked across the room, pulled a wooden chair away from the wall, sat, and casually crossed his legs. Iris noticed that the starched cuff of his white shirt bore a monogram stitched in navy blue. He was wearing a heavy gold identification bracelet on his left wrist and an expensive-looking gold watch on his right.

Davidovsky began speaking to the visitor at length, apparently updating him on what had transpired so far. The man alternately knitted then raised his eyebrows as he listened, occasionally looking at Iris with a pleasant expression that revealed little. His finely detailed lips had a natural lift at the edges, as did his eyebrows, making him appear as if he was smiling even in repose.

While Davidovsky was talking, the man pulled a gold cigarette case and a gold lighter from his jacket pocket. He clicked open the case and held it toward Iris who shook her head, then took one and lit it.

The detective grimaced as he spoke, as if he were delivering bad news. He lifted his hands with resignation. It was clear to Iris that he was being deferential to the other man.

The man patiently and attentively listened until Davidovsky had finished, after which he directed a few questions in Russian to the detective who passed them on to Iris.

'This big art deal that your friend Fillinger talked to you about, this art was owned by someone in Moscow?'

'I don't know.'

'Fillinger must have spoken to you of the Club Ukrainiya.'

'No.'

Davidovsky made a comment to the small man who said something back.

'But he told you of Nikolai Kosyakov?' Davidovsky asked Iris.

'No.'

Davidovsky looked at the man, apparently seeking guidance.

Iris volunteered, 'You should find Todd's partner, Enrico Lazare. He could tell you about the art deal.'

The man eyed Iris skeptically and in a way that made her very uncomfortable, in spite of his apparent cheerfulness. She tugged on the hem of her dress again then tightly crossed her arms over her chest, hunching against the chill in the room.

He rose to tap ash into the overflowing glass ashtray on the desk. He slowly sat back down, looked at Iris with green-black eyes, then surprised

17

her when he said in perfect and careful English, 'I find that hard to believe, Miss Thorne.'

'Well, believe it. Believe everything I've told you. I have nothing to hide. Now it's time for you to take me back to my hotel.' She rose and took a step toward the door.

Dmitri quickly moved from the filing cabinet to block it.

Iris didn't sit back down, but stood in the center of the room. She put her hands on her hips.

The fox-faced man openly studied Iris's legs. 'You and Todd Fillinger were lovers.'

Iris boldly leaned toward him. 'We were *friends*. Furthermore, I don't see what my relationship with Todd has to do with anything.'

He reached inside his jacket and pulled out an envelope from which he took several sheets of folded stationery and what appeared to be a photograph. From another pocket he produced a pair of wire-rimmed half-glasses which he placed on his nose. As he scanned the pages, the edges of his lips curled even more. 'Paris. No finer place to fall in love. Wouldn't you agree?'

In horror, Iris realized he was reading the letter Todd had sent her. She took a step toward him. 'That's my letter! It was in my hotel room.'

Ignoring her, he got up and handed the letter to Davidovsky.

Davidovsky smiled as he looked at the photograph of Iris and Todd in front of *Le Café des Quatre Vents*. 'You were lovers after all.'

'Yes, and so what?'

The small man again sat and fastidiously crossed his legs. Her rancor seemed to amuse him. He drew on his cigarette and waved it in Iris's direction. 'Miss Thorne, you would be more comfortable sitting down, wouldn't you agree?'

Scowling, Iris returned to the hard chair.

Davidovsky's questions became more pointed. 'Why are you in Moscow, Miss Thorne? You expect us to believe you came all this way to investigate investing in art galleries with a man you say you haven't had any contact with for five years?'

'Yes, I do.'

The door suddenly opened and a tall, slender man with a long face and lank blond hair came in. He didn't wait to be acknowledged. 'I'm Dean Palmer, consular officer with the US Embassy.'

Iris tipped her head back on her shoulders and murmured, 'Thank God.'

'You took Ms Thorne into custody three hours ago. I'm sure she's told you everything she knows about Todd Fillinger's murder.'

'Actually, we were just starting to make progress,' Davidovsky said.

'Witnesses saw two men on motorcycles shoot at Fillinger with automatic weapons then flee the scene,' Palmer said. 'This looks like an ordinary, mob-style hit. I know for a fact that Mr Fillinger was having a

18

dispute with the local mob and that they had threatened his life. Obviously, Ms Thorne had nothing to do with the crime. Ms Thorne is an American citizen. Under the authority of the US Ambassador, I'm escorting her to her hotel.'

Davidovsky stood behind his desk. He was a tall, broad man. 'Mr Palmer, I don't care who you are. My interrogation of Miss Thorne is not complete.'

The balding man walked over to Davidovsky, spoke quietly into his ear and handed him a US passport. Iris exchanged a bewildered look with Palmer.

Davidovsky held up the passport. 'Until we complete our investigation, I must request that Miss Thorne remain in Moscow. We will retain her passport to ensure that she does.'

Iris gaped at him while Palmer voiced his outrage. 'You can't do that! You have no authority.'

Davidovsky opened the top drawer of his desk and tossed the passport inside. 'We will be in touch.'

Iris glared at the balding man. He met her eyes. He looked pleased.

Palmer took Iris's arm and pulled her into a corridor full of crime victims standing in long lines. At too few desks at the front, sunken-cheeked Militsiya officers were making out reports in longhand on green forms.

Outside the aging police station, Palmer told Iris, 'Let's go one street over. We'll have a better chance of getting a cab there. We'll probably end up walking to your hotel. Cabs aren't usually out this late. The drivers are afraid of being robbed.'

They walked through the quiet streets which were wet from rain. Iris was surprised that a city which seemed defined by noise and activity during the day had transformed into something so silent at night.

Palmer shook his head. 'I can't believe they confiscated your passport.'

'You've never seen that happen before?' Iris rubbed her hands up and down her arms. Her teeth were chattering.

'No.' He took off his sports jacket and handed it to her. 'I'll talk it over with the Ambassador first thing tomorrow.' He looked at his watch. 'It *is* tomorrow.'

Iris gratefully slipped her arms into the jacket. 'Thanks. Who was that bald man?'

Palmer nervously rubbed his hands together as they walked. 'I don't know.'

'He asked me about Nikolai Kosyakov and the Club Ukrainiya.'

He stopped walking and frowned at her. 'He did?'

'Who's Kosyakov?'

He began walking again. 'Kosyakov is said to be the richest man in Russia. He bought this run-down mansion and turned it into Moscow's first private club, the Club Ukrainiya. Everyone who's anyone in the city belongs to it. All men, of course.'

19

'Is Kosyakov Mafia-connected?'

'What Russian businessman who got rich overnight isn't?'

'Maybe he's the one Todd was afraid of.'

'Could be.'

'Did you know Todd?' Iris stepped lightly in her strappy high heels. The uneven and broken asphalt, easily felt through the shoes' thin soles, made her feet ache.

'A little. We frequented some of the same places. I'd heard that he'd stood up to the Mafia. They're going to be this city's downfall, if you ask me. Todd had guts. He's a hero in my book.'

'Davidovsky and that bald guy were interested in this art deal Todd was into,' Iris said. 'I wonder why. I wish I could talk to Todd's business partner, Enrico Lazare. Do you know him?'

'I've heard of him, but never met him.' Palmer saw a taxi, a beat-up Lada, with its roof light illuminated. 'Finally, a bit of luck.' He ran into the street, almost in the taxi's path, and waved his arms. He directed the driver to the Metropolis Hotel.

'I don't have any cash on me,' Iris apologized.

'Don't worry about it.'

Now that she was safely on her way back to the hotel, she began to weep. 'I'm sorry. I just—'

Palmer put his arm round her shoulders. 'You don't need to explain. You've held up remarkably well, considering everything that's happened. You held your own under a three-hour investigation by the Russian police.'

'Yeah, wearing nothing but a cocktail dress and do-me heels.'

They both laughed. He fished a handkerchief from the rear pocket of his gray slacks.

Iris dabbed her eyes with it. 'I don't know what I'd've done if you hadn't shown up.'

Palmer patted her arm. 'Don't mention it.'

The taxi pulled up in front of the Metropolis Hotel. A uniformed doorman sleepily rose from where he had been sitting at a desk just inside the glass doors.

'So what now?' Iris asked Palmer.

'We need to get your passport back and get you on a plane to Los Angeles.'

'Do you think there will be any problems?'

'Well, there usually are. Let's hope for the best.'

Iris shook Palmer's hand and stepped from the cab. The taxi waited until she walked into the hotel, which she did quickly, cutting a wide circle round Todd Fillinger's blood.

20

Chapter 3

Iris opened her eyes to darkness and was disoriented. After a moment, she remembered where she was and, with a sick feeling, what had happened. Heavy shutters and thick drapes across the windows prevented her from seeing whether it was day or night. The bedclothes were only slightly disturbed. She reached out her arm, which felt thick and heavy, and turned the digital clock on the nightstand to see the face. It took her a moment to realize that it wasn't 1:00 in the morning, shortly after she'd gone to bed, but 1:00 in the afternoon.

She stumbled to the windows, pulled the cord to open the drapes, and cranked open the rolling metal shutters until the windows were half revealed, letting in gray light from what appeared to be a dismal day. She staggered back to the bed, sat on the edge, held her head in her hands, and tried to rub away the dense feeling from her eyes. When she became more fully awake, she tried to blot out the memory of Todd lying on the hotel's marble steps, covered with blood. It wouldn't budge.

Hot tears sprang into her eyes and she sobbed, her shoulders heaving. She cried for Todd and for herself. The moment quickly passed, emotion overwhelmed by reality, in the face of which her tears seemed useless. All that was left was a hollow feeling in the pit of her stomach.

She toddled to the brilliantly white-tiled bathroom, turned the shiny silver spigots, splashed water on her face, then took the hotel's thick terrycloth robe from the hook behind the door and put it on.

She opened the doors of a tall armoire, revealing the square, black eye of a Japanese-made television. On top was the remote control. She clicked on the power, finding comfort in this universal technology. Mindlessly surfing the handful of channels, she clicked past an ordinary line-up of news, cartoons, and old movies. Then she was startled to see the familiar, overly made-up faces and big hair of *Simply Maria*, a Mexican soap opera she'd watched at home. There, her scant Spanish had allowed her to follow the plot loosely but here the dialogue had been dubbed into Russian.

She clicked the volume down but left the show on and perused the English-language section of the hotel guide. She was starving. As she suspected, breakfast was no longer being served. Even worse, the hotel did not offer room service.

She let out a long moan.

21

In the walk-in closet, she located her carry-on bag, which had been moved from where she'd originally stashed it. Everything had been slightly rearranged. The thought of the dapper balding man from the police station and his thick-fingered henchmen sifting through her belongings gave her the creeps. From a zippered pocket, she took the cheese and crackers airline snack she'd saved and hungrily gobbled it down. She found a plastic liter bottle that she'd filled with tap water before she'd left and savored the taste of home.

Still bleary-eyed, she sat on a brocade chair by the window and picked up the telephone from the round table next to the chair. She punched the number for an outside line, then the country code for the US, and finally the number for Garland's office in New York. Thankfully, the call went through without a hitch. Garland's secretary got him off the call he was on to speak with her.

'World traveler!' he enthused. 'How are you?'

'Umm . . .'

His bright tone turned somber. 'What's wrong?'

She told him everything, with only a few tears.

'An old fraternity brother of mine has an influential position in the State Department. I'll call him after we hang up, then I'll get on the first flight over there. Are you going to be in your room for a while?'

'I don't think I'll leave my room. Although I may starve to death.' Iris rubbed her temples. A dull pain had started behind each eye. 'Or die from caffeine withdrawal.'

'It would do you good to drink less coffee.'

'Garland, I love you, but this is not the time for me to begin a moderation program.' Iris pinched the bridge of her nose and winced. There was only one way to remedy a caffeine headache – simple painkillers had no effect – and there was no caffeine in the room. 'Hey, have you heard of a Russian businessman named Nikolai Kosyakov? The police asked me whether Todd knew him and mentioned Kosyakov in connection with Todd's art deal. Dean Palmer later told me that Kosyakov's one of the richest men in Russia and probably Mafia-connected.'

'That name does sound familiar. Wait a sec . . .'

There was the sound of papers rustling. Iris envisioned Garland sitting at his large desk in his Manhattan office which overlooked the World Trade Center and the Brooklyn Bridge. He was probably wearing a starched shirt with a button-down collar, braces printed with a subdued design, and a silk tie, maybe one of the more fashionable ones she had bought him in an effort to have him dress less conservatively. She wanted to go home. This was the first time in her life that she wasn't able to move freely. Tears welled in her throat as she listened to the crackle of her old life that was transmitted through the telephone line. She swallowed them back down. Garland was probably more upset over her circumstances than she was. Going to pieces wouldn't do anyone any good.

'Yeah, here it is,' Garland said. 'In last week's *Business Week*, the article's called "Russia's Rockefeller". He looks like a slippery kind of guy.'

'Could you fax it to me here?'

'Sure.'

She thumbed through the hotel guide until she found the fax number which she gave to him.

'I'm going to get on these phone calls. I'll call you back as soon as I find out anything.' He paused and inhaled deeply. Iris imagined him pressing his lips together with determination. 'Iris, don't worry. Everything's going to be fine.'

'I miss you. I wish I hadn't come. I should have taken your advice.'

'You had good reasons for going. Come on. Don't revisit your decision.'

'I love you.'

He made the small noise that he made whenever she told him that. A noise as if he was savoring something good. 'I love you too.'

She hung up and glanced at the television screen that was still showing *Simply Maria* and tried to decide what to do next. Her rumbling belly decided for her. She pulled a handful of roubles from her purse which had been miraculously returned to her room the previous night along with her coat. She shoved the money into one of the robe's pockets, started to set the purse back down, then reached inside it again, this time taking out dollars in different denominations. She also took out a small brush and yanked it through her hair which was severely crimped on one side of her head from her long sleep.

Standing and readjusting her robe, she grabbed the hotel guide and her *Russian for Travelers* dictionary, left the room and walked into the hallway. A businessman who was leaving his room at the same time gave her a hard look. She nodded and smiled then padded after him in bare feet down the thick carpeting. He cast a glance at her over his shoulder. Now irritated, she gave him a narrow look back.

Iris was disappointed to see a different *dezhurnaya* from the night before sitting at the desk at the end of the hallway. This one was also wearing a pink uniform, but hers was marked with smudges and spots. She was older than the other one and thick; her square figure tested the dress's buttons. Her hair was dyed raven black and stiffly molded into a cap of curls, the careful style contrasting with her soiled garment. Heavy eyeliner was drawn into points at the corners of her eyes. She and the businessman warmly exchanged a greeting in Russian as he handed her his room key. He walked to call the elevator and the concierge turned her Cleopatra-painted eyes on Iris.

'*Pree-vyet,*' Iris greeted the woman, smiling and bowing slightly. The woman nodded back, casting a critical glance at Iris's bathrobe and bare feet.

Iris opened the hotel guide to the section that described the hotel's meal

23

accommodations in four different languages. The woman pursed her lips when Iris pointed to the section that described breakfast. She pulled the guide from Iris's hands and pointed to the lunch section then tapped the face of her watch with a polished, pointed fingernail.

The businessman got in the elevator, leaving Iris and the concierge alone. Iris pointed at the breakfast again and then pointed toward her room. When the concierge frowned, not understanding, Iris opened the traveler's dictionary and found the phrase, 'in my room'. She held the book open for the concierge and pointed to the Cyrillic letters.

The woman vigorously shook her head and uttered in clear English, 'No.'

From her pocket, Iris produced about ten dollars worth of roubles. The woman looked at the money for a second as if she was considering Iris's proposition then shook her head. Iris tried again, this time with a twenty dollar bill. Slowly, the woman raised her hand and took the money, quickly slipping it beneath the desk.

'*Spasíbo*,' Iris thanked her, clasping her hands and bowing.

The concierge picked up the receiver of the telephone on her desk and Iris added, '*Kófe*,' then held her hands apart to indicate the size. Big. She produced a five dollar bill from her pocket and handed it to the woman which managed to provoke a smile from her.

At the door of her room, Iris heard her telephone ringing. She opened the door and bolted across the room to answer it.

'Iris, it's Dean Palmer.'

'Dean, hi.'

'How did you sleep?'

'Like the dead. I just came back from bribing the concierge to have breakfast brought to my room.'

'You're learning the ropes quickly.'

She winced against her headache. 'Think it'll work on those cops?'

'It's an option, but I don't think we need to try that just yet. Look, the Ambassador has been talking with the powers that be about your case. I have to tell you that Davidovsky is being difficult about letting you go home.'

'Oh, no.'

'No need to be alarmed,' Palmer quickly added. 'It's probably a case of the police not wanting to look like they caved in to our request. I fully expect this to be resolved in twenty-four hours.'

'I'm trying to remain calm.'

'That's the best thing you can do. I've been in contact with Tracy Fillinger, Todd's sister.'

Iris cranked open the metal shutters all the way and looked at the city that had again come alive. 'In Bakersfield, California?'

'That's her. She can't afford to travel to Moscow to settle Todd's effects and asked if I'd take care of it for her. She says she doesn't want anything.

24

She figures that Todd was such a nomad, he wouldn't have much worth the expense of shipping. I'm going out to Todd's apartment today to check things out. Would you like to go with me?'

'Yes, I would. Thanks for asking.'

'I'll be by in an hour.'

Shortly after they hung up, Iris's food arrived. A waiter pushed a cart loaded with covered dishes and a big jug of coffee into the room. He got busy setting up a table next to the window. In the center, he placed a rosebud in a glass vase.

No room service, my eye, Iris thought to herself.

Folded in half and stuck between the dishes was Garland's fax. The waiter handed it to Iris and continued working.

In a cover note, Garland wrote that tomorrow was the soonest he could get a flight into Moscow, but he'd keep trying for something earlier.

Iris gave the waiter a generous tip and read the *Business Week* article as she wolfed down her food. The story on Nikolai Kosyakov displayed a photograph of him standing on the marble steps in front of the neoclassical façade of the Club Ukrainiya. Kosyakov had a sturdy face with broad cheekbones, a square chin, and narrow eyes. His thick salt-and-pepper hair was neatly trimmed around the sides but showily puffy on top. He was wearing a light suit and an open-collared shirt. He wasn't looking into the camera but was frowning at the ground as he talked into a cellular phone.

Iris wasn't completely disappointed that Garland couldn't arrive sooner. She had some business she wanted to take care of on her own.

Chapter 4

Dean Palmer and Iris took a taxi to a shiny new skyscraper of cream-colored marble and brass. Right after they exited the taxi, a group of pre-teenage boys started following them.

'Pickpockets,' Palmer whispered to Iris, stepping up their pace.

The building doorman burst onto the sidewalk, swinging a heavy board and yelling at the boys. They scattered, but not before the doorman thwacked one, the board cracking against his leg, knocking him to the ground.

'Good Lord!' Iris cried.

The boy scampered to his feet and escaped before the doorman could swing again.

Palmer tried to explain, 'It's the only thing he can do to keep them away.'

As the doorman held the door for them, Palmer spoke to him in Russian. He grinned modestly in response.

In the lobby, thick oriental carpets covered the polished marble floor. The building was as quiet as if it were vacant. Iris and Palmer entered an elevator lined with burnished brass and he pressed the button for the fifteenth floor.

'Todd told me that Moscow had been good to him,' Iris remarked. 'I guess he wasn't kidding. Do you have any idea what the rent is on a place like this?'

'Easily five thousand dollars a month.'

'Wow.'

'Todd did well here in a short period of time.'

They exited the elevator and walked down the corridor to the last door on the left. Palmer unlocked it and pushed it open. 'The police have already searched the place.'

After crossing a small entryway, they entered a large, airy living room. The corner apartment was spacious with high ceilings and two walls of windows that overlooked the Kremlin, St Basil's Cathedral, and the Moskva River. An open kitchen and an adjacent dining area were at one end. In the living room was a brick fireplace with a large gold-framed mirror above it. A hallway to the left led to the bedrooms and bathrooms.

The apartment was minimally and coolly furnished with a glass and chrome dining room set, a navy blue leather couch and armchair, and a glass coffee table.

'This doesn't look like the bachelor pad of a nomadic freelance photographer,' Iris commented. 'Todd had a beautiful apartment in Paris, too. He had a knack for making money.'

'Appears so.'

Iris ran her hand across the back of the couch, savoring the smooth texture of the leather. 'Are you sure his sister doesn't want any of this?'

'That's what she told me.'

'Seems like it would be worth her while to have his furniture sold and the money sent to her.' She walked to the coffee table on which a photograph in a silver frame was displayed. She slid her backpack on to the sofa and picked up the photograph, lightly touching the surface with her fingertips and smiling sadly.

She explained to Palmer who was looking over her shoulder, 'It's a picture of me and Todd in Paris. We were at a party at a friend's house. He'd found that beret laying around somewhere and put it on my head.'

'The two of you look happy.'

After a long pause, she said, 'We were.' She set the photo back on the table.

'What happened?' Palmer scraped back the lank strands of hair that drooped onto his forehead. Wearing khaki pants and a navy blue blazer, he looked like Mr Preppy USA except for the dark circles under his eyes.

'I broke it off.' She shoved her hands into her jeans pockets. 'And I broke his heart.'

'Why?'

'Good question. I've been searching for the answer myself. I just had to run away. I don't know if it was too much, too fast – which it was – or if I was spooked by the idea of commitment.' Iris didn't care that she was revealing secrets to a stranger. She wanted to talk about it. 'We were going to get married and I left him standing at the altar in a little chapel in Paris while I packed my bags and took a taxi to the airport. That was five years ago. Part of the reason I came to Moscow was to explain, or try to, anyway. To at least tell him I'm sorry.'

'Did you get the chance?'

'Yes.'

'How did he take it?'

'He was . . . OK. But I could tell he hadn't gotten over it.' Iris walked to the window and stood looking at Todd's newly adopted city. One in a string of cities. She had told herself that it had been the same with her. She was just one of many. That was part of the reason she'd run from him. He had said he was ready to settle down, but the rootlessness that had first attracted her had come to seem too big to tame. But she could have been wrong.

Palmer picked up the photo and handed it to her. 'Take it.'

'If things had been different between Todd and me, maybe he wouldn't have ended up shot full of holes on a Moscow street.'

Palmer touched her arm. 'You can't blame yourself. People make their own choices.'

'I know. But you think of the events that shape your life . . . If a few things had gone differently for me, I'm not so certain how I would have ended up. I never had a big support net under me and neither did Todd. His mother died in a car accident when he was ten. His father started drinking after that. He was raised by his older sister. He was good at playing the carefree, man-about-town role, but there was a sadness to him. I saw it when we were in Paris. I saw it yesterday. I never quite grasped him. He was something of an enigma.'

'Let's have a look around and get out of here. Go have a drink somewhere.'

'Sounds good to me.'

'If you see anything else you want to take, go ahead.' Palmer walked into the kitchen with Iris following. He began opening cupboards, finding a few dishes and cooking utensils. He glanced at her. She drew down the corners of her mouth and shook her head.

They walked through the living room and down the corridor, entering a small room. Palmer flipped the wall light switch. A red bulb in the middle of the room glowed dimly. A black curtain was pulled over the windows. Jugs of chemicals and packets of photographic paper were stored on shelves against the wall. Shallow plastic trays were side by side along a high table. Photographs were pinned with clothes pegs to cords strung across the room.

'Todd's darkroom,' Iris commented. She unclasped some of the photographs and looked at them. 'I know this building. This is the Club Ukrainiya.'

Palmer took the photograph that she held out to him. 'It is, isn't it? How did you know that?'

'My boyfriend faxed a *Business Week* article about Nikolai Kosyakov to me at the hotel. So there is a connection between Todd and Kosyakov. Most of these are interior shots. I wonder why he took them and how he got permission.'

She started pulling down the photographs. 'I'm taking them.'

Palmer helped her. After they had them all, they went into Todd's bedroom. The bed was made but the spread was wrinkled and the pillows propped up as if someone had been reclining there.

Iris spotted a large, square portfolio leaning against a wall. She hoisted it onto the bed and unzipped it. It was full of photographs, both loose and mounted. She dropped in the photos of the Club Ukrainiya, zipped it up and set it by the door. 'I'd like to take that.'

From a desk in the corner, Palmer picked up a large photo album. He flipped through the pages. 'This looks like samples of his magazine work.'

Iris looked over his shoulder. In the bright light from the window, she got a good look at Palmer's yellowish complexion for the first time. She had noticed his thinness when she'd first met him. Seeing him now in broad daylight, she wondered whether his sallow complexion and the circles under his eyes were indications that he was ill.

'Good stuff, huh?' He looked up at her and she returned her attention to the album.

'I'll take that too. I'll deliver them to his sister. I'm certain she'd want something of Todd's. Bakersfield is less than a two-hour drive from Los Angeles.' She put the scrapbook inside the portfolio.

'That's very kind of you, Iris.'

Returning to the desk, she picked up a pad of paper with writing on it. 'Looks like he was writing his sister a letter when he was killed. Listen to this:

Dear Tracy,

Sorry I haven't written in a while, but things have been a little chaotic for me lately. What else is new, right? Ha, ha. Moscow's a great city. I've got a great business going with a partner, a Corsican named Enrico Lazare. We buy and sell fine art to the rich people in Moscow. It's a perfect job for me and we're making tons of money. I'll wire you some tomorrow. Don't try to send it back. It's the least I can do.

Things are tense for me right now. The Russian Mafia is trying to elbow in on our business. They expect everyone who runs a business to pay protection money. I've had an altercation with them. Lazare thinks I'm nuts to live in Moscow. I thought I could handle the heat, but now I'm not so certain.

'That's all he wrote.' Iris pulled the letter free from the pad, folded it and slipped it into her pocket. 'He says he's going to wire his sister money. He must have a bank account. That should go to his family.' She started opening the desk drawers and going through them. 'I don't see any bank statements or anything.'

'A lot of people don't trust Russian banks. Maybe his partner handled their money. But I'll look into it when I get back to my office.'

'Odd. I can't see any bills or check stubs or even a phone book.'

Palmer shrugged. 'I barely knew the guy.'

The doorbell rang. Palmer glanced at his watch.

'Are you expecting someone?' Iris asked.

He shook his head. 'I'll go see who it is.'

Iris continued rifling through the desk drawers, not finding anything of a personal nature. She walked to the nightstand. On top was an ashtray with a cigarette stubbed out in it. She'd never seen Todd smoke. If he'd picked up the habit, surely he would have taken a puff during the hours they'd spent together the previous afternoon. She tilted the ashtray, rolling the butt to see the brand. 'True' was printed on the delicate paper in fine blue lines.

She found an empty envelope in the desk, tapped the butt into it, folded it and slipped it into her jeans pocket. She heard Palmer and a woman talking in the next room. She cocked her head to listen, but they were speaking in Russian. The woman was laughing now, which Iris found odd under the circumstances.

She entered the large walk-in closet and fingered Todd's clothing. The garments were understated but expensive. She pushed aside the hangers and searched against the closet's walls and in the corners. Perplexed, she picked up the portfolio and left the bedroom. From the hallway, she saw Palmer with two young women in the living room. One was admiringly drawing her hand down the length of the couch.

Reaching the darkroom, Iris flipped on the red light and looked around. She scratched her head and took another look, making certain she hadn't missed anything. She switched off the light and joined Palmer in the living room.

The women both had long, curly black hair and were wearing tight jeans, tight sweaters, boots, and dramatic costume jewelry. Their makeup was too bright. The one who had been fondling the couch was now examining the contents of the kitchen cupboards. The other was sitting on the couch with her hands draped across the back, apparently chuckling at something Palmer had said. She stood when Iris came into the room.

'These are Todd's friends,' Palmer explained, not introducing them by name.

Iris smiled thinly and nodded at them while she leaned Todd's portfolio against the side of the couch. The woman who had been sitting moved to shake Iris's hand and the one in the kitchen came into the room to do the same thing.

Iris noticed that a bedsheet was covering the large mirror over the fireplace. 'What's this doing here?' When she raised a corner, the sheet fell away, partially exposing the mirror.

One of the women gasped then rushed to cover the mirror again. She smiled apologetically at Iris who looked quizzically at Palmer.

He explained. 'It's a superstition. She thinks mirrors are windows into the netherworld and doesn't want Todd's spirit to reenter the world of the living through it.'

The women gathered their designer handbags and animatedly spoke to Palmer as they walked to the front door. After shaking his hand, they left.

'Do you need more time here?' he asked Iris, quickly skirting the issue of the two women.

'What did they want?'

He reached to tuck the sheet around the mirror's edges. 'To say goodbye to Todd, I guess.'

'They didn't seem to be very broken up over his murder. Frankly, they seemed to have come to pick over his bones.'

'Iris, I've told you what I know.'

She put the framed photo of her and Todd inside the portfolio and tossed off a question. 'Where's Todd's photography equipment?'

Palmer thoughtfully raised his eyebrows. 'Good question. Maybe he used a studio.'

'In Paris, he worked out of his apartment. Even if he used a studio, he'd still have darkroom equipment.'

Palmer walked to the door and opened it. 'This whole incident has been very strange.'

'And it's getting stranger.' Iris walked past him and into the corridor. He closed the door behind them.

'I know you didn't know Todd very well,' Iris began, 'but did you ever see him smoke?'

'No. Why?'

'Just wondering.'

Outside, the cab they'd arrived in was still waiting. Saying she was tired, Iris turned down Palmer's offer of a drink. He instructed the driver to return to the Metropolis Hotel.

Iris gazed out the window, thinking about Todd's apartment and what she had and hadn't found there. Suddenly she said, 'Todd's driver, Sasha. His bodyguard. He drove us from the airport. Where is he?'

Palmer took a small leatherbound notebook from his inside jacket pocket and slipped out the pen that was encased in it. 'Sasha, you say?' He scribbled on the pad. 'I'll look into it.' He wrote a few more notes. 'Then there's the issue of whether Todd had any bank accounts. And what else?'

'Missing photography equipment.'

'Right.' His responses were clipped.

'I doubt you'll find it, but it should be reported.' Iris absently stroked her neck then turned to Palmer. The whites of his eyes looked yellow. 'A ring. Todd was wearing it on his left pinky finger. It was my class ring. I gave it to Todd in Paris. Do you think you could get it for me?'

Palmer made a note and drew a star by it. 'If it wasn't stolen in the mortuary, I don't see why I can't get it for you.'

'He was also wearing a watch. Looked like an antique, gold with a rectangular face.'

Palmer noted that as well.

Iris frowned as a thought occurred to her. 'His body.'

'Tracy Fillinger said that Todd talked about being cremated in the event of his death. The mortuary will do that as soon as the police release the body.' He raised an eyebrow, as if coming to an unwelcome conclusion. 'I guess we'll ship the ashes to his sister.'

'Oh, no.' Iris grimaced. 'The poor woman.' She shook her head, then touched Palmer's arm. 'I'll take them to her. I want to go there anyway to give her these things of Todd's.'

Palmer brightened. 'That would be extraordinary, Iris. Tracy was really

32

broken up over Todd's murder. From what you said, it was just the two of them left. I'm certain that would bring her a lot of comfort.'

'It's the least I can do.' Iris sighed. 'For all the people Todd knew, it seems like he didn't have many friends.'

'As you said earlier, he was an enigma. He still is.'

The taxi stopped in front of the hotel. Iris handed Todd's portfolio to a doorman.

'I'll call you tonight, Iris, just to touch base. Or sooner if I've found out anything about your passport.'

Iris waved him off and watched as the taxi turned the corner. She handed the waiting doorman some roubles and asked him in English to take her things to her room and to call her a taxi. He raised his hand and the first one waiting in a nearby queue pulled up to the curb next to her.

'Club Ukrainiya,' she told the driver.

Chapter 5

The taxi slowed on a street of dingy concrete block buildings and stopped in front of closed black iron gates embellished with brass ovals between the bars. The brick columns supporting the gates were painted a yellow ochre color. An iron statue of an eagle about to take flight topped each one. Beyond the gates, a gravel path lined with trimmed boxwood and classical sculptures on pedestals led to the great house that was surrounded by a vast lawn and many trees.

Two men wearing what seemed to be the bodyguard's uniform of black leather jackets and dark slacks hung around in front of the gates. One had a thatch of sandy brown hair and looked to be barely out of his teens. The other looked as if he'd been around. He had a soft belly, slicked back hair, and a tough expression. He was talking on a cellular phone. Both of them eyed Iris when the taxi stopped in front of the gates.

The driver asked for the fare in Russian and Iris didn't feel like sorting out the language differences. She pulled out a handful of roubles in different denominations, fanned them in her hand, and held them toward him. The driver took what seemed an excessive amount and she didn't protest.

Iris didn't like the looks of the two guys but, in her experience, the world tended to be kind to attractive women, so her chances with them were good.

Taking her traveler's dictionary from her purse, she flipped through the pages as she walked over to the younger man. He had earnest eyes and seemed too kind for his profession.

In the book, she pointed to the phrase in Russian that meant, 'Do you speak English?'

He rubbed his finger across his upper lip and shot a glance at the older man who was still on the telephone. 'Little.'

'I want to see Nikolai Kosyakov.'

The other man ended his call and walked to join them. He put his hands in his pants pockets, pulling back his jacket, revealing the bottom of a shoulder holster above his thick waistline. Looking at the other guard, he hitched his greasy head in Iris's direction. The younger guard explained Iris's request while the other man produced a package of unfiltered Camel cigarettes from his shirt pocket, tapped it against the side of his hand, pulled a cigarette free with his lips and lit it with a gold lighter. From their Russian dialogue, Iris picked up the name Kosyakov and nothing else.

The older man drew heavily on the cigarette and fixed Iris with a steely gaze as he exhaled smoke. 'Who are you?'

'I'm Iris Thorne.' She repeated her name in response to his frown. 'Iris Thorne. Please tell Mr Kosyakov that I'm here. It's very important.'

'I don't know you.'

Iris was tempted to make a smart remark, but smiled instead, trying sugar instead of vinegar. It didn't seem to work. 'I'm a friend of Todd Fillinger.' She pronounced it again, slowly. 'Fillinger.'

That got their attention. The older man pulled a two-way radio from his jacket pocket and spoke into it, dragging on the cigarette, consuming the rest of it and throwing the butt on the ground, not bothering to mash it out. Something clicked and the two gates slowly swung open in the direction of the house.

The older guard had obviously finished with Iris. He moved several yards away and stood with his back to her, once again talking on the telephone, a fresh cigarette between his lips. She quizzically looked at the other man who jerked his head toward the house.

Iris walked down a gravel path, the soles of her hiking boots crunching against the small gray stones, and admired the marble statues of Greek gods that led to the two-story neoclassical mansion. She passed a huge oak tree that grew in a circular bed filled with wood chips; a flock of black birds resting there took flight. She inhaled slowly; the air here seemed sweeter than in the city. Ironically, this stroll across the property of the man who may have murdered her friend was the first bright spot in her Moscow visit. She had no reason to feel safe, but the beautiful house and well-tended grounds calmed her. She could have been on the campus of an Ivy League university in the States.

Marble steps ascended to a colonnade of six Corinthian columns which were topped with a pitched roof inset with a large clock. Two rows of evenly-spaced windows lined the face of the long building. The windows and doors were finished with molding painted shiny white, as was the colonnade. The rest of the house was painted yellow ochre.

She climbed the white marble steps and unseen hands slowly opened the tall, carved door. She entered a large rotunda whose floor was laid with an intricate mosaic. She involuntarily let a long sigh escape as her eyes trailed up to the domed ceiling, lined with gold leaf which reflected the light of a large chandelier in the center. The crystal teardrops cast tiny, shimmering rainbows across the floor and walls. Piano music, laughter, and the buzz of conversation came from a distant room.

'Good afternoon.'

She hadn't noticed the young man standing a few feet from her. After staring at the floor, her eyes had been immediately drawn to the gold ceiling. She closed her mouth, which had dropped open. 'Oh, hello.'

Two men with flushed faces stopped their animated conversation to look questioningly and, Iris thought, reproachfully at her before brushing past. They went out the front door, trailing the odor of alcohol.

Iris knew she didn't belong there and that she might end up doing more harm than good, but she wanted to take the chance. Kosyakov might be the only one who could get the police to let her leave the country.

'Miss Thorne,' the young man said, smiling timidly. 'This way, please.'

His shoes squeaked against the marble floor. As they walked, the sound of the laughter and music grew louder. They passed a large room cluttered with sofas and armchairs. In it were about a dozen men. Someone was playing a grand piano that stood in a corner. There was cigarette smoke and the clinking of ice against crystal. The conversation dimmed as Iris passed. Someone shouted something, everyone laughed, and Iris's escort blushed. He shot her an apologetic glance. She smiled and shrugged.

As they walked, Iris admired the paintings and tapestries that covered every wall, the statues and vases in every corner and on top of every table, and the cabinets full of crystal and china.

'Mr Kosyakov is an art collector?'

'Yes. He loves beautiful things.'

Finally they reached another tall door divided into panels and painted white like the house's other woodwork. The boy pulled down on the brass door handle and Iris walked onto a polished parquet floor covered by a large oriental carpet. This room was also cluttered with furniture, art, and ornaments. The walls were covered with nubby silk in a soft peach color. A large desk of dark wood – Iris guessed it was mahogany – and a heavy chair with a high back that gave it a throne-like quality took up one side of the room. Brocade drapes were pulled open, giving a view of a manicured garden.

'Please be comfortable,' the boy said to her. 'Can I offer you a beverage?'

Iris sat on a couch against one wall, slipping her backpack from her shoulder and setting it on the floor. 'No, thank you.'

Without another word, he headed toward the door.

'Uh . . .' Iris turned to ask him a question, but saw only the tall door quietly closing. *You're into it now*, she scolded herself.

She looked at her watch, then around the room. Several magazines about architecture and art, most of them in English, were strewn across a coffee table in front of the couch. She flipped through them absent-mindedly. She thought of Garland and hoped he hadn't called her at the hotel. He'd be worried to find that she wasn't there.

The sun spilled across a corner of the desk and illuminated a vase on a pedestal next to it. The vase was blue and white and decorated with frolicking cherubs. Iris suspected it was Wedgwood. Also caught in the sunbeam was a round hole in a corner of the desk. Near it, a long, narrow groove sliced across the top. The silk wall covering next to the vase was marred with several small holes. She stood and moved to get a closer look when the door opened.

The neat, fox-faced man who'd entered the police interrogation room and given her passport and Todd's letter to Detective Davidovsky entered the room. Iris gaped at him, her heart beginning to pound.

'Miss Thorne, what a pleasant surprise.' He extended his hand and when she gave him hers, he warmly shook it. His hand was as small as a woman's. 'You look startled to see me. Understandably so. We've never been formally introduced. I am Konstantin Markov, head of security for Nikolai Kosyakov.' He gestured toward the sofa. 'Please, sit down.' He sat in a wing-backed chair next to the couch. 'Didn't Yuri offer you refreshment?'

Iris sat, her resolve wavering. She drew a trembling hand through her hair, looping it round an ear, detecting a hint of his musky cologne on her palm. 'Oh, yes. He did. Thank you, but no.'

'Unfortunately, Mr Kosyakov is attending to his oil interests on the north shore and cannot meet with you today. How can I help you?'

Iris was nonplussed by his polite formality, which was in stark contrast to his accusatory demeanor at the police station the previous night. She didn't know where to begin.

He calmly waited, his green-black eyes under a fringe of dark lashes resting on her without animosity. If anything, his finely lined lips and sculptured eyebrows with their natural lift made him appear pleased to see her.

She blurted the first thing that came to her mind. 'You told Detective Davidovsky to keep me in Moscow. Why?'

He crossed his legs. His black shoes were highly polished. 'I suspect you already know the answer to that.'

'I told you everything I know about Todd Fillinger.'

'I disagree,' he said without changing his pleasant yet slightly distant expression.

'Then we're even. I don't think you're telling me everything you know about Todd's murder.'

Markov sat perfectly still. 'What would you like to know?'

'What is the connection between Todd and Kosyakov?'

The light from the window shone on his fringe of neatly-trimmed black hair and his bald pate. 'You and Mr Fillinger were such close friends. I find it hard to believe that he never mentioned Kosyakov to you.'

Iris crossed her legs as well, unconsciously aping Markov's behavior. In her jeans and hiking boots, she felt inappropriately casual in the elegant surroundings. 'I'd never heard of Kosyakov until his name was brought up at the police station last night. Now I know a great deal about him.' She unzipped her backpack at her feet and pulled out the *Business Week* article. She unfolded it and held it up for Markov to see.

His eyes darkened slightly. He apparently didn't care for this profile of his boss.

Iris read from the article. ' "Kosyakov denies having Mafia connections but an unnamed source is quoted as saying, 'You don't get that rich that fast in Russia without mob connections.' " '

Markov didn't respond and didn't look as if he was about to.

Iris returned the article to her backpack. 'Todd told me the Mafia was trying to extort money from him. Before he was murdered, he was writing a letter to his sister, telling her the same thing.' She took the letter from the back pocket of her jeans and handed it to Markov.

He pulled his wire-rimmed half-glasses from his inside jacket pocket, slowly opened them, and set them on his nose. He read the letter, then punctiliously put his half-glasses away again. He handed the letter back to Iris without comment. His expression was as genial as before but his attitude had subtly chilled.

Markov's lack of response and remote air was getting on her nerves. 'It's clear that Kosyakov had Todd Fillinger murdered and you're keeping me in Moscow until you find out how much I know about it. It wouldn't be good for public relations if I left here and told the world business community that Russia's top entrepreneur is nothing more than a dressed-up street thug.'

Markov smiled with amusement, drawing his closed lips tightly across his teeth.

It burned Iris up.

'I recognize that American women are bolder than what we're accustomed to here in Russia, but I must confess that your attitude takes me by surprise, Miss Thorne.'

Undeterred, Iris went on, 'Well, Mr Markov? Was Kosyakov shaking down Todd Fillinger?'

Markov chuckled brightly.

Iris blushed. Her skin felt prickly underneath her denim shirt.

Markov touched a tear in the corner of his eye. 'You're mistaken, Miss Thorne. Frankly, Mr Kosyakov has more pressing business than to . . . What was your term? *Shake down* a small-time photographer who pretended he was a celebrity.'

'What happened in this room?' She stood, circled the coffee table and walked to the desk. Without rising, he turned to watch her.

'These look like bullet –' The oriental carpet squished wetly underneath her feet. She quickly stepped off it and tested the area with the toe of her boot. Several square feet of the carpet were wet. It also felt as if something was underneath it.

She reached down, grabbed a corner of the carpet, and pulled it back, revealing wet white toweling that was stained pinkish-red. She dropped the carpet and staggered backward, looking at Markov with dread.

He dispassionately watched her with two fingers pressed against his lips.

She stood in the center of the room. 'What happened here?'

'Curious,' he said finally. Without uncrossing his legs, he reached under the corner of the mahogany desk.

Within seconds, there was a quick rapping on the door then the fresh-faced young man opened it.

Markov gazed out the window, his head turned away from Iris as if he were deep in thought. After a moment, he returned his attention to her. 'Yuri will show you out.' He stood and extended his hand. 'Thank you for your visit, Miss Thorne. It has been very enlightening.'

Chapter 6

Iris sat in the Metropolis Hotel's posh bar, nursing her second vodka tonic and eating salted pistachios. She wanted to get rip-roaring drunk, to blow herself into a fuzzy fog, but with the way things were unfolding in Moscow, she didn't dare. She was homesick for a glass of California Chardonnay, which she would sip while sitting in her backyard in her Adirondack chair, gazing at the Pacific Ocean that changed its colors like a mood ring.

A German businessman in a group at a nearby table kept shooting glances at her, the stares lingering longer the drunker he became. She'd turned down their offer to join them, but this man seemed to think that her refusal didn't really mean no. Several Korean businessmen were looking her way as well, despite her denim and hiking boots and limp hair, flattened by the dampness in the air. She was the only woman in the bar who was not accompanied by a man. The other women there – waif-like things in expensive furs and trashy dresses – were on the arms of men. She looked out the window at where Todd had fallen and counted the hours until Garland was to arrive.

He was flying in the next afternoon. He'd been on the phone to everyone, pulling every string he had to spring her and promised that he'd have the situation resolved by the end of the week.

She felt oddly calm about the whole thing. Garland was involved now and he'd take care of it. It had taken her a while to shrug off the desire to micro-manage everything in her life. But once she'd learned to trust him, she'd found it was easier when two shared the burden. Garland was coming to Moscow and he would take care of things.

She was more preoccupied with the question of Todd and what had happened to him. She thought about herself and the dippy period of her life when she'd almost married a man she hardly knew. She had wanted Todd so badly that she'd fooled herself into thinking that they didn't need to know each other longer. They were soul mates, kindred spirits who already understood each other on a deeper, more profound level, making the details trivial. It seemed silly now. Much had changed for her in five years. She'd changed. Todd hadn't. He was still running, searching. They had intersected at a point where she had been running too. She could have told him what she was thinking. It would have been the decent thing to do. He didn't deserve that. He didn't deserve any of it.

41

She downed the last of her drink and raised her glass in the direction of the waiter. He nodded at her. She dragged her finger through the salty residue left by the pistachios and sucked it off to the undisguised salacious interest of the German. She was high enough not to care.

She was relieved to see the group of German men start to leave. Her fan lingered, weaving on his feet, his features lax from too much alcohol. The booze had also laid bare any façade that might have disguised his true motives. Iris scowled at the table top, avoiding eye contact. His friends pulled his arm and managed to drag him away. She relaxed.

The waiter brought her drink. 'Were you able to find my cigarettes?' she asked.

'Sorry, no. When the hotel tobacco shop didn't have them, they called a bigger store. No one has heard of this brand, True.'

'I guess low tar and nicotine cigarettes are not popular in Moscow.'

He smiled. 'No, they are not.'

'Can I order a sandwich that I can take to my room?'

'Certainly. I'll have something prepared for you.'

She examined the bill and slowly calculated a hefty tip for him, not fast with numbers even when she was clear-headed. The waiter spoke to someone who approached the table. When she finished settling her tab, she looked up to see the double chins and barrel chest of Detective Davidovsky. The waiter picked up the check and quickly exited.

'Detective Davidovsky,' Iris said, somewhat thickly. 'What a surprise.'

He flipped her passport onto the table in front of her. 'Thank you for your cooperation in the Todd Fillinger murder investigation. We have all the information we need from you. You're free to leave Russia.'

Iris opened her passport to her grinning photo. She repeated his message to make sure she'd heard correctly. 'I can go home?'

'Yes, you are going home.' He stood with his hands straight by his sides.

'Oh.' She slipped the passport into her backpack on the banquette next to her. 'Great. Well, I guess I can finally enjoy my visit to Moscow.'

'There's a direct flight to Los Angeles leaving in four hours.'

'My boyfriend's arriving tomorrow. Now that everything's resolved, I'd like to see some of the sights.'

Davidovsky said more pointedly, 'You are leaving for Los Angles in four hours. I will wait while you gather your belongings and escort you to the airport.'

Iris rose behind the table, with a foot on the floor and her knee on the banquette. 'Wait a minute. First you won't let me leave, now you won't let me stay. What gives?'

'You're interfering in a murder investigation.'

'Interfering? Because I tried to see Nikolai Kosyakov? Because I found out that someone was shot in his office?'

'I'll wait in the lobby while you pack your things. You have half an hour.'

Iris slid from the booth, hooking the strap of her backpack over her shoulder. 'Fine. No problem. But I'm not leaving until I get Todd Fillinger's remains.'

'Remains?'

'His ashes. I'm taking them to his sister. Is that all right? Dean Palmer is making the arrangements. You'll have to ask him when they'll be ready.'

Without a word, Davidovsky walked to the bar and gestured for a telephone, which was promptly set in front of him. He watched Iris as he made a call.

Before long, he returned to her. 'Dean Palmer will meet us at the airport with the urn.'

Chapter 7

After the airplane had crossed the desert, greater Los Angeles leapt from the darkness like a bogeyman from underneath a child's bed. The lights upon endless lights brought tears to Iris's eyes. It was her hometown. As the plane made its descent into LAX, she took in the landscape of houses, backyards, and dots of blue from swimming pools illuminated in the night. Separate lives, tiny stakes in this arid landscape, cobbled together by a web of streets and freeways, powered by gasoline, tire rubber, and dreams. Land's end. Making it here wasn't a guarantee of making it anywhere else, but few cared.

It was 10:00 p.m. when Iris, gritty-eyed, left the plane and walked through an almost deserted terminal. She'd carried the urn on the plane with her to ensure there was no luggage screw-up. It was taped inside a tall, corrugated cardboard box and was heavy. She held it cradled in one arm. In her backpack, she'd folded the brief articles about Todd's murder that she'd found in Moscow's two English-language newspapers. Neither of them said much or mentioned her name, for which she was grateful.

She'd asked the Russian businessman sitting next to her on the plane whether there was any mention of the murder in the Russian newspaper he was reading. He found a small piece about it which he read to her. This one said that Todd had been waiting on the steps of the Metropolis Hotel for an American friend, but no name was given. Good. All she wanted to do was put the incident behind her.

She had suspected she'd have some trouble getting through customs with the urn. She was escorted out of line and sent to a small, glass-walled office where an African-American man in a brown uniform asked her to remove the urn from the box.

As Iris opened the box, she tried to explain, sensing she was being somewhat incoherent. She'd slept little on the plane and her body clock was haywire. 'A friend of mine was murdered when I was in Moscow. I'm taking his ashes, which are in the urn, to his sister, Tracy. His name was Todd. Todd Fillinger. Tracy, the sister, lives in Bakersfield.' Her sentences were short and simple. It was the best she could manage.

The customs agent helped Iris pull the urn from the box. 'Huh,' Iris said with surprise when she saw it. It was antique brass and gently curved with a round lid and a broad base. 'This is really nice.'

The officer soberly looked at her. 'Haven't you seen it before?' He held the urn under a high-intensity lamp on the table and slowly turned it.

'No. A consul officer from the US Embassy in Moscow told me that the Embassy was going to purchase an urn.'

He pulled a pair of latex gloves from a box and put them on.

She winced as he opened the urn.

'He said it was the least they could do for the family.'

'They find out who murdered your friend?'

Iris retracted her lips with disgust as she watched the officer probe the ashes with a metal rod. The soft gray material clung to the rod and the light caught the particles that were released into the air. She tried to breathe shallowly, fearing she'd inhale them. 'No. It was a Mafia hit. He refused to pay the mob protection money.'

The officer tapped the urn all over with the rod. 'You never saw this urn empty?'

'That's correct. You can call the Embassy in Moscow. The consular officer's name is Dean Palmer.'

He pressed the lid back on the top then picked up the urn between both hands. 'Wait here.' He left the windowed booth, closing the door behind him.

Iris rested her elbows on her knees and her head between her hands. 'Am I ever going to get home?' Her stomach loudly rumbled with hunger. 'Am I ever going to have a decent meal again?'

After several minutes, the officer returned with the urn. He slid it back into the cardboard box and refastened the tabs of tape.

'Did you dump it out?' Iris asked.

'X-rayed it.' He handed her the box. 'Let me give you a tip. Never accept a package from a stranger and never take such a package on an aircraft.'

'Never again. On my word.'

'Welcome to Los Angeles.'

Iris loaded her suitcase, the box containing the urn, and the portfolio of Todd's photography onto a luggage cart and headed for the exit. A small group of people was waiting for the arriving passengers just beyond the glass doors separating the customs clearance area. Iris wove past them, her eyes focused on the doors that led outside, when a woman holding a handwritten sign caught her eye. On the square cardboard in block letters was IRIS THORNE. For a moment, Iris thought that Garland might have ordered a limousine for her which didn't make sense because he knew she'd driven her car to the airport.

The woman, wearing a V-necked T-shirt printed with the LA Clippers logo and cut-off jeans that dangled loose threads of fabric from the unfinished edges, wasn't dressed like a limo driver. Her streaked blonde hair was combed into a high ponytail which was held by a bright yellow scrunchie on the crown of her head. She scurried over when she saw Iris peering at her.

'Iris Thorne?' she asked, holding the sign higher between both hands.

'I'm Iris Thorne.'

'I'm so glad I didn't miss you. I waited and waited. Oh, I'm Tracy Fillinger, Todd's sister.' The woman's eyes and nose were red as if she'd been crying.

'Tracy? Well, hi. What a surprise. I, ah . . . How . . .?'

'Dean Palmer told me the flight you were on and I thought I'd meet you and save you the trip to Bakersfield.'

'That's very nice. You didn't have to do that. It wouldn't have been any trouble for me to drive to Bakersfield.'

'I wanted to. You've already done so much for Todd. I can't thank you . . .' She pulled a crumpled wad of tissues from her pocket and dabbed her eyes.

'It must have been a terrible shock for you.' Iris patted her bony shoulder. She was very thin.

'It hasn't really sunk in yet.' She sniffed and looked at Iris's luggage on the cart. 'I don't want to keep you. You must have had a long day.' She pointed to the rectangular box. 'Is that the urn?'

'Yes. Look, I have some things of Todd's that I took from his apartment. Would you like to have a cup of coffee or something? I have a letter he was writing you before he—'

'I'd like to, but I have kids at home. The neighbor's staying with them. If I could just take the urn.'

Iris squatted to pick up the urn and warned Tracy as she handed it to her, 'It's heavy.'

She held it like a baby against her shoulder. 'Wow, it is heavy. Thanks again.' She quickly turned to leave.

'I'll call you about these other things of Todd's.'

'Sure, yeah,' Tracy said over her shoulder.

'Wait!' Iris fumbled in her purse and found Todd's watch wrapped in a tissue. 'This belonged to Todd.'

Tracy slowly walked over. Her eyes brightened when she saw the timepiece. 'Thanks.' She plucked it from Iris's hand and again sped toward the exit.

Iris watched her push through the outside doors and disappear down the sidewalk. She realized she was unconsciously twisting the class ring she was wearing, the one that Dean Palmer had managed to retrieve from Todd's corpse.

Chapter 8

Iris was asleep in her own bed in her own house in Casa Marina, a small community spread across tall hills next to the ocean, just north of Santa Monica. The 1920s bungalow, painted yellow with white trim, was tiny, with two bedrooms and one bathroom. A wooden sunburst motif decorated the façade beneath the pitched roof and a halved sunburst topped each of the two large front windows. The house had an ample front and backyard, the front door reached by a meandering brick path lined with rose trees, the beds filled with seasonal flowers. The pansies she'd planted in April were still blooming in September. She'd paid dearly for the charming bungalow, much more than the size or design would indicate, because of its ocean-front location. The steep cliff at the edge of her backyard dropped straight to Pacific Coast Highway several hundred feet below. On the other side of the highway was broad, sandy Casa Marina Beach.

The sound of the front door opening didn't wake Iris who was sleeping soundly in her bedroom in the back of the house. It was the footsteps, clacking against the hardwood floor, made by someone who didn't seem concerned about keeping quiet, that finally roused her. She sat up in bed with a start. She didn't own a gun. She'd thought about it a million times, but finally decided a gun presented more potential problems than it was worth. Instead, she kept a wooden baseball bat under her bed. There was little danger of it being used inappropriately.

Iris didn't grab the baseball bat but stumbled out of bed and padded down the hallway in bare feet, not bothering to put a robe over her cotton jersey pajamas printed with a Western design of cowboy hats, boots, and lassos.

'Morning, Marge,' she said to her neighbor, scaring the seventy-year-old woman within an inch of her life.

'Good Lord! Iris, I didn't know you were home.' Marge was standing at the kitchen sink, filling a plastic watering can. It was 6:30 a.m., and she was dressed in a pink knit suit with a collared jacket, slim skirt, and high-heeled pumps. Every hair on her champagne-blonde do was in place. Her reedy hands were festooned with several heavily-jeweled rings. One hand rested against her chest where it had flown when Iris startled her. An enameled diamond-inset bumblebee brooch was pinned to the shoulder of her jacket.

She dried her hands on a dishtowel, studied Iris with bright blue eyes, and asked, 'How was your trip?' It was the polite question to ask and Marge was always exceedingly proper, but Iris wondered whether the older woman had already figured out the answer.

'It was fine. I'm glad I'm home.' Iris waited for Marge to ask about the American who was gunned down, perhaps even mentioning him by name, but she didn't. Perhaps it hadn't yet made it into the press here. Hopefully, it wouldn't. Marge and Iris's mother were friends and Iris was hoping to avoid her mother's inappropriate anxiety over a situation that had already passed.

'You're home a couple of days early.'

'I wrapped up my business there sooner than I thought.'

Marge easily hoisted the heavy, full watering can from the sink and headed toward the potted ferns next to the dining room window. 'Wasn't the Hermitage just *mar*-velous? Didn't you just *love* it?' She was enthusiastic about all the good things life had to offer and her enthusiasm was contagious.

'Incredible.' Iris hated lying to her, but she wanted to put the Moscow affair behind her. If her mother got wind of it, it would live in perpetuity.

'And St Basil's Cathedral?'

'Didn't make it there.'

'You will.' Marge watered the ferns as she spoke. 'You'll be back. Moscow has a way of calling you back.' The older woman had traveled most everywhere and had gone in style. She'd certainly had her ups and downs, but there was one thing about Marge, she knew how to live.

Iris smiled thinly, thinking it would be a cold day in hell before she set foot in Russia again. 'Why are you here so early?'

'I have *such* a day before me.' Marge watered the ficus in the corner of the living room, her heels loud against the floor. On her way back to the kitchen, she pressed her fingertips against Iris's arm. 'You must come for cocktails tonight and tell me all about your trip. I want to know *everything*.'

'I don't know if I can, Marge. I'm going into the office today and I might be late catching up.'

'I'm having martinis and canapés at five as usual. If you're around, stop over. I've invited Kiki and Roger from up the street. Kiki's father is staying with them and they want me to meet him. I told them I'm always *delighted* to meet an attractive man. I can use a little male interaction, if you know what I mean.' She nudged Iris in the ribs. Marge's directness sometimes embarrassed her. 'It's been a little dull since Frosty died. But no marriage. I told Kiki, I've buried three husbands. I refuse to buy one more cemetery plot.'

Marge turned the slender gold watch where it had slid round her tiny wrist to face her. 'I've got to *run*. Your house is in great shape. No news to report. Ta-ta!' Her feet wobbled slightly on her high heels as she walked to the front door.

After Marge left, Iris started coffee brewing and dug through her refrigerator. She found bagels, jam, and yogurt. She sliced a poppy seed bagel in half, slipped it into the toaster, and poured the first dribbles of coffee that had brewed into a stoneware mug. It was too strong and very hot, but tasted great to her.

She hoisted the portfolio of Todd's photography onto the dining room table and unzipped it then sat down and started going through the contents. On top was the silver-framed photo of her and Todd in Paris. She stood it on the table and looked at it, resting her head on her laced fingers. His eyes were shining, happy. She looked more closely, searching for the hint, the clue, the subconscious knowledge that his life would be short. She looked for the tragic end that had to have been imprinted on his cells, waiting, waiting for its time.

What did she see in her own eyes? Was there a hint of the betrayal that would unhinge Todd's life? Was her decision to run home already germinating in a corner of her mind? Was the bright spot that appeared to be a reflection from the flashbulb really the flash of deception? The harder she looked, the simpler the image seemed. All she saw were two people in love, blissfully unaware of the future.

She leisurely ate breakfast and dressed, having no need to hurry since she wasn't even supposed to be in the office this week. She was too edgy to relax around the house and thought she'd save her vacation days for a better time. It was only Wednesday, and she'd been out of the office just two days, but things could have easily gone haywire in her absence.

At the mouth of the mighty Interstate 10, Iris floored her give-me-a-ticket red 1972 Triumph TR6 for all it was worth. She orange-lined it with pleasure, flying past the Christopher Columbus Transcontinental Highway sign, the convertible top down and her hair whipping her face. This was LA. The air was hot, the sky was brown, drivers occasionally shot at each other, and the profundity of the culture was open to discussion, but dammit, at least people drove between the lines.

Iris threw her head back on her shoulders and crowed. It felt so good, she did it again. She glanced around at the other drivers. Everyone was still looking straight ahead, not paying her any attention at all. She loved this city.

She descended into the parking garage of her office tower, going round and round until she found the spot marked: RESERVED FOR I. THORNE. She parked the Triumph between the massive Mercedes and Lexus on either side, smiling with satisfaction. *Here* she was somebody. *Here* she had some pull. Screw Moscow. Screw Davidovsky and Markov. To hell with all of them.

Humming her tuneless, happy song, she ascended in the polished chrome-lined elevator with a few other people on their way to work. They wore the defeated expressions of those beginning another routine day. Their small angst touched her. She stopped humming out of respect for their mood. If they only knew how good they had it. *This is the United States of America, people*! she exclaimed to herself.

She barreled out of the elevator that accessed the parking levels and circled to the bank of elevators that accessed the office levels, her pump heels smartly retorting against the polished granite floor, when she spotted what appeared to be a display of some sort in the lobby. A long queue of people, some carrying flowers, a few with candles, snaked through the lobby and out the front door. Iris walked over to investigate.

She was about to ask the security guard Benny, whom she'd known for the five years she'd worked in the building, what was going on, when she saw her boss standing near the front of the line.

Sam Eastman was the divisional manager over all the McKinney Alitzer offices in the western states. Since Iris had been promoted to branch manager two years ago, against Sam's wishes, she and Sam had finally arrived at a position of mutual respect, if not love. They'd reached an unspoken understanding. Sam would stay out of Iris's way and let her run the LA branch the way she wanted to as long as the branch was exceeding quota, which it had during every quarter since she had taken it over. So what was Sam doing in her arena while she was supposedly out of town? It confirmed to her that she couldn't let her guard down for a minute. She picked up her pace, tightening her grip on her briefcase.

'You're very welcome. Remember, this experience was made possible by McKinney Alitzer,' Sam said as he handed a brochure to a woman then meaningfully clasped her shoulder with his hand. She took the brochure and dabbed a wadded tissue to her eyes. She was weeping.

'Sam,' Iris said, 'what's going on?'

'Oh, Iris,' he gushed, clutching a wad of McKinney Alitzer Financial Services brochures. 'Isn't it wonderful?'

He was standing next to a wood desk that was slightly tilted, the feet elevated by bricks on one side. Bright lights on poles lit the desk and shone on Sam's skull between the thin strands of light brown hair that he combed across his head in an attempt to cover his bald spot.

'That's my desk!' Iris exclaimed, noticing a rectangular burn mark on the top. 'I made that mark when I left my curling iron on.' She watched in disbelief as a woman knelt and kissed a corner of the cherrywood desk she'd ordered when she was promoted to branch manager.

Sam handed the woman a brochure. 'McKinney Alitzer can make a financial miracle happen for you.' He cocked his head and gave Iris a simpering smile, his eyes glassy. 'It overwhelms me.' He gently placed his hand on Iris's upper arm. 'Let me be the first to show you who's been watching over you.' He pushed through the crowd to reach the other side of the desk. 'Excuse me, please. This is the woman who owned the desk.' He rotated his hand a few inches above the front left corner. 'There she is.'

Iris squinted at the area Sam indicated. 'Who?'

'The Virgin Mary. See her? There, in the grain of the wood.' He sketched an image in the air above the desk with his finger. 'See her profile and her robes around her face coming down around her shoulders?'

'Where?' Iris asked, turning her head this way and that.

'Right there.' He again delicately painted the image, being careful not to touch the desk. 'See her?'

'That?' Iris exclaimed incredulously. 'That's a smudge!' She moved her thumb toward the desk.

Sam roughly grabbed her arm before she made contact. 'Iris, no!'

She looked at him curiously and slowly pulled her hand away. 'Sam, what's this about?'

'One of the cleaning crew saw it while you were on vacation. The word spread like wildfire. I quickly realized that something of this magnitude had to be shared.'

Iris backed out of the crowd into an open area. 'Please put my desk back in my office.'

He rapidly shook his head. 'Can't do that, Iris. It belongs to the world now. We bought you another desk, even nicer than this one.'

'Sam . . .' She looked into his pale blue eyes that glowed with excitement but in a way that made him seem slightly mad. She thought it best not to discuss the situation here. 'Sam, I'll be going upstairs now.' Dazed, she started walking toward the elevators.

'Iris,' Sam called after her. She turned. 'Now I know the secret of your success over the past few years.'

Iris smiled limply and continued walking.

She exited the elevator on the twelfth floor and pulled open the heavy glass doors marked in brass letters: MCKINNEY ALITZER FINANCIAL SERVICES. Her pump heels made small depressions in the thick mauve carpeting. It was almost 9:00 a.m. and the office was in full swing, having started the day at 6:00 a.m., shortly before the New York Stock Exchange opened.

She turned left and entered the sales department, passing the partitioned area for the junior investment counselors and sales assistants called the bull pen. All of them had their headsets on and were giving it all they had.

'Buy!'

'Diversify!'

'Wealth!'

'Growth!'

'Now!'

One of her new guys promptly removed his feet from his desk when she cast a glance at him as she walked by. She realized she was probably still scowling after the incident in the lobby. She hadn't meant to alarm the guy. Oh well. She was glad to see that she hadn't lost her power to intimidate.

People smiled at her as she passed, then exchanged words behind her back. Iris was fully aware of what was going on. She'd worked for the man

53

long enough to know the game. Now she was the man. She wasn't supposed to be in the office until the following Monday and it was only Wednesday. They had counted on a few more days without the boss around. Poor flowers. Life's tough, ain't it?

Along the suite's outside walls were the offices of the senior investment counselors. Amber Ambrose and Kyle Tucker had offices there and Iris had recently moved Sean Bliss into the golden corridor. She haphazardly flitted her fingers in their direction, after which Amber rose from her desk and stuck her head into Kyle's office.

'I know,' Iris muttered to herself. 'I'm baaack.'

One of the two large corner offices belonged to Iris's top producer, Liz Martini, who was known around town as the broker to the stars. She was married to Ozzie Levinson, one of the top Hollywood talent agents. Liz broadly waved at Iris from behind her desk, rattling several diamond tennis bracelets on her skinny, tanned wrist. At least Liz was genuinely glad to see her. Liz and Iris had been friends since Iris's first days in the industry. Liz had taught Iris the ropes. Her stable of well-to-do clients including a slew of Hollywood first wives – Liz's specialty – was part of the reason that the LA branch was one of the firm's highest producing offices.

Iris occupied the other large corner office directly across from Liz. In an alcove outside Iris's door sat her assistant Louise. Louise's chair was vacant but the items on her desk – a pad, pencil, stack of reports, and the ceramic cup with the fitted top that Louise used for tea – indicated she'd just stepped away.

Iris turned through the doorway of her office and was startled to see a woman sitting at her new desk.

'Who are you?'

The woman gave Iris a look that could shoot daggers and relaxed into Iris's chair. The chair was upholstered in cream-colored leather that had a texture like butter. It was Iris's favorite piece of office furniture and she'd had a huge battle with Sam Eastman over buying it. The woman, who appeared to be in her twenties and was wearing a short knit top that revealed a pierced belly button, seemed a little too comfortable sitting in it. She balanced the pencil she was holding between her index fingers and said, 'I should be asking you that question.'

Iris threw her briefcase onto one of the tapestry-covered Queen Anne-style chairs that faced her desk and marched over to the woman who continued to regard her insolently. 'I don't know who you are, but get the hell out of my office.'

'Dawn, I've warned you for the last time.'

Iris was relieved to hear Louise's voice behind her. Louise had been assistant to the branch manager for twenty years. Iris hadn't seen a problem yet that Louise couldn't handle.

'I'm waiting for Kyle,' Dawn protested.

54

'Out!' Louise pointed toward the door. 'Before I call building security.'

Dawn stood, gave Iris an up-and-down look, then sauntered out of the office, her hips marking a sultry rhythm.

Louise pushed an errant strand of gray-streaked blonde hair into her French twist. 'She's a hairdresser in the lobby salon. She's dating Kyle Tucker and is obsessed with him, if you ask me. She keeps sneaking into the office. I'd better make sure she leaves. Glad you're back, Iris.' She left to follow Dawn.

Iris sat at her new desk. It was cherrywood, like her old one, but was slightly bigger and had finer details. At least Sam had had the common sense to trade up.

She opened the drawers. All of her belongings had been transferred into it, but everything was unnervingly neat. She felt as if she'd entered a parallel universe that looked and felt like her old world but was subtly different, like she'd stepped through the looking glass.

'Hi, Sunshine.' Liz Martini walked in unannounced and without asking. She dropped into one of the chairs facing Iris's desk and carelessly crossed her legs, her tight skirt traveling up her tanned thighs. Her thick, dark hair was scooped onto the back of her head where it was held by a rhinestone banana clip. Corkscrew curls dangled around her pixyish face. 'What are you doing here?'

Iris shook her head, not knowing where to begin. Liz was the only person in the office she trusted enough to tell what had happened in Moscow, but it was more than she wanted to get into at this moment. 'It's unbelievable, but I'll tell you later.'

'Tell me now.'

'*Liz.*'

She raised her hands in surrender. 'Did you see Sam-I-Am in the lobby?'

'How could I miss him? What's going on?'

Louise answered, setting a full mug of coffee on Iris's desk. 'I think he's having personal problems.'

'Losing his mind is more like it,' Liz suggested.

Iris sipped. 'Just when you think you've seen everything, Sam takes ridiculousness to new heights.' She peered at her mug which was printed with the slogan BUDGETS ARE FOR WIMPS. 'What happened to my mug?'

'I scrubbed it,' Louise responded.

Iris skeptically took another sip of coffee and made a sour face. 'Now it doesn't taste good anymore,' she teased.

Louise crossed her arms over her chest. 'I had to scrub it twice with cleanser to get off the caked-on coffee and lipstick.'

'I'm gone two days and all hell breaks loose,' Iris joked.

'Just goes to show, you'd better not leave.' Louise didn't seem to be kidding. She turned on her heel and left.

'Does she know something I don't?' Iris asked Liz.

Liz leaned forward and spoke in her low-modulated voice used for office secrets. 'I know something no one's supposed to know yet. The home office is very upset with Sam-I-Am's exploits downstairs. They've been unhappy with him for some time, but this incident clinched it. I heard they're going to ask him to retire.'

'Retire?' Iris leaned back in her chair. 'Wow. I never liked the SOB and he did everything he could to make my life miserable, but retiring would kill him. This job is his life. He's only fifty-nine.' She looked out of one of the two floor-to-ceiling windows that met in the corner of her office.

'That's not all,' Liz continued. 'I heard they're going to offer the regional manager job to you.'

Iris whipped her head round to look at Liz, who was wrapping a tendril of hair over her finger. 'Who told you this?'

'Dave Ross. He was in a meeting with Jim Hailey. You can't breathe a word or all our asses will be grass.'

Iris was stunned.

'Wouldn't that be great, Iris? You'd be the firm's only female regional manager in the country. After a few years as RM, it'll be on to New York and the big money. You're on the fast track, baby. You and Garland would finally be on the same coast.' Liz released the lock of hair and it sprang into a curl. 'You don't seem excited.'

'I am, I . . . I just got off a plane from Moscow twelve hours ago. Everything's hitting me all at once.'

Liz stood. 'Company car, big expense account, big bonus, no office to show up at day after day, no BS problems to handle. All you'd have to do is kick the behinds of ten branch managers.'

'Well, I've never met a promotion I didn't like.'

'Can't hardly wait to find out.' Liz left and Iris swiveled her chair to look out the window behind her desk which faced west. It was too smoggy to see downtown LA much less all the way to Catalina Island, a treat permitted only on rare crystal-clear days. She swung back to her desk and began sorting through a stack of square pink telephone message slips. She'd told Louise that it was fine for people to leave messages on her voice mail, but her assistant continued to take handwritten messages. People tended to ramble on the voice mail, Louise said, and it was a waste of Iris's time.

Iris saw that she had just missed a call from Garland. She'd missed him at his office this morning when she'd called before she left for downtown. Louise's neat schoolbook writing said: 'Made reservations for a Palm Springs weekend. Pick you up Friday night.'

Iris closed her eyes and visualized lying in the sun, a waiter bringing a margarita, Garland walking from the pool after a swim, water trailing down his toned physique. The image sustained her through the rest of the morning.

The day passed quickly. Iris looked up from her work when Liz Martini rapped on her door frame. She was surprised to see Liz with her briefcase in her hand and her purse slung over her shoulder. By the Waterford crystal clock on her desk, Iris saw that it was 3:00. The office was almost empty.

Liz stood with her hand on her narrow hip, accentuating her large, surgically enhanced breasts underneath her clingy jersey sheath. She was thin and rich and firmly believed neither could be overdone. 'Hey, Miss Workaholic, some of us are going to have a drink downstairs. Why don't you come?'

'That sounds good.'

'You haven't even told me what happened on the trip and why you came back so soon.'

Iris rolled her eyes. 'It's a story.' She downed the last of her coffee and set her mug on the corner of the desk. She stood and tossed a file into her briefcase, which was open on the credenza against the window behind her.

Louise appeared in the doorway behind Liz. 'I'm leaving for the day, Iris, but there's a woman in the lobby who would like to see you.'

Iris took the business card that Louise handed her. The engraved type on thick paper stock said:

Rita Winslow
Dealer in Fine Art and Antiquities
33 New High Street
London SW4

'She looks like she has money,' Louise added, anticipating Iris's question.

'I'll see you downstairs after you're finished, Iris,' Liz said before leaving.

Iris flicked the business card, testing the stiffness of the paper, and told Louise, 'Please show Ms Winslow in.'

57

Chapter 9

Rita Winslow did look as if she had money, in the understated, tailored manner of people who were raised with it and saw no need to flaunt it. She was a tall, big-boned woman in her fifties, with a long face, strong jaw, and plain features. She wore little makeup and was dressed in a crisp oatmeal-colored linen suit. The small amount of jewelry she wore was not expensive, but her shoes and handbag were. Her light brown hair was cut short with thick bangs that brushed her forehead. She had a pleasant smile, revealing two overlapping front teeth. She looked as if she'd be comfortable around sailboats, guns, and horses.

'Pleased to meet you, Ms Winslow,' Iris said as she shook the woman's large hand.

'I prefer *Mrs* Winslow,' she said in a soft, English voice.

Iris nodded deferentially and gestured toward one of the chairs facing her desk. The woman's formal mannerisms were rubbing off on her. 'Please sit down.'

'Thank you, but could we speak privately?' Winslow shot an edgy glance at the open door.

'Of course.' Iris moved to close it, even though the office was now deserted. She relaxed into her leather chair and folded her hands in her lap. 'How can I help you?'

Winslow leaned forward, clutching her handbag between both hands, pressing her thin lips together as if undecided about how to begin. 'May I express my sincere condolences on the death of your friend, Todd Fillinger?'

The comment took Iris by surprise. 'Well . . . Thank you. That's very kind.' She looked askance at Winslow. 'Did you know Todd?'

'I knew Todd when he lived in London.' Winslow gazed out the window, shaking her head sadly. 'Terrible tragedy. Very unfortunate.' Returning her attention to Iris, she squared her broad shoulders and brusquely said, 'Let me get to the purpose of my visit.' She crossed her ankles and tucked her feet underneath the chair. 'I'm trying to recover a small statuette which has been stolen from me. I understand you have it. I'm willing to pay you twenty-five thousand dollars for its return, no questions asked.' She fixed her pale gray eyes on Iris, who was baffled.

'A statuette?'

59

Winslow's posture stiffened. 'The fox, Miss Thorne.'

'Fox?' Iris repeated, to the obvious irritation of Winslow, who impatiently shifted in her chair.

'Yes, Miss Thorne. The fox.'

Now angry at the intrusion and the woman's sudden change in attitude, Iris pushed back her chair and stood behind her desk. 'I think you've mistaken me for someone else.'

'You are the Iris Thorne who was in Moscow with Todd Fillinger the day he was murdered?'

'How do you know about that?' Iris asked warily.

Winslow ignored her question and accusingly demanded, 'Why did you leave Moscow so suddenly?'

The woman's headmistress's tactics worked on Iris, who dutifully responded. 'I had no choice. I was escorted to the airport by the police.' She planted her hands on her hips and asked a few questions of her own. 'Who are you? And how do you know so much about me and Todd Fillinger and Moscow?'

Winslow smiled slyly. 'Twenty-five thousand dollars, Miss Thorne. That's a great deal of money. I'm prepared to hand it to you right now.'

'I can't help you.'

'I think you're lying.'

'I think you should leave.'

Winslow's square jaw became rigid with disapproval. 'You're becoming tedious, Miss Thorne.' She stood her handbag on her lap, opened the brass clasp, and took out a lace-edged, monogrammed handkerchief. She carefully folded the fabric into a point and touched it against her upper lip. The delicate handkerchief looked incongruous in her broad hand.

Iris glared at her. 'Who told you to come here?'

Winslow slowly returned the handkerchief to her handbag. 'Someone who has good reason to believe that you have the statuette.'

She set her handbag on the seat of the other chair, stood, and rapidly walked around the desk to where Iris was standing, shoving her out of the way with an outstretched hand.

'Hey!' Iris protested.

'I'd sincerely hoped it wouldn't come to this, Miss Thorne, but you leave me with no choice.' Winslow opened a desk drawer and begin rifling through it.

'I'm calling security.' Iris grabbed the telephone receiver and started punching in numbers.

Winslow didn't pause or look up from her work. 'That will bring you a temporary fix, Miss Thorne, but I won't stop until I get what I want.'

Iris set the receiver down and slowly walked to the other side of her desk. In a quick movement, she snatched Winslow's purse from the chair and dumped the contents onto the seat.

That got Winslow's attention. 'Just what do you think you're doing?'

She petulantly glared at Iris with her lips pursed, her lipstick melting into the fine lines around her mouth.

'Don't forget to look through the filing cabinet. It's not locked.' Iris quickly pawed through Winslow's belongings.

She found a plastic key for the classy Peninsula Hotel in Beverly Hills and a folded piece of hotel stationery with Iris's home and office addresses on it in flowery handwriting. There were two linen handkerchiefs with Winslow's embroidered initials, a small steel box of licorice candies, a mirrored lipstick case with a tube of rose lipstick, a gold pressed-powder compact, a package of Dunhill cigarettes, a gold cloisonné lighter, a passport, wallet and a small, pearl-handled gun.

'I have never in my life . . .' Winslow quickly rounded the desk, grabbed her purse from the chair and began scooping her things into it, but not before Iris had picked up the wallet, passport, and gun from the pile and scurried to a corner.

She slipped the gun into her skirt pocket and proceeded to examine Winslow's belongings more closely. The wallet was of fine leather and crammed with US dollars, Deutschmarks, pounds sterling, francs, and lire in paper and coin and several credit cards. The British passport was for Rita Winslow and was stamped with multiple visas. Iris flipped through the pages. There was no Russian entry stamp, but she did see that Winslow had entered the United States in Miami, Florida, a week ago.

Winslow dimly watched Iris with her hands folded across her chest.

'How did you get my address?' Iris demanded. 'How did you know I was in Moscow with Todd? The murder was barely reported in the Moscow newspapers and I wasn't mentioned at all.' She rudely tossed the wallet and passport at Winslow who bolted forward to catch them.

'One has one's methods, Miss Thorne.'

'You come in here, search my office . . . At least show me the courtesy of telling me what the hell is going on.'

'I want the fox, Miss Thorne.' A muscle below Winslow's eye twitched. 'Twenty-five thousand dollars is very generous. If you don't cooperate, things can become unpleasant for you.'

A tall man with chiseled features, olive complexion, and dark wavy hair entered the doorway. He pointed the gun he held at Iris.

Iris, eyes wide, backed toward the window.

'Fernando, darling,' Winslow said. 'There's no need for weapons. Miss Thorne and I are having a nice chat.'

'Why is it taking so long?' he said to Winslow while his sleepy eyes were focused on Iris.

'Fernando, come now.'

He slipped the gun into the back of his pants waistband where it was hidden by his sports jacket.

'Enough.' Iris picked up the telephone receiver with a trembling hand. Winslow pulled the hem of her jacket, straightening it, and brushed the lapels. 'Miss Thorne, if you did smuggle the fox into the United States from Russia, I would not recommend calling the police. In my experience, they do not look kindly upon international smugglers.'

Iris hesitated before punching the last number.

'You brought something back with you from Russia, didn't you?' Winslow's eyes gleamed.

Beads of perspiration pricked Iris's skin. She remained frozen with her hand still poised above the telephone dial.

Winslow condescendingly went on, 'I can assure you that the authorities won't care when you bat your pretty blue eyes and tell them you didn't *know* you had smuggled stolen art.'

Iris set the phone back in the cradle and tried to ignore Winslow's smug expression.

'As you've ably discovered, I'm staying at the Peninsula Hotel. If you change your mind about the fee, please call me. May I have my gun, please? Don't worry, if I'd wanted to use it, I would have.'

Iris took the gun from her pocket and handed it to her.

Winslow put the weapon inside her purse then gave Fernando a lascivious look, drawing her fingers slowly down his cheek. 'Shall we go, darling?'

In the doorway, Winslow turned back to Iris. 'And don't even think about doing a deal for the fox on your own. I do not look kindly on amateurs muscling in on my business. Have a nice evening.'

Chapter 10

Iris unlocked the front door of her house and was pleasantly surprised to discover that it had not been ransacked. At first, she didn't think it had been entered at all, then she found small things out of place, drawers carelessly left ajar, and an empty wine glass that had been washed and left in her dish drainer next to a saucer that had also been washed. The odor of cigarette smoke hung in the air. She found the Dunhill cigarette butt and ashes in the kitchen garbage. Winslow and her henchman had gained access by cutting a small half-moon into the glass of a side window. At least they were neat.

Iris kicked off her pumps, re-washed the glass standing in the dish drainer, and poured what was left of a bottle of Chardonnay into it. At the sound of laughter in front of her house, she peeked out her windows to see Kiki and Roger from up the street heading toward her neighbor Marge's house. They were followed by an older man carrying a large bouquet of flowers – Kiki's father. Iris thought he and Marge would make a cute couple.

Too edgy to sit down, Iris picked up her remote phone and called Garland while she paced around her living room. He wasn't home. This was the normal pattern of their weeks, leaving messages and connecting about half the time. It was no way to build a relationship. She knew that. He knew that. They'd talked about it, but neither of them wanted to move cross-country. Maybe what Iris's mother had told her was true. She was too set in her ways ever to get married. Iris had dismissed the comment as fatalistic and bleak. Certainly, two bright, determined people who wanted to be together could work things out. She left a message telling Garland she was looking forward to Palm Springs that weekend. They'd lie in the sun and engage in conspicuous consumption like capitalists.

Thoughts of a romantic weekend away only momentarily distracted her from the incident with Rita Winslow and the sultry Latino. She kept replaying her experience last night with the customs officer. If she'd smuggled something it must have been inside the urn, but how?

The officer said he'd X-rayed it. Certainly he would have seen the statuette that Winslow described – unless of course the urn was lined with lead.

From a bookcase in the guest bedroom that she'd set up as an office,

Iris located her road atlas of California. She changed into loose jeans and a T-shirt, brushed her hair, freshened her makeup, grabbed a jacket, Todd's portfolio and a jug of water and headed out the door. At the corner gas station, she gassed up the Triumph.

Iris reached the Bakersfield city limits in an hour and a half. She pulled into a gas station to ask directions to Tracy Fillinger's house. Todd had given her Tracy's address when they'd lived in Paris. She'd kept it in a box where she stored the addresses of people with whom she'd lost contact. She didn't throw the addresses away. It seemed like throwing the people away.

The house was white with dark blue trim and looked as if it had been recently painted. A nylon banner with bright flowers hung from a pole attached to the porch roof. Terracotta bunnies nestled in a flowerbed. When Iris drove up, the front porch light clicked on.

With difficulty, she pulled Todd's portfolio from where it had been wedged into the front passenger seat. She walked up the cement path to the house. A dog fenced in the backyard of the neighbor's house began to bark.

Iris rang the doorbell and before long a tall man with neatly trimmed, receding wavy hair answered.

'Hi. I'm sorry to bother you, but is Tracy Fillinger home?'

The man appeared surprised and amused by Iris's question. 'Tracy Fillinger?'

Behind him, Iris saw a girl and a boy of about ten and twelve years old sprawled on the floor too close to a large television. 'Is she here?'

'Yes, she's here. I just haven't heard her called by that name in a while. We've been married for seventeen years. Who can I say is calling?'

'Iris Thorne. I'm a friend of her brother Todd.'

He looked at her with heightened interest. 'Todd? Oh sure.' He turned inside the house and yelled, 'Tracy!' then said to Iris, 'Come on inside.'

The kids rolled on the floor to look at Iris, then returned their attention to the television.

'Here, let me.' He took the portfolio from her and leaned it against the arm of an easy chair. 'I'm Richard Beale.'

Iris shook his hand. 'Nice to meet you.'

The furnishings in the room were comfortable and practical. The sole excess was the large-screen television that occupied most of the far wall.

A woman walked across the dining room from the kitchen, wiping her hands on a dishtowel. She had short, dark hair and a rotund figure that was somewhat camouflaged by the oversized blouse she wore over black leggings. She smiled at Iris and looked at her husband for assistance.

'This is Iris Thorne,' he said. 'She's a friend of Todd's.'

The woman held her hand out. 'Pleased to meet you.'

Iris tentatively accepted her hand and squinted with confusion. '*You're* Tracy Fillinger?'

'Yes. Well, that was my maiden name.' She exchanged a glance with her husband. 'Is something wrong?'

Iris rubbed her forehead. This was not the woman she'd met at the airport. 'You can't be Tracy Fillinger.'

Richard took a step forward. 'Ma'am, we don't mean to be rude, but why don't you tell us what you want?'

'Do you have a sister?' Iris ventured.

'No,' Tracy answered. 'There's just me and my brother. Kids!' she shouted, turning toward them. 'Go watch television in the back, please.'

Iris pressed her fingers over her mouth as she pictured handing the urn to the woman she thought was Tracy Fillinger at the airport. She remembered her edginess and tears, which Iris had attributed to grief. What a fool she'd been. It was all a ruse to string her along, to dupe her into transporting the urn into the States and delivering it. Rita Winslow was right – Iris was a smuggler. And Dean Palmer, her supposed one ally in Moscow, was behind it.

Then something else occurred to her. Palmer had probably never contacted the real Tracy Fillinger about Todd's murder. She slowly exhaled. 'Umm . . . can we sit down?'

Tracy gestured toward a blue couch and sat next to Iris while Richard took the leatherette easy chair. No one seemed relaxed.

Iris nervously rubbed her hands together. There was no good way to deliver bad news.

Tracy folded the dishtowel, tossed it on the coffee table, and guessed what was on Iris's mind. 'Did something happen to Todd?'

Iris looked her over. It was clear that this woman bore more of a familial resemblance to Todd than the woman at the airport. Iris took a breath and spoke quickly. 'Todd was murdered in Moscow a few days ago.'

Tracy sucked in air.

'He was shot to death while he was standing in front of a hotel. The police don't know who did it, but they suspect the Russian Mafia.'

Tracy stared intently at Iris. The silence in the room was deafening. Iris babbled to fill it. 'I was there when it happened. I went to Moscow to see Todd and to discuss investing in a chain of art galleries he'd wanted to get started. I'm very sorry to have to tell you this. I'm so sorry.'

Tracy sat back on the couch and looked at her husband. 'Well . . . We'd figured Todd for dead lots of times, hadn't we, Richard?'

He clasped his hands between his splayed knees and nodded.

Tracy explained. 'Long periods would pass when we wouldn't hear from him. It almost became a joke between Todd and me. Todd would show up out of the blue and we'd tell him, "We'd figured you for dead," and then we'd all laugh.' Tracy emitted a choking sob. Her husband winced in sympathy. She covered her face with her hands and cried.

Iris briefly stroked her arm then dropped her hand, feeling like an unwelcome intruder.

Richard rose from the chair to kneel on the carpet next to his wife, wrapping both his arms round her. At this, she cried harder, as if she could let go knowing there was someone to lean on, someone who wouldn't let her completely tumble down. Richard handed her the dishtowel, his face grave.

'My Todd, my baby,' Tracy wailed.

Iris wiped tears from her own cheeks.

'Poor, poor baby. He never had a chance.'

After a while, Tracy's sobs subsided. Richard left the room and returned with a box of tissues and two glasses of water. Iris drank greedily.

The discussion quickly returned to the practical. 'What happened to the body?' Tracy asked.

Iris's face burned. She couldn't bring herself to tell this woman that she'd handed her brother's ashes to a stranger. 'They cremated the body in Moscow. A consular officer at the US Embassy knew Todd and said he'd talked about wanting to be cremated when he died. I don't know what happened to the ashes.' It wasn't a complete lie. 'I brought back that portfolio from Todd's apartment. It has samples of his photography. I thought you might want them.'

She walked round the coffee table and picked up the portfolio. From it she took the scrapbook of Todd's magazine work.

'Todd had some nice furnishings in his apartment. I can try to get them for you.'

'That would be very kind but don't go to too much trouble. They're probably not worth the cost to ship them.'

Tracy moved a potted plant on the coffee table and some knick-knacks to make room. She began slowly turning the stiff pages lined with plastic film. 'Death Valley. I remember when he shot these photos for a travel magazine.'

There was a photo of a city marker apparently in the middle of nowhere. Two donkeys were dozing next to it. The sign said: 'FURNACE CREEK. Pop: 78. El: – 190.

'Todd loved Death Valley. We went there a couple of times when we were kids, on family vacations. When we were still a family.' She started to weep. 'Everyone's gone now. They're all gone.' She snatched a handful of tissues from the box on the coffee table.

Iris reached into her purse. 'Here's a letter Todd was writing you before . . .'

Tracy unfolded the plain, white paper. 'He was writing me a letter? I hadn't heard from him in . . . must be three years or more.'

'Really? The tone of the letter doesn't sound like years had passed.'

After reading the letter, Tracy refolded the pages and pressed them flat on top of the scrapbook. 'I'm glad he was doing something he enjoyed. Sounds like he was finally settling down.'

'He looked good. Very successful. He had a . . .' Iris stopped before mentioning the Mercedes. What had happened to it?

'When did you meet him?'

'I met him about five years ago when he lived in Paris.' Iris was intentionally vague.

'Iris, Iris . . .' Tracy regarded her with new interest. 'I remember Todd talking about you.'

Her husband leaned forward to get a closer look.

Iris shifted uneasily.

Tracy pointed at her. 'You sent a letter here for Todd. He'd left Paris and was living in London. He'd come home for Christmas. My goodness, he had all these expensive gifts for the kids. Remember that, hon?'

Her husband nodded.

'Anyway, I gave Todd your letter. I'd had it here for a couple of months.'

'He read my letter?' Iris asked.

'Yes.' Tracy hesitated. 'He read it. Then he balled it up and threw it in the fireplace. I didn't ask him about it. Probably wouldn't have done any good anyway. Todd was kind of a private person. Inward, if you know what I mean. You never really knew what he was thinking. All he said was that you were someone he'd met when he was living in Paris.'

'We dated for a while.'

'I figured it was something like that.'

Iris changed the subject. 'This is the house Todd was raised in, isn't it?'

'Yes. Richard and I moved in after my father became ill. Would you like to see Todd's old room? His nephew has it now, but he keeps his uncle's football trophies on display. He wants to play football someday too.'

'I'd like that.'

Iris followed Tracy through the small house. A large, sunny bedroom with French doors was at one end, the style and size incongruous with the rest of the house. Iris figured they'd had it added on. The two children were sitting on the bed in there, watching a television installed in a wall unit with shelves cluttered with photographs. The kids turned their attention briefly away from the tube to glance at the adults.

Tracy introduced them. 'That's Emily and that's Richard Todd. Say hello to Iris, she's a friend of your Uncle Todd's.'

They gave a lackluster greeting.

Tracy led the way to a small bedroom at the end of the hall that was boldly decorated in navy blue and red. Posters of heavy-metal bands were thumbtacked on the wall next to posters of bikini-clad supermodels of the moment. Brass-and-chrome football trophies were displayed on a book-shelf. Tracy picked one up and handed it to Iris.

'I didn't know that Todd played football,' Iris confessed.

'Todd was the best player East Bakersfield High's ever seen,' Richard enthused. 'I was assistant coach when he was on the team. After graduation, he got a football scholarship to USC. He was disappointed

67

when they put him on second string. I told him everybody's got to start somewhere. Then he got hurt in his third game and that really got him down. I told him to rebuild his muscles, go back the next season and give it his all, but . . .' He shrugged. 'Lost his spirit, I guess. It's hard to go from being a star at your hometown high school to playing with guys as good as or better than you are.'

Iris replaced the trophy on the shelf. 'Todd went to USC? I thought he went to Cal State Fresno.'

Tracy swatted dust from a trophy. 'That's where he transferred after he left USC. We tried to get him to go back for his second year. Even his coach talked to him, but I guess he was too afraid of not making it. Todd was a big, tough guy on the outside, but he was pretty fragile deep down. Cal State Fresno was where his buddy Mike was going.'

Iris scanned the other trophies. 'It's odd that he never talked about football, seeing that it was such a big part of his life. He never talked much about his past at all. I guess his mother's death when he was so young really affected him.' She felt silly for making such an obvious statement. 'Well, of course it did. It had to.'

Tracy and Richard became very still and Iris sensed she'd said the wrong thing. Tracy said, 'Todd told you about what happened to our mother?'

'She died in a car accident when Todd was ten. Didn't she?'

Tracy raised a corner of her mouth in dismay. 'She died when Todd was ten but it was no accident. It's always been sort of a family secret, but since everyone's dead, I guess it doesn't matter anymore.' She took a deep breath. 'My mother was murdered. Shot to death by her lover. They were boozing one night in a hotel and . . . something happened and he shot her. They arrested him and he went to prison. Got out after a few years and disappeared. My dad knew about my mom's chasing around, but he really went downhill after she died. He drank before. Drank a lot more after. Managed to keep his job at the post office and put food on the table, but that was about it. Retired with a pension. I was left to raise Todd. I was sixteen. We kind of made a home of sorts. My dad was here, but he was a shadow.'

'My God.' Iris rested her hand on Tracy's arm. 'I'm sorry. I had no idea.'

'Now you tell me Todd's been shot to death.' She bitterly shook her head. 'Some family, huh? It's not going to be that way for my kids. My kids are going to have a normal life.'

'Of course they are, hon,' Richard said soothingly.

Tracy raised her chin. 'Now you know everything about the Fillingers.'

Iris smiled sympathetically; she felt she knew less than before.

Chapter 11

Iris peeked through a crack in her living room drapes as she spoke on the telephone. 'It was there last night when I got home around ten o'clock and was still there this morning. It was gone when I went outside to bring in the paper about an hour ago. Now it's back.' The late model navy blue Thunderbird with darkly tinted windows was parked across the street near the rise in Casa Marina Drive. 'No, I haven't seen anyone. I think the driver's still in it. Could you please check it out? Thank you.'

Iris looked at her watch. It was 6:00 a.m. She was half an hour late hitting the road for the office. She couldn't seem to get back in gear. She drank the last of her coffee and glanced over the photographs from Todd's portfolio that she'd spread over her dining room table. Before leaving Bakersfield the night before, she'd asked Tracy Beale if she could take Todd's work with her, promising to return it soon. She wanted to sort through it, hoping she might learn something about Todd or find a clue about the statuette, although she didn't know what. It was the only thing she had.

She clomped into the kitchen in her pumps and set the coffee mug in the sink, folded the newspaper into her briefcase, snapped it closed, grabbed it and her purse and was about to head outside when, through her dining room windows, she saw a black-and-white pull up next to the Thunderbird. A police officer got out of the passenger door and walked round to the other car's driver's side. Iris saw the officer talking to someone inside. Soon after, the Thunderbird pulled away from the curb and descended Casa Marina Drive.

Even though it was late for Iris, it was still early for most worker bees to begin their day. The lobby of the office building was still quiet and the display Sam Eastman had made of her desk hadn't yet attracted any visitors. Iris took the opportunity to get a closer look at the controversial image.

She bent over in front of the desk and turned her head this way and that without seeing a figure of a woman cloaked in a robe. She fixed her eyes on the spot then slowly backed up, treating it like one of those swirl and flower-crammed prints with a 3D image hidden in it that one has to look at just right to see.

'Boo!'

Iris jolted into the air, flinging her briefcase across the slick granite floor. She wheeled round, eyes wide.

Liz Martini's bemused smile fully displayed the small dimples in her left cheek, enhancing the impish looks created by her diamond-shaped face and big brown eyes. 'Whoa, girl!' She held her hands out to each side as if trying to steady a large beast. 'Calm down. Thatsa girl.'

Iris bent over and snatched her briefcase from the floor, not caring who saw her backside. 'That's a heck of a way to come up on somebody.'

'A little jumpy, are we?'

'Yes.'

Liz's good humor turned to concern. 'What's wrong, kiddo?'

Iris opened her mouth to speak, then exhaled in exasperation. 'I don't know where to begin. I don't want to talk about it here and I need to get upstairs.'

'Hey! Let's have lunch today.' Liz made most ideas sound like the best thing she'd ever heard.

'Love to.'

Liz clamped a well-manicured hand on Iris's wrist. 'Let's splurge and go to Hugo's. I'll call and make sure they reserve Ozzie's table for us. You'll feel better after some good food and a nice long chat. OK?'

'Terrific.'

'Great!' A natural-born salesperson, Liz put a sales spin on even the most minor transaction, describing the features, the benefit for the buyer, and asking for the close.

'What is Sam-I-Am doing here *again*?' Iris watched as her boss energetically walked toward them carrying a paper carrier bag.

'Wait, isn't that his Monday green suit? It's Thursday, so it should be brown suit day.' Liz dramatically grabbed her long, dark curls. 'This is so confusing.'

'Good morning, Iris, Liz.' Sam Eastman set the bag on the floor and rubbed his hands together with enthusiasm that was not reflected in his washed-out blue eyes. From the carrier bag he pulled out a yellow bedsheet printed with white and green flowers. He began draping it over the desk.

'Sam!' Iris said. 'No more making miracles with McKinney Alitzer?'

'New York called me and said they didn't think it was an appropriate marketing campaign for the firm. I guess someone saw it on the news.'

'What's going to happen to the desk?' Iris asked.

'I'm buying it from the firm. Going to put it in my house.'

Iris looked at her watch. 'Gotta go. See you, Sam.'

'Bye, Sam,' Liz chimed.

As they walked to the elevator, Iris said to Liz, 'At least that insanity is coming to an end. Sam looks pretty chipper for someone being forced to retire. Maybe there's no truth to the rumor you heard.'

'That was no rumor.'

In the elevator, Iris said, 'I can't see me as regional manager. I've spent my entire career with McKinney Alitzer in this office.'

'You'd be great.'

Iris arched an eyebrow. 'More money. More power. Sure, I could get used to it.'

They exited the elevator on the twelfth floor and Iris pulled open the glass door of the suite for Liz to pass. They walked through the Sales Department, heading for opposite corners when they reached the end of the suite.

Iris greeted her assistant then went into her office where Louise had already unlocked the door, opened the drapes, and turned on the lights. The clock on Iris's desk said 7:15 and she was afraid that it was already too late to call Moscow. She wanted to inquire about obtaining Todd's possessions for his sister. She also wanted to put Dean Palmer on notice that he wasn't going to get away with what he'd done – even though she didn't quite understand exactly what it was.

Louise brought Iris a cup of black coffee in her BUDGETS ARE FOR WIMPS mug. Iris took a sip and said, 'I swear the coffee tastes different since you washed this mug.'

'It can't possibly.'

'It does. Thanks for thinking of me while I was gone.'

'You? I did it for me. I was sick of looking at the filthy thing.'

'Could you please close the door after you, Louise?'

Louise complied, looking slightly surprised. Iris felt a sting of betrayal. She had no secrets from Louise, who was the soul of discretion. But since Iris didn't know what she was into or how deep she was into it, she thought it best to keep things quiet.

She dialed the US Embassy in Moscow. 'Dean Palmer, please.'

The young-sounding woman who answered the phone put Iris on hold. Soon, a man came on the line. 'Dean Palmer is not here at the moment. Can I help you?'

'It's very important that I speak with him. Do you know where he can be reached?'

'I'm sorry, I don't.'

'Can you have him call me when he comes in?'

'What does this concern? Maybe I can be of assistance.' His voice was overly solicitous, making her suspicious.

'This is Iris Thorne. I'm a friend of Todd Fillinger, the American who was gunned down Monday night. I was with Todd just before he was shot and was questioned by the Moscow police. Dean Palmer came to the police station that night and rescued me. I'm back in Los Angeles again and I have to talk to him about that incident. It's very important.'

'Hold on.'

Iris slumped in her chair and stared blankly out the window at the smoggy September day.

A new male voice came on the line, older and deeper than the other one. 'Miss Thorne, this is Bob Davies, Chief Consular Officer. How are you?'

Iris rolled her eyes. 'Just fine, thank you.'

'The fact of the matter is, we're also very interested in locating Dean Palmer.'

'He's gone?'

'Yes, he's disappeared. Yesterday, after he didn't show up for work or call or answer his phone, I sent someone over to his apartment in the Embassy compound. When Dean didn't come to the door, we went in. He'd cleaned it out.'

Iris sat in stunned silence.

'Is there anything I can help you with?'

'I'd like to recover Todd Fillinger's possessions for his sole heir, his sister Tracy in California. Dean took me to Todd's apartment on Tuesday. It was full of expensive furnishings. Dean told me he'd been in contact with Tracy and that she didn't want any of Todd's belongings, but it was a mistake.'

'A lie, Miss Thorne. It was most probably a lie. I'll send someone over to Mr Fillinger's apartment, but I doubt whether we'll recover anything.' Davies slowly drew in a breath. 'Dean Palmer is a heroin addict. We'd suspected for some time that he'd been selling visas and passports to finance his habit. We were setting up a sting to trap him when he slipped away.'

Iris thought about the two women Palmer had let into Todd's apartment and how they were admiring the furnishings. She now knew why Todd's photography equipment was missing. 'What about the urn?'

'What urn?'

'Never mind.' She already knew the answer and didn't want him to know that she had played a role in Palmer's scheme. 'I trusted him. I feel like a fool.'

'If it makes you feel any better, so do I.'

Liz Martini pulled her Rolls-Royce Silver Shadow into the circular driveway in front of the pink stucco façade of Hugo's. Her toy poodles, Thelma and Louise, one black and one apricot, both wearing small pink bows in their ears, flew between the front and back seats and the shelf in the rear window, yipping gaily. Iris tried to subdue them without success.

'Iris, just throw them off. I apologize. The girls are always jetted after they've had their hair and manicures done.' From the glove compartment, Liz took out Chanel leashes of leather braided with gold chain. Iris spotted Liz's .38, which she knew was loaded. Liz carried a matching gun in the trunk and maintained a virtual arsenal in her home in the Malibu colony. She was an expert shot, practicing weekly at the Beverly Hills Shooting Club.

A flurry of parking valets opened the big car's doors. Liz managed to grab one of the dogs, a valet nabbed the other, and they snapped on the leashes. From the back seat, Liz took a cut crystal bowl which she filled with bottled spring water. She squatted next to the dogs who jumped on her Vera Wang sheath dress and licked her face with abandon.

'Mommy's gonna order you a nice filet mignon. Just be patient, sweethearts.' She slipped the valet ten dollars. 'Thanks, Miguel.'

Iris casually watched the goings-on. She'd become accustomed to Liz's extraordinary habits a long time ago.

Miguel and another valet simultaneously opened the restaurant's tall, white, double doors by their huge, round doorknobs.

Hugo's had been a Los Angeles institution since it opened in the 1950s. It hit hard times in the seventies and was shuttered for about ten years in the eighties. Frail old Hugo refused to cave in to developers who pursued him to sell his large corner lot on the stretch of Wilshire Boulevard known as the Miracle Mile. He also refused to sell a single fixture, martini shaker, or autographed celebrity photo.

In 1991, his grandson obtained financing to reopen the place and restored it to its 1952 kitschy glamor, re-upholstering the deep booths in petal pink, tuck-and-roll vinyl, re-finishing the French provincial furniture in the original white with gold trim, and giving a facelift to the chubby cherubs and oversized mirrors decorating the walls. The white marble fountain with the statue of Venus in the grand lobby again sprayed water in five different rotating patterns, each change accompanied by a different colored light that shone from the base. Martinis, aged beef, cigars, and the rat pack were in vogue again and Hugo's was hotter than ever.

A deferential maître d' showed Liz and Iris to Liz's husband Ozzie's A-list table in the corner of the main room where they could see who came and went. Shortly after they were seated, someone from a neighboring table came to greet Liz. Then a waiter with a stiffly starched long, white apron tied round his waist took their drink order. Liz ordered an Absolut limon martini and a filet, medium, cut into small pieces for her dogs. Iris ordered a glass of Chardonnay.

'To you, darling.' Liz raised her brimming glass.

'To me,' Iris agreed.

Liz let out a small noise of pleasure as she took a sip. 'Now what's gotten you all shook up?'

'Todd Fillinger was machine-gunned to death in Moscow, almost in front of me.' Iris slowly turned her wine glass by the stem against the table as she waited for Liz's expected horrified response. Then she told her everything, feeling relieved at finally being able to unburden herself. She told her about Detective Davidovsky, the police station, and the elegant yet unnerving man who turned out to be Konstantin Markov, head of security for the rich and powerful Nikolai Kosyakov. She told her how she went to the Club Ukrainiya to seek out Kosyakov and instead found bullet holes and a blood-soaked carpet. Then there was Dean Palmer, the urn, and Todd's mysterious partner, Enrico Lazare.

She described her speedy exit from Moscow and meeting the woman who claimed to be Tracy Fillinger in the airport and how she saw Todd's real sister in Bakersfield. And then there was the visit from the stately but dangerous British woman, Rita Winslow, and her sultry partner, Fernando, who had searched her house and offered twenty-five thousand dollars to return some fox statuette, no questions asked. Finally, she'd found out that Dean Palmer wasn't who he pretended to be.

Before Iris finished, Liz had ordered a second round of drinks, called Louise on her cellular phone and told her that she and Iris wouldn't be back that afternoon.

'I'm afraid to call the police. Winslow told me that if I did transport stolen art into the States, the police won't care whether I was aware of what I was doing or not.' Iris nibbled the clams casino she'd ordered as an appetizer.

'She's right. The police send drug mules to jail all the time. I saw a story on *Sixty Minutes* about a woman who thought she was transporting a friend's paintings from Columbia. They turned out to be filled with cocaine between the canvas and the backing. The police didn't care that she didn't know anything about it.' Liz stabbed her oysters Rockefeller. 'Maybe it's not the statuette itself that's valuable. Maybe it was stuffed with jewels or drugs.'

Iris set her fork down and leaned against the pink vinyl. 'I don't know what this fox statuette is. It had to have been small enough to fit into the base of the urn.' With her hands, she framed an area about eight inches in diameter.

'You were really in love with Todd Fillinger, weren't you?'

Iris indecisively pulled down the corners of her mouth. 'I like telling myself it was more lust than love, but then I realize I'm trivializing it. It was more than that.'

She dabbed a corner of soda bread into an empty clam shell to gather the last of the garlic, bread crumbs, and butter. 'I am so unlike Todd. We happened to meet at a point in my life when I was as loose and carefree as he was. I'd finally finished my MBA after years of going to school at night and working fulltime. I'd quit my teaching job and moved out of my apartment which was five miles from where I'd grown up. My things were in storage. I hadn't even looked for a new apartment and had no idea where I wanted to live. I was starting a new job in a completely different line of work in four months. For the first time in my life, I was completely untethered.'

Liz pulled the martini olive from its decorated toothpick with her teeth. 'And open to meeting someone like Todd. How did you meet him, anyway?'

'I'd planned a long trip to Europe before I started McKinney Alitzer's

74

training class. Didn't have a firm itinerary in mind. My first stop was Paris. I'd rented a room in a charming little hotel. On the corner was *Le Café des Quatre Vents*. Café of the Four Winds. That's where I first saw Todd. He went there a lot, with friends or alone. He seemed to know a ton of people. He always had at least one camera with him and was usually carrying a tripod and a shoulder bag with equipment. He was very friendly with the couple who owned the place.' Iris rubbed her forehead. 'What was their name?' She shook her head, giving up.

A waiter brought their entrées. Liz had ordered liver and onions and Iris had lamb chops.

Iris attacked the spinach soufflé side dish with her fork. 'At first, I thought Todd was French. I'd only heard him speak French and he was fluent in it. I later found out he had a gift for foreign languages. Anyway, we'd exchanged a few glances and one evening he walked over to me.'

'And you ended up in bed.'

'*Excuse* me! That was the next night.'

Liz smiled.

'My three-month European tour didn't take me much farther than the Parisian countryside and to Cap D'Antibes on the Riviera to stay with friends of Todd's. I was so swept away by him, by Paris, by the whole thing, I never wanted to leave. Soon, the time came for me to make a decision. I had a fantasy of staying in Paris with Todd. He'd take pictures and I'd cook *à la Americain* and write a novel or draw in pastels and live a Bohemian life. But I suspected I couldn't live that far from home forever. Todd had a solution – we'd get married. I'd go home, start my new job. He'd close up his affairs in Paris and come over later.'

'Sounds wonderful. What happened?'

'I ran. While he was waiting in a small chapel with two friends, I was in a taxi heading for the airport.'

'Really?' Liz twirled her fork in a mound of caramelized onions. 'You didn't even say goodbye?'

'I left a note on the bed. "Adieu, Todd." ' Iris chuckled sadly. '*Quelle* drama, huh? I just had to go. I felt like I would die if I didn't. I guess I had a panic attack. I didn't want to tell Todd my plans because I was afraid he'd talk me out of it. He could have, easily. Maybe I just had cold feet.'

'The whole thing seems so unlike you. It's as if you're talking about someone else.'

'Doesn't it? When I think about my time in Paris, it seems unreal, like it was a movie I saw rather than something that actually happened. All I can say is that I was different then. My life was different. I'm not trying to excuse what I did. It was rotten. Probably the worst thing I've ever done to anyone.' Iris pushed the bare bones remaining from her lamb chops around the plate with her fork. 'At least I was able to apologize to Todd before . . .' She slowly set down the fork and folded her hands in her lap.

'How much does Garland know about you and Todd?'

'Everything, except for the squishy parts. He knows Todd and I were engaged and that I left him at the altar. Garland had the class not to pry. He's never asked about the men in my past, happily for me. My past has been, to put it mildly, a bit more checkered than his. I assured him he had no reason to feel jealous or threatened by my going to see Todd and I don't think he was jealous. He mostly questioned Todd's motives for inviting me to Moscow.'

'Justifiably.'

'Garland is a rock. Todd was cotton candy.'

Liz ate about a third of her entrée then asked the waiter for a take-out container. 'You may never find out what really happened in Moscow.'

'I have to try. Todd didn't deserve to die the way he did. And I didn't deserve being used as a pawn.'

'What are you going to do?'

'Rita Winslow knows what happened. I'm going to pay her a visit.'

Chapter 12

The rooftop pool on the Peninsula Hotel's tenth floor sparkled bright turquoise-blue in the hot late-afternoon sun. Cabañas of striped forest green and white canvas with scalloped edges, the roofs pulled into circus-tent peaks, lined the pool. Hollywood power players dressed in swimwear and suntan lotion conducted business from lounge chairs with associates in business suits. The young and the beautiful wore as little as possible and tried to be noticed. Waiters in crisp khaki slacks and white polo shirts kept things lubricated.

The front desk clerk told Iris that Mrs Winslow could be found in her cabaña. It was 90 degrees, but Iris left on her jacket as she walked across the patio. It gave her a more commanding air. The heat didn't bother her.

She found Rita Winslow sitting in a pool chair, straddling a small table inside a cluttered cabaña. She was wearing a one-piece bathing suit with a gauzy wrap over it. Large sunglasses were perched on her head. In a tall glass at her elbow, a lime wedge floated in melted ice. Photographs and photocopies of art and art books and magazines were scattered about. The cabaña was outfitted with a fax machine, scanner, document shredder, and several telephone lines. One of the hotel's plush terrycloth robes and a mesh bag crammed with magazines and toiletries hung from a bamboo coat rack in the corner.

Winslow was furiously typing on a laptop computer and did not look up when Iris stood outside the tied-back canvas door. 'Miss Thorne. How nice to see you again.' She finally turned her attention from the computer screen. Her upper lip was damp with perspiration. 'Please come in.' She moved papers and books from a mesh-covered chair. 'I'm glad you've changed your mind about the fox.'

Iris sat down. 'Why did you search my house if you were planning on offering me twenty-five thousand dollars for the fox?'

Winslow plucked her sheer bathing suit cover, demurely pulling it closed. 'You can't blame me for trying to save money. The fox is rightfully mine. I've already paid a million dollars for it. I shouldn't have to pay you anything to recover it.' Her smiled was forced, as if they were having a polite conversation about local politics at a tea party and found they disagreed.

'Possession is nine-tenths of the law.'

Winslow's smile faded. 'You said you had information about the fox.' She looked at her watch. 'Well?'

Iris casually crossed her legs, pleased that she had piqued Winslow. 'All in due time. First, I want some information from you.'

Winslow slitted her eyes. 'I'm very pressed for time today, Miss Thorne.'

'Who told you about me?'

'A reliable source. Very reliable.'

'Who?'

'Now, Miss Thorne, you don't really expect me to divulge the names of my sources. One spends too much time cultivating them to simply turn them over to anyone who asks.' She smiled smugly as she tapped a cigarette from a pack and lit it with her cloisonné lighter. Her attention was drawn to something outside the cabaña.

Iris followed her gaze and saw Fernando, the handsome man who had come into her office with Winslow. Even with the glut of beautiful people poolside, he attracted stares as he strolled across the patio. He stopped a waiter and ordered a drink then made his way to the cabaña. Winslow's eyes widened appreciatively as she watched him, then narrowed when he turned to observe a lithe young thing walk past.

He had to duck to enter the tent.

Winslow stretched to grab his hand, beaming at him. 'Did you have a good nap, darling?'

'Yes, I feel very refreshed.' He spoke with an accent, lisping some of his words in the manner of the Catalonia region of Spain.

Winslow pulled his face close to her, clutching his thick wavy hair between her fingers, and kissed him on the mouth.

Fernando briefly returned the kiss. When he tried to straighten up, Winslow pulled him down again. He forcefully removed her hand from his head, wiping at the lipstick he correctly assumed was on his face. 'Rita, we have a guest.'

She leered at him, appearing to enjoy this rough play.

'Hi, I'm Fernando Peru.'

Iris had been feigning interest in the goings-on by the pool. She looked round when Fernando introduced himself.

He added, 'Rita's business associate.' He seemed to feel an obligation to explain that he was more than her toy boy. 'We weren't properly introduced yesterday. I apologize for coming into your office carrying a gun.'

Winslow lecherously eyed him. 'Yes, he usually only enters a room with his gun out for me.' She ran her hand underneath the hem of his shorts on the inside of his thigh.

He grabbed her wrist before she reached his crotch. 'Now, Rita . . .' He roughly retracted her hand then sat in a chair several feet away.

She rubbed her wrist. 'Don't look so concerned, Fernando. I'll stop

78

embarrassing you in front of your little friend.'

Iris would have preferred being almost anywhere else.

'Fernando, our Miss Thorne has as much told me that the fox is hers now by virtue of possession.'

'You do have the fox?' Fernando asked.

'I have a connection to it.'

The waiter brought Fernando's drink and Winslow became irritated at the interruption. 'Would you like something?' she brusquely asked Iris who declined.

After the waiter left, Winslow asked, 'Are you working for Enrico Lazare?'

'Maybe.'

Winslow's gray eyes bored into Iris, her masculine features imperiously stern. There was a long silence. At last, she sniffed and took a puff of her forgotten cigarette. 'Todd Fillinger and this . . . Corsican thought they could set themselves up as art dealers just like that.' She snapped her fingers. 'They thought it was so easy. If Rita Winslow can do it, anyone can do it.' She pressed the cigarette out in a glass ashtray.

Fernando Peru absently stroked his chest, his hand inside his silky Hawaiian-print shirt. His eyes met Iris's. He quickly looked away when Winslow glanced at him, but not before she caught him.

She gave him a reproving look and went on, 'After everything I did for Todd,' she sneered. 'To have him muscle in on *my* business like that. Loyalty doesn't exist anymore.'

'Come on, Rita,' Fernando said. 'Todd found the fox. If he wanted to cut someone else in on the deal, that was his call. The set-up was tricky. He felt he needed help.' He picked up his drink and took a sip from it, dabbing his fingers which were damp from the condensation on the glass against the cocktail napkin. 'You can't control everything.'

She glared at him. 'As you keep reminding me with little trophies called Susie and Julie and Boom-boom. Little reminders to let me know that I can't control you.'

Fernando sat motionlessly. Finally he said, 'Rita, you're suspicious of me and you have no need to be.'

'Oh, don't I?'

'Rita, Iris came here to talk about the fox,' he said gently.

'Yes, of course. The fox. Well, Miss Thorne, where is Lazare? I take it he has my fox.'

Iris took her jacket off, the heat finally getting to her. 'Mrs Winslow, I have information and sources which I prefer not to reveal, just like you.'

'Todd and Lazare planned to rob me all along,' Winslow muttered almost to herself. 'Then Lazare double-crossed Todd. That's what he gets for playing with fire.' She pointed a broad index finger at Peru. 'And you played right into their hands.'

'I was in the subway with Todd, remember? He didn't expect that any more than I did.'

'What subway?' Iris asked.

'You don't know?' Peru asked. 'That's where Todd told me to—'

'Ah, ah!' Winslow warned. 'She should know about that.'

Iris tucked a damp lock of blonde hair behind her ear. 'I was only told what I needed to know. That's all the information Todd gave me and all I wanted.'

Peru continued in spite of Winslow's admonition. 'Todd told me to meet him in the Park Kultury metro station. I brought the rest of Rita's money and he was bringing the fox. Right after I got there, some guy robbed both of us at gunpoint. He took our guns and was handcuffing me to a bench when Todd ran away. The guy shot at him but missed.'

Iris listened with rapt attention. 'What happened in Nikolai Kosyakov's office?'

Winslow raised her hand and Peru closed his mouth, holding the comment he was about to make. 'I find it hard to believe that no one told you about that.'

'Like I said before, Mrs Winslow, they didn't fill me in on the details.'

'Then you don't need to know the details.'

Iris crossed her legs and saw Peru sneak a glance at them. 'Todd was my friend. I'd like to know what happened to him.'

'Rita, what difference could it make now?' Peru argued.

'You couldn't have been that close.' Winslow eyed Iris suspiciously. 'I don't remember Todd ever mentioning you.'

'I met Todd in Paris several years ago,' Iris responded. 'If you knew Todd, then you know that he was a very private person. He rarely spoke of people or events in his life.'

Peru raised his eyebrows with recognition. 'I remember Todd talking to me about you. Iris from Paris. Sure. You lived with him, right?'

'Yes.'

'I see now,' Winslow said. 'You were in love with Todd.'

Iris didn't respond.

Winslow continued anyway. 'You weren't the only one, my dear. Todd had that effect on women. Our Todd left a long swath of broken hearts across two continents.'

Iris felt her cheeks coloring. She quickly changed the subject. 'Fernando, how long did you know Todd?'

'A long time.' Peru nodded at the memory. 'We met in Barcelona, where I'm from, in nineteen eighty-eight. We hooked up again when Todd moved to London after he left Paris.'

Winslow patiently watched them with her head in her hand, her index finger pressed deeply against her cheek. 'This is all very interesting, but I don't have time to rehash both of your social histories. Let's get to the point. Who brought you the fox in Moscow and where is it now?'

Iris boldly stared back. 'Not until I get some information.'

Winslow flipped her hand away from her face and looked at Peru and back to Iris as if she was mystified. 'That's all we've been doing, Miss Thorne. Giving you information. Now let's get to the point of your visit. Where is the fox?'

Iris stood and folded her jacket over her arm. 'I thought we could have a polite conversation, Mrs Winslow. Apparently not.'

Winslow openly looked Iris over. 'I'm not dealing with you any longer. I find you tedious. Tell Lazare I want to speak with him directly.'

'He doesn't want to speak with you. I'm your best chance at recovering the fox, so you'd better be nice to me.'

Although his face was still immobile, Peru seemed amused by their interchange. He continued to stroke his chest, his eyes moving back and forth between the two women.

'This is a dangerous game, Miss Thorne,' Winslow cautioned.

'If you paid a million dollars for the fox, it must be worth more than twenty-five thousand to you to get it back.'

Winslow arrogantly tipped her head back and regarded Iris down the length of her nose. 'Be careful, Miss Thorne. You're entering into what I sense is unknown territory for you. You may get in over your head.'

Iris took her sunglasses from her purse, put them on, and without a word turned to leave.

Winslow said to her back, 'I'll pay you fifty thousand dollars.'

Iris looked at her over her shoulder. 'That'll cover my fee.'

'Two million for the fox, including your fee, and not a penny more.'

Iris shrugged. 'It's a question of supply and demand.'

Winslow's mouth grew pinched.

Iris stepped into the sunshine of the seemingly endless late summer day and left.

The valet drove Iris's Triumph TR6 onto the gently sloped driveway in front of the hotel, put it in neutral and pulled the parking brake. The loud ratcheting sound of the brake being engaged roused Iris from her thoughts. She raced toward the valet, madly waving her arms.

'Hey! Stop! The parking brake . . .'

The valet noticed the red car starting to roll slowly toward the street. He leaped for the door, threw a leg inside and mashed the brake pedal.

'. . . doesn't work.' Iris pressed her hand over her pounding heart.

The valet cut the engine and left the car in gear. Iris put some money into his hand, got into the car and restarted it.

She'd gone several blocks in the impatient Beverly Hills traffic, turning right onto Wilshire and right again onto Robertson before she noticed that the navy blue Thunderbird with the tinted windows that had been parked across the street from her house the previous night was following her. She took a few unnecessary turns just to make certain. The car stayed closed behind her.

With one hand on the wheel, she fished her cellular phone from her purse and punched in 911. She got a rapid busy signal.

'Son of a bitch!'

She tried again. Again she heard the rapid busy signal. 'Dammit! Stupid cellular service!'

She sped through a yellow light that was about to turn red. The Thunderbird ran the red light to keep up with her. She turned right onto Olympic, darting through a small opening in a group of pedestrians. The Thunderbird was slightly delayed but soon caught up with her. She drove into a gas station, cutting through the bays, almost hitting a man who was shoving a hot dog into his mouth as he came out of the minimart.

She screeched to a stop in front of the garage where two mechanics wearing grease-covered overalls looked up from their work at her.

Iris bolted from her car, leaving its door open and the engine running. 'Help!'

With horror, she saw the Thunderbird pull up behind the Triumph. From it exited a solidly built man wearing a gun in a shoulder holster. He walked briskly toward her as if he saw no need to run because he knew he'd catch her.

'Call the police! That man is chasing me!'

One of the mechanics started to run toward Iris then stopped when the man from the T-bird firmly grabbed her upper arm. Iris thrashed in his grasp.

'FBI. Ms Thorne, please stop kicking me.'

Iris stopped fighting him long enough to get a look at the badge and identification card he was holding.

'Everything's under control. Let's remain calm. No one's going to get hurt. Sir, would you please be kind enough to park Ms Thorne's car by the wall over there, lock it and bring me the keys? We're going to leave it parked here a while. Is that all right?'

The mechanic nodded and jogged to the Triumph.

'Ms Thorne, I'll gladly let you go if you promise not to run away.'

'I wouldn't have had a reason to run if you hadn't been chasing me,' she snapped.

He released her and handed over the keys that the mechanic gave him. 'Why don't we sit in my car and have a little chat?'

Iris looked at the dark-windowed Thunderbird and shook her head. 'Not until you tell me what this is about.'

In a gesture that indicated it had been a long day for him, he ran his hand over his deeply lined face which was heavily marked with acne scars across his cheeks. He appeared to be in his fifties. 'That's precisely the reason why I'd like to chat with you in my car.'

'Why there? Why not here?'

'It's cool inside the car, Ms Thorne. OK?'

'Can I see your identification again, please?'

His jaw stiffened but he patiently complied with her request. She scrutinized his ID then grudgingly handed it back to him.

Without a word, he opened the passenger door. A blast of chilled air hit her. The engine and the air conditioner were still running. She slid across the navy blue fabric seats. When he closed the door, she detected a slight coconut odor. He'd opted for the piña colada fragrance at the car wash. Something about the small extravagance made him less intimidating to her. She looked around. Tossed across the back seat was the jacket that matched his dark gray suit pants. Several file folders and a briefcase were also in the back seat.

He opened the driver's door, slipped behind the wheel, and faced her with one leg propped on the seat. He held his hand out. 'Name's Roger Weems.' He elongated the vowels, having a southern accent that Iris hadn't noticed until now. His handshake was strong. He smiled quickly, out of politeness, displaying straight but small teeth, then grimaced as he ran his finger inside the collar of his white button-down shirt and pulled at the knot in his tie. Circles of perspiration had darkened the fabric at his armpits. 'I do believe it's a hundred degrees today.'

He took a rumpled handkerchief from his back pocket and wiped the back of his neck and around the edges of his thick, black hair that was styled in a crew cut. The hair on top of his head stood straight up and was cut so close at the sides, his scalp was visible.

Iris jumped when he put the car in gear and released the parking brake with a thud. 'Wait a minute. You said we'd talk in the car.'

He started to pull out of the gas station. 'We have several matters to discuss and I think it's best if we talk in my office. I'm over in the Federal building in Westwood, just a few miles from here.'

'I'm not going anywhere with you.' Iris opened the door and was about to leap from the slowly-moving car when he stepped on the brake and threw the transmission into park.

'Now, just hang on one second, here.' His words were clipped. He punched the button on the glove compartment and took out a small digital camera. 'Would you mind closing the door? You're letting all the cool air out.'

Iris ignored him and remained sitting with one foot in and one outside the car.

The vertical lines down each of his cheeks grew deeper but he said nothing as he switched on the camera and held it so Iris could see the tiny screen on the back. He clicked through a series of photographs, all shots of her poolside meeting with Rita Winslow and Fernando Peru.

Iris swallowed hard, her throat suddenly dry.

'Who are these folks, Miss Thorne?'

Iris raised her hand to point, but it was trembling. She tucked it under her thigh. 'That woman is a client of mine, Rita Winslow. And that's her driver, Fernando Peru.'

Weems tapped a finger on the small screen. A long, white scar cut diagonally across the back of his right hand. 'Rita Winslow, low-level British aristocrat, passes herself off as an art dealer, owns a shop in London. She's actually a well-established fence for stolen art. Fernando Peru, Winslow's lover. Does her dirty work, moves the art and the money. And that's you.'

He turned off the camera and looked at Iris. 'You smuggled a piece of stolen art into the United States from Moscow, Miss Thorne. Let's go to my office and have a little chat about that.'

Iris pulled her leg inside the car and closed the door.

Chapter 13

Weems drove conservatively on the surface streets, stopping at yellow lights and letting other drivers merge in front of him without attitude. He didn't hum, play music, or attempt idle chit-chat. Iris didn't notice the silence. She turned the vents that were spouting overly cool, piña colada scented air away from her then sat quietly, looking out the window at people going about their business – busy, pressed for time, happy, or not feeling any particular way at all. Unlike her, they were free.

'Do I need an attorney?' Her voice came out in a schoolgirl pitch. She cleared her throat.

'There's no need for an attorney, Miss Thorne.' He spoke loudly for the small space. 'We're just going to have a chat. I'm not going to arrest you.' He glanced in the side-view mirror and changed lanes. 'Unless you refuse to cooperate.'

He activated the turn signal. Its rhythmic clicking sounded to Iris like a time bomb.

'Cooperate?'

'Let's just go to my office where we can sit across a table and discuss things.'

He pulled into the outside parking lot behind the Federal Building, a tall, boxy structure of white cement that looked as blank and indifferent as the entity it housed. A broad, neatly trimmed lawn and large trees didn't soften it.

The lobby was crowded with people of all sizes, colors, and social status. It was a cross-section of the city's population that was rarely gathered under one roof.

Weems maintained a strong grip on Iris's upper arm as he maneuvered her through the crowd. They might have been a couple here to obtain passports for a long-awaited overseas cruise. He even gazed down at her and smiled, his teeth as small and square as Chiclets, his eyes betraying a hint of triumph. She wanly smiled back. Through his suit jacket, she felt the hard butt of his gun against her arm.

With a key card, he accessed a restricted area of the building and took an elevator to the tenth floor. Exiting there, they reached a thick, bullet-proof glass door with the seal of the Department of Justice in the center. Weems opened and closed his hand to a young receptionist sitting behind a large, curved desk inside. The door clicked and Weems let Iris walk in ahead of him, finally releasing his grip on her.

'Good afternoon, Meghan. Any messages?'

'Hi, Roger. A few.' She handed him several slips of pink paper and amiably smiled at Iris.

An inner door off the reception area opened and a group of men entered the lobby on their way out of the suite. Some of them were more casually dressed than Weems but they also had short-cropped hair, compact physiques, and an edge in the way they carried themselves. Weems and the other men acknowledged each other without speaking.

Weems walked to the inner door and pulled it open after he heard it click when Meghan unlocked it. He again let Iris pass first, then walked next to her through a spacious area of partitioned cubicles with offices along one wall. Men and women were at work, just like at any other office, but here many of them were wearing guns.

The glass wall that faced west overlooked Olympic Boulevard across West LA and Santa Monica to the ocean. It probably offered a terrific view, but today the ocean was barely visible through the smog that an inversion layer had held trapped in the Los Angeles basin for the past several weeks.

Weems walked quickly through the suite, finally reaching a set of wood doors with polished brass fixtures. He held one open and Iris walked ahead of him into an expansive conference room. A long rectangular table surrounded by high-backed chairs was in the middle. On one end was a large-screen television, a VCR, a large white board on wheels, and several easels with pads of paper, the used pages rolled over the top. The windows in this room looked north over the UCLA campus and the hills of Westwood and Bel-Air, all encased in thick smog.

Iris didn't pay attention to the view. She was looking at the clutter strewn across the conference table. There were thick art books, some of them with their pages open, stacks of file folders, official-looking reports bound with tinted mylar covers, a multi-line telephone, and a statuette of a fox.

'Whew!' Weems exclaimed as he took off his jacket, pulled a hanger off a coat rack in the corner and hung it up. 'They tell me you don't feel the heat out here because it's dry. I'm from Louisiana and I'm here to tell you, heat is heat. Humid, dry – makes no difference.' He unbuckled his shoulder holster, hung it with the gun inside next to his jacket, and began plucking at his shirt where it adhered to his skin.

'Would you care for coffee or something to drink?'

'Just water, thanks.'

Weems opened a small refrigerator in a corner and took out two chilled plastic bottles of water.

Iris examined the statuette. The fox was rendered as if it was slinking away, fluffy tail carried low between its haunches, its head turned back to look over its shoulder, ears pricked, lips retracted in a sly smile. It was about five inches long and four inches high at the tips of its ears. It appeared to have been dipped in gold at one point, but the coating was peeling off, revealing dull lead underneath. Small red gems were set in its eyes. It was covered with rows of white gems set down its back and on the tuft of its tail. Several were missing. Many were cracked and stained.

'That's a forgery I picked up in Buenos Aires twelve years ago.' Weems set the frosted plastic bottle of water on the table in front of Iris. He twisted the cap of his bottle, breaking the seal with a snap. 'Probably looked authentic when it was first made but . . .' He sucked his teeth, making a noise of distaste.

Weems clapped his hands and rubbed them together with delight. 'Rita Winslow not only contacted you directly, but she doubled what she's willing to pay for the fox. Not like her to dirty her hands like that. This is going good.' He paced next to the table as if he was too excited to sit. 'She wants the fox bad. I think we can turn this puppy around.'

Iris gaped at him. 'You were listening to our conversation?'

He blinked with surprise. 'Of course.' Composed again, he put his hands on his hips and stared evenly at her. 'You claimed to have a connection to Enrico Lazare and the fox. It's best if you come clean now, Miss Thorne, before you dig yourself into a deeper hole. Everything's off the record. Tell me what you know and maybe we can work something out. Why don't we both have a seat?'

He pulled out a chair and waited for her to sit.

'Know?' She backed away from him. 'I don't know anything. I don't have anything to do with this damn fox. I don't even know what it is!'

'That's not what you told Rita Winslow.'

Iris became increasingly exasperated and frightened. She gestured toward herself. 'I'm an innocent victim in all this.'

'Do tell.'

'You *have* to believe me!'

He patted the top of the vinyl-covered chair. 'Miss Thorne, please.'

She sat and folded her hands in her lap.

Weems sat in a chair across from her. He leaned close with both elbows on the table. 'Look. I'll tell you what *I* know. I was close, Miss Thorne, close to recovering one of the most famous pieces of missing art in history and arresting Rita Winslow and Fernando Peru, who have slipped through my fingers for years. I had a bead on the fox and there was no way Winslow and Peru were getting away from me this time. It was going to be the arrest of my career. Then you showed up and everything went to hell in a handbasket. I don't know who you are, Miss Thorne, or why you're involved in this, but you are involved in this and you're going to start talking or your comfortable life as you know it will be over.'

Iris remembered the bottled water, grabbed it from the table, broke the plastic seal on the top and took a long drink. She slowly screwed the top back on and set it in front of her, still grasping it between both hands. She released a long sigh and began, 'Look, this is exactly what happened.' She relayed the chain of events that took her to Moscow less than a week ago to the poolside meeting with Rita Winslow that afternoon.

Weems tipped back his chair, his hands laced behind his head, and slowly rocked as he listened.

Iris concluded her story. 'I thought I'd visit Rita Winslow and string her along, letting her think I could get the fox, hoping I'd find out who murdered Todd Fillinger and set me up.'

'That wasn't a good idea, Miss Thorne.'

'Well, yeah. I kind of figured that out. I just don't know who put her onto me.'

Weems grinned, not concealing his delight. 'A little birdie told her.'

Speechless, Iris bolted from her chair and walked to the window. When she turned to face him, she was furious. '*You* put those creeps onto me? Do you realize they pulled a gun on me in my office and broke into my house?' She jerked her head at him. 'And you sit there with that smug, self-satisfied smirk on your face, pleased as hell for having accomplished this.'

Weems continued smirking. She had a dreadful suspicion that she was playing right into his hand.

'How did you find out about me?'

'We have our methods, Miss Thorne.' He picked up the bogus fox, stood, cradled it in his arm and stroked it as he walked around the room. 'But this is an interesting turn of events.'

Iris's bluster faded. She leaned against the window, tipping her head back to touch the glass. 'What is this fox anyway? Why are people getting killed over it?'

Weems slowly drew his hand across the fox's back. 'It's known as the Tsarina's Fox, sometimes called the Snow Fox.' He pulled one of the art books toward Iris and tapped his finger against a color photograph. 'That's the only known photo of the original piece.'

Iris leaned closer to the heavy book to get a better look.

'It was made for Catherine the Great, commissioned by her lover and adviser Prince Potemkin, to commemorate one of the greatest triumphs of Catherine's reign, the annexation of the Crimea in seventeen eighty-three.' He stopped playing with the fox and set it on the table with a sharp thwack. 'The original is solid gold, eighteen carat. The eyes are set with rubies and the fur is depicted in blue diamonds – very rare, each one flawless – ranging in size from a half to five carats with a total weight of about three hundred carats.

'The fox remained in the Winter Palace in St Petersburg until the Russian revolution in nineteen seventeen when it disappeared. It turned up in nineteen twenty-three, on display in the Bremen Museum in Germany. Museum records indicate it was a gift from an unknown donor.

More likely, one of the servants of the Tsar's household fled with a few priceless ornaments. The museum probably purchased the fox on the black market, then falsified records to make it look like a legitimate gift.

'The fox remained in Bremen until the city was overrun by the Nazis at the end of World War Two when it dropped from sight. It was presumed lost until twelve years ago when it was spotted in Buenos Aires. I flew there, but the closest I got to it was this replica. But it definitely had been there. I found an old jeweler who swore he reset blue diamonds on a solid gold statuette of a fox. The man who brought him the fox was not from Argentina. The jeweler thought he looked like a Gypsy. In any case, the man waited while the jeweler repaired the fox, never taking his eyes off it, and paid him handsomely in cash. The jeweler commented on the unique piece, but the man wouldn't talk about where he got it or its history. I searched every corner of Buenos Aires looking for the Gypsy.' He unconsciously drew his fingers back and forth along the scar on his hand.

Iris took a couple of long drinks from the bottle of water while she listened to Weems with rapt attention.

Weems paced beside the table, his hands on his hips. 'After that, I heard nothing about the fox for a decade. Then Todd Fillinger went to the Club Ukrainiya in Moscow to take photographs of the restored mansion for an architectural magazine. Nikolai Kosyakov's secretary Irina, an occasional girlfriend of Fillinger's, showed him her boss's latest acquisition. She told Todd how Kosyakov bragged about taking the fox from a Hungarian businessman who owed him money, along with the Hungarian's thumb. Apparently, Kosyakov wasn't aware of the fox's value or history until it was stolen from him.'

Weems walked to his jacket, reached inside the pocket and took out a pack of Juicy Fruit gum. He held the pack toward Iris who declined. He took out a piece and shoved it in his mouth.

'What's the fox worth?' Iris asked.

'Hard to tell exactly. Estimated to be worth about twenty million.'

'Did Todd tell Winslow about the fox?'

'He did. Winslow immediately knew he was talking about the Tsarina's fox and told Fillinger she'd pay him five hundred thousand dollars for it. Fillinger mulls it over for a few days, calls Winslow back and says the gems on the piece have to be worth at least a couple of million, plus robbing Kosyakov will be very dangerous. He told her he didn't have the expertise to do it on his own. He wanted to bring in his associate, Enrico Lazare. The whole deal would cost Winslow a million dollars. Winslow agreed.'

'How do you know so much about what happened?'

Weems looked at her as if the answer was obvious. 'I've been in this business a long time, Miss Thorne. I have many sources.'

'Was Todd Fillinger one of your sources?'

He looked askance at her. 'I can't say.'

89

'Who was shot during the robbery at the Club Ukrainiya?'

'One of Kosyakov's security men. It happened the day you arrived in Moscow. Two masked men broke into the club and stole the fox from Kosyakov's office. We believe the robbers gave the fox to Fillinger who then met Fernando Peru in the Park Kultury metro station. Peru had already given Fillinger a five hundred thousand dollar deposit from Winslow and was carrying the balance on him. As Peru and Fillinger were completing the sale, they were robbed by a sole gunman. Peru was handcuffed to a bench. Fillinger escaped only to be shot to death an hour later on the steps of the Metropolis Hotel. Somehow the fox got in the hands of Dean Palmer who put it in the urn for you.'

'Do you know about Dean Palmer?'

'I know all about him. I also know he's disappeared.'

'What about Enrico Lazare?'

Weems shook his head. 'Don't know much. Interpol is in Corsica trying to track down information on him.'

'So who stole the fox and murdered Todd?'

'Enrico Lazare with the help of Dean Palmer.'

'What about me?'

'Well, I wasn't certain about you until today, but I think you were a lucky coincidence for Palmer and Lazare. Fillinger must have told either one or both of them about your planned visit and his former relationship with you. Palmer knew that after Todd's murder, he could play on your feelings for Fillinger to get you to bring over the urn, no questions asked.'

'The Customs officer X-rayed the urn at the LA airport and didn't see the fox. Was the urn lined with lead?'

'Probably. It's a common way of doing these things.'

Iris felt a glimmer of hope. 'Now that you know how I got involved in this thing, I guess I can go, huh?'

Weems scratched his pitted cheek. 'I want you to help me.'

'Help you? How?'

'The only way to get the fox and to flush out Fillinger's murderer is to arrange a buy.' Weems's jaw worked with the gum. 'I want you to pose as the agent of an anonymous buyer.'

Iris was incredulous. 'What?'

'Palmer's already sent out word that he has the fox and he wants to unload it fast. He's been in contact with a known stolen art fence out of San Francisco, a fat little slime ball named Douglas Melba. Melba couldn't resist blabbing all over town about how he's fencing the Tsarina's Fox. All you have to do is make a phone call to Melba. Set up a time, place, and a price. Something you do every workday anyway, right?'

'Why me? Why not an FBI agent?'

'Because I'd rather use a civilian. Crooks have radar for the law. And you're already involved.'

Iris sat down and crossed her legs. She looked away from Weems, who was intently watching her. After a long pause and with weariness in her voice she looked at Weems and said, 'I'm not doing it.'

'Then I have no choice but to arrest you.'

Iris's jaw dropped. 'Arrest me? You can't do that! I'm an honest, tax-paying citizen.'

'Miss Thorne, I'm glad you pay your taxes and vote, but you did smuggle stolen art into the United States.'

She clenched her fist. 'I don't know that for certain and neither do you.'

'Maybe I can prove it and maybe I can't, but while I was trying to make a case, you'd have a hell of a lot of explaining to do to your employers and clients. The Securities and Exchange Commission would love to lay their hands on something like this after all those long hours investigating dull stuff like insider trading. They'd be like flies on horse manure stumbling over themselves to get a chance at this.' Weems became glib. 'Of course, we'd try to keep such an investigation under wraps, but you know how things can leak out.'

Iris slipped down in the chair and pinched the bridge of her nose between her fingers.

Weems sat next to her, his hands folded on the desk. He dropped the sarcasm and spoke soothingly. 'Miss Thorne, some person or persons crafted an elaborate plan to rob and murder a good friend of yours. They took advantage of your honest nature and desire to do the right thing, pulled you into their criminal web of deceit and put your life in danger. I can't speak for you, but I'd have a hard time going the rest of my life not only having to look over my shoulder but knowing that I could have brought the people responsible for these heinous crimes to justice. But instead of choosing to be a hero, I chose – out of fear or just not caring enough – to do nothing.'

Iris watched Weems's battered face as he was talking, the sweet fragrance of the chewing gum reaching her. She knew his words were chosen to push her buttons and they had hit their mark. Though the message was overblown, she felt he was being sincere. 'I'd like to think it over.'

'It's now or never.'

Iris shifted uneasily in the chair.

He pressed his palms together as if in prayer and continued in a gentle voice, 'All you have to do is make a phone call. A single phone call. Set up a meeting. Go to the meeting. It'll be in a public place, in broad daylight with undercover FBI agents everywhere. I won't tell you there's no risk, but it's minute. It'll be safer than crossing Wilshire Boulevard during rush hour. . . or flying to Moscow by yourself.'

'OK.'

'OK?' Weems formed his mouth into an O. 'OK, Weems, leave me alone or OK, you'll do it?'

'I'll do it.'

He grinned broadly, exposing both rows of his small, even teeth, and extended his hand. When she took it, he clasped his other hand on top and squeezed hard. 'OK!' he laughed.

Chapter 14

In contrast to their quiet drive to the Department of Justice office, Iris and Weems were chatty on the way back to the gas station. Iris was nervous and welcomed the distraction. Weems told her how he'd started with the FBI twenty years ago after he'd graduated from the University of Louisiana and spent three years in the army, doing two tours in Vietnam. He was a lieutenant in the signal corps and a communications specialist, working behind the front lines, but he still saw a lot of action. He was sent home after he was wounded by a sniper near the Cambodian border.

'Were you in the hospital for long?'

'Just a year and a half,' Weems said casually out of the side of his mouth. He didn't elaborate.

'Then you joined the FBI?'

'Went straight to Quantico for training. My first assignment was on a team investigating a string of warehouse robberies in Brooklyn. The goods were showing up in California. We'd tracked this truck that we suspected was loaded with electronic equipment and one night we were waiting for it to cross into New Jersey. We'd pulled it over on a quiet, rural road when this punk comes out of the cab with guns blazing. A couple of guys on the team took him out, but I just stood there.' Weems fixed his dark eyes on Iris. 'I mean, I saw and heard that flash of gunfire in the night, and I was paralyzed. Guys were yelling at me to get down, bullets were flying . . .'

Weems became somber. 'I thought, this could be a problem. The FBI thought so too. They put me in mail fraud. I figured my career was over before it even started. After a few months, *long* months, something crossed my desk that changed my life.

'An antique dealer in Philadelphia, an old guy by the name of Rhys Coverdale, filed a complaint. He'd spotted a Louis the Fourteenth sideboard and two chairs in a catalogue mailed to him by a London art dealer, Rita Winslow, which he suspected had been stolen from the estate of a Philadelphia Main Line matron who had died two years previously. Coverdale had been hired by the executor of the estate to inventory the art holdings. He did so. When it came time to divvy up the property, about a dozen pieces turned up missing.

'When he saw the sideboard and chairs in Winslow's catalogue, he spoke with one of the heirs who told Coverdale to buy them. When they arrived, the pieces had markings and design characteristics that Coverdale remembered when he'd inventoried the dead woman's estate. Unfortunately, he hadn't made a note of them at the time, so there was no way to prove that Winslow was dealing in stolen goods. I gave Winslow's name to Interpol. My experience with Rhys Coverdale piqued my interest in stolen art. I took classes in art history and asked to be a liaison with Interpol in the stolen art detail. That was seventeen years ago.'

They reached the gas station where Iris had left the Triumph. The gas bays were still open but the garage was gated and dark.

Weems pulled up next to the Triumph.

'Is that when you started pursuing Winslow?'

He left the Thunderbird's engine running and put it in park, then slid in the seat to face Iris, his arm across the back of her seat. 'Not quite. I tucked her name away. About six years later, I got a tip that a middleman for a wealthy art collector in Bethesda, Maryland, was going to Buenos Aires to buy the Tsarina's Fox. Rumor had it that the fox had surfaced after being in someone's attic or something for years. Winslow got the same tip. We both ended up in Buenos Aires. We both got ripped off. But at least I found out that the fox existed.'

'Were you sold the fake that's in your office?'

He responded cautiously. 'Something like that.' He scratched his cheek with his index finger. 'Look, I want you to make this phone call to Dean Palmer's middleman on Saturday. That'll give me a day to set things up. Everything is cooking now. If we don't move fast, it's going to slip through our fingers again.' He clutched the top of the steering wheel.

'Wait a second. Why are you so hot to get Rita Winslow?'

He answered matter-of-factly. 'She blew my deal for the fox. She's a bad person. I don't like bad people.'

'Is she the one who did that to you?' Iris pointed at the long, white scar across the back of his hand.

Weems removed his hand from the steering wheel and let it fall into his lap. He didn't answer right away. 'No.'

'Since I'm involved in this fox situation, I think I deserve to know the whole story. I want to know what I'm getting into.'

'Miss Thorne, it's not in your best interests to know the whole story. You only need to know this. You have the power to bring to justice the person who murdered your friend and set you up as a stolen art mule. You'll have the force of the Federal Bureau of Investigation backing you up. I need to have your absolute commitment to this. Do I have it?' He stared at her without blinking.

Iris met his stare. 'Yes.' She opened the car door. 'What's the next step?'

'I want you to come to the office Saturday at two o'clock.'

'OK. I'll be there.'

Weems waited as she got into the Triumph, cranked the engine, and left the gas station. He drove behind her for several blocks. She couldn't see him behind his tinted windows. He turned south on Robertson Boulevard and she continued home.

Automatic timers had turned the lights on, making Iris's small house look warm and inviting. She pulled a stack of mail from the brass box next to the front door and walked inside. After a hectic day at the office, she usually loved the quiet and solitude of her home. She rarely felt lonely. Tonight she did. The silence seemed oppressive, as if it had physical mass that enveloped and bore down on her. She normally enjoyed the solid retort of her pump heels against the hardwood floor. The old house's thick walls and heavy floors made her feel secure and happy with what she'd accomplished. She had earned all this. It was real. It was something she could put her arms round. It had stood the test of time. It was hers. Now each footstep seemed to mock her, chiding that it was all hollow and meaningless, that she'd anchored her dreams to a false star.

The knowledge that catastrophe could come down on her closely watched, carefully managed life was always there. Loved ones die in car crashes. People contract terminal illnesses. It happens every day. She prayed, like everyone else, that it wouldn't happen to her. Now catastrophe had visited her in the form of a solid gold, jewel-encrusted statuette of a fox.

She felt desperate to call Garland and tell him the whole story. Since she'd returned from Moscow, she hadn't really leveled with him. She had wanted some time to get to grips with all that had happened but things kept moving too fast, she hadn't had the chance to get any clarity on the situation. And she was embarrassed.

She hadn't told Garland the whole truth. She did go to Moscow to apologize to Todd about dumping him. It was an incident in her life that had haunted her and she saw an opportunity to put things right. But she didn't tell Garland that the main reason she had gone was simply to see Todd. She had been overwhelmingly in love with him. If she was honest, she had to admit that the intensity of her emotions for Todd exceeded what she felt for Garland. She and Garland were a low simmer while she and Todd had burned hot. She knew her relationship with Garland was more stable and enduring in the long run and they'd definitely rung the bell, but Todd always haunted her. She suspected her desire to see Todd was a way to put some distance between herself and Garland, to keep from committing to him completely, to prove to herself that she was still free. She couldn't quite make that small step from dating to being a couple. You and me. Me and you. For ever. Yikes!

Garland had probably already figured it out. It amazed and dismayed her that she, who had thought herself so complex, was so transparent to him. He was wise enough not to stand in her way. So she had gone to Moscow. And Moscow had come home with her.

95

She opened the doors of the armoire and turned on the television inside. The canned laughter of a sitcom filled the room with false gaiety. She had the feeling of being trapped at a cocktail party where she wasn't having fun, a smile frozen on her face, a drink warming in her hand. She walked through her house, picking up things, putting them down, without any real purpose. She hadn't eaten since her big lunch with Liz earlier that afternoon, but she wasn't really hungry. She wondered whether she'd made a mistake by agreeing to help Weems.

She decided to take a shower when her front doorbell rang. Through the rectangular peephole that was covered by a small, tarnished brass door, she saw Fernando Peru on her front porch.

He was smoking a cigarette and had wandered to the edge of the porch. He turned toward the door when the hinge on the peephole cover squeaked, moving his face close to the opening which was covered with a brass grille on the outside.

'Iris, I'm sorry to bother you, but if you'd talk to me for a few minutes . . .'

'Sure.' Iris unlocked and opened the door and grimaced as Peru tossed his cigarette butt into the flowerbed beside her porch. 'Come in. Would you like some coffee or something?'

He walked in and looked around. 'That would be nice.'

He smelt of faded cologne and fresh cigarette smoke, a combination that Iris found pleasant on him. 'Come into the kitchen.'

She picked up the remote control from the end table between the love seat and sofa and clicked off the television, then crossed the room, passing beneath the arched opening that led to the small dining room. The kitchen was separated from it by a high tiled counter lined with bar stools. She busied herself grinding coffee beans and filling the ceramic sugar bowl and creamer set that she used only when she had guests. 'I don't have decaffeinated. This is full octane.'

'Never drink decaf.'

'Me either.' She set the sugar and cream on the table.

'Rita's at some reception at the British Consul General's house.' He picked up the framed photograph of Iris and Todd and looked at it as he talked. 'She likes that sort of thing. Rubbing elbows with the rich and famous. She says it's good for business, but she likes it just because she likes it.' His Catalonian accent made the letter 's' sound like a soft 'z'.

The coffee started brewing, filling the room with its aroma. Iris hadn't a clue why Peru had come to see her and wondered if it had been smart to let him in. She sensed it was OK and that he was OK. She was grateful for the company. Not knowing what to say to him, she foraged in her pantry for something to serve with the coffee.

'I came to apologize for the way Rita acted this afternoon.' Peru shook his head as he stood the photograph on the dining room table. 'She can be very cruel sometimes.'

Iris found a box of Graham crackers, took a bite of one, frowned when it bent from staleness between her teeth, and tossed the remainder and the box in the trash. 'And she enjoys it.'

Peru smiled knowingly.

'Why do you stay with her?'

'Good question.' He didn't answer it. 'I wanted you to know that you weren't just some woman in Todd's life. I mean, yeah, Todd had girlfriends. Lots of them. But he loved you.'

Iris remembered an amaretto cake that a client had given her the previous Christmas. She dug it out of the freezer and started to unwrap it.

'Please don't go to any trouble for me.' Peru gestured toward the boxed cake and the long knife Iris was forcing through the frozen core.

'No trouble.' Iris grunted as she sliced the cake. 'That was a rotten thing for Rita to say, especially after what happened to Todd.'

'She's mad that she was ripped off. She's trying to make everyone pay. I wanted you to know that you were special to Todd.'

Iris stopped fooling with the cake and looked at him.

His eyelids with their thick lashes drooped seductively. 'He left Paris because of you. He was distraught after you left. Paris lost its magic for him. I told him to come to London. He stayed in Rita's flat for months. It was like he was broken.'

Iris felt empty inside. She carefully arranged the cake slices on a china plate and carried it to the table. She took cups, saucers, and dessert plates from the china cabinet in the dining room and arranged them on the table, the china rattling with a brittle noise. In the kitchen, she got out silverware and napkins.

'After a few months, he snapped out of it. We did London. Partied till we dropped. He was the same old Todd again. And like the old Todd, it wasn't too long before he moved on.' Peru slowly sauntered around the room as he talked. 'Went to Prague for a while. Made that scene. When Prague got too tame for him, he moved to Moscow. But I don't think he ever really got over you.'

Iris poured coffee into the cups. 'Please sit down.'

Peru took a chair after Iris sat. 'Todd was a good guy. A complicated guy, but good at heart.' Peru tapped his chest over his heart with his fist. 'So sad, what happened to him.' He stirred several spoonfuls of sugar into his coffee.

Iris drank her coffee black. She lifted a piece of amaretto cake onto a plate, broke off a corner with her fingers, and slowly chewed. It had defrosted but was ice cold. She considered putting the slices in the microwave but decided not to bother. Her urge to engage in mindless busywork had passed. 'Yes,' she finally responded to Peru.

'Especially when you consider that the people who murdered him will probably get away with it.'

'Who do you think did it?'

'Lazare. It had to be Lazare.' He looked at her over the top of the cup which he held in both hands. His sleepy eyes definitely had the power to seduce.

'Have you ever met him?'

Peru lowered his eyes to indicate he hadn't and took another sip of coffee.

'What about Dean Palmer, an American, a consular officer at the US Embassy in Moscow?'

'No, I haven't heard of him. Who is he?'

Iris was vague. 'Someone Todd knew.' Almost as an afterthought, she asked, 'Do you know whether Todd smoked?'

Peru became thoughtful. 'I never saw him smoke. Why?'

Iris shrugged. 'Just wondering.'

Peru gazed morosely out the picture window. 'Poor Todd. He didn't deserve it. I wish there was some way . . .' His voice trailed off into silence.

'There is,' Iris said firmly.

Peru brightened. 'Do the Moscow police have a lead?'

'Not that I know of. But there's another way.' She nodded as if finalizing a decision with herself. 'There's a way.'

'What is it?'

'I can't say, but something just became clear to me. You're right. We have to at least try to seek justice. We can't lay down and let the bad guys win.'

'If there's anything I can do to help you, let me know.'

'I will.'

Peru placed his empty cup on the saucer and touched a napkin against his lips. 'I'd best be going. Rita will be back soon.' He pushed back the chair and stood.

Iris stood as well.

'Thank you for seeing me. I'm glad I talked with you.' He walked to the front door and opened it.

Iris followed him onto the porch and walked with him down the steps and onto the brick path.

He held his hand out to her. When she took it, he clasped her fingertips and raised the back of her hand to his lips.

Out of the shadows at the side of the house walked Rita Winslow. She was trembling with rage. 'I never dreamed you would betray me this way, Fernando. After everything I've done for you.' The pitch of her voice grew higher as she raised both fists in the air. 'You were nothing when you met me!' She slammed them against Peru's chest until he grabbed her wrists. 'Nothing! Nothing!' Tears streamed down her cheeks.

Iris darted back toward the open front door as Peru tried to calm Winslow. 'Rita, please. I met with Iris to talk about getting the fox for you. That's all it was. That's all, sweetheart.' He kissed her tightly closed fists. 'Are you going to calm down now? Can I let you go?'

He released her hands and she spun away from him, stumbling across the lawn. She pressed the back of her hand tightly against her mouth and held the other out as if she needed it for balance. Iris cowered against the doorframe, her hand on the door ready to slam it if necessary, and watched the woman with a mixture of fear and pity.

Winslow turned to face Peru, standing on the grass with her feet spread. 'You had Todd murdered, didn't you? Your good friend Todd. Murdered him and stole my money and gave the fox to that bimbo,' she pointed angrily at Iris, 'to bring into the States. I wondered why you wanted to come straight to LA, straight to Iris Thorne. Now I know why. Now I know.'

Still standing in the doorway, Iris spoke up. 'Rita, I told you I can get you the fox. That's all Fernando came to talk to me about.'

'Then get it,' Winslow snapped. 'What's taking so long?'

'I have to make arrangements,' Iris responded.

'Arrangements,' Winslow said bitterly. 'I know what kind of arrangements. You're going to sell it out from under me, aren't you?'

'Rita,' Peru said soothingly.

Winslow darted a polished fingernail at them. 'Just a word of warning. Don't underestimate me. I'm on to you. Both of you.' She stomped across the yard and down the street. In a moment there was the sound of a car engine turning over and accelerating as it drove away.

'Wow,' Iris said from the porch.

'Don't worry about it. I can handle her.' Peru got into his car which was parked in front of Iris's house and left.

Iris remained on the porch. The silence seemed deafening in the aftermath of Winslow's outburst. She glanced into the flowerbed then walked down the steps and reached into it, picking up the cigarette butt that Peru had tossed there when he first arrived. She looked at the brand. Marlboro. The person who had smoked the True cigarette in Todd's bedroom the night he was murdered was still unidentified.

Chapter 15

The next morning, Iris walked into the McKinney Alitzer suite with her head held high, her gait brisk and unwavering, her gaze sure, even if her eyes were grainy from lack of sleep. She had put on her pale yellow silk suit which was fresh from the cleaners. It always made her feel snappy even if she was dragging. She smiled at her crew as she walked through the suite. Since she'd barely slept the night before, the many things on her mind not letting her rest, she was up earlier than usual and had beat most of her employees into the office. The ones who were already at their desks were surprised to see her. The ones who were used to coming in late but managed to skirt in just before Iris did would be even more surprised to see her. It was good to keep them off base. Iris reflected that everyone, herself included, had become a bit too relaxed during the extended bull market which had floated all boats. This was potentially risky business.

'Morning, Louise,' Iris sang to her assistant who was dunking a tea bag into a cup of hot water.

'Well, good morning. You're here bright and early.'

'Early, anyway.' Iris went into her office, which Louise had already opened, put her purse in the filing cabinet and hung her jacket on a hanger behind the door. She grabbed her mug which she still hardly recognized after its scrub and polish and strode into the lunchroom at the other end of the suite. She opened the door and was stunned to see Kyle Tucker in a passionate embrace with Dawn, the girl who had been sitting at her desk when she'd returned from Moscow.

They were equally stunned to see her. Kyle harshly pushed Dawn away as if the gesture would undo what Iris had seen.

'Good morning.' Iris walked to the coffeemaker.

Dawn scowled at Kyle then left the room, smoothing her hair. Kyle swiped his hand across his mouth, but he didn't get all the lipstick that had rubbed off on him. 'Iris, I'm sorry about that.'

'Kyle, wasn't that the woman who I heard has a fatal attraction for you?'

His pale schoolboy complexion was bright red. 'She is not a fatal attraction. Who's spreading these rumors?'

'I don't want to see her in the office again.'

'Sure, of course. I understand.'

101

Iris left the lunchroom without looking at him. On her way back to her office, she told the receptionist to call security if she saw the woman who had just left loitering in the suite. Iris was back in her office and had just started going through her phone messages when Lisa Roman, one of her new hires fresh out of business school, poked her head inside the door.

'Do you have a minute, Iris?'

'Sure. Come in.' Iris tried not to look irritated about being interrupted. 'Sit down.'

Lisa smiled in a manner that seemed calculated to look competent yet engaging. Iris had practiced it herself in the mirror many moons ago. 'As you know, I've been over one hundred and twenty-five per cent of quota each of the six months I've been here and—'

There was a high-pitched squealing noise in the bull pen, as if an animal had been stepped on.

'No more, Liz!'

Iris recognized the voice of David Wayne, the latest in a string of Liz Martini's sales assistants.

'It's just for two hours. Jeesh!' Liz Martini retorted. 'Did he hurt you, baby?' she cooed, then snapped, 'I swear you stepped on her on purpose.'

Undeterred, Lisa continued, 'Since I've been performing at such a high level, I feel I've earned my own sales assistant—'

David Wayne stomped into Iris's office. He sneezed violently. 'I told her I'm allergic to dogs, Iris. She keeps bringing these *animals* into the office! Why do you permit this?'

Lisa scowled at David for having interrupted what appeared to be a carefully prepared presentation.

Liz pushed past him into Iris's office, cradling a miniature poodle under each arm. 'It's just until the vet opens at ten, for goodness sakes. He acts like it's a federal offense.'

Wagging his finger at Liz, David pronounced, 'This is a place of business. Not a kennel.'

Kyle Tucker pushed into the office carrying a fire extinguisher. 'I'm sorry, Iris. I tried to stop her—'

Lisa petulantly stood and said, 'I was having a meeting with Iris. Iris, please!'

'Louise!' Iris shouted. 'Look, everyone except Lisa leave. I'll deal with you one at a time.' She noticed the fire extinguisher. 'Kyle, what . . .?'

Liz and David were arguing, Kyle and Lisa were trying to get Iris's attention when Sam Eastman, Iris's regional manager, appeared with two removal men. 'Iris, I'm giving you back your desk with the Virgin's image on it. My wife says it's causing too much trouble at home.'

Iris's phone rang. The display indicated Louise was calling.

'Iris, Garland's on the phone.'

'Can you tell him I'm—'

'No, I'm not telling him you're not here. Here he is.'

'Hey!' Iris shouted over the commotion. 'Everyone leave my office now.' She spoke into the telephone, 'Hi, sweetie,' then shouted at the group, 'Now, please!'

Sam was behind her desk and had started removing things from her drawers.

'Sam!'

'Oh, I didn't know you meant me too.'

She gave him a pained look and he slunk from the room.

'What's going on there?' Garland asked.

'What isn't going on is probably the better question.' It was only then that she noticed the heavy static on the line. He was probably calling from an airplane. 'How are you? What's up?'

'Flying to your arms, sweetheart.'

'Flying to . . .?'

'Palm Springs weekend, remember? I'll be at your house around two. I rented a car. We can load it up and we'll be in the desert in time for cocktails.'

'Oh.' Iris had completely forgotten that they had planned to go away. Roger Weems had called her after Fernando Peru had left the previous night to make certain she hadn't changed her mind about meeting on Saturday to set up the buy of the fox. She couldn't get out of it. She knew Weems wouldn't let her.

'What's wrong?'

'I can't go out of town this weekend.'

'Why not?'

'I can't talk about it here.' She nervously twirled a strand of her hair.

'What's going on?'

'Just come to my house like you planned. I should be home by two. If not, you know where the key is hidden.'

'Is this something I should be worried about?'

'No! No, it's, ah, just a funny thing that happened.' She laughed nervously. 'You'll see. It's kind of different, but it's nothing, really.'

'OK.' His tone was guarded. 'See you then.'

Everyone she'd chased out of her office filed back in right after she'd hung up the phone. She set up times to meet with each one of them, and they scowled about having to wait to voice their grievances. She started with Lisa Roman who finished her pitch about why she deserved her own assistant, but not before Sam Eastman had come back in and began removing things from Iris's desk.

'Sam,' Iris pleaded. 'I'll take care of this. When are you bringing the desk?'

'Now. I want to do this now.'

Lisa barely controlled her irritation at being interrupted again. Iris quickly brought their discussion to a close. 'I'll get back to you on that, OK, Lisa?'

When she had left, Sam commented, 'I didn't care for her attitude. I wouldn't let her talk to me that way.'

Iris's nerves were frayed. 'Sam, I am very busy right now. Could you please—'

Louise buzzed her. Iris picked up the phone. 'Yes, Louise.'

'It's Jim Hailey from New York.'

Iris guiltily looked at Sam. 'I have to take this call in private, Sam.'

He looked put off. 'Oh, sure.'

Iris closed the door behind him. Jim Hailey, the head honcho in New York, was calling her. She wondered if the rumors about Sam Eastman's forced retirement were true.

Fifteen minutes later, she'd found out. They were true. Hailey offered her the regional manager position. She asked for a few days to think about it.

Iris had intended to beat Garland to her house, but the rest of her day had been as nutty as the way it had started and she didn't leave the office until two o'clock. Kyle's girlfriend had slipped into the suite and set a fire in his garbage can, miffed at how he had pushed her in the lunchroom. Iris pacified Liz's allergic assistant and received a verbal promise from Liz that she wouldn't bring the dogs into the suite – a promise that Iris knew would be broken the next time the dogs had an appointment with the veterinarian or beauty parlor. She'd stalled Lisa Roman for a few days. And Sam persisted in returning her desk.

Garland had considerately parked the rental car in the street, leaving Iris's narrow driveway open so she could pull the Triumph into the garage. She unlocked the door and found him sitting at the dining room table, as she had feared.

Without a word, he rose to meet her at the door and they hugged and kissed and hugged some more. She pressed her cheek against his and tightly closed her eyes. She had missed him terribly.

After they'd separated, she nonchalantly looked through her mail and asked, 'How was your flight?'

'It got up OK and it came down OK, so I guess it was fine.' He strolled into the dining room and gestured at the clutter that now covered it. 'What have you got here?'

When Iris couldn't sleep the night before, she'd spread out the photographs that she'd taken from Todd's Moscow apartment. She didn't know what she was looking for but hoped that some clue might be hidden among them. 'Oh, I was just looking through the stuff I brought from Moscow.' She quietly added, 'Todd's stuff.'

'Looks like some sort of shrine to the guy.'

She smiled meekly.

'What's going on?' It was said with deep concern rather than accusingly. She exhaled at length then walked to the china cabinet and took down two wineglasses. 'I have some Chardonnay open or would you like a Merlot?'

'Chardonnay's fine.'

While she got the wine and glasses, she told him the other big news. 'Jim Hailey called me today. He's forcing Sam Eastman to retire and he's offered me the regional manager position.'

'Iris, that's great!' Garland swept her into his arms and gave her a big hug and a kiss. 'What did you tell him?'

'That I want to think about it.'

'But you're going to accept it.'

She held her glass up and he clicked his against it. 'I want to think about it. Sometimes that office makes me want to scream with all the personalities and pettiness and power struggles. Sometimes I would kill to get out of there.'

'So what's the problem?'

'I want to think about it, that's all. Let's go outside.' She walked out the kitchen door, down the side yard, and into the backyard. She swatted at the dust and smog particles that had accumulated on the two Adirondack chairs with a paper napkin. She and Garland sat, putting their glasses on the matching table between the chairs.

'So tell me what's going on,' he said.

She took a long drink, then told Garland the story of the fox. He listened without expression but Iris could tell he didn't like what he was hearing. He didn't comment until she'd finished.

'So Weems wouldn't tell you the real reason he has such a hard-on to get Rita Winslow.'

'He said I didn't need to know.'

Garland tapped his index finger against his lips. 'You don't need to participate in this. Weems can't force you. He can't even prove that anything was in the urn you brought back. You said the customs agent at the airport even X-rayed it. It's all speculation on Weems's part. Walk away, Iris.'

'He said he'll arrest me.'

'Let him. Call his bluff. If he does, we'll take it from there. The way the FBI's reputation has been in the dumper lately, he won't have a leg to stand on.'

'But I want to do it. Todd Fillinger was murdered. Someone has to pay for it.' She pushed her empty wineglass away from her.

Garland gave her a stern look. 'Fine. Let the authorities take care of it. Why do you have to be involved? Weems can find someone else to set up this buy.'

'He says I'm the best one to do it and I agree with him. I'm not in law enforcement. Weems says crooks can smell a cop a mile away.'

'Bull. Police do undercover work all the time.'

'And I'm already involved in it. Winslow and Peru think I can get them the fox.' Iris cupped her hand against her forehead, shielding her eyes from the bright late-afternoon sun. 'Inserting someone new into the mix could jeopardize everything.'

Garland's jaw grew rigid in a way that she knew only too well. He said nothing.

'Garland, all I have to do is make a phone call—'

'And meet with some creep.'

'With FBI agents everywhere.'

Garland rose from the chair and held his hand out for her to do the same. He put his arms round her and she rested her head against his shoulder.

'I don't mean to be a jerk about this, Iris,' he said quietly. 'I just don't want you to get hurt.' He held her away from him and looked into her eyes. 'I don't know what I would do without you.'

She blinked back tears, touched by the depth of his feeling for her. 'It'll be all right. It's kind of exciting in a way.'

He gave her a wry smile. 'I figured that was part of it.'

She dragged her knuckle underneath her eye. 'But the main reason is to find out who murdered Todd and set me up.'

He dropped his arms to his sides. 'Frankly, that's been the hardest part for me, knowing that you're still in love with Todd.'

'That's not true.'

'I know you didn't go to Moscow to investigate investing in art galleries. Any investing you wanted to do, you could have done from the comfort of your own home. You hate leaving LA. I can hardly get you to New York, much less Moscow.'

She backed a few feet away to see him clearly. In the bright sunshine, she saw things perhaps more clearly than she wanted. He wasn't accusing or angry. He was simply reciting the facts, facts which she had finally admitted to herself were true. As she had suspected, Garland had had it figured out from the beginning but had had the grace to let her work it out on her own. He was only speaking up now because things had got out of hand.

'I believe you went to Moscow to apologize to Todd face to face for leaving him at the altar, but that's not the main reason you went. You went to see him, pure and simple. You went to see *him*, Iris.'

'Yes.'

'Because you were still in love with him.'

She backed into a chair and sat with a plop, drained of energy. 'No.' She wiped a tear from her cheek. 'I *was* in love with him. Five years ago. Very much.'

He walked to the edge of the yard and stood looking at the sparkling ocean.

'Todd and I were going to get married. I don't know what happened. All of a sudden, I felt like I couldn't breathe. I felt like if I didn't get away,

I would die. I ran, all the way back to Los Angeles, I ran.' She looked at her hands in her lap. 'I don't know what happened. Then Todd's invitation came and I thought, if I saw him, I would finally figure it out.'

Garland turned to face her. 'Did you?'

'No. I'm more confused than ever.'

'In my humble opinion, I've figured it out,' he said brusquely then drank the rest of his wine. 'You fell in love with a con artist. On some level, back in Paris, you knew. Those excellent instincts of yours made you come home.'

'That's hard for me to believe.'

'Iris, Todd Fillinger ended up shot full of holes on a Moscow street because he participated in a multimillion-dollar art heist. One of his cohorts double-crossed him.'

Iris shielded her eyes from the sun with both hands. 'I was shocked to find out that Todd was involved in the theft of the fox. I wonder if he was desperate or something.'

'If I can go a little farther without you getting pissed off at me, I propose that he intentionally involved you in his scheme. A good con artist knows his mark. If he couldn't lure you to Moscow by guilt alone, he'd toss in an investment opportunity. There was most likely an element of revenge in it on his part. He was probably going to hide the fox in your luggage or in some gift he was going to give you. Then the whole thing blew up in his face. But his buddies knew you were the perfect courier, so they hatched a scheme to use you anyway.'

'I think I'm a better judge of character than that, Garland.'

'You're an excellent judge of character now, but you were pretty green when you came to work at McKinney Alitzer. You've changed a lot since then.'

Iris closed her eyes. Bursts of yellow and red exploded on the insides of her eyelids.

He walked behind her and massaged her neck and shoulders. 'You don't owe Todd anything.'

'What about his sister and niece and nephew? What about me? That drug addict Dean Palmer played me like a harp, like I was the biggest pushover he'd ever seen.'

'Let it go, Iris.'

'I want to finish it.'

He knelt on the grass in front of her. 'Now you are pissing me off.'

'I'd like to have your support.'

'It stinks, Iris. The whole thing.'

'I know. So are you with me?'

'Could I be any other way?'

She brushed his lips with hers. He kissed her amorously. She broke their embrace and said, 'I'm starved. You want to get some Chinese?'

It was clear that Chinese food wasn't what was on his mind. He smiled crookedly. 'Whatever makes you happy, sweetness.'

'You make me happy.'

That pleased him. He helped her up from the deep chair and watched CNN while she got ready.

They made love after they returned from having dinner. Both of them exhausted, they turned out the lights at nine o'clock.

In the darkness, Garland asked her, 'Any other men from your past I should know about?'

The question startled her. She was glad he couldn't see her face. She'd never talked to Garland about the other men in her life. It didn't seem important or something that he needed to know. His life had taken a much more traditional path than hers. She'd done plenty of things that she wasn't proud of, done them out of naiveté, insecurity, desire to be loved. Whatever the reason, they were still stupid. More importantly, they were in the past, never to be repeated. Of that, she was certain. Garland was right, she had changed a lot in five years. Her past had been troubled and dark. Her future was bright and warm. Only the Tsarina's Fox stood in her way.

'None that you should know about,' she answered truthfully. 'None that matter. You're the only one that matters from now on.'

They both fell asleep quickly. In spite of herself, Iris dreamed of Todd Fillinger and *Le Café des Quatre Vents*. He looked as she remembered him in Paris, with no beard and a husky build. He moved close to kiss her and she stroked his smooth cheek.

Chapter 16

'That Rita Winslow.' Roger Weems chuckled and shook his head. He was dressed casually, wearing khaki slacks and a white polo-style knit shirt. Even dressed down, there was a military attitude in the knife crease in his pants and the way his brass belt buckle was precisely squared. He tossed the bogus fox up and down like a football as he spoke. It seemed to be a good-luck charm for him. 'She's a funny old bird, isn't she?'

'She seems to have Fernando Peru on a short leash,' Iris said.

Iris and Weems laughed while Garland, who was sitting at the conference table reading an entry about the Tsarina's Fox in one of the large art books, wore his irritation with the scene on his sleeve.

He interrupted their laughter and directed a comment to Weems. 'Just for the record, I want you to know that I don't like this plot you've got Iris roped into.'

Weems scratched his head through his crew-cut, black hair. 'All due respect, Mr Hughes, but Miss Thorne stepped into this patch of quicksand herself.'

'You're manipulating her desire to solve the murder of her friend.'

'Just doing my job, Mr Hughes. Just doing my job. Certainly, a man like you can appreciate that.' Weems cocked his head at Iris. 'You're not getting cold feet on me now, are you, Miss Thorne?'

'No, I want this thing resolved.'

'Good deal. That's what I like to hear.'

'Could you please call me Iris? Since we're sort of in business together now.'

'Iris it is.' Weems's southern accent elongated the I. 'And call me Roger.' He touched his chest with his right hand. The scar across the back looked longer than Iris remembered.

The conference room door opened and a man pushed in a cart covered with telephones, tape recorders, and other devices.

'Here's Jimmy. Great. Go ahead and do what you need to do to get everything set up.' Weems held his hand out to indicate the new man. 'Iris, this is Jimmy Decker. Jimmy, Iris Thorne. And this is . . . Mr Hughes.'

Garland didn't ask him to be less formal.

'Jimmy's going to set up our communications.' Weems gathered the papers and books that were scattered across the table into a pile. 'Don't mind us, Jimmy.'

Weems sat at the head of the table. Iris took a seat across from Garland, who was facing the window.

'Iris, I received some information from Interpol on Enrico Lazare,' Weems began.

Iris eagerly leaned forward.

'He's an up-and-coming drug lord.'

She frowned. 'A drug lord?'

'In the past few years, he's become very influential in the European heroin trade which is centered in Corsica. He's exceedingly ruthless. Murdered his way to the top.' Weems opened a manila file folder and slid a black-and-white photograph across the table to Iris. 'That shot was taken at his sister's wedding reception held last year at the estate of another wealthy Corsican on the island.'

Iris studied the photograph. It was obviously taken at a wedding but snapped from far off and enlarged until the details had blurred. The bride was in a full-skirted white dress with a long veil. There appeared to be many guests. The man who Weems indicated was Lazare was visible in profile. He had long dark hair, pulled back into a ponytail, a prominent nose, and was wearing a black tuxedo with a bow tie. 'It's hard to tell, but he doesn't look like anybody I remember from Paris.'

Weems slid across a few more photos. One of them showed Lazare facing front. None of them was clear.

'Dean Palmer was a heroin addict. That explains his connection to Lazare.' Iris pushed the photos over to Garland, avoiding making eye contact with him.

'Interpol hasn't received any reports on Lazare for over a month. It's rumored that he recently had plastic surgery to disguise himself. He may be recuperating from his surgery in a secret location.'

'Is there any indication that Lazare had a legitimate business dealing in art with Todd Fillinger?' Garland asked.

'Based upon our information, Lazare was purely a drug dealer,' Weems said. 'Which doesn't exclude his involvement in stealing the Tsarina's Fox. He's in drugs for the money. The fox represents money too, lots of it. Todd brought in Lazare because he needed muscle to steal the fox. Lazare steals the fox, kills Todd, keeps the fox to sell another day.'

Iris voiced what she knew Garland was thinking. 'Todd lied to me about buying and selling art to wealthy Russians.'

'It appears so, Iris,' Weems admitted.

'And he was the kind of character who was involved with drug dealers,' Garland said. 'Seems to me Todd Fillinger is your link between Palmer and Lazare. You have the big-time dealer and the user on the street. You have to have a middleman. Is there any indication that Todd was a drug dealer?'

Iris watched Jimmy set up the telephones.

'We don't have any information about that, but he could have been. Moscow is a booming town for vice of all shapes.' Weems put the photographs back into the folder and opened another one. 'I also received information from Detective Davidovsky in Moscow. He's obtained a report of the calls Todd Fillinger made on his cellular phone in the weeks before his death. Nothing too remarkable here.'

He scanned a photocopied phone record on which someone had scribbled notes in the margin. 'There were calls to Rita Winslow's London shop and her flat. Some to Nikolai Kosyakov's Club Ukrainiya.'

'Any that can be traced to Lazare?' Iris asked.

Weems shook his head. 'There's only one that turned out to be a dead end. But it's intriguing because he made it ten minutes before he died.'

'He must have been on his way to meet me,' Iris said.

'Curiously, the call was to an ophthalmologist's office in Visalia, California.'

'Visalia?' Garland repeated.

'A Dr Hart. We tracked it down, but no one in the office had heard of Todd Fillinger. The doctor's assistant checked the records and Fillinger wasn't a patient.'

'Visalia is about an hour north of Bakersfield, where Todd's sister and her family live,' Iris commented.

'It's worth following up on, but right now our best shot at getting to the bottom of this is flushing out Enrico Lazare and Dean Palmer.' Weems looked at Jimmy, who was sitting at the opposite end of the table wearing headphones. 'How's it look, Jimmy?'

He held his thumb up. 'Ready whenever you are.'

Iris swallowed drily. 'Could I have some water, please?'

'Certainly.' Weems rose and walked to the small refrigerator in a corner of the room. 'Mr Hughes?'

'Sure, thanks.'

Weems returned with several small plastic containers of water. 'Now, this is the deal. You're going to be calling an art fence by the name of Douglas Melba, this fat little SOB who lives up in San Francisco. He's working for Dean Palmer who contacted him and said he wants to sell the fox. Your name is Margo Hill. You represent a well-known art collector who wants to remain anonymous.'

Iris picked at a loose cuticle on her finger. 'What if he demands to know who the buyer is?'

'Don't tell him. He won't ask. This is typical of how these deals go down. No rich collector wants it known that he's bought stolen art, although many of them do.'

Iris rattled on nervously, 'What if he's suspicious of me and starts asking questions like how long I've worked for the collector and how did I meet him?'

Weems responded patiently. 'He won't. He'll want to set the time, date, and price and get off the phone.'

Garland interjected, 'Won't Lazare or Palmer be suspicious if they've never heard of Margo Hill?'

'She's a rich guy's executive assistant. They don't need to have heard of her. And she doesn't need to sound smooth. They'll think this isn't something she does every day. Look, it's real easy. If either Lazare or Palmer get suspicious, there's no deal. They'll just walk away.'

Garland had fixed Weems with a steely gaze. Iris knew this look. He wasn't saying much, but he didn't have to. 'This fence, Douglas Melba, he's someone you know.'

'Right.' Weems waited for the rest of Garland's thought.

'Then why don't you simply follow him until he leads you to Palmer or Lazare and arrest the lot of them?'

Weems picked up the bogus fox and sharply banged it against the table. 'Because of this, Mr Hughes. We want the fox. Once I have the fox, I can get everyone. Getting the fox, that's the main thing.'

'What about the price?' Iris sucked on the bloody spot where she'd pulled off her cuticle.

'Ask him his price then haggle with him a little. That's right up your alley, isn't it?'

'What are we willing to pay?'

'Try to keep it near six million. That's a good black market price. We'll give you a case full of money. He'll give you the fox. We'll trail the money to Palmer.'

'Where's Lazare?' Garland asked.

'In the shadows. He's got Palmer doing his dirty work for him. Our best shot at getting him is to get Palmer then put the squeeze on Palmer. Once we get the fox, then we'll arrange to sell it to Winslow. Then I'll have it all. After that, I may just get out of this business.'

Garland raised his hand in a warning gesture. 'Wait a minute. What do you mean, we'll arrange a sell to Winslow? I thought Iris's involvement ended with her setting up a purchase of the fox.'

'It's a two-part deal, Mr Hughes. The buy, then the sell.'

'I'm very familiar with how the marketplace works, Mr Weems. But that wasn't your original deal with Iris. And you said not five minutes ago that the main thing you wanted was the fox.'

'Maybe I didn't state it explicitly, but it was implied that Iris would follow through to the end. Rita Winslow believes that Iris is getting the fox for her. I can't throw someone new in the mix. I'm too close to wrapping my hands round this, Mr Hughes. I'm not giving up now.'

'Iris, this guy is full of crap. He's as bad as these crooks he's chasing.' Garland stood. 'Come on, let's go.'

Iris looked from Weems to Garland.

'Now hold on just a second, Mr Hughes,' Weems said as he stood. 'I

112

explained to you earlier that if your lady friend backs out of this, there will be severe consequences for her.'

'And I just explained to you that you're full of crap. You have an obsession about getting this fox and a vendetta against the Winslow woman. I don't know what's behind it and I don't care, but Iris doesn't need to be part of it. Iris, let's go.'

'Garland, please,' Iris said. 'I'm going to do this. I know you don't like it and I'm sorry.'

'But fuck you, Garland. Right?'

'Garland—'

He was out the door before she could finish.

Iris scowled at the closed door. Jimmy, seated at the end of the table, busied himself with his electronic equipment. Weems studied Iris.

Finally, she said, 'Let's do it before I lose my nerve.'

Weems clapped his hands once, his enthusiasm restored. He obsequiously pulled Iris's chair out when she got up and guided her to the opposite end of the table, pulling another chair out for her to sit down. 'Price, time, and place. Tell him you want to meet in Los Angeles in a public place. A bus station or airport or something like that. You won't meet him in some hotel room somewhere. I need to surround you with agents.'

'Should I mention a place?'

'I don't want him to get suspicious. Let him suggest a place. I'll check it out. If I don't like it, you'll call him back and tell him to pick someplace else. But impress on him that your boss wants the deal done tomorrow or the next day at the latest. Tell him the fox is hot and if the plans take too long, he's afraid word of the sale will get around.'

Iris nodded.

He looked at his watch. 'It's almost three. I got word to Melba that we'd call by then. We'd better do it. Ready?'

'As I'll ever be.'

Jimmy punched in a telephone number. Iris picked up a telephone handset. Weems pressed one side of a headset to his ear.

The phone rang twice then a man answered. He sounded tired. 'Hello.'

'Douglas Melba, please,' Iris said.

'Who's calling?'

'This is . . .' Iris paused for a second.

Weems winced.

'Margo Hill.'

'OK. This is Melba.'

'I'm calling about the fox. My boss wants to buy it.'

'Six million.'

'Six?' Iris began to relax and get into the flow. 'That's a little steep. That's more than my boss wants to pay.'

Weems closed his eyes and nodded slowly.

'What does he want to pay?'

'No more than five.'

'Can't do it. Can't go any lower than five seventy-five.'

'Five fifty. That's his final offer.'

Weems widened his eyes at Iris.

Melba exhaled into the phone. There was a long pause during which no one in the conference room moved.

'OK, five million, five hundred thou. Cash.'

'Of course. When and where?'

'Let me get back to you on that.'

Iris shot a worried glance at Weems. He put up a hand to indicate it was OK and scribbled SOON on a pad of paper.

'That's fine,' Iris said into the telephone. 'But my boss wants the deal completed tomorrow or the next day.' She watched as Weems scribbled on the pad of paper. 'He's afraid word will get out if it takes too long.'

Weems turned the pad so she could read it.

'Understood,' Melba said in his flat voice. 'Where can I call you?'

Iris read the number that Weems had written down and also read what he wanted her to say. 'That's my private line at my employer's office. If I don't answer, just leave the time and place on the phone machine. You don't have to say who it is. I'll know. But it has to be in the LA area.' She quickly added, 'And a public place.'

'Public. I don't know if I can go for that.'

'Look, I'm coming by myself. I'm not going to meet you in a hotel room or something. You can understand that.'

Weems clenched his fist and shook it, indicating Iris was doing well.

'OK, fine,' Melba said. 'I'll call you back tomorrow.'

'OK. Goodbye.'

Weems drew his finger across his throat and Jimmy disconnected the call. As soon as they were off, Weems threw his arm round Iris's shoulder and hugged her hard. 'You were great, Iris! It couldn't have gone better.'

'Good work,' Jimmy agreed.

'Thanks. I feel a little shaky.' Iris's hand trembled as she took a sip from the plastic water bottle.

'Do you need a ride home?'

'I don't know. I can't believe that Garland would have left me here, but maybe he did.'

'I'll drive you.'

Iris left the building with Weems, who continued grinning, showing his small white teeth. He guided her through the almost vacant building with his hand on her upper arm as he had done the day he first brought her here. But today, the gesture was protective and warm.

She still felt shaky and stepped carefully as if her legs might give way. She didn't know if it was because of the phone call alone or because Garland's departure had sunk in. On the one hand, she wished she'd gone

114

with him and left Weems to follow through on his threats. On the other, she was angry at Garland for trying to control her. Maybe he didn't agree with what she was doing, but he should at least respect her decision. His outburst had surprised her. She'd never seen him act so emotionally before. He was jealous of Todd, a dead man. She was certain of one thing, she didn't know what she would do if Garland wasn't waiting for her.

She didn't have to figure it out. He was sitting on a cement bench next to the parking lot, his elbows on his knees.

'Looks like your ride's still here,' Weems said. 'I'll call you as soon as I hear from Melba.' He quickly proceeded to the parking lot, paying his respects to Garland as he walked past.

After being roused from his thoughts by Weems passing by, Garland turned to see Iris approaching. He smiled at her and she stepped up her pace.

'I thought you'd left me.'

'I could never leave you,' he told her. 'I just . . .' He scratched his head, rumpling his auburn hair. 'I don't know you as well as I thought I did. It's a bit jarring, that's all. I don't understand how you could have been in love with a man like that.'

'Todd was always nice to me. He wasn't involved in anything criminal when I knew him.'

'You don't want to admit it.'

'Garland, Todd Fillinger wasn't a criminal when I knew him. He slipped downhill after that. Peru said he was depressed.' She stroked his face.

'Iris, people don't become criminals overnight. Todd was into some pretty heavy stuff. I can understand why you wouldn't want to admit to yourself that you were in love with a creep.'

Iris smiled sadly at the ground, not agreeing with Garland but feeling it was pointless to pursue the issue. Out of the corner of her eye, she saw Weems's navy blue Thunderbird drive past. 'It doesn't matter. Todd Fillinger is dead. I'm in love with you, not him.'

'I can understand one thing about the SOB. I'd be depressed if you left me.' He took her hand from his cheek and kissed it. 'I'm sorry I stormed out like that. This whole thing stinks. Your motives for getting involved are perfectly honorable, but I don't trust that Weems farther than I can spit. People like him prey on nice, well-intentioned people like you. Call me jaded, but I think people in law enforcement are one step away from being crooks themselves.'

He unfolded her hand and placed it against his cheek again. 'The thought of something happening to you or someone hurting you makes me nuts.'

'Nothing's going to happen to me. It's going to be fine. And by Monday night, it'll all be over.' She looped her arm in his and they walked to the car.

Chapter 17

Iris lay in bed for a long time, listening to Garland sleep. It was still dark, early on Sunday morning. She didn't want to get out of bed this early on principle and she didn't want to wake Garland, a light sleeper under normal circumstances. She carefully pulled the goosedown comforter up to her neck, lay on her back with her hands folded across her chest, and gazed at the wooden Venetian blinds covering the sliding glass door on the far wall. Beyond it was a redwood deck with steps down to her small backyard.

She made plans to get quotes from contractors on replacing the wobbly sliding glass with French doors. She'd also get quotes on having all the windows re-hung. After decades of earthquakes and land erosion that had torqued the house and its foundation, none of the windows worked properly. The hardwood floors could use refinishing. She should have the chimney cleaned before winter.

She thought about the holidays and decided to host Christmas this year. She wondered about her mother and sister and two nephews and her darling niece and felt an overwhelming desire to see them. She'd call them today and make plans. She thought about her dad and what she and her sister called his new family. He'd had five children with his second wife Sonja for whom he'd left his first family to marry when Iris was fourteen. Twenty years had passed before Iris had gone to see him with her sister Lily a few years ago. It was surprising to learn that his eldest son was eighteen. Iris now called her father occasionally, but they weren't close. Not like when she was little. For some reason, her father wanted her to get to know her half-brothers and sisters, kept gently suggesting it, but she could never muster anything more than mild interest in them, as if they were kids who lived round the corner or something. They were virtual strangers to her, sharing nothing but some genes.

She thought about all kinds of things as she listened to Garland's deep, even breathing, wishing she could be where he was. Finally, she heard the first bird of the morning sing, bright and sharp. Soon, it was joined by a second voice. Then the blackness visible through the Venetian blinds turned a pale gray and the birds began singing in earnest. She watched and listened and made more plans and tried to think about anything but Todd Fillinger.

Slowly, she slipped from the bed, the cool air raising goose bumps on her nude skin. She padded to the boudoir chair in the corner, grabbed the sweats she had tossed there the previous night, and pranced from the room, the hardwood floor creaking with every other step. She quietly closed the door behind her, spying Garland, still asleep, creeping into the warm spot she had left.

Just outside the closed door, she shivered as she put on the sweats. She started the coffee brewing and went outside to bring in the newspaper. It was foggy, the air thick and white. It would break up by 10:00 a.m. and the late September day would be bright and sunny.

Her tennis shoes were on the front porch next to his. She banged hers against the side of the steps, knocking off most of the sand from the night before when they'd crossed the bridge that spanned the four busy lanes of Pacific Coast Highway and went down the long, spiraling staircase on the other side to Casa Marina Beach. They'd taken a long walk on the sand, stopping at a local joint for beer and a platter of fried calamari, clams, and shrimp. By the time they'd started back, the tide was coming in, submerging areas of the beach, forcing them to scale jagged rocks. The froth from the waves splashed them and they were halfway drenched but laughing by the time they got back.

She rubbed the tennis shoes against the dew-covered grass, removing the rest of the sand, put them on and walked to the flowerbed where the newspaper was on top of her pansies. She'd have to call and complain again. A snail's slimy track meandered across the brick path. She followed it to where it disappeared into the flowerbed, pulled the snail from between the pansies, took it to the street and stepped on it, the shell crunching wetly under her tennis shoe.

Back inside the house, she filled a mug with coffee and started gathering the contents of Todd's portfolio that were still spread across her dining room table. In spite of herself, she started looking through them again.

The scrapbook held clippings from magazines and books where his work had been published, and samples of his studio work, held in place on the black cardboard pages by a thin film of plastic. There was the article about Death Valley featuring Todd's photos that Todd's sister Tracy Beale had noticed. She'd commented that Todd had loved Death Valley. Iris had not known that about him.

She turned to a photograph of an elderly woman sitting in a rocking chair in a structure that appeared to be made of bottles and mud. The article talked about squatters who lived on government land without running water or indoor plumbing. This woman was known as the bottle lady and she had built her house out of mud and items she found in the desert. The sweeping vista of Death Valley's Zabriskie Point was captured in a wide-angle photograph.

Iris found more magazine shots: an Art Nouveau hotel in Prague; stars making the scene at Manhattan's Studio 54; antique shops in London,

118

with one of Rita Winslow in front of her place; a lavish wedding reception for the daughter of a wealthy Russian at his country *dacha*; a spread on the work to finish Gaudi's Sagrada Familia in Barcelona.

She smiled at photos of French celebrities, including one of the French Madonna signed '*Pour Todd, avec love*'. Iris remembered when the singing star had stopped by the café and Todd had introduced her. Lots of people came to see Todd at the café, many of them well-to-do. Iris had thought it odd at the time, since it was a ramshackle old place in an unfashionable neighborhood, but didn't question it.

There were studio shots of attractive young women, apparently taken for their modeling portfolios. Shots of nude women were mingled with traditional family portraits. An elderly woman posed with her two cats.

Iris closed the scrapbook and began digging through the zippered portfolio. The photos in it were loose and clumped at the bottom of the large case. There were proof sheets of wedding photos, more shots of pretty girls, both clothed and in different stages of undress. There were Polaroid snapshots. Here was Todd arm in arm with a group of people. Here he was arm in arm with another group of people. And yet more people. He had moved so frequently, leaving everything behind, she wondered whether any of these people could have meant anything to him. He was alone.

The photographs covered five countries on two continents and ran the gamut of styles. What was Todd looking for? What was he running from?

She smiled at a fading Polaroid of the husband and wife who owned *Le Café des Quatre Vents*. They were an older couple. His face was bloated and mottled from years of drinking too much cheap red wine from the bottles he refilled at the *cave* down the street. She had a face that was still pretty and took pains every month to dye the gray from her black hair that she wore in a twist pinned to the back of her head. They had a grown son who worked in a nearby bank and a daughter who lived in the south.

Iris tapped the snapshot against her forehead, trying to remember their name. It came to her. Monsieur and Madame Mouche. Mr and Mrs Fly.

She sorted through another handful of photos and was surprised to find nude shots of her. She'd forgotten all about them, but seeing them brought the event back to her. It had not been forgotten after all but just stored away, like a flower pressed between the pages of a book she'd long ago finished reading and returned to the shelf.

Todd had taken the shots using only the sunlight that streamed through the tall windows of his apartment. She had just risen from bed and was angry with him. They had argued the previous evening. He'd left the apartment and hadn't returned until the next morning when he'd found her wrapped in a sheet, sitting by the window, looking at the city.

His apartment was spectacular and the photographs captured it well. On the top floor of an eighteenth-century building, it had fifteen foot-high ceilings, ornate crown and base moldings, marble floors, polished antique brass fixtures, a modern kitchen, and a view of the Seine with the Eiffel Tower in the background.

The first time he'd brought her there, she commented that his business must be going well.

Todd had looked at his surroundings and smiled. 'I've finally figured it out.'

So it confused her when she'd come back from shopping one day to find Todd sulking and drinking.

'The *Paris Match* job,' he told her when she asked what was wrong. 'I didn't get it.'

'I'm sorry, Todd. Something else will come along,' she said, to be encouraging. 'It always does. You're doing well.'

He gave her a dark look that stunned her with its ferocity. 'I'm a fucking failure,' he snarled. 'My life's a complete waste.'

She was taken aback by his comment. 'This is just a small disappointment.'

He looked at her incredulously. 'You have no idea, do you?'

'About what?'

'About me. About what it means to be me.'

Trying to be helpful, she sat near him and quietly asked, 'What's going on, Todd?'

He sneered at her. 'Like you would have a clue.'

Iris was stunned by this caustic side of Todd; she'd never seen it before. She was unprepared to go where the conversation was heading. She walked into the kitchen and began putting away the groceries she'd bought. While she was doing that, she heard the front door slam.

She'd paced the floors most of the night, worried sick about him. He'd returned the next morning carrying croissants and chocolatines from her favorite patisserie. She was madder than hell and he irritated her by thinking it was cute, so cute that he wanted to take pictures of her just as she was, sitting in the natural light, draped in a sheet.

Iris flipped through the handful of photographs. She thought her face looked ragged but her body looked good. Todd knew how to pose her to capture her best angles. She remembered that as he was taking shots and adjusting the sheet over her nakedness, she had found herself becoming aroused. Her expression in the photographs changed as her anger gave way to desire. They had made love on the floor in the sunbeam of a Paris morning. Afterward, she hadn't completely forgiven him, but she wasn't done with him either. The questions were still all there, but she didn't care. His was an intoxicating life, unlike anything she had ever known, and she hadn't had her fill.

The toilet flushed. Garland was up.

She quickly put away Todd's photos except for the nudes of her which she slipped into a kitchen drawer. Her cheeks were hot. The recollection of

120

that time with Todd had made her blush as if she had been caught betraying Garland.

He padded toward her in bare feet, his hair rumpled, wearing the cotton bathrobe he kept at her house. He kissed her and his mouth tasted like peppermint from having just brushed his teeth.

'I didn't hear you get up,' he said as he poured himself coffee and then held the pot over her empty mug. She nodded and he filled it. 'I was out like a light.'

'You must have needed the rest.' Her face felt cool again. Thankfully, the flush had left.

He hugged her from behind. 'You're the one who needs the rest, sweet pea. What time did you get up?'

She shrugged. 'Early.'

'Maybe you should try to take a nap later today.'

She put her hands on top of his which were holding her waist. This was what love really was.

He kissed her on the back of the neck then let her go. 'Any idea what you want for breakfast?'

'I don't know. I don't have a thing in the house. I haven't had time to go to the store since I've been back.'

'I don't feel like eating out. Let's cook something here. I'll run down to the store. How about some pancakes and country sausage?'

'Sounds good. Oh, and some fruit.'

He started walking to the bedroom. 'Go ahead and take a shower, and I'll be back in a few minutes.'

She was still standing in the kitchen, looking through the newspaper which she'd opened on the breakfast bar, when he walked back through the house, now wearing jeans and a sweatshirt printed with a logo from his alma mater.

After she heard his car go down the hill, she pulled the photographs from the kitchen drawer and took them into the smaller bedroom that she used as an office. She fed them through the paper shredder, the images still visible yet shattered on the even slivers of paper that fell into the trash can.

Of course Todd must have been dealing drugs. How else could he have afforded that de luxe Paris apartment? He had a few photography jobs during the time she'd stayed with him, but that paltry amount of work couldn't have earned enough to support his lifestyle.

She ran her hand around the trash can, mixing together the fragments of photographs.

Then there were all the people Todd knew and the comings and goings at *Le Café des Quatre Vents*. She had taken it at face value, all of it. She hadn't thought about it. She didn't think she needed to. It was a wild and nutty fling. That's all she'd thought it was until Todd had told her he felt differently. Then she began to feel she was in love with him. Garland

121

would say he conned her, but that seemed too simplistic. She was in love with Todd, but with the Todd that he had allowed her to see. She could have attempted to peel back the layers but didn't care to. He'd painted a pretty picture and she'd decided she liked the picture just fine.

But after Todd had stayed out all night, things changed. The dream began to unravel for her while he started to cling to her in a way he hadn't done previously. There was an edge of desperation to it. She saw a fragility that he hadn't revealed before. He kept asking her if she was still returning to Los Angeles at the end of September to start her new job. When she'd first started up with him, she'd had a wild notion of tossing caution to the wind and sharing his Bohemian lifestyle, but she'd settled down over the course of the three months she'd spent in Paris. She was beginning to feel homesick. And the intensity of his emotions was starting to scare her. It was as if he wanted to absorb her, like a balm; as if he thought she could save him, as if she was his last hope. She cared for him deeply, but it was beyond her to save him.

One night, a week before she was to leave, he proposed marriage to her on bent knee. She said yes, touched by the earnestness in his face, swept away by the vision of their life together, rendered in brilliant colors. He didn't have a ring for her, but would get her one.

She said, 'Here, I'll give you a ring instead.'

He squeezed her class ring onto his pinky finger. 'I'll never take it off.'

'And you never did,' she said aloud, still trailing her hand through the shredded photographs. She touched a tear at the corner of her eye.

Todd had made plans for a small wedding three days later, right before she was due to go home. Now she was the one who became duplicitous. She had to get away, to run. She became obsessed with the idea that he was a wounded man, although she couldn't pinpoint why she felt that way. She'd convinced herself that the glint in his eye was madness.

It seemed so dramatic and overblown now, sitting here years later in her quiet house with her steady, sure man. It was a sweeping gesture, a style worthy of Todd, picking up and fleeing with no forwarding address. She despised herself for it. It was rather like stomping on a puppy.

Todd wasn't a bad man at heart. Garland would disagree, but she refused to believe that about Todd. In the years that had passed since she'd left Paris, many of them spent without love, she'd thought about the life with Todd that she had thrown away. She'd fantasized that with some stability in his life, they might have turned out fine together. But something had made her run. There was no getting around that. She had decided it had been a flaw in her.

She had gone to Moscow to say she was sorry and to touch those months in Paris one last time.

She picked up the trash can, carried it through the house and out the kitchen door, depositing the contents in the large Dumpster at the side of the house. The fog was starting to burn off sooner than she'd anticipated.

She went around the house into her backyard and stood looking at the ocean, which was a deep sapphire blue today.

'Hi ho, neighbor.'

Iris squinted through the tall hedge that separated her yard from the one next door and saw her neighbor Marge wearing gardening gloves and carrying a basket full of cut flowers and a pair of shears.

'Come over and I'll give you some flowers for your table. Everything is blooming *so* beautifully this year,' she enthused. 'I just can't *believe* how lucky we are!'

Iris slipped between the hedge and the white picket fence at the end of Marge's yard where it met the cliff. As she skirted through, she faced the house and did not look down to Pacific Coast Highway several hundred feet below.

Even though it was still early, Marge was dressed in a knit suit and heels, not a hair out of place. She smiled, her eyes bright in a sprightly face that did not disguise her age but seemed eternally youthful. It said more about spirit than wrinkles.

'Here, take all you want, Iris.' She started picking the prettiest blooms from the basket.

'Marge, you keep those for yourself.'

'Oh, *non*-sense. I want you to have them. I saw that your Garland is here. These will make a nice bouquet for your breakfast table.'

'Thanks, Marge. Well, I guess I'd better get dressed. Garland will be back from the store soon.'

'And I'm off to church. You did promise to come with me one day.'

Iris nodded.

'Is something wrong, Iris? You seem a bit blue.'

'I was thinking about absent friends.'

'Anyone in particular?'

'A boy I knew. He's dead now. I thought I was in love with him, but I was never certain whether it was real.'

Marge waved dismissively with her gloved fingers. 'If you felt it, it was real. Love's a little bit stupid that way.'

Iris felt her chest tighten as the tears welled up. She took a deep breath.

'Cheer up. Don't dwell on the past. We all do the best we can.' Marge cocked her head in the direction of the street. 'That sounds like Mr Garland Hughes, and if I know him, he's returned with a big bag of groceries to make you breakfast.'

'Thanks, Marge. Have a nice day.'

Marge called out to Iris when she was halfway back in her yard. 'Miss Iris, do me a favor. Do not waste one moment of this *gorgeous* day thinking about things you can't change.'

Iris waved at her and returned to the house. She picked up the aroma of cooking sausage before she opened the door.

The phone rang just as she stepped inside. It was Roger Weems. The buy was set up for 8:00 the next night, Monday, at a restaurant named Greentree in Pasadena, a city just east of Los Angeles.

Iris hung up and told Garland the plans. They didn't talk about it again the rest of the day. It was indirectly addressed when Garland changed his airline reservation to depart Tuesday morning instead of that afternoon.

Chapter 18

Monday morning, Iris took refuge in her work. She had more than occasionally thought of making a job change and now one was before her. Jim Hailey needed a response from her about the regional manager's position by the end of the week. Lately, she'd considered hanging out a shingle and starting her own investment management firm, luring her top clients and employees to follow her, being her own boss. Today, she relished going to a job that she could do in her sleep. She wanted to see the same old faces and do the same old thing. They were sojourners on the same journey. She hadn't quite seen it that way before, but she now felt a bittersweet affection about the Los Angeles branch office and those who worked there.

Everything felt warm and familiar, from the people she'd seen in the corridors and elevators for years whom she'd never spoken with to the buzz of the bull pen as her sales staff struggled to make quota. She smiled warmly across the network of cubicles, making eye contact whenever she could. She sensed that they cringed slightly as she walked by, their smiles wavering on their lips. She was glad to see them but they weren't glad to see her.

Kyle Tucker walked in behind her and after a quick, 'Morning, Iris,' skirted to his office on the opposite side of the suite.

'Hi, Kyle,' she said to his back. 'How was the weekend?'

'Great,' he replied, cutting her off when he unlocked his door and went inside his office. Iris suspected that normally friendly Kyle wanted to avoid a discussion of his somewhat psychotic love interest, Dawn.

She saw Amber Ambrose at her desk in the office next to Kyle's. Iris raised her hand in greeting but dropped it when Amber, not missing a beat on her phone call, spun her chair to face the window, her back to the suite. Iris was positive Amber had seen her. This was typical of Amber who was frosty to her face and gossipy behind her back. Iris reflected on how much energy it must take for Amber to maintain such a level of hostility. Fortunately for Amber, her sales production was good.

Finally, Iris reached the end of the suite and Louise sitting at her desk. Louise looked up from typing on her computer and perfunctorily said, 'Good morning, Iris.'

'Good morning, Louise,' Iris said back, feeling miffed by the cool reception she'd received on a day she felt warm and fuzzy about her workplace. She hung up her suit jacket on the hanger behind the door and put her purse in the top drawer of her filing cabinet. She tucked her brightly printed silk blouse, which she had selected that day for its cheerfulness, into her skirt, assessing the tightness of her waistband as she did so. Her hand slipped in easily. She hadn't gained weight over the weekend. At least that was good news.

She picked up her coffee mug and studied its BUDGETS ARE FOR WIMPS slogan. For the first time, it impressed her as harsh. Opening her center desk drawer, she fished around for spare change and pocketed a few coins. Closing the drawer, she remembered the image of the Virgin and bent this way and that trying to spot it. When she couldn't she considered it a bad omen.

'Louise,' she said in a normal speaking voice.

For over twenty years, Louise had listened to the whims of the branch managers who had occupied that corner office. Iris didn't have to call a second time. Louise was already in her doorway, peering at her over the top of her half-glasses.

Iris pointed at the desk. 'The image, I can't find it.'

'I had the desk refinished over the weekend. It was becoming more trouble than it was worth.'

'Refinished? But you didn't ask me.'

'In the past, you've told me to handle any administrative details like that without bothering you.' Louise stood with both feet firmly planted on the floor, poised like a runner at the starting line, ready to get on with it. 'Do you want me to run such things by you now?'

Iris shook her head. 'Thanks, Louise.'

She took her mug to the lunchroom. When she opened the door, several sales assistants and junior brokers who had been laughing and talking suddenly clammed up and dispersed. Alone in the lunchroom, Iris filled the mug with coffee and fed coins into the vending machine. A packet of six Oreo cookies dropped into the aluminum bin.

Back in her office, Iris sat on the credenza against the southern-facing, floor-to-ceiling window. She ate the Oreo cookies, first twisting them apart then scraping the creamy filling off against her bottom teeth, and gazed out the window toward the hills of northeast Los Angeles where she had grown up. She pressed her cheek against the window to get a better look, not able to make out much more than a dim outline through the smog.

When she was a girl, she'd sit at the top of the hill above her house and gaze at the skyscrapers of downtown LA and wonder if she'd ever leave the neighborhood, have money, see the world, fall in love. She had done all those things. Now she looked back at where she'd come from, wondering if her life would ever be that simple again.

'Oreos on the credenza. Something's up.'

Iris turned to see Liz Martini stride into her office, wearing a double-knit wrap-around dress in a psychedelic print, her wavy, long, dark hair blow-dried smooth and cascading past her shoulders. She walked to the window and peered out. 'Ugh, look at this smog.'

Iris slid round and crossed her legs. 'No one in the office likes me except you.'

'And I just put up with you.'

'I was really happy to come to work today and see everyone, but no one was glad to see me.'

'Iris, it's *Monday*. Plus, you've spent years actively cultivating a healthy wariness of you on the part of your employees. Who cares if they like you? They're producing!' Liz put a hand on her bony hip. 'What's going on?'

'I wonder if it's all worth it. To have success but at what price? Garland and I are never together for more than a week at a time. He's always jetting all over the place. I've turned into the ice princess. My male co-workers used to call me that to get my goat when I first started in the industry, but it's become a self-fulfilling prophesy.'

'But that's not you, Iris. It's your work face. You're just doing what you have to do to get the job done.'

'Part of it is. It's not a complete act. I can be cold and calculating. I've manipulated people to get what I want. I've betrayed people.'

'Oh, Iris. You run a big office, you have responsibilities. If you were a pansy, people would walk all over you. Cold and calculating – when you have to be. Manipulating – occasionally. But you've betrayed people? I don't think so. What set you down this slippery slope?'

Iris twisted two halves of an Oreo apart then tried to press them back together. 'I thought a lot about Todd Fillinger over the weekend. I betrayed him. I should have been honest. I never intended to marry him.'

'Well, duh. Like I hadn't figured that out.' Liz drew a cookie from the cellophane package with her long acrylic nails and bit it in half. 'You should have told him the truth, but you didn't and it was rotten. You apologized to the guy in person. Now he's dead and you feel even worse. Let it go, Iris.'

'Garland and I kind of had a fight about it over the weekend.'

'Don't risk making Garland mad over this. That's really stupid.'

'There's the issue of the fox,' Iris said, lowering her voice. 'Things have become more complicated since I last spoke to you.'

'You mean with that British woman?'

'Shhh!' Iris warned.

Liz spoke more quietly. 'Forget about her. Tell her to get lost. My advice is to walk away while you still can.'

Iris stood and brushed cookie crumbs from her skirt. 'You're right. It's not my job to set the world straight. If someone wants to come after me, let 'em give me their best shot.'

'That's my girl. That's our piss-and-vinegar Iris.'

Iris squared her shoulders and tossed the remaining cookies in the trash where they landed in the metal container with a thwack. From the doorway of her office, she scanned the suite with a gimlet eye. 'That new guy keeps flirting with everything in a skirt. Look at him with the mailroom girl. She's too timid to tell him anything. His sales figures haven't been good enough for him to waste time bothering other employees.'

Liz whispered in Iris's ear, 'Give 'em hell.'

'A softer, gentler Iris. Yeah, right. What was I thinking?' She hitched up her skirt and strode into the suite.

Iris corrected the errant junior investment counselor and made a sweep of the office, chatting, suggesting, encouraging, but above all scoping out the scene and taking mental notes. She lingered in Amber Ambrose's office making chit-chat simply because she knew it annoyed her. She was also giving herself time to see if her decision would stick. After an hour, she still felt the same way. To hell with the fox and Weems. She had returned to her office to call Weems and tell him her decision when Louise buzzed her.

'Mrs Winslow is here to see you. She doesn't have an appointment. Are you in?'

Iris pondered the possibilities. She was bound to have to face her sooner or later. 'Show her in, please.'

Winslow and Iris greeted each other cordially.

'Miss Thorne, so nice of you to see me on such short notice.'

'Mrs Winslow, this is a distinct surprise.' Iris closed the door while Winslow sat in one of the chairs facing her desk. Still standing next to the door, Iris said, 'If you're carrying a gun, I want it now.'

With a blink of her bloodshot eyes, Winslow dropped her pleasant expression and scowled. 'I'm here alone on your territory. I'm not giving up the only protection I have.'

Iris threw up her hands. 'This is a business office. I don't come to work packing heat. Either give me your gun now and I'll put it in this filing cabinet or you'll have to leave.'

Winslow's jowls grew longer as she pursed her lips. She snapped the brass clasp on her fine leather handbag, pulled out the chrome-plated, pearl-handled gun and handed it butt end first to Iris. Iris deposited it in the top drawer of the cherrywood filing cabinet and pressed a button on the top, locking it. She sat behind her desk.

Prudishly clutching her handbag on her lap between both hands, Winslow said, 'I thought you were negotiating with Lazare to purchase the fox for me. Why haven't I heard from you?'

'Mrs Winslow, I'm glad you came to talk to me.'

'I'm not in the habit of seeking people out. You were supposed to reach me.' Winslow's knuckles were white from tightly holding the purse.

'Look, I have to be honest with you. I can't get you the fox. When I went to see you at the Peninsula Hotel, I didn't know anything about the fox. I led you on just to see if I could find out what happened to Todd Fillinger.'

Winslow's eyes bored into Iris. Her jaws were tightly clenched and a muscle in her cheek pulsed.

'I'm telling you the truth,' Iris insisted. 'I was not involved in stealing the fox from you. I went to see Todd in Moscow to examine investing in art galleries. After he was murdered, a man named Dean Palmer who worked for the US Embassy there gave me his ashes in an urn to bring to Todd's sister in Bakersfield. I brought them back to the States and a woman who said she was Todd's sister took them from me at the airport. That's all I know. That's the God's honest truth.'

'Don't toy with me,' Winslow rasped.

Iris was stunned into silence by the viciousness of her tone.

'I can't believe the ends Fernando will go to in order to betray me.' Winslow picked up the handbag from her lap and slammed it onto the seat of the chair next to her. 'I gave him everything, even freedom when he wanted it, within limits, of course. I asked little in return, only that he stay with me and help me run my business. But again and again he—' She clapped her hand over her mouth but not before a sob escaped.

Iris sat motionlessly then abruptly began rummaging in a desk drawer for a box of tissues. She offered them to Winslow but the other woman had already pulled a monogrammed, lace-edged handkerchief from her handbag and was dabbing her eyes with it.

'Mrs Winslow, don't get the wrong idea about Fernando Peru and me. He showed up at my house that night of his own accord. He wanted to tell me some things about Todd Fillinger. He filled in the gaps about what happened to Todd after I left Paris. You have to admit, you wouldn't let us discuss Todd when I came to see you at the hotel.'

Winslow's teary moment passed. She quickly stuffed the handkerchief into her purse and went on as if nothing had happened. Her demeanor was again steely. 'Don't lie, Miss Thorne. It doesn't suit you.'

'I'm not lying!' Iris protested. 'Mrs Winslow, I'll admit I lied to you when we met at the hotel, but that's the only time. All my cards are on the table now. I just want to be free of this whole situation.'

'I must confess that your story has a certain earnestness to it. Did Roger Weems help you cook it up?'

Iris sat as still as if she had been slapped.

Winslow gloated smugly. 'Little girls like you. So cocky. So sure of yourself. Sitting here in your bright corner office with your expensive clothes and your cheap antique reproductions. Assuming that someone like me is past her prime, easy to trick. Well, I see *all* and I know *all*.'

Iris recovered, although she sensed it was too late. She answered with a half-truth which was harder to pin down than an out-and-out lie. 'Weems showed up and asked me about you and Fernando Peru and the fox. I told him exactly what I told you.'

'And he went away and left you alone after that?'

'Yes.'

Winslow laughed cruelly. 'I know Roger Weems better than you. I don't know what scheme he's brewing, but he's not going away until he gets what he wants.' She took a packet of Dunhill cigarettes and the cloisonné lighter from her purse, placed a cigarette between her lips and lit it.

Iris didn't have the guts to tell her there was no smoking in the building. She dumped paperclips from a hammered silver tray into a drawer and slid the tray across the desk.

Winslow posed with her elbow cocked, hand held high, the cigarette squeezed between her fingers. She swung her arm to her mouth and took a puff, leisurely exhaling a long stream of smoke. 'How much did Weems tell you about me? About his history with me?'

'Not much.'

'Did you ever wonder why he works alone?' Winslow knocked ash into the silver tray.

'I wasn't aware that he does.'

'Let me tell you something about Roger Weems. He wants the Tsarina's Fox and he'll do anything to get it. It goes beyond logic and reason. It represents for him his darkest hour. Like Captain Ahab and Moby Dick. If he can get the fox and me, he'll redeem himself.' Winslow's eyes were bright. 'I'm part of the prize. Very much so.'

She again tapped ash into the tray then settled back into her chair. 'Twelve years ago in Buenos Aires, an old woman died. Nothing remarkable, except this old woman was the Argentinian widow of a former high-ranking member of the Nazi party who had fled Germany for South America at the end of World War Two. Her adult children cleaned out her house and found, wrapped in velvet, tucked away in a corner of an old trunk, an unusual jeweled statuette of a fox.' She laughed quietly at the vagaries of life. 'They took the statuette to a very respected jeweler who immediately recognized not just the value of the gems but the artistic value of the piece. He took it to a professor of art history at the university. Before long, I received word through my network that the Tsarina's Fox had been found. I immediately made plans to travel to Buenos Aires with my associate at the time, Paolo.

'With some mild persuasion on the part of my middleman, the professor was encouraged to part with the fox. In the meantime, Roger Weems and his partner, a sweet young man by the name of Greg Kelly, had also heard that the fox had been located and were en route to Buenos Aires. You see, the Bremen Museum had offered a longstanding, substantial reward for the fox. Weems was able to convince someone at the FBI that the statuette fell under their jurisdiction. Roger Weems knew of me but we had yet to meet.'

Winslow gazed out the window behind Iris's head as if seeing the events of the past projected there. 'Paolo and I met the middleman on a quiet street near midnight, as arranged. I wasn't happy with the location but it was the one acceptable to the middleman. After that night, I swore I'd never be that foolish again.' She smiled ruefully. 'But of course I was. It seems that we are always that foolish again. The middleman gave me the fox and I inspected it in the dim light, was satisfied, and paid him. We were standing in the middle of the empty street, shaking hands, when out of the darkness Greg Kelly walked up holding a gun. From the other side of the street came Roger Weems, also armed.

'Before anyone could say a word, the middleman pulled a gun and started running away, shooting all the while. Kelly returned the fire. Paolo was dead before he had a chance to draw his gun. Kelly was out of bullets and was running for cover to reload when the middleman shot him in the back.'

'What about Weems?' Iris asked.

'Weems just stood there.' Winslow's expression was sardonic. 'In all that gunfire, he just stood there with his gun in his hand. He was not three feet from the middleman, but he let the guy shoot his young partner to death. Bullets were flying everywhere and Weems stood in the middle of it like a statue. I didn't carry a weapon back then. I dropped to the pavement as soon as the shooting started. Then I remembered the fox. It was on the ground beside Paolo. Weems had gathered his wits by this time and kicked me in the side of the head, knocking me out. When I came to, a few minutes later, I saw Weems kneeling next to Greg Kelly in the street. I grabbed the switchblade that Paolo always kept in his right boot, snuck up on Weems and slashed his hand, making him drop the useless gun he was still holding. I grabbed it and told him to give me the fox. Bleeding profusely from his hand, cursing me throughout eternity, he finally turned it over.'

Winslow pressed out her cigarette in the tray. 'It wasn't until I returned to the hotel that I discovered I'd purchased a fake. It was an excellent facsimile and given that it was dark, I had made an honest mistake. Knowing that Weems would soon track me down thinking I had the real fox, I quickly left the hotel, leaving the bogus statuette behind. I understand that Weems still keeps it as a memento.'

Iris listened with her hands steepled, resting her chin against her thumbs. 'Didn't Weems get into trouble with the FBI over that incident?'

'He simply fabricated a story about what happened in which he portrayed himself as a hero rather than a coward. I've since learned that the sight and sound of gunfire at night causes him to have a flashback of when he was shot in Vietnam. He becomes paralyzed with fear. Greg Kelly died because of Roger Weems. Weems, as befitting a man of his character, lays the blame at my feet.'

Winslow drew her handbag onto her lap, opened it, and took out a mirrored lipstick case. She spread rose color on her thin lips. 'Much blood had been shed over this fox.' She angled her eyes at Iris. 'Weems is here because he thinks the fox is here. He sought you out for the same reason I did. But something is going on, and I can't quite get my arms round it. The only explanation is that you're lying to me. You and Fernando. I don't know what you two are plotting behind my back. I'll leave you with this: you will get me the fox. I don't care what you have to do to get it.'

Iris was now sorry she'd attempted to back off from her story about having a connection to the fox. Instead of chattering away to this woman, she should have kept her mouth shut. All it had accomplished was to confirm in Winslow's mind that she was not to be trusted. Garland was right, none of these people were clean. And she was hopelessly caught in the drama they'd been acting out for years. She attempted to walk away from the fox one final time. 'What if I can't get it for you?'

'Then I'll kill you. May I have my gun now, please?'

Iris hesitated.

'Miss Thorne, I'm not going to kill you as long as you're of use to me. But you will not have Fernando. That I cannot permit.'

Iris took a small key from her desk drawer and opened the filing cabinet. 'What if I get you the fox? What about then?'

Winslow tucked the gun back into her handbag. 'Oh, so you've swung back to the position that you *can* get it?'

Iris had finally learned not to say anything.

'Once I get the fox, I will happily go on my way.' Winslow stood and smoothed her seashell-pink tailored dress. The delicate color, like the hanky, seemed to mock the size of the big-boned woman. 'All this may sound overly dramatic and excessive to you, but it means that much to me. You have no idea. Good day, Miss Thorne.'

Chapter 19

Iris didn't tell Weems about Winslow's visit. She didn't tell Garland either. Since the only way out of this situation was through it, there was no point in getting everybody riled up. She had no doubt that Winslow would follow through with her threat if she did not produce the fox. To eliminate Winslow from her life, she needed Weems's help. To get his help, she had to follow through with his scheme to buy the fox from Douglas Melba then sell it to Winslow. She repeated the plan in her mind like a mantra: buy and sell, buy and sell. It was a cruel perversion of what she did every day in her professional life.

In Weems's office, Garland watched the goings-on with resignation and barely suppressed anger, an attitude that Iris had become familiar with since her involvement in this ordeal.

Weems flitted around like a maid of honor attending the bride with a commensurate level of giddy excitement while a cadre of agents outfitted Iris with audio transmission wires and a bulletproof vest. When she had gone home before coming to Weems's office, she had put on a bathing suit top which covered as much of her as a brassiere, but kept her from feeling as if she was wearing her underwear in public while the FBI wired her for sound. She'd also selected a thick denim shirt – nothing thin or clingy, according to Weems's instructions – comfortable jeans and hiking boots. The jeans and hiking boots were her idea. In case something happened and she needed to run.

Weems cradled the bogus fox as he described the set-up, for at least the fifth time now. 'At this Greentree restaurant, we'll have agents posing as diners in the area where you'll be sitting. We didn't clear out the restaurant because we don't want Melba casing the place ahead of time and noticing something's amiss.'

Garland drummed his fingers against the tabletop. 'The people at the restaurant know what's going on?'

'No. We couldn't take the chance that someone in the restaurant would tip off the other side.'

Garland persisted, 'What if the restaurant employees or owners are on the other side? What if Lazare owns this place?'

'Mr Hughes, we'll have agents sitting all around Iris, at every table. They're there right now, already in place. Deals like this are very straightforward, done every day.' Weems sliced the air with a flat hand as if demonstrating how straight everything is. 'The choice of location is excellent. The restaurant has large windows and there's a hotel right across the street that gives a clear view of the restaurant where we'll be monitoring communications.'

'But this place was not of your choosing,' Garland interrupted. 'The bad guys selected it for the same reasons you outline. Their people will be watching what's going on too.'

'Undoubtedly, Mr Hughes,' Weems agreed. 'That's a given.'

'But Dean Palmer knows what Iris looks like. When he sees it's her and not this Margo Hill, he'll know something's up.'

Iris put on the denim shirt and buttoned it over the various contraptions she was wearing. She unzipped her jeans and tucked in the tail.

'We've anticipated that.' Weems rapidly snapped his fingers in the air at no one in particular. A man brought over a box from which Weems took a wig of long, brown hair. 'Ever wonder what you'd look like as a brunette, Iris?'

Iris brightened at the idea of being in disguise. She ran her fingers through the long hair and quoted an old commercial for hair coloring, 'If I have one life, I want to live it as a blonde.' She began tying up her shoulder-length blonde hair with the bobby pins an agent handed her. 'But I'll make this one exception.'

'Mr Hughes,' Weems continued, 'my guess is Enrico Lazare will not send Dean Palmer to oversee the deal. If Lazare doesn't come himself, he'll send a trusted associate. Dean Palmer is nothing more than Lazare's flunky. Lazare would never count on a drug addict to pull off an operation like this.'

Iris looked in a hand mirror that an agent held for her and brushed the wig. If she wasn't in danger of losing her life, she would have enjoyed all the attention. She swung the long hair over her shoulder and gave Garland a vampish look. 'Peel me a grape, darling.'

He was not amused.

Weems, on the other hand, was ebullient. He grabbed Iris's shoulders from behind and gave her a playful shake.

An attractive young man entered the room.

'Hey!' Weems exclaimed, holding out his arm to welcome the new-comer. 'Iris, this is Don Vinson. He's going to come with you into the restaurant and take the hotel key from Melba.'

They shook hands and exchanged pleasantries. Iris introduced Vinson to Garland.

Now serious, Weems pulled out a chair and sat facing Iris, their knees almost touching. He pressed his palms together as if in prayer. 'OK, tell me how this goes down.'

'Don and I will drive up to Greentree. While Don leaves the car with the valet and gets the claim check, I'll take the briefcase with the money from the trunk. We'll walk into the restaurant and ask the host for a window table. I tell him I'm Margo Hill and I'm waiting for a gentleman. Would he show him to my table when he arrives?'

Weems nodded.

'We'll sit down, look at the menu, and chat a bit. We'll both order cappuccinos. I'll take the cellular phone you'll give me and set it on the table. When Melba arrives, he and Don will take the briefcase into the men's room and count the money. After Melba's satisfied the money is there, they'll return to the table and give the briefcase back to me. Melba will give Don the key to a hotel room across the street where he's left the fox. Don will leave. After he verifies that the fox is in the room and it's real, he'll call me on the cellular phone. I'll hand the briefcase to Melba. He'll leave.' Iris paused. 'Then what?'

'Come over to that hotel room to see the fox and have a glass of champagne, Iris Thorne!' Weems exclaimed.

'So what happens then?' Garland asked.

'We follow the money to the bad guys.' Weems looked at his watch. 'OK, it's six o'clock. Let's get you and Don on your way. You'll get to Pasadena early, so drive around a bit.' He extended his hand to Iris. 'Good job.'

'Thanks. I'll feel better about it when it's over.'

Weems turned to Garland who was hanging on the fringes of the group as if he felt like a fifth wheel. 'Mr Hughes, why don't you drive over with me? We'll watch everything from our communications center then you won't have to wait to find out that everything went fine.'

Garland smiled. 'Thanks, I didn't expect you to invite me along after I was so prickly about this whole thing.'

Weems slapped him on the back. 'I didn't expect anything less. I'd be the same way if I were in your shoes.'

'But I think I'll wait for Iris at her house,' Garland said. 'She'll be nervous enough without me there.'

'Are you sure?' Weems still rested his hand on Garland's back. 'Well, if that's the way you feel about it.'

Iris was privately relieved, as Garland knew she would be. She'd only worry about him worrying about her.

Weems gave Garland a gentle nudge toward Iris. 'Say goodbye to your hero, here, until you meet again in just a few short hours.'

Garland and Iris looked into each other's eyes with an intensity that almost made Iris lose her nerve, as if they were trying to peer into the other's soul. Iris lightened the moment by giving him a quick peck on the lips and a hug. 'See you soon.'

'See you soon,' he repeated, reluctantly letting her go.

On the drive to Pasadena in a nondescript late-model American sedan, Iris nervously chatted with Don Vinson about nothing of any significance.

They arrived about forty-five minutes early. For the first time Iris could remember, she had hoped for more traffic so they wouldn't be left with time on their hands.

They drove around Pasadena's residential neighborhoods and looked at the stately old homes on the tree-lined streets. Iris pointed out the 'Leave it to Beaver' house on one street and a few others that frequently appeared in commercials or movies. Many of Pasadena's cozy two-story houses behind neatly appointed front lawns were favorite filming locations, providing a comfortable Midwestern look just beyond the palm trees of Los Angeles.

It was twilight when Vinson stopped the car in front of Greentree. Through the tall windows that faced the street, Iris noticed that the large bar and restaurant were busy with patrons dressed as if they'd come from work. With Vinson wearing a sport jacket and tie, she felt conspicuously underdressed, something she hadn't thought about when selecting her attire. She shrugged it off. This was one occasion she was glad she'd chosen practicality over style.

Vinson took a claim check for the car from a valet while Iris pulled the heavy briefcase from the trunk. Vinson took it from her and opened the restaurant's glass door.

Across the bar at the entrance to the dining area, the host looked up at them from behind a podium and smiled with practiced congeniality. 'Good evening. Welcome to Greentree.' He looked crisp and freshly shaven and had a slight olive tint to his skin that gave him a Continental air.

'A table for three by the window,' Iris said.

'Do you have a reservation?'

Iris gave Vinson a panicked look. No one had mentioned a reservation to her. It was just the sort of stupid oversight that could mess everything up.

'Margo Hill,' Vinson answered. 'For eight o'clock.'

The host raised his eyebrows and ran his finger down a large page covered with handwriting. 'Of course. Would you like to wait in the bar until the third party arrives?'

Iris shook her head. 'We'd prefer to go to the table now. We're waiting for a man who's short and . . . rotund. Please show him to our table as soon as he arrives.'

The host ducked his head, indicating he understood and handed two large menus to a waitress who'd suddenly appeared at his elbow. Iris and Vinson followed her to a table set for four right next to a window facing the street. They sat opposite each other. The waitress handed them menus and gathered the extra place setting.

Iris opened the menu and scanned it without seeing a thing. She closed it and breathed a sigh of relief. 'One down.' She removed strands of synthetic hair from her cheek and smoothed the wig with both hands.

Don leaned close and spoke into Iris's ear. 'Our people are all over this place. Those two guys there, that woman and man there. And outside, see that homeless guy standing on the corner? He's one of ours.'

Iris rolled her shoulders in an attempt to reseat the awkward bulletproof vest and glanced at the terraces off each room of the hotel across the street. The wrought-iron railings held window boxes crammed with bright flowers. The hotel looked small and inviting, a nice place for a weekend getaway for her and Garland. Now she wished she hadn't let him wait at her house. She would have liked to think that of everyone watching her from that hotel, there was someone there whose sole interest was her wellbeing.

The waitress returned and they ordered cappuccinos.

'Will you be ordering dinner?' she asked, narrowing her eyes with disapproval when Iris handed her the menu and said they would not.

'Very good.' She sharply spun on her heel and left, probably calculating the tip she'd lost waiting on two deadbeats who were occupying one of her prime tables during the dinner rush.

Vinson attempted to engage Iris in pleasant conversation, but she was too rattled to focus on anything. She gave him clipped, disjointed responses while she scanned the street for the approach of a squat, overweight, balding man. The street lights came on as dusk set in.

Vinson was talking about basketball, which would not have held Iris's attention under any circumstances, when she saw a man fitting Douglas Melba's description walking as quickly as his chubby legs would carry him toward the restaurant. Her heart began to pound and she nearly rose from her chair which made Vinson stop mid-comment.

Melba was dressed completely in black. A heavy gold chain bracelet was visible beneath the rolled-up cuffs of his shirt and he wore a necklace under the V of his open collar. His pants rode low on his hips and were belted underneath his protruding belly. His eyes traveled across the diners sitting next to the window, stopping when they landed on Iris.

'It's him,' she hissed.

Vinson took a quick glance then hitched his eyebrows, indicating that Iris was correct.

The waitress chose this moment to bring the cappuccinos. Iris barely noticed her. She was watching Melba who had stopped on the sidewalk a few feet from where she and Vinson were sitting. He was standing stock still, not looking inside the restaurant at her any longer but at something across the street.

'Great, thanks,' Vinson told the waitress as she arranged their cappuccinos. He casually dropped a lump of sugar into his cup and stirred it, almost too pointedly ignoring Melba.

Iris followed the direction of Melba's gaze and saw a man standing in the open doorway of a terrace off a room on the hotel's third floor. The room was dark, but the lights from the street and passing cars were sufficient to illuminate him in silhouette.

'Iris,' Vinson warned. 'Relax.'

'Wait a second, something's . . .'

Vinson turned to see what had distracted her and they both watched as the man on the terrace stretched his arm into the light cast by a street lamp. With his fist closed, he turned his thumb down.

Melba abruptly turned and quickly started walking back down the street.

Vinson bolted from his chair, startling the restaurant's patrons. 'Melba's leaving,' he shouted to the undercover agents who were now out of their seats. 'Grab him! Cauble, get Zajac and find out who was on that terrace, fourth room from the left. Don't let him get away!'

They scattered dishes and chairs as they ran from the restaurant. Diners rose from their chairs, some angry, others fearful, all of them wanting to know what was going on. The maître d rushed in and demanded an explanation from Vinson.

Vinson quickly flashed his identification card. 'FBI. Get everyone to stay calm.'

The explanation didn't satisfy the maître d. 'You can't come in here and—'

Vinson pushed past him, grabbing Iris by the arm and pulling her with him. She was only too willing to go. They were halfway to the door when they heard screaming coming from the kitchen in the back of the restaurant. Kitchen workers streamed into the dining room. Fear turned to pandemonium when Fernando Peru staggered out, his shirt soaked with blood.

Chefs wearing white toques, their jackets splattered from preparing food, gave Peru a wide berth. People rushed the front entrance, pushing and shoving, knocking over chairs and tables. Somebody bumped into a waitress whose arms were loaded with dinner plates which hit the tile floor with a tremendous clatter, sending food and shards of china everywhere.

'Weems!' Peru shouted, clutching his middle. 'It's over!' He stumbled, leaving a bloody handprint on a linen tablecloth when he tried to steady himself. 'Weems!' he bellowed. 'It's over.'

'Peru,' Vinson said, approaching him. 'What happened?'

Peru spotted Iris and breathlessly crept toward her, grunting with pain. He tightly grabbed her hand. 'Rita knows, she knows!' His eyes were wild.

Someone yelled, 'She's got a gun!'

Vinson tore Peru's hand from Iris and forced her to the ground, kneeling next to her and drawing his gun. 'Fernando, get down!'

Rita Winslow burst from the kitchen. She raised her arm, aiming her gun at Peru who was still unsteadily standing. The remaining people in the restaurant cowered underneath tables.

Winslow's eyes were glazed. 'I warned you, didn't I?'

'Drop the gun,' Vinson said.

'Rita, please,' Peru weakly begged, weaving on his feet.

'Winslow, drop it,' Vinson again ordered, but Winslow didn't seem to hear him.

Iris, prone on the floor, started crawling behind an overturned table. People close to the door made a break for it. Winslow didn't notice anything except Peru.

Vinson didn't ask her a third time. He opened fire, hitting Winslow multiple times. She went down, but not before she fired a final shot at Peru.

Roger Weems burst into the restaurant. His face contorted with horror at the scene.

'Are you all right?' Vinson asked Iris. After she nodded, he approached Winslow, kicking her pearl-handled gun away from her hand which lay limp on the ground. He pressed his fingers against her neck although her unblinking stare indicated she was dead. He left her and attended to Peru.

Iris climbed to her feet, shaken but fine. She crept to where Weems and Vinson were crouched next to Peru and was mystified by what she saw.

Weems had rested the fallen man's head in his lap and held his hand between both of his. He was muttering, 'Oh man, Fernando. Don't check out now.' He grimaced and bitterly shook his head. 'Come on, man. Hang on. You're going to make it.'

'Help's coming, buddy,' Vinson said, patting Peru's arm.

'Don't leave me, man,' Weems said with a hitch in his voice.

Peru was mumbling barely coherently, his voice a whisper. 'She found out. She found out.'

'Don't talk, Fernando,' Weems said.

'I got away to find you but she followed me.' Peru smiled, his mouth full of blood. 'Rita told me she'd never let me leave her.' He laughed and began choking. 'She didn't, did she?'

Weems looked away, his face a mask of grief.

Peru grabbed Weems's shirt. 'I'm sorry, man.'

'It's not your fault,' Weems reassured him, forcing himself to look at Peru. 'Don't talk any more.'

Paramedics bustled into the restaurant, shoving aside tables and chairs. They pried Peru's fingers from Weems's shirt and began cutting his bloody clothes off him. Weems stayed nearby, barking orders. A paramedic spotted Winslow and had the courtesy to cover her with a sheet.

Vinson pulled Weems away. 'Roger, let them do their work.'

'Right, right.' Weems wandered outside.

Iris followed.

The street was filling with onlookers. The local police had arrived.

'Vinson,' Weems said. 'Take care of the local law, will you?'

Vinson started to leave when Weems stopped him with an outstretched hand. 'Why did Melba run?'

139

'There was a guy on the hotel terrace over there.' Vinson pointed to the room. 'Gave a thumbs-down.'

Weems squinted at the window. 'Who the hell is checking it out?'

'Cauble and Zajac.'

Weems distantly nodded. Vinson left to talk to the police. Weems looked down at his blood-splattered clothing then watched with casual interest as two FBI agents who had been posing as restaurant patrons shoved a handcuffed Douglas Melba into the back seat of a car.

Iris approached Weems and was about to speak when the paramedics pushed a gurney carrying Peru into a waiting van. Winslow's body was still on the floor. The coroner would come for her later. Iris and Weems silently watched the van weave through the crowded street, siren blaring, lights flashing in the twilight.

He finally looked at Iris. His face was grave.

Hers was angry. 'Fernando Peru was your *informant*?'

He sighed as if barely controlling his patience. 'Miss Thor . . . Iris, I'm a little busy right now. There's plenty of time to discuss this later.' He began walking across the street.

'We're going to discuss this now.' She jogged to keep up with him. 'You lied to me, Roger.'

Ahead of her, he raised both hands in an elaborate shrug.

Chapter 20

Agent Cauble walked quickly through the hotel lobby and met Weems as he came through the door.

'Rooms three thirty-one and three thirty-three are registered to Enrico Lazare,' Cauble told Weems as they both started walking toward the elevator. Iris scurried to keep up.

The staff and patrons of the hotel were already alarmed by the events at Greentree – many faces were pressed against the lobby windows – before Weems arrived in his bloody garments. The front desk employees whispered among themselves and kept their distance.

'Son of a bitch,' Weems spat. He rapidly punched the elevator call button after Cauble had already done so then paced back and forth, his hands on his hips.

Cauble continued filling him in on what he had found out. 'Lazare registered last night around nine. The front desk clerk who signed him in is due to start work in half an hour, so hopefully we'll get some information from her. We haven't found anyone who remembers seeing a man who fits Lazare's description.'

'What about the garage? Anyone leave in the last half hour?'

The elevator doors opened and Iris barely slipped in behind them before the doors closed. They didn't seem to notice that she was there.

'Zajac's down there now,' Cauble responded.

'How did Lazare pay?' Weems asked.

'Cash. Each room was three hundred dollars a night for two nights. That's a lot of cash.'

The doors opened on the third floor and Weems barreled out into the corridor. The doors to rooms 331 and 333 were open. They entered 331.

The room looked undisturbed. The bathroom soap was still wrapped, the bed was unwrinkled, the drapes were closed, and the air was stale and warm.

'Iris,' Weems said without looking at her. 'Look out the terrace window and tell me if that's where you saw your mystery man.'

Iris patted the drapes until she found where the two halves joined and peered out. The street below was crowded with police cars, a coroner's van, officers directing traffic, a mob of onlookers, and media personnel and equipment. She let the drapes fall closed. 'I can't say for sure. Maybe

141

if you had someone stand here, I could sit in the restaurant and see.'

Weems swatted the air as if batting away an irritating gnat. He stomped through an open door into an adjoining room. Iris and Cauble followed.

This room had been occupied. The bedspread was creased. The bathroom had been used. The drapes and the sliding glass door to the terrace were open. On a desk near the terrace were a half-empty jar of macadamia nuts and an empty miniature bottle of Absolut vodka from the mini bar. Ice was melting in a glass and in a plastic ice bucket printed with the hotel's logo.

Weems ordered, 'No one touch anything.'

Although the command was general, Iris suspected it was directed at her specifically.

'Cauble, get someone up here to fingerprint these rooms.' Weems roamed around like a dog marking new territory.

Cauble took a cellular phone from inside his jacket and quickly punched in a number.

Weems walked onto the terrace, his hands still on his hips, his legs apart. His shoulders rose and fell as he sighed deeply. 'Iris,' he said without turning. 'This is where you saw the mystery man.'

It wasn't a question. 'Most likely.'

'Uh-huh,' Cauble said into the phone.

Iris caught sight of herself in the mirror over the dresser and remembered that she was still wearing the wig. She hooked her fingers under the cap near her forehead and peeled it off and started pulling out hairpins, shoving them into her jeans pocket.

Cauble ended his call and said to Weems, 'They found out from Melba how the deal was supposed to go down. Palmer told him to go to the front desk at seven thirty and ask if there was a message for him, Melba. He picked up an envelope with the key to room three thirty-one.'

Weems crumpled a stick of Juicy Fruit chewing gum into his mouth, then held his hands in front of him, looking at Fernando Peru's drying blood. His eyes dimmed as he turned his hands. 'Keep talking. I'm going into the other room to wash up.'

Cauble moved to the doorway that connected the two rooms. 'Then Palmer told him to disappear until eight o'clock sharp when he was to walk north on Raymond Street to Greentree. Before he reached the restaurant windows, he was to look across the street at the hotel. Someone would be standing in the open doorway of a third-floor terrace and give him a thumbs-up if the deal was good and a thumbs-down if it wasn't.'

'What do you mean, if it wasn't?' Weems came into the room again. His hair looked damp and freshly combed.

'If something was wrong. If he saw the thumbs-down, he was to walk away and go back to San Francisco and wait for Palmer to call. And if it was a thumbs-up, he was to go in the restaurant, verify the money was good, and give Margo Hill the key to room three thirty-one. Her associate,

Vinson, would go to the room and make sure the fox was there then call her at the restaurant. Then Melba would take the case of money and drive to the LA Airport, parking structure four, top level, and wait there for someone to pick it up.' Cauble made a noise of dismay. 'Something got really fucked up.'

'Thumbs-down. What spooked him?' Weems gave Iris a piercing look, his jaw noisily working the gum.

She balled up the wig and started to set it on top of the television when Cauble took it from her. She generously scratched her scalp.

She was about to comment on Weems's accusatory stare when Agent Zajac entered the room with a young Asian woman. She was wearing the hotel uniform of navy blue blazer and skirt. A brass name tag was pinned to her lapel. She was clearly unnerved by the scene.

Zajac introduced her. 'This is Jeannie Cho. She registered these two rooms yesterday evening to Enrico Lazare.' He handed Weems a hotel ledger card that bore Lazare's signature.

'Miss Cho,' Weems said in an unnecessarily booming voice from across the room. 'What do you remember about Mr Lazare?'

She held her hands by her sides, trying to maintain a calm, professional demeanor. 'He was tall. I'd say around six feet. Clean-shaven. I couldn't see much of his hair because he was wearing a ball cap, but it seemed neatly cut and was dark brown. He also had on dark glasses.' She tried to avoid looking at Weems's bloody clothing and focused on his face.

'Did he speak with an accent?'

'Yes. It was hard to tell what, maybe French or something European. He didn't say much. he wanted the two adjacent rooms for the night. I tried to chat with him about the weather and such but he didn't seem to want to talk so I dropped it.'

'Ball cap?' Weems drew a circle in the air above his head. 'Do you remember the logo? Was it a team cap?'

She frowned as she searched her memory. 'Lakers. That's right. I asked if he'd seen the game last night. He said it was great.'

'In a French accent, he said it was great.'

She nodded.

'Show her that photograph of Lazare.'

The desk clerk looked carefully at the photograph Cauble handed her and shrugged. 'It could be him, I can't really tell.'

Weems smoothed his short black hair with his hands as he walked across the room. 'Thank you, Miss Cho.' He was again looking out the open sliding glass door that led to the terrace.

Jeannie Cho tentatively looked at the other agents in the room while stepping backward toward the door. When she reached the doorway, she turned and quickly left.

'Zajac, what about the garage?' Cauble asked.

'No one except hotel employees have left in the past—'

'Wait a minute,' Weems interrupted, turning from the terrace, raising both hands. 'A frog who likes basketball?'

There were muffled snickers.

'The French don't do basketball,' Weems said.

'Maybe Palmer was here,' Cauble suggested.

'Maybe,' Weems agreed. 'Still doesn't explain why the deal went south. What spooked the man on the terrace?'

Cauble shifted his weight on his feet. 'He could have recognized one of the agents. Maybe he saw Peru.'

Walking yet again onto the terrace, Weems leaned against the railing and peered at the restaurant across the street. 'But Peru came in the back, through the kitchen. Melba had already left before Peru entered the dining room.' He faced the room, resting against the railing, and studied Iris.

She spoke. 'If Dean Palmer was in this room, that wig wouldn't have fooled him for more than a few minutes. Once he saw it was me, he would know something was up.'

Weems flicked his hand in the direction of Cauble and Zajac. 'Why are you two standing around? Zajac, find out where that fingerprint guy is. Cauble, check on Peru's status and help Vinson with the local cops.'

Soon, Weems and Iris were alone. She stood with her hands clasped behind her back. He still leaned against the terrace railing, methodically chewing the stick of gum.

'Just say what's on your mind, Roger.'

'Why did you spook our mystery man?'

'Why are you convinced it was me?'

'Call it intuition. I have a feeling you know more about Enrico Lazare than you've let on.'

Iris wagged her finger at him. 'Now wait just a minute. I've been one hundred per cent honest with you from the get-go. You, on the other hand, have lied to me from day one.'

Weems looked bewildered. 'Don't tell me you're sore about Fernando Peru? I told you I had an informant.'

'Peru was wired when I met Winslow at the Peninsula Hotel, wasn't he? That's how you found out everything that was said. Then you sent Peru to my house that night. You sensed I was wavering in helping you to buy the fox so you told him to come over and pour it on about how much Todd Fillinger loved me, to punch my guilt buttons about poor Todd and how he has no one to seek justice for him, didn't you?'

'Just doing my job, Iris.' Weems's voice crackled with false sincerity. 'Come on, aren't you being just a tad emotional about the whole thing?' He expansively held his arms open. 'After all, we both have the same goal here.'

'You manipulated Rita Winslow. You knew she was insanely jealous of Peru. You led her on, told Peru to suggest that maybe he was double-crossing her after all, hoping she'd crack. You played her, just like you played me, and it unfolded just the way you wanted it to. She gave you a reason to take her out. Finally you got revenge for Buenos Aires and Greg Kelly.'

Weems paled.

Now Iris became smug. 'Rita Winslow paid me a little visit earlier today and told me some secrets about you, Roger Weems.'

'Why didn't you tell me?'

'Why didn't *you* tell *me*, huh?' she shouted. 'Winslow is dead and Peru is shot full of holes because of you.'

'You're not going to shed any tears over that squirrelly old Winslow bird, are you?'

'I bet you're not going to shed any tears about Fernando Peru either. Used him up and threw him away.'

Weems's eyes widened as anger rose inside him. 'Fernando was not supposed to get shot. He's a good man. He'll pull through this, then he'll head for Miami where he has a woman and a little girl. They're what finally made him decide to turn on Winslow. She was a lunatic when it came to him. He'd tried to leave her before and she'd stalked him all over the world. He was afraid for his woman and child. He'd finally had enough and wanted to go straight. I am very sorry about Fernando Peru. But he'll make it and he'll finally be free of that lunatic Rita Winslow.' He gingerly touched the blood drying on his clothes. 'I'm not as callous as you think I am, Iris.'

She leaned against the desk and absently picked up a paper cocktail napkin that had been folded into accordion pleats.

Weems came inside and didn't comment on her disturbing the desk top. 'So where does that leave us? The fox is still out there. Todd Fillinger's murderer is still out there.'

Iris stared at the cocktail napkin, turning it in her hand. She moved to stand in the terrace doorway and peered at the table where she'd sat in the restaurant.

Weems paced the room, outlining possible scenarios. 'Lazare and Palmer will still try to unload the fox. Maybe they'll wait for the situation to cool off. Nah, they're thieves. All they care about is getting money and getting it now.' He took a long breath. 'I can still use you, Iris.'

She continued staring into the restaurant's windows, gingerly holding the creased napkin by its edge.

Don Vinson entered the room, his face grave. 'Roger, it's Fernando.'

The kinetic energy drained from Weems. He seemed to grow smaller.

'He didn't make it,' Vinson said. 'I'm sorry.'

Weems pressed his lips together and nodded. 'Thanks for letting me know. I'll catch you later.'

After Vinson left, Weems rubbed his hands over his face, leaving them there for a long time. When he finally pulled them away, Iris was looking at him with disdain.

'Iris, I need you more than ever.'

She watched him dispassionately.

'We can still get the fox and Todd Fillinger's murderer.'

She collapsed the folds of the napkin until it was a narrow rectangle and slipped it into her jeans pocket. Quickly unbuttoning her blouse, she pulled it off, ripped open the Velcro fasteners on the bulletproof vest, shrugged it off and flung it on the bed as hard as she could. She wrenched free the wires of the listening device, bundled it up in her hand and threw it, missing the bed and hitting the floor. She buttoned her blouse again, not bothering to tuck it in.

As she headed out of the room, Weems grabbed her arm. 'Iris, please, I need you. Do it for Fernando.'

She jerked away as if he had burned her. 'Screw you.'

She had left the hotel and reached the sidewalk before she realized she didn't have a ride home and that her purse was in Weems's office. Standing in the street arguing with a Pasadena police officer who was trying to keep him from the scene was Garland. Iris couldn't remember ever being so glad to see someone in her entire life. She ran and leaped on him. He twirled her round.

'They reported the shooting on the news and said a woman had been killed. I was so worried, Iris.'

'It was Rita Winslow.'

'My Lord.'

'Peru's dead too. The fox is still missing. But I'm all right.' She repeated it as if to convince herself. 'I'm all right.'

Chapter 21

Iris fell into a deep sleep as soon as her head hit the pillow. Several hours later, she opened her eyes in the darkness, wide awake, and didn't have to look at the clock to know it was 3:00 a.m. It was a form of insomnia. Over the years, she'd endured all of insomnia's variations and she had a medicine cabinet full of potions from gentle herbal teas to prescription knock-out pills. Sometimes nothing worked. She sensed this was one of those times.

Right now, she didn't mind being awake while everyone else slept. The clutter of life was cleared away for the time being. It was just her, the darkness, and her thoughts.

She looked at Garland who was on his back, breathing deeply, face slack, mouth slightly open. His familiar face looked foreign without his personality to animate it. She watched him sleep. Sleep. It was so mundane, available to everyone, but completely inaccessible to her by any natural means.

Her bed now seemed like a torture device. There was no point in enduring further torment. She quietly slipped from underneath the covers, pulling them up over Garland. Tiptoeing across the room, she grabbed from the floral print boudoir chair the jeans and denim shirt she'd worn the previous day and hadn't found the energy to hang up. She slipped her fingers in the crack of the walk-in closet door and opened it a few more inches, cringing when the hinges squeaked, standing frozen when Garland stirred. When he fell quiet again, she snatched her tennis shoes from the floor and a sweatshirt from a hook on the wall and carried the bundle of clothing from the room, breathing a sigh of relief after she closed the bedroom door behind her.

She made a pot of coffee. She dressed in the clothing she'd brought from the bedroom, neglecting to don underwear which added to her slightly off-center feeling from starting her day in the middle of the night.

Unzipping Todd's portfolio which she'd leaned against the dining room wall, she reached inside and took out the framed photograph of her and him at *Le Café des Quatre Vents*. The Café of the Four Winds. She hadn't appreciated the irony until now. No wonder Todd had chosen it as his hangout.

She stood the photograph on the breakfast bar and climbed onto a stool with a mug of steaming black coffee. Something occurred to her that she'd never thought about before. Why did he hang out there? He didn't live close to the café. His grand apartment was a good half-mile and a number of similar café bars away.

Slipping from the stool and digging in the portfolio again, she found the fading Polaroid snapshot of Monsieur and Madame Mouche. She stuck it in the corner of the picture frame and wondered whatever happened to the couple as she drank the coffee as quickly as its heat would permit. She watched the clock on her kitchen wall, the hands in the shape of a knife and fork, slowly tick off the minutes: 3:47 a.m. Almost four o'clock, which was very early to be up but more or less officially morning. It was almost noon in London, 1:00 p.m. in Paris, and 3:00 p.m. in Moscow. Four major cities, four different stories. All of them with one common thread: Todd Fillinger.

She pulled Todd's scrapbook toward her on the bar and found the article on London antique stores with its photograph of Rita Winslow proudly standing in front of her shop. Iris knew a bit of Fernando Peru's life but almost nothing of Winslow's. She used the title Mrs but had she ever married or did she use it because it commanded more respect than Miss? Did she have children? Who ran the shop in her absence? Do they know she's dead?

Iris thought sadly that perhaps she had no real friends, that she had invested too heavily in the attentions of handsome young men whose interest in her didn't extend beyond what she could do for them. She suspected that Winslow finally realized she'd invested poorly and that's why she clung so desperately to Fernando Peru, as if she felt that as long as he stayed with her, she could pretend it was real, that life was beautiful. Like Todd Fillinger had clung to her, lassoing a star that was doomed to burn out but hanging on for dear life anyway.

Iris propped the scrapbook open to Winslow's photo on the bar next to the shot of her and Todd. She ducked her head to see the wall clock. It was finally 4:00. It was early, but it was morning. The sooner the night ended, the better.

Rummaging in her kitchen cabinets, she located a thermal carafe and a squat-bottomed commuter mug. She filled the commuter mug with coffee and poured the rest into the carafe. She set out another mug, a spoon, and the artificial sweetener that Garland liked. He would know to get the creamer from the refrigerator. Iris always chided him that he was turning his coffee into a milk shake with all the flavorings he added to it. She, however, was a coffee purist, only drinking hers strong and black.

On a piece of paper from a gummed pad, she left a note: 'Went for a walk. Back soon.' She intentionally didn't leave the time, knowing he'd worry if he knew she'd left while it was still dark.

She propped the note against the empty coffee mug then spent a moment taking in the little domestic scene. It warmed her.

Digging her finger around the ceramic bowl in which she tossed all her keys, she picked out the spare key to the front door that was on a plastic fob printed with her dry cleaners' logo. She quietly closed the front door behind her, stood on the porch, and pulled on her sweatshirt.

The air was cool and clear. The fog hadn't rolled in that night. The sky had paled slightly, just enough to turn from blackness to midnight blue. There were still a few stars and a thin crescent moon high in the sky. It grew faint as she watched it, slowly fading as night gave way to day.

She walked down her brick front path, eagerly stepping on two snails and making plans to put snail poison in her flowerbeds that weekend. She began a mental list of a million other household chores. It was only Tuesday but she could hardly wait to get started on them. Mindless, back-breaking chores and a trip to the home warehouse where she'd wander through and load her cart with things she never knew she needed until then.

It had been only a week since Detective Davidovsky had approached her in the bar of the Metropolis Hotel and told her she was leaving on the next flight to Los Angeles. It had been a week and a day since Todd Fillinger had met her at the Sheremetevo Airport. It seemed impossible that only a week had passed since then.

She walked in the middle of the street which was reinforced by thick pilings buried deep in the ground. Some of the pilings were visible, the asphalt draped over them like sheets on unused furniture, where the ground had eroded around them. The hillside community of Casa Marina was slowly crumbling. Passage was restricted to residents and guests to preserve the fragile environment. There were no gates or guards to enforce this, just a sign at the entrance of Casa Marina Drive and eagle-eyed residents who weren't above stopping unknown cars and asking drivers their business.

Iris walked past her neighbor Marge Nayton's house and looked at her neat yard and garden. Even though Marge was in her seventies, she kept up her yard and did most of her household maintenance herself. Iris had even seen Marge on her roof, cleaning her rain gutters. She decided to ask Marge what to do about snails. Marge would know. She was a font of practical and impractical information.

Next to Marge's house was the first of three narrow cement staircases that traversed the hill, connecting the three streets that partitioned it like the layers of a wedding cake. Several of Los Angeles's older neighborhoods had staircases like these, all of them constructed in the 1920s, well before cars outnumbered people in the city, as they did now.

Iris quickly descended the sixty steps, finally accustomed to the width that was narrow and the depth that was high by today's standards. Thick natural vegetation, most of it bone dry at the end of the summer, grew on either side of the steps, providing privacy for homeless people who lived there. The steps were not the safest place to be alone in broad daylight, not to mention in the darkness of early morning. But after everything that had

149

already happened to her, Iris felt strangely invulnerable.

A bird sang. The first bird of the morning. Iris smiled. At least she wasn't the only one who was up.

Iris and Marge's homes were on the first tier of the terraced hillside. At the bottom of the hill three hundred feet below was Pacific Coast Highway. The steps stopped well before that at a bridge that crossed the highway and led to the beach on the other side. Iris stopped in the middle of the bridge and leaned against the sturdy wire mesh dome that encased it, preventing people from throwing objects or themselves on the cars below. Traffic on the highway was lighter than normal but was still flowing. Traffic never completely disappeared from major thoroughfares anywhere in the city anymore.

The bridge's interior walls were covered with spray-painted graffiti. An odd assortment of litter had worked its way against the corners. There were the usual fast-food and soda containers, crumpled cigarette packs and butts, and a few bits of clothing – a single shoe, a belt. And then there was garbage unique to the beach environment: suntan lotion bottles, a broken beach chair, a good towel accidentally dropped, a child's rubber flip-flop with a plastic daisy decorating the strap.

Iris stretched her arms up against the wire mesh which was moist to the touch. She watched the cars pass beneath her, traveling north or south with their lights still on. People on their way.

She remembered the big Mercedes in which Todd Fillinger had picked her up from the airport in Moscow and the intimidating driver, Sasha.

'Moscow has been very good to me,' Todd had told her. She had bought it, all of it, hook, line, and sinker. What a pushover.

She turned and jogged across the rest of the bridge, skipping down the spiral staircase at the end, trailing her hand against the steel railing. At the bottom she almost collided with a homeless person who was coming from the beach with a sack of treasures – *objects perdus* now *objects trouvés*. She started running, not looking back, struggling in her tennis shoes on the soft sand. She bent over and pulled them off without untying them and kept running, reaching the smooth wet sand left behind by the receding tide. She didn't stop. Her clothing felt heavy and restrictive and it chafed because of her lack of undergarments, but she kept running, pumping her arms with a tennis shoe in each hand. She ran fast, as fast as she could, not needing to pace herself because she didn't know how far she was going. She just needed to run.

'You grew a beard.'

'It's cold in Russia.' Todd had smiled at her, brightening his handsome face. 'I need all the fur I can get.'

'I like it. I never imagined you with a beard.'

'You look great,' he'd told her. 'Just like I imagined you.'

She'd been flattered and touched by his attention, at the knowledge that he'd thought of her.

She kept running, the wet sand yielding to her footsteps, pleasantly abrading the soles of her feet. She felt a small, sharp pain in her heel, as if she might have stepped on a broken shell or God only knew what, but she didn't stop. She panted heavily, growing tired, but not slowing down. After a while, she realized she was crying and didn't know when she'd started. The salty tears ran freely down her face, mixing with her perspiration and the sea air. She didn't touch them, saving her arms for pumping. One of her tennis shoes flew from her hand and she didn't stop for it.

'You've lost weight,' she'd said after hugging him through his fine cashmere sweater. He'd always been burly. A football player's physique. She hadn't found out he'd been a football player until she'd visited his sister. A small detail casually left out. Not an active lie. Not yet.

'Been busy,' he'd told her.

He was nervous, on edge, looking over his shoulder, ducking people who got too close. When she couldn't help but notice, he explained, 'I got cross-wise with the Russian Mafia. It wasn't too smart, but I just got fed up. It had to stop somewhere.'

Where did reality end and the show in which she was playing a role unknown to her begin?

The tide had retreated sufficiently to allow her to run round a tall outcrop of jagged rocks and easily access Sand Dollar Beach. Its secluded location made it a favorite spot for nude sunbathers. Since it was usually hard to get to, surrounded by rocks and a tall cliff, the police generally left the free spirits alone. The beach was empty so early in the morning.

The moisture on Iris's face ran onto her lips and she licked them, tasting salt. She walked into the surf. A wave rolled in, submerging her ankles. She tossed her one tennis shoe safely onto the beach then crouched down and trailed the fingers of one hand through the frothy foam.

'My class ring. You're still wearing it.'

'I told you I'd never take it off.'

She'd been touched by that, too. Impressed, frightened, warmed, curious – she'd done it all on cue. She'd been that predictable.

'I sent you a letter to your sister's house in Bakersfield. Did you get it?'

He'd looked at her clear-eyed and, she now knew, lied, 'No.'

She'd sat there in the King's Head pub in Moscow, filled with smoke and Brits and Americans drinking and playing darts and apologized to him for leaving Paris the way she had. She'd traveled half-way around the world to do the honorable thing, to relieve herself of a five-year burden that, it was clear to her now, had been completely unnecessary for her to carry.

He sat, stony-faced, and listened to her while she twisted her guts inside out. 'Iris, what's past is past. No hard feelings.' He listened to her explanation about why she ran and folded a cocktail napkin into tiny accordion pleats. 'If I was still that angry with you, I wouldn't have asked

151

you to go into business with me, would I?'

The surf swirled about her calves, drenching her jeans. She reached into her jeans pocket and pulled out the folded cocktail napkin she'd found in the hotel room. She compressed the careful pleats then held one end and released the other, making a fan, like Todd had done in the pub. This napkin had to be nothing more than a nutty coincidence. She had seen Todd Fillinger shot full of holes on a Moscow street. She had seen him dead. Nonetheless someone, probably using field glasses, had recognized her at the Greentree restaurant. Someone knew her well enough to spot her even with the wig. Someone who had a habit of toying with paper napkins had known it was her.

She needed more proof. If she told a single person that she thought Todd Fillinger was alive, they'd think she'd flipped her lid once and for all. And if Todd was alive, who had died on the Moscow street wearing Todd's clothes and jewelry?

She tore the napkin in half. Baring her teeth and whimpering, she tore it again and again until it was the size of confetti and threw the pieces into the surf. Bits stuck to the damp skin on her hands and she madly swatted at them as if they were poisonous. She submerged her hands in the sea foam, washing them clean. She watched the waves churn the paper, rolling it over and over, until she couldn't see it anymore. She turned round, picked up her tennis shoe, and started home. Along the way, she found her other shoe.

On the steps of the bridge, she sat down, brushed the sand from her feet, and put on her shoes. Traffic on Pacific Coast Highway had picked up. No one had their lights on. She looked up through the mesh dome and realized it was finally daylight.

Chapter 22

Iris was at first glad then perplexed when she saw that Garland was still asleep. Then she realized it was only 6:00 a.m. She'd done a lot in her insomnia-fueled state, but that wasn't unusual for her. Some years ago when she'd shared an apartment, she'd risen in the dead of night full of nervous energy. Her roommate was surprised when she'd awakened to find that Iris had rearranged the living room furniture.

The sight of the coffee and the note she had left for Garland made her smile. She folded the note twice and slipped it into her jeans pocket, an emblem of love taking the place of that creased napkin.

In the bathroom mirror, she had to laugh at how bad she looked. Her hair was twisted and matted and her face was streaked with sweat and tears and mottled with makeup left over from the previous day which she hadn't bothered to remove. She hadn't even brushed her teeth. She stripped off her clothes, climbed into a hot shower, and scrubbed her skin until it was pink and her scalp until it tingled. She looked in the mirror again. She couldn't do much about the circles under her eyes, but at least she was clean.

Wrapped in her terrycloth bathrobe, she carried a mug of coffee into Garland, sweetened and lightened the way he liked it. He had moved into the spot she had left, a subconscious gesture that always touched her.

He opened his eyes when she sat on the corner of the bed. 'Good morning.'

'Good morning.'

'You look nice and fresh.' He propped a pillow against the headboard and pulled himself up to lean against it.

She gave him a peck on the lips and handed him the coffee.

'Did you sleep well?' he asked.

'For a while.'

He frowned with concern. 'How long have you been up?'

'A while.'

He stroked her cheek. 'You're going to get sick, sweetpea, if you don't get some rest.'

'I won't get sick. Not right away, anyway.'

'Why don't you stay home from work today?'

'Maybe I will.' She pulled back the covers and slid in next to him. It

153

was warm inside the bed. She laid her head on the pillow and closed her eyes. They felt grainy and stung beneath her eyelids.

The next thing she knew, Garland was kissing her on the cheek. She opened her eyes to see him dressed in a suit. He smelled of soap and toothpaste.

'I've got to get to the airport. I have that rental car to return.'

'Mmmm,' she mumbled. Airports and rental cars to drop off. It was an ongoing scene in their relationship. When they'd first started dating, she relished the mixture of togetherness and privacy their long-distance romance meant. The simple fact that she had someone warmed her throughout the day and night, even when he wasn't around. It was great to belong yet remain autonomous. But lately, she'd wanted him too, not just the idea of him. She felt a pang thinking of waving goodbye at her front door. 'What time is it?'

'Nine.'

She bolted up, wide-eyed.

'Relax. I called Louise and told her you had the flu.'

She drowsily slid back underneath the covers. 'Did she ask you about Greentree? Have you seen the news?'

'It's the only thing that's on the local news. Weems has done a good job of damage control. So far, Winslow's and Peru's deaths have been explained as a betrayed woman who came gunning for her lover and inadvertently came across an off-duty FBI agent who took her down. I haven't heard any mention of you, Douglas Melba, or the fox.'

'Thank goodness for that.' To herself, Iris speculated that Weems had shielded her because he still had plans for her.

Garland stood over her, looking down. 'What's wrong?'

'What do you mean?'

'You're shaking your head.'

'Oh.' She shrugged. 'I don't know. It's nothing.' She climbed out of bed.

'You don't have to get up.'

'I want to walk you to the door.' She took a step on the hardwood floor and winced. She leaned on him and looked at the bottom of her foot. Her right heel had a semicircular cut in the middle. The morning run came back to her. It seemed surreal. Without this physical proof, she might have thought it was a dream.

'How did you do that?'

'I went for a walk early this morning.'

'Barefoot?'

She raised her eyebrows.

He decided not to investigate further and walked through the house to the front door next to which was his familiar array of wheeled Pullman, briefcase, and laptop computer case.

She held open her arms to hug him. He unfastened the belt of her robe

154

and slid his hands against her smooth skin and pulled her close. His clothing, rigid and cool, smooth here and harsh there, felt oddly alluring against her nakedness. She rubbed against him, relishing the sensuality of the different textures. Their quick goodbye kiss soon turned passionate.

She pulled him toward the loveseat, hopped on the back, and let the open robe fall from her shoulders. He unzipped his pants and let them fall to the ground. She wrapped her legs round his back. Their lovemaking was brief and intense. Afterward, they remained in an embrace, his arms keeping her balanced on the sofa's narrow back. Inevitably, after both of them had waited a respectable but brief period, they sought out timepieces. He glanced at his watch and she turned to catch the face of the antique mantel clock above her fireplace. Without speaking, he dressed and she pulled the robe loosely round her. At the door, he gathered the handles of his various encumbrances and after a quick kiss, he left.

She walked onto the front porch, squinting at the harsh, hazy sunlight, and watched him load up the car. She raised her hand as he pulled away from the curb then walked to the edge of the lawn in her bare feet, only lowering her hand after he had paused at the bottom of the hill, leaned over to blow her a kiss through the passenger window, rounded the bend, and was out of sight. She pulled the edges of the robe round her and looked at the empty street.

Her neighbor Marge came out of her house just then, dressed in a pale blue sheath, a string of pearls against her collarbone, three-inch heeled pumps, her hair combed into a bouffant with a deep wave on one side. Judging from the many framed photographs in Marge's house, she had worn variations of the same hairstyle her entire life. She'd also maintained the same weight, as slender now as she was as a young girl. The photographs were a testimony to a life structured by high standards and lived consistently well and with style and grace. Iris had never seen Marge in a bad mood or anything other than pleasant and considerate. She'd buried three husbands and had a grown son whom she rarely saw yet was not bitter, because she refused to be.

It was only in the past few years that Iris realized what an achievement that was. How easy it is to let go, to slip down. Her own life seemed to have been a series of histrionics. It was how she had been raised, with people screaming at each other and throwing things to get their point across, with mixed success. And the career she'd chosen wasn't known for its subtlety. But slender, bird-like, chipper Marge with her perfect hair and careful, ageless clothes showed Iris there was another way. Iris was ready for another way, a different life. Change was imminent, closing in, like a dark sky heavy with rain on the verge of release. She'd lived her life one way but something else was waiting in the wings.

She waved at Marge. 'Morning!'

Marge walked across her lawn, not paying attention to the dewy grass on her shoes and met Iris across the row of rose bushes, still lushly

155

blooming in many colors, that divided their properties. 'Good morning to you, Iris. Did I see Garland leave?'

'Yes, back to New York.'

'If you get too lonely this evening, come over for a cocktail.'

'Martinis at five o'clock sharp.' Iris smiled. 'Our Marge.'

'Rituals give us a safe harbor in a chaotic world, don't you agree?'

'Yes, I do. I don't have any rituals, other than working, getting ready for work, and coming home. Everything else in my life is constant chaos.'

'That's certainly honorable and productive. And necessary.'

'But it's not enough.'

Marge drew her finger along the wave in her hair. 'We'll put our heads together and see if we can cook something up for you.'

'Have you ever been in love with somebody and you later found out that everything that person was, everything they pretended to be was a lie?'

'Are you talking about the dead boy who you mentioned to me the other day?'

Iris nodded.

'As for me personally, no I can't say that I have. When you get to know someone, they're sometimes different than the way you first thought they were, but you seem to be talking about something more serious.'

Iris scrunched her toes against the damp grass. 'I suspect this guy was bad from the beginning. I don't know if I was conned by him or if, on some level, I knew it all the time.'

'I don't believe that someone can completely hide an inherently evil nature. But I don't believe you would ever fall in love with someone who was completely bad.' Marge touched the pearls at the base of her neck, gently straightening them. 'Why do you think this about him? Did you discover something he did that was wrong?'

'Yes, something very wrong.' Iris blinked at the grass. 'The worst. It's completely turned everything I ever thought about him on its head. I feel betrayed . . . and stupid.'

'Love is blind,' Marge said brightly. 'And your affair with that boy is in the past. You've chosen well with Garland.' She turned the tiny gold watch on her bony wrist to see the face. 'I've got to *fly*. I'll see you for cocktails?'

'Let me take a rain check. I'm not certain whether I'll be around this evening.'

Marge reached across the rose bushes and clamped her hand round Iris's wrist in a reassuring gesture. 'Cheer up, Miss Iris Thorne. Don't lose the present by dwelling in the past.'

Iris watched Marge back out of her driveway in her vintage, two-toned Buick Roadmaster, her head barely reaching above the steering wheel, and thought to herself that she'd be only too happy to leave the past behind, to hack it away like seaweed twisted round her ankles, keeping her

156

from swimming freely. But if the impossible was true and Todd Fillinger was alive, could she ever feel safe? He had recognized her from the hotel terrace. He didn't know whether she had recognized him.

She felt compelled to find out when Todd's betrayal had started. Had the whole thing been a lie from the beginning or had he only gone bad later? Part of it was wanting to see how stupid she had been. Finding out wouldn't accomplish anything, but she wanted to know.

After Marge's car had rounded the bend at the bottom of the hill, Iris went back inside her house. In the kitchen, she made another pot of coffee then went into her home office. She sat on the floor in front of the closet and began pulling out boxes of photographs, letters, mementos, and tax and financial documents. Some boxes were labeled and some weren't. Finally she found an old shoe box on which was written 'Paris' with a black marker. In it were photographs, postcards, a charcoal drawing a street artist had made of her, and small souvenirs. She ignored them all, the wistful, bittersweet haze through which she used to view her time in Paris now completely blackened. She rapidly searched through the box until she found a round cardboard coaster imprinted with the name, address, and telephone number of *Le Café des Quatre Vents*.

After opening the blinds covering the windows in the corner, letting sunshine into the dark room, she sat at her desk with the coaster in front of her and dialed the operator to obtain the country code for France. She spent a moment composing what she was going to say, refreshing her paltry knowledge of French by looking up a few words in an English-French dictionary she'd located on her bookshelf and jotting down a few phrases. She kept the dictionary at her elbow.

She dialed. Shortly, she was connected to the café, its phone emitting a quick double ring in the European style. A man answered.

'*Allo, café.*'

Iris took a deep breath and asked in French if she could speak to Monsieur or Madame Mouche. After a pause, the man responded that they hadn't owned the bar for over four years.

'*Ils ont pris leur retraite?*' Did they retire? '*Je voudrais les contacter.*' I'd like to contact them.

'*Non, malheureusement, Monsieur Mouche a été tué.*' The man went on to explain that the owner was shot to death and his wife was wounded.

'*C'est horrible. Qu'est-ce qui s'est passé?*'

He said there had been a shoot-out in the café. Two men came gunning for a drug dealer who apparently owed them money. The Mouches had got caught in the crossfire. '*Apparemment, il a payé les Mouche pour qu'ils le laissent dealer dans leur café.*'

The man described how a drug dealer convinced the Mouches to let him use the café as a front for his drug sales, paying them a percentage of his deals. After her husband's death, Madame Mouche sold the café and moved to the south to live with her daughter.

157

Iris asked what happened to the drug dealer. '*Qu'est-ce qui est arrivé au dealer?*'

'*Il s'est cassé.*' He split. No one saw him again. The man knew just one thing about him. '*C'etait un Americain.*'

'*Merci beaucoup.*' Iris hung up. Of course Todd had been a drug dealer. It had all been there for her to see – the lavish lifestyle without any discernible source of income, the mysterious comings and goings, the series of visitors in the café, the envelopes of photographs and contact sheets that Todd handed out in exchange for rolls of cash. She had just gone along with it. She hadn't wanted to look too deeply. Maybe that's one of the reasons Todd had fallen for her. She had accepted him at face value. But it wasn't her normal mode of operation. He'd simply caught her during a blip in her life.

From a desk drawer, she took out a plastic sandwich bag that held the True cigarette butt she'd taken from Todd's bedroom in Moscow. She squared it on the desk.

The doorbell rang. She padded across the hardwood floors and area rugs to the front door where she unlatched the molded brass cover over the peephole. On the other side, grinning broadly, revealing his snake teeth, was Roger Weems.

'Good morning, Iris. Just wanted to stop by and make sure you're all right after last night.'

Iris straightened her robe and unlocked the door.

Weems stood on the porch with his hands behind his back. 'I called over to your office and your secretary said you were home sick.'

Iris felt a flush of panic. 'You didn't say who you were, did you?'

'Oh no, no. I wouldn't do that, Iris. I have a deep appreciation for the spot I've put you in.' He presented her with a bouquet of assorted flowers he'd been hiding behind his back. 'To brighten your day.'

Iris took them and impassively thanked him. 'Would you like to come in?' She didn't want him in her house, but she'd expected him to show up sooner rather than later. She might as well hear what he had to say now. She walked through the arched entrance to the dining room. 'Would you like some coffee? I've just made a fresh pot.'

'That would be very nice.' He trailed behind her, looking around at everything in a manner that was a bit too practiced to be mere curiosity. Standing in the dining room, he picked up the framed photograph of her and Todd in front of *Le Café des Quatre Vents* and sadly tsked-tsked. 'His murderer is still out there, Iris.'

She busied herself putting the flowers in a glass vase of water and didn't respond. He was just lobbing a ball over the net to see if she'd swing.

He looked at the photograph Todd had taken of Rita Winslow in front of her antique shop. 'Old Rita.' He made a small noise of appreciation as if remembering a fallen war buddy. 'Hell of a gal. Todd took this picture, huh?' He squinted at the photo credit. 'Sure enough.'

Iris set the sugar bowl and creamer on the table then put out napkins and spoons. Her good china was getting a workout lately. 'So what happened to Douglas Melba?' She poured coffee into a cup and set it on a saucer on the table. She put a trivet in the center and positioned the vase of flowers on it.

Weems sat down. 'Thank you so very much, Iris.' His manner was subdued, even deferential. It amused her. He'd do, say, or be anything to get what he wanted. 'Douglas Melba,' he carefully repeated. 'We didn't have any further use for him. I think the Pasadena police asked him a few questions as a witness to the shooting, then let him go. We didn't rat him out to the local cops. He's of more use to us running loose on the street.'

'Do you think Lazare would use him as a middleman again?'

'He might. We still have a bug in the phone in Melba's office. Of course, he's probably figured that out. I'm having some guys out of the San Francisco office put one in his apartment. I guess we shall see what we shall see.'

'What about the guy who was in the hotel room?'

'Who? You mean Enrico Lazare?'

Iris felt her cheeks color with the slip. She had to remember always to use Lazare's name. 'Yeah, Lazare.'

'Gone. See ya, baby.'

The bright morning sun showed how badly Weems's face was scarred from acne. Deep vertical wrinkles rent his cheeks, making him look older than his years. Iris didn't know whether it was simply a long, hard life that had aged him or if the darkness in his heart was slowly eating him away.

'So what happens now?'

'We wait, we watch, we listen. Lazare will try to sell the fox again.'

Iris pulled her robe more closely around her. She was glad that Weems had politely not paid any attention to her attire. She realized she was hungry. She hadn't had anything to eat yet but wanted to wait until Weems left before preparing something. She didn't want to break bread with him. 'So soon?'

'All Lazare cares about is money. The sooner he sells the fox, the sooner he gets the money. Word about the fox is in the wind. The longer he delays, the greater the chance he'll get caught.' Weems barely squeezed the tip of his blunt index finger into the delicate handle of the china cup. He raised the cup to his lips and sipped. The white scar on the back of his hand shone in the light streaming through the big windows.

Iris didn't have anything more to say. She waited. She didn't have to wait long.

Weems pulled on his earlobe and pursed his lips as if in pain. He entreatingly opened his hands toward her. 'Iris, you've got to help me. I understand how you feel about me, but you have to look at things from my perspective. I couldn't tell you about Fernando Peru secretly working for

159

me. The risk of ruining the operation was too great and that information could have put you in danger. I knew that Winslow was close to the edge. Fernando told me she'd sensed something was up, that she'd accused him of being involved with another woman. But I in no way suggested to her that the other woman was you. The bloodshed last night was completely unanticipated.' He shook his head with the horror of it then raised his hands toward himself, his dark eyes burning. 'What did I gain from that? Nothing! My entire operation blew up in my hands.'

'You got to see Rita Winslow die.'

'I would have preferred to see her rot in jail for the rest of her life.'

'No, for you, it's better that she's dead. Now she'll take to the grave how you stood by while your partner Greg Kelly was shot to death.'

His face became taut, deepening the lines in his face. He swallowed as if tasting her remark to see how he liked it. He let it pass. 'I'll be the first to admit I've done a lot of things in my life that I'm not proud of. But now I'm asking you, someone who has as great an interest in seeing justice done as I do, to set aside our differences and work with me as an equal partner to retrieve the fox and find Todd Fillinger's murderer.' He locked his eyes on her.

She looked away, pondering Weems's statement. Finally, she said, 'What do you want me to do?'

He brightened. 'First, I want to know why you spooked Enrico Lazare.'

'Why are you so certain it was me? It could have been your agent Vinson I was sitting with. Lazare could have recognized one of the other agents sitting in the restaurant. Maybe Peru tipped him off. Why are you focused on me?'

'OK. Fair enough. Look, Melba believes you're for real.'

'Still? Being swarmed by FBI agents didn't clue him in that I was working for you? I find that hard to believe.'

'Sure it did, but we convinced him that you were as surprised by the whole thing as he was. Melba's desperate to complete this deal. He's seeing a hunk of change disappear before his eyes. Right after we released him, he called your number—'

'My number?'

'Margo Hill's number. Couldn't wait. He apologized for the deal blowing up. He figured the FBI had his phone tapped. He's calling from a secure location and wants to know if your buyer still wants the fox. He'll wait for you to get back to him. In the meantime, he'll contact the seller and make sure he still wants to do business with you.'

'And you want me to do what?'

'Leave a message for him at the Bay City Diner in San Francisco. Say it's Margo Hill for Douglas Melba and the answer is yes.'

'Then what?'

'Tell him when he can reach you. You'll come into the office like you did before and we'll wait for his call. If it was you who spooked the seller, then he won't want to come near you and we'll learn something. If not, we'll arrange another buy.'

'Another buy.'

Weems pinched his fingers together, demonstrating the precision of the new operation. 'Next time, it'll go smoothly. Like clockwork.'

'Smoothly.'

'Like clockwork.'

Iris watched his greedy, eager eyes on her, waiting for her response. She sighed and gazed out the window, appearing to wrestle with a decision when all she was really doing was letting him twist in the bitterness of his unfulfilled ambition and the opportunities he'd let slip through his fingers. She'd already made her decision when she'd left the hotel room the previous night. She turned cold eyes on him and simply said, 'No.'

His neck grew blotchy and the flush moved quickly toward his scalp. 'What do you mean, no?'

'It seems clear enough to me.' She stood and began gathering the cups and saucers. This party was over.

He watched her as if he couldn't believe they'd reached the end. 'You can't just back out now.'

Iris looked back at him over her shoulder as she walked toward the sink. 'What are you going to do? Arrest me?'

He stood, almost knocking over the chair, and tried another tactic. 'Iris, you're all I've got.'

'If I'm all you've got, you're really in deep do-do.'

Without another word, he left, slamming the front door so hard her windows rattled.

Chapter 23

Bakersfield was known for oil and agriculture. After crossing the Tejon Pass through the Tehachapi Mountains then descending four thousand feet into the San Joaquin Valley, the road became long, straight, and dusty and traversed the core of California. The mountains that shielded the vast, agriculturally rich valley had a long history. One of the area's most unusual events was its selection as the site for the installation of Cristo's yellow umbrellas which were clumped across the rolling hills like bright fantasy poppies. Tragically, the wind force in the pass was underestimated and gusts of wind broke one of the huge umbrellas loose from its base, crushing a woman. More commonly, icy and snowy conditions on the pass during winter resulted in numerous jack-knifed trucks, making wintertime driving between LA and Bakersfield a dicey proposition.

About two-thirds of the way to Bakersfield, the Country and Western stations on the radio came to outnumber all others with Spanish-language stations coming in a close second. Iris found a station that played *banda* music which was sort of like Mexican polka. The bouncy rhythm kept her going. She drove past workers wearing straw cowboy hats bending in cultivated fields and oil pumps with insect-like heads bobbing up and down in the dry earth. The Triumph hummed along.

Tracy Beale's neighborhood comprised square city blocks and small, neat houses on postage-stamp lots. The nondescript neighborhood could have been anywhere in the West where the land was vast but the developers were greedy. Iris drove past East Bakersfield High School where the football team and the band shared the athletic field, practicing in the autumn afternoon. The team was wearing practice uniforms and the band was in street clothes. Iris parked the Triumph and leaned against the chain-link fence to watch them.

She got back into the Triumph and drove to the school entrance where she parked in a lot at the front, which was reserved for teachers, administration, and guests. Parking there made her feel her age. It was 2:00 p.m. and classes were still in session. Kids were hanging around the cement benches in front of the old school. None of them wore lettermen's jackets and club sweaters like in her high school days. An unofficial uniform of baggy pants and oversized shirts prevailed.

The main building of the aging school was brick with an ornate portico over the large double-door entrance. Embossed in cement over the portico in angular letters that were barely legible was this quote from Socrates: THERE IS ONLY ONE GOOD, KNOWLEDGE, AND ONE EVIL, IGNORANCE. There was a quote in a similar vein over the main entrance of Iris's high school and she had been inspired by it. To her it meant there was something greater to be accomplished than belonging to the right clubs and being accepted by the popular and beautiful kids and going to the hip parties, although those were life-and-death issues to her at the time.

She walked up the broad curved steps and entered the building, which was dim and cool inside. She arbitrarily turned right and went down the hallway. Before long, she was stopped by a heavyset, hard-eyed woman who crooked a finger at her. She automatically cringed from having been caught where she wasn't supposed to be, her high school experience permanently imprinted on her.

'Do you have an appointment?' the woman asked. 'Are you a parent?'

'Uh, no.' Iris figured it would be useless to lie to this woman who had probably heard every story and had a low tolerance for bull.

'What is your business here?' She wore frosted pink lipstick on oversized lips. Her chubby cheeks wobbled when she spoke. Iris would have paid to find out the school kids' nickname for her.

'Frankly, I have no official business here. An old friend of mine, Todd Fillinger, is a graduate and I—'

'Todd Fillinger!' She beamed, her eyes almost disappearing behind her fleshy lids which bore smudges of blue eye shadow. 'I was his homeroom teacher for three years. Have you seen him? How is he doing?'

'He's living in Moscow and doing very well.'

'I'll be damned.'

'He's a photographer, traveled the world. His pictures have been published in many of the biggest magazines. Moscow's a wild and woolly place to be at the moment, but he's making money hand over fist. I drove up from LA to see his sister, Tracy—'

'Tracy Beale. Her husband Richard's our football coach. He's probably out working with the boys if you want to see him.'

'No, I just . . . Todd had such fond memories of East Bakersfield High that I wanted to see it and . . . tell him how it looked.'

The hall monitor warmed to her, seeming to hold her in higher regard now knowing that she was a friend of Todd's. 'You go right ahead. Down at the end of the hallway we've got a display of East Bakersfield's athletic triumphs. There are some pictures of Todd there too.' She grew wistful as if revisiting a sweet past. 'Tell Todd hi for me if you see him. I'm Miss Collins. Ruth Collins.'

'Will do, Miss Collins.' Iris headed down the hallway floored in well-worn burgundy linoleum, amusing herself by conjuring a scene between Todd and his homeroom teacher. It was just like Todd to charm someone like Miss Collins, to extol her finer points to his sarcastic, big-men-on-campus friends to the extent that they wouldn't be certain whether he was kidding or not. Todd's work had stood the test of time. She could show Miss Collins a videotaped confession of the crimes which she suspected Todd of having committed and Miss Collins probably would not believe it. She would not have believed it herself if she hadn't been sucked into his scheme which she hadn't quite figured out yet.

School elections appeared to be underway; the hallway was draped with banners hand-painted in tempera: BE FOXY, VOTE FOR ROXY; JOHN 4 PREZ. Large glass cases lined the walls, filled with testimonials to primarily athletic triumphs with academic achievement given a nod via a display of the school's entry at the science fair and a photo of the nerdy-looking kids who participated. Some things never change.

A case at the end was devoted to what appeared to be East Bakersfield's glory days of football. It was crammed with trophies and photographs. A jersey was pinned to the back wall, Fillinger, number 14. The school had retired his number in honor of their greatest quarterback ever. There was a black-and-white photograph of Todd with one arm held aloft for balance, the other ready to let a football fly, eyes squinting as he maintained a bead on his target. Even Iris emitted a swoon. The photo caption indicated that Todd's target was running back Mike Edgerton who caught the long pass and ran forty five yards for the conference-winning touchdown.

There were other photos of Mike Edgerton and Todd who were affectionately called East Bakersfield's Terrible Twosome. Edgerton, while not quite as ruggedly handsome as Todd, was tall and dark with a captivating smile.

Iris felt a pang of loss as she surveyed Todd's early triumphs, feeling sorrow for promise unfulfilled. His natural athletic ability, good looks, and charisma could have sustained him through a happy and successful life. It should have been easy for him. But the normal bumps in the road had made him spin out of control. His mother's murder when he was ten and his father's subsequent slow decline must have robbed him of the inner strength to endure. There was an essential goodness in him that inspired love and loyalty from clear-thinking people. Iris had hooked into that. So had Miss Collins. Both of them had fielded plenty of crap in their days to know the difference. Iris was convinced that Todd was corrupted by circumstances. She didn't condone his actions, but guessed he acted out of desperation. If he had wanted to punish her for dumping him, he could have taken action long ago. He had carried around a little kernel of resentment for years. Something had finally made him act on it.

Miss Collins startled Iris when she walked up behind her. 'Todd was a handsome cuss, wasn't he? Did he keep his looks or did he lose all his hair and gain weight?'

Iris looked down at the short woman who was built like a refrigerator. Her hair was tight and frizzy from a bad permanent wave and stood high on her head, displaying a narrow strip of gray where her blonde dye job needed a touch-up. Iris would have detested having this woman as a teacher. Miss Collins would have intimidated the hell out of the insecure teenager that she had been and probably would have enjoyed it. Today, Iris appreciated Miss Collins's forthrightness. 'Still handsome. Still a charmer.'

'When he went to USC to play football, everyone here was certain he was on his way to the major leagues. We were all real disappointed when we heard he'd dropped out after just one season. I called him myself. "Sure you got injured," I told him. "So what? Pick your ass up and get back in the game." '

'What did he say?'

'Promised he was going back.' Miss Collins smiled sadly, dimpling her chubby cheeks. 'Even then I knew he was funnin' me. That's what teachers live for, to see their students make something of themselves.' She turned her bright eyes on Iris. 'But you say that Todd did.'

'Todd's sister told me he transferred to Cal-State Fresno after USC.'

'That's what I heard. His buddy Mike Edgerton was going there.' She tapped a too-pointed fingernail polished in frosted pink that matched her lipstick against the display glass. 'Todd and Mike. Mike and Todd. The Terrible Twosome. They were like frick and frack, those boys were. Friends since kindergarten.'

'Is Mike still around?'

She raised her eyebrows which were drawn where her natural brows had been plucked out. 'I heard he lives not far from here. Haven't seen him in years. They rarely come back, you know. Never come by to say hello. They don't think of us as people.' She turned and began walking down the corridor, her broad haunches rhythmically raising and lowering her full skirt, making it swish round her legs. 'Take your time. Just wanted to make sure you found what you were looking for.'

Iris stayed a few minutes longer then walked out, nodding to Miss Collins who was harassing some kids who claimed one of them had left a needed book in a classroom.

Tracy Beale's street was quiet, waiting for the school-aged kids and wage-earners to come home. Through the screen door, Iris saw Tracy energetically pushing around a vacuum cleaner, its long cord extending the length of the living room. Iris pushed the doorbell several times before Tracy heard it. The silence seemed to ring in the air once the vacuum cleaner was shut off.

Tracy rushed to unlock the screen door, her face moist with perspiration. 'Iris, I'm so glad you stopped by. Come in. Ignore the mess. I was trying to get the house straightened up.' She pulled the corners of her mouth in opposite directions as if she wasn't sanguine about the prospects. 'Excuse me just a second while I get this out of the way. Have a seat.'

Iris leaned Todd's portfolio which she was returning to his sister against the easy chair that had been occupied by Richard Beale during her first visit. Iris had made photocopies of what she wanted, keeping the framed photo of her and Todd for herself. She sat on the couch and watched Tracy loop the electrical cord round hooks on the side of the vacuum's handle. She pushed it into the hallway where Iris heard a door opening and closing.

'I want to make myself presentable,' Tracy called out to her. 'Won't be a minute.'

'Take your time. I'm in no hurry.'

Iris mentally framed how she was going to tell Tracy the truth about Todd. She'd rehearsed several speeches aloud as she drove north on Interstate 5 then headed north on Highway 99 to Bakersfield. Now, sitting in the Beale house where gap-toothed school photographs of Todd's niece and nephew were proudly displayed, she wondered what would be accomplished by spilling the beans about Todd. She thought about the nephew's bedroom and how he cherished the football trophies his uncle had won. She thought about Todd's brother-in-law recounting his triumphs. Inevitably, in such a small community, word would get back to Miss Collins at the high school. Iris no longer saw the overriding, immutable value of truth above all else. Todd was a beautiful dream. She would gain nothing other than a sadistic jolt of revenge by sullying the dream with tales of Todd the drug dealer, Todd the con artist, maybe even Todd the murderer.

Tracy came back. She'd changed from shrunken leggings and a baggy top to black jeans with a print blouse worn over them. 'Thanks for returning Todd's things.' She sat on the couch.

'I called the American Embassy in Moscow and asked about his furnishings and other effects.'

Tracy listened attentively.

'There's nothing left. His apartment was cleaned out. The Embassy representative said everything's probably been sold by now.'

'Well . . .' Tracy said quietly, 'thanks for looking into it. I'm grateful for what you managed to bring back.'

'You're welcome.'

Tracy scratched at something on the palm of her hand, her brow furrowed. Suddenly, she wailed, 'Where did you go? Where did my sweet little boy go?' She pressed her hand against her mouth and looked at Iris as if she might have an answer, her eyes filled with tears. 'I'm sorry.' She jumped from the couch and left the room.

Iris leaned her elbow against the arm of the chair and rubbed her forehead.

Tracy returned clutching a wad of yellow tissues, composed but her eyes still teary. She sat on the couch again, her previous energy and good spirits displaced by weariness. 'It's funny. You don't see someone for a long time or very often. Someone you love. But you get used to it. You

167

learn to live knowing that they're in the world and that becomes enough. It's all you expect. The occasional phone call or card or visit and the knowledge that they're in the world and happy . . . hopefully. Living, making their way, like anyone else.' She blew her nose. 'Your relationship with that person begins to exist more in memories than in the real world, but it's OK. You accept it. Then you hear they're dead. Gone. And what's changed really? What in my day-to-day life has changed? Nothing. But the world seems a bit dimmer. It's as if the person threw off a light, a glow, and now the world is dimmer.'

They sat in silence that spoke volumes, Tracy weeping and wiping her tears with yellow tissues and Iris chewing her thumb, holding her grisly secret, and staring at the blackened logs in the dead fireplace on the other side of the room. After Tracy's weeping had subsided, Iris offered some information.

'I heard from Davidovsky, the Russian police detective handling Todd's case.'

Tracy perked up.

'They have a lead on the murderers. Someone recognized the two men who shot Todd from the motorcycle. They're known criminals, professional assassins from Chechnia. Davidovsky said they're bound to be long gone although the police are on the lookout for them. They also traced the phone calls Todd made on his cellular phone and were able to track them all down. None amounted to much but there was one they couldn't figure out. It was made ten minutes before Todd was shot to death. It was to a Dr Hart in Visalia. An ophthalmologist. It was a short call, just a few minutes. But no one at the doctor's office recalls getting a call from Todd or even knew who he was. He's wasn't a patient.'

Tracy frowned and twisted the tissues between her hands. 'Dr Hart? Visalia, you say?'

'An ophthalmologist.'

'I think that's where Mona works.'

'Mona?'

'Mona Edgerton. She's married to Todd's best friend, Mike. Was Todd's best friend, anyway. Mike lived two doors down from us. Todd and Mike grew up together. All through school, Mike was Todd's only close friend. Todd knew lots of people. He was the personality kid. You probably knew that. But he didn't get close to people easily.'

Iris nodded ruefully.

'That's odd.' Tracy dropped a handful of tissues on the coffee table. 'I wonder why Todd called Mona all the way from Russia.'

'Why is it odd?'

'Well, I . . . I didn't think Todd had been in touch with Mike and Mona. Course, I don't know who he kept in touch with. I spoke with Mona . . . must have been a few months ago. She didn't mention Todd, but then she and Mike have been having their own problems.' Tracy fell quiet and Iris sensed she was holding something back. Her hand flew to her cheek. 'They won't know about Todd. Oh no.' She grabbed her lower lip between her teeth. 'I can't tell them something like that over the phone.'

'Visalia's about an hour or so from here, isn't it? I'd like to talk with Mike and Mona. Do you want to come with me?'

Tracy glanced at her watch. 'Two o'clock. Kids will be home soon.' She drummed her fingers against her cheek. 'Sure. I'll call the neighbor and ask if she'll watch the kids. Our kids play together all the time anyway. Shouldn't be a problem.' She stood. 'I'd rather not be alone when I tell the Edgertons about Todd. I might lose my nerve otherwise.'

While Tracy made arrangements for her children, Iris looked in the telephone book and found the listing for Adolph Hart, M.D., in Visalia.

Tracy reappeared with a brown paper lunch bag and a cardigan. 'I made a couple of sandwiches and packed some drinks.' She shrugged. 'Once a mom, always a mom.'

Chapter 24

Highway 99 from Bakersfield to Visalia cut flat miles through vast cultivated fields of America's salad bowl. Tracy asked Iris to leave the top down on the Triumph. Iris gave her the extra scarf she kept in her glove compartment to tie round her head and they drove mostly in silence as was demanded by the wind, the road, and the roar of the Triumph's engine.

When they reached Visalia, Tracy thought she remembered the way to Dr Hart's office and they made a wrong turn or two but finally reached a complex of one-story medical offices with an attached, uncovered parking lot.

'Aren't you going to put the top up?' Tracy asked, concerned about the Triumph.

'If anyone wants to steal it, they can slit the canvas top.'

'I guess you're right.' Tracy began purposefully walking toward the low brown buildings without waiting for Iris to finish untying her scarf. Tracy was halfway across the parking lot before she turned to wait for Iris. 'I'm sorry. I guess I'm a little scatterbrained today.'

'It's all right.'

Dr Hart's office was in a corner suite. He shared it with an optician and another ophthalmologist whose brass placards were on the door beneath his. The waiting room was decorated in soothing pastels with ersatz Impressionist art on the walls. Tracy approached the reception window behind which several women were at work. A tall, slender man with thinning hair and shiny gold-framed glasses was leaning against the counter, writing on a patient chart.

'Can I help you?' asked a woman seated closest to the window. A plastic name tag on her pink jacket identified her as Chris.

'I'm here to see Mona Edgerton,' Tracy said brightly, perhaps trying to disguise any hint of foreboding in her voice.

The doctor looked up from his notes and the other two women stopped what they were doing to glance at one another. Chris turned to the doctor, as if for assistance. He circled the counter, opened the door, and walked into the waiting room.

'Are you a friend of Mona's?' he asked Tracy.

'Why?' She took a step back. 'Is something wrong?'

He frowned. 'I'm Dr Hart. Mona Edgerton was murdered over the weekend.'

Tracy gasped and reached out in Iris's direction. Iris put her arm round her.

The doctor explained what had happened. 'When she and Mike didn't show up for dinner Sunday evening as planned, Mona's parents went over to the house. They found her in the bedroom on the floor. She'd been strangled.'

'What about Mike?' Iris asked.

Dr Hart shook his head. 'Gone. Mona had told her parents he was taking a backpacking trip in the Sierras for a couple of weeks. He was due to return last Saturday.'

Tracy let go of Iris and moved to a chair where she slowly sat down.

Two of the office staff were weeping. One of them rose from her desk and left the area.

Iris pressed for more details. 'Do the police have a motive? Had Mike threatened his wife? Were there problems?'

'They had their problems like anyone else,' Chris volunteered. 'They'd had financial difficulties lately. Mike's been unemployed for about five months. He was an account representative for a business machines company in town and he got downsized. Mona told me he was getting pretty depressed. Then about three weeks ago, she came to work all smiles, and told me Mike was going backpacking in the Sierras by himself for two weeks. She was glad that he'd decided to do something, anything. She was happier than I'd seen her in a long time.'

'Did Mike frequently go backpacking?' Iris wondered if her questions sounded overly direct.

'He used to,' Chris replied. 'He was a big outdoorsman. But with the job and everything, he didn't have time to take long trips. Mona couldn't care less about it. They did some camping in tents and stuff, but not way out in the backwoods, like Mike used to do. Mona was looking forward to having some time apart. Things had been tense at their house. Mona had been trying to get pregnant for ages. Before Mike got laid off, they'd started fertility treatments, which cost a fortune. They really wanted a baby. Then he lost his job and—'

'Mike couldn't have killed Mona.'

Everyone looked at Tracy who had been sitting quietly with her hands clasped in her lap. Now she clutched the chair arms, her knuckles white. 'I practically raised that kid. He was my brother's best friend all through school. I knew him. He couldn't have murdered his wife. He adored Mona and she worshiped the ground he walked on. It couldn't have happened that way.'

The doctor opened the door, went into the back office, and began searching the counter. Finding what he was looking for, he wrote on a pad and held the notepaper through the open window. 'If you have information

172

that might help the police in their investigation, I know they'd love to talk to you. A detective named Russ Proctor is handling the case. Here's his phone number.'

Iris took the paper from him.

'The police station's less than a mile from here if you want to go by.'

'Thank you. I think that would be a good idea, huh, Tracy?'

Tracy stood and agitatedly chewed her fingernails. 'I would like to do that. Somebody's got to tell me what's going on here.'

'I'm so sorry to have been the bearer of bad news,' the doctor said. 'I'm certain everyone in town knows about Mona. You must not be from around here.'

Tracy abruptly left the office without another word.

'No,' Iris responded, watching her leave.

'Poor woman,' Dr Hart commented. 'It's a big loss. Everyone loved Mona.'

'One thing happened that was strange, that I keep thinking about,' Chris said. 'The last time I saw Mona was Friday. She'd taken half a day's vacation that day and left the office early. Late in the afternoon, she came by to pick up something she'd forgotten and she was dressed to the nines. She had on this very expensive-looking pant suit with this beautiful silk blouse. I knew she hadn't bought it in Visalia. Our little stores around here don't carry clothes like that. So I asked her where she got the fabulous outfit. She got this big smile on her face and told me she'd ordered it from the Saks Fifth Avenue catalogue. I didn't say anything, but I thought it was odd, them trying to make ends meet on her salary alone and her coming in here like that. I mean, she had new shoes, purse, jewelry, everything. Mona must have known what I was thinking because she said, "Don't look so concerned, Chris. Things are going to be very different for me from now on. You'll see." And then she left.'

Chris touched the corners of her eyes. 'I didn't tell the police. I wonder if I should.' She looked at Dr Hart who was standing next to her.

'It couldn't hurt,' he said. 'Maybe she just went a little nuts and maxed out her credit cards.'

'Thank you again,' Iris said. 'I'd better see to my friend.'

Iris found Tracy sitting on the edge of a cement planter outside the door.

'What's happening, Iris? What's going on?'

Iris gently pulled Tracy's arm. 'Let's go talk to this detective.'

Detective Russ Proctor brought Iris and Tracy back to his desk where they'd interrupted his late lunch of a tuna salad sandwich and a bag of ruffled potato chips from a Subway sandwich shop. The women urged him to finish his meal before talking with them.

Proctor wiped his thick moustache with a paper napkin. 'Busy day. Had a gang shooting on the south side. Two down.'

Iris was surprised. 'You have gang problems here?'

'Gangs are everywhere now. But we've had gangs for a long time. Mostly Latino. Recently, Eighteenth Street, the big LA-based gang, has been trying to carve out a presence.' He was tall and well-built with curly brown hair that he attempted to wear smooth. His bright blue eyes were incisive and watchful. 'What information do you have about the Mona Edgerton murder?'

Tracy sat on the edge of the wooden chair. 'I've known Mike and Mona Edgerton for years. My brother Todd grew up with Mike. They were best friends. They were roommates at Cal-State Fresno. That's where Mike and Mona met. I can tell you without any doubt that Mike did not murder his wife. He doesn't have it in him to do anything like that. He's a very gentle person. Kind and giving.' She clenched her fist. 'He couldn't have murdered Mona. He just couldn't have.'

Proctor listened without reaction, carefully dragging the napkin down his moustache after each bite of the sandwich. He popped the last corner in his mouth and balled up the wrapping. 'Do you know Mike Edgerton's whereabouts last Saturday night or since?'

'No, I haven't seen him for, it must be two months,' Tracy confessed.

'What about your brother? Do you know the last time he saw Mike?'

'No, I don't. I haven't been in contact with my brother much over the past few years. But I know he called Mona Edgerton's work last . . .' Tracy looked at Iris.

'Monday. Two Mondays ago.'

'Do you know what they talked about?'

'No,' Tracy responded.

'I'd like to talk to your brother. You say his name is Todd. Same last name as yours?'

Iris was about to tell the detective the critical missing detail that Tracy seemed unable to reveal when she spoke up. 'My brother is dead. He was murdered the same night he called Mona Edgerton.'

Proctor raised his eyebrows, the most emotion he'd displayed since the women had arrived. 'Where?'

'In Moscow,' Tracy explained. 'He was living there.'

Proctor jammed the straw into the ice at the bottom of his jumbo-sized Coke. 'What happened?'

When Tracy hesitated, Iris jumped in. 'Mafia. That's what the Russian police think. Todd was in business there. The Russian Mafia's a real problem for businessmen.'

'Damn.' Proctor gave his head a quick shake. 'Why would he call Mona Edgerton? Were they having an affair?'

'No.' Tracy looked at the ground and added, 'I don't think so.'

'Had they had one in the past?'

The question made Tracy uncomfortable. She shifted her position in the chair and re-crossed her legs. Iris waited for Tracy to reveal the piece of the Mona, Mike, and Todd story she'd left out earlier.

Tracy took a deep breath. 'I hate to even tell you about it because I know how it's going to look. I'll never in a million years believe that Mike Edgerton murdered Mona.'

Proctor leaned back in his wooden swivel chair which creaked under the pressure and patiently regarded Tracy. He seemed prepared to wait as long as necessary. 'Mona Edgerton was strangled in her bedroom apparently by someone she knew. There was no evidence of a forced entry or a struggle. If you have any information that might help us solve this case, her family would be very appreciative.'

Tracy's face looked drawn and pale. 'My brother Todd transferred from USC to Cal-State Fresno at the beginning of his sophomore year. He moved in with Mike who'd started at Fresno out of high school. Todd is . . . was a real charmer. Good-looking, lots of girls, lots of buddies. Mike was different. He was a good-looking guy too, but he was kind of shy and quiet. They made a good match, the two of them. Mike was a leveling influence on Todd and Todd got Mike out of the house.' Tracy paused and picked an invisible piece of lint from her black pants.

'Todd met Mona at a party and they started dating. Mike hardly ever had any dates, so Todd and Mona would sometimes take him with them when they went out. Todd was pretty serious about Mona, but I guess he had a funny way of showing it.' She gave a weak smile. 'Mona said she thought he was mad at her half the time. He'd be loving and sweet, then he'd turn around and be distant and cold. Sometimes he'd disappear for days.'

Iris reflected on her similar experiences with Todd in Paris.

'One day, Todd came home from class and found Mike and Mona in bed together. They told him they hadn't been seeing each other romantic-ally for very long and were going to tell him about it soon but couldn't find the nerve. Without a word, Todd loaded everything he could into his Dodge Cougar and left. None of us heard from him for weeks. We notified the police and everything. No word. We were terrified. After three weeks, Todd called. He'd driven across the country, traveling here and there, sleeping in his car on the side of the road, and ended up in New York City.' She sighed sadly. 'This was a kid who'd never been out of California until then.'

Iris thought to herself that Todd had never stopped running.

Tracy brightened when talking about her brother's adventures. 'In New York, he started doing a lot of photography. He'd always been interested in it. He got involved in the club scene there and took pictures of celebrities, which he sold for a lot of money. His photography took him all over the world. He ended up in Moscow.' The last word hung in the air like a discordant musical tone. She twisted her wedding ring.

Proctor concocted an ending to the story. 'Mike and Mona get married. Years go by. They eke out a modest living. As you said, Mike was a soft, likeable guy. Not a go-getter. He loses his job. Can't find another one. She can't get pregnant and now can't afford the fertility treatments either. Somehow she gets in touch with her old boyfriend Todd who's leading this glamorous life. Who contacted who first doesn't matter. They have an affair, maybe Mona flaunts it to Mike and it tips him over. I think your brother's murder in Moscow was a coincidence. I know how you feel about Mike, but given everything you've told me, Mike Edgerton is still our only suspect in Mona Edgerton's murder.'

Tracy clutched her arms and leaned forward against her crossed legs as if she was in pain. 'I don't know what to think any more. It's like the world's been turned on its head.'

Iris rose to get a closer look at a bulletin board on the wall next to Proctor's desk. Pinned to it was a color photograph of a man and woman wearing bright sweaters standing in front of a Christmas tree. 'Is this Mike and Mona?'

Tracy turned to see. 'That's the Christmas photo they sent last year.' Her face puckered and she quickly looked away.

Proctor took a box of tissues from a desk drawer and set it on the edge of his desk.

Iris carefully studied the photograph. Mona was an attractive blonde with long, straight hair that fell past her shoulders and a big smile. Mike was considerably taller than her, broad-shouldered but very lean. He wore a thick, full beard. 'How tall is Mike Edgerton?'

'He's six foot one,' Proctor answered.

'Brown eyes?'

'Brown hair, brown eyes. On the slender side. Weighs about one-sixty.'

'Do you have a copy of this photograph?'

'Sure. We've been handing out fliers throughout the county.' Proctor flipped open a file folder on his desk and handed both Iris and Tracy a black-and-white copy of the photograph. On the bottom it said: 'This man, Michael Allan Edgerton, is sought for questioning in the murder of his wife Mona.' It was followed by a description of when and where he was last seen and a detailed list of his physical characteristics.

'You've got everything down to the scar above his left eyebrow,' Tracy remarked.

'Is it accurate?' Proctor asked with a hint of concern.

'Oh yes.' Tracy folded the paper into quarters and put it in her purse. 'He got that when he and Todd were about thirteen. They were fooling around on their skateboards on our street and Mike went face first into the curb. I drove him to the emergency room. Took ten stitches. Left about a two-inch scar. Slit his eyebrow in half. The hair never grew back there.'

Russ Proctor stood and handed Iris and Tracy his business card. 'If either of you see or hear from Mike Edgerton, call me any time, day or night.'

176

Chapter 25

By the time Iris had returned Tracy to her house, her husband Richard had ordered a couple of pizzas to the delight of their two children. They invited Iris to eat with them and she accepted even though she knew it meant a long return drive over the pass in the dark. She wanted to prolong her visit with the Beales. They were the only ones other than herself who had a personal interest in Todd Fillinger and Mike and Mona Edgerton. They weren't aware of the big picture that she hadn't completely pieced together. Over the course of the day, she had come to the conclusion that her decision to withhold her horrible suspicions about Todd from Tracy was sound. No good would come of it and it would only bring this woman and her family more grief. As it stood, Tracy's grief over Todd and the Edgertons remained pure, not tainted by the fox and the people who would kill and maim just to own it.

'Honey, let me cut that in half for you,' Tracy said to her daughter.

'I can eat it like this.' The girl struggled to hoist the generous slice of pizza into her mouth, refusing to be singled out and treated differently from her older brother.

Tracy watched her daughter happily chewing a bite of pizza, grease rimming the girl's lips, taking a parent's pleasure in the mundane aspects of her child's life.

They were all sitting at a redwood picnic table and benches on the backyard patio. The heat had broken with the setting sun and the streets came alive with kids on bicycles and skates and dogs barking at them. Dinner dishes were washed and put away as the cool evening air settled across the dry land. The neighbor's kids screamed and yelled as they played on a jungle gym in their backyard, the tallest point visible above the cedar-plank fence separating the two yards.

A large avocado tree, its branches still heavy with fruit, grew in a corner of the Beales's rectangular yard. Bare dirt encircled its base where the shade was too dense for grass to grow. Judging by the toy cars, plastic farm animals, and dolls scattered around well-worn tracks in the dirt, the big old tree was a favorite spot for the kids to play during the heat of the day.

'Rich! You still eating?' a boy yelled to the Beales's son from the top of the jungle gym.

'Pizza!' he yelled back, throwing the neighbour a thumb's-up.

177

'I try to keep junk food to a minimum,' Tracy explained to Iris. 'This is a treat for them.'

'Have they had the F-U-N-E-R-A-L?' Richard asked, spelling the word to prevent arousing the morbid interest of his children.

'No fair spelling!' the girl protested.

'F-U-N . . .' nine-year-old Rich started spelling aloud.

'I didn't think to ask about it,' Iris said. 'They found . . . I mean, the situation was revealed on Sunday. Maybe it's scheduled this week.'

'Funeral!' the boy happily announced. 'Who died?'

'Why don't you kids take your dinner and eat it in front of the television?' Tracy suggested.

'You mean it?' the girl asked with delight.

'Go ahead,' Tracy confirmed. After they'd disappeared inside the house, she commented, 'We're breaking all the rules tonight. Oh well.'

'Looks like you run a tight ship,' Iris observed.

'I try to. Todd and I grew up in chaos. I promised myself that if I ever had a family, we would act like a family is supposed to act.' Tracy pushed her half-eaten slice of pizza around her plate. 'The only models I had were "Father knows Best" and "Leave it to Beaver" on television and Norman Rockwell paintings. And the Edgertons. They were a real family to me. After my mom was murdered, Mike's mother helped us out a lot.'

'I'm surprised she didn't tell us about Mona,' Richard said.

'She's probably in shock,' Tracy said. 'It just happened.'

'More iced tea, Iris?' Richard raised the plastic pitcher over Iris's glass.

'Thanks,' she nodded, wishing she had something stronger.

'You try and you try and things just go to hell anyway.' Tracy spoke to the empty seat across the table from her as if she was trying to explain to an unseen guest who had demanded an answer.

Richard covered his wife's hand with his. 'We're fine, Tracy. You, me, and the kids, we're fine and we're going to be fine.'

'I can't help but wonder if I'd been a better sister to Todd—'

'Tracy,' Richard scolded, removing his hand from his wife's. The abruptness with which his tone changed suggested that this topic was visited frequently. There was no need for him to hear his wife out. It had all been said time and time again. His opinion had been formed long ago. 'You were just a teenager when your mother was murdered and you'd been taking care of Todd a long time before that. Your mother was never home. She was too busy chasing around to care about you and your brother. After she died, you had that drunken excuse of a father to deal with, until his liver finally gave out.'

Tracy looked at him with hurt eyes, the truth still painful after all the years that had passed.

'Todd was the one who threw away every chance he ever had,' Richard continued. 'As soon as things didn't go his way, he was out of there. You can only do so much for a person, Tracy. You did all you could.'

'I know, but I think about the years when I didn't try to keep in touch with him. Knowing that he was wanted was important to Todd.'

'You finally stopped trying to track him down all over the world and he didn't make a single effort to contact you. We're the ones who've lived in the same place for almost twenty years. He couldn't find the time to call you? Todd was really good at doing this guilt number on you. It was like a test. I want you to show me how much you love me. And no matter what you did for him, how far you went, it was never enough. Isn't that what Mona told you about why she left Todd? He wanted more, more, more from her. It was like he set up hurdles for her to jump. He was a bottomless pit. But when it came to her, he held back. Tracy, he's got you in the same loop.'

Tracy wept quietly. 'Does anything good ever come out of a bad family? Or is it just struggle, constant struggle to be normal? I feel like I've lived my whole life looking over my shoulder, waiting for that dark cloud, the family curse to catch up with me. No matter how careful or watchful I am, it's there waiting. Waiting for a careless moment to suck me down. I try to protect my family with rules, discipline, a clean house, church on Sundays. To the outside world, mine has to be the most dull life imaginable, but no one knows how hard I've struggled to have just this and how much I fear that the whole thing sits on a precipice, ready to tumble over. I'm mad at Todd for that. I thought I had it beat.' She shook her head. 'But it was only sleeping.'

Richard reached his hands across the table to clasp his wifes'. 'Come on, Tracy. Don't do this to yourself. What happened to Todd happened to him and not to us. OK?'

Tracy managed a smile but it seemed it would take a lot more than Richard's supportive words to convince her. 'And I'm mad at Todd for leaving me.'

'You're hardly alone, Tracy.'

'I know that, Richard. But Todd was there. He was there. He saw. I feel like there's no one left who understands what happened. I know you think you understand, Richard, but you can't completely. It's too big to explain in words. Unless you were there, you can't really know what it was like. Mother, father, brother . . . all gone. I'm the only one left.'

Richard squeezed his wife's hands and said nothing. This was an impasse that was not going to be bridged tonight.

Iris asked a question that had been on her mind. 'Was Todd in love with Mona?'

Tracy nodded. 'She was his first real love. You know Todd, women flocked to him. He had his pick. Then Mona came along. Todd never said much about it, but I could tell. He fell hard.'

Iris recalled the attractive woman in the Christmas photo then realized that Tracy was scrutinizing her.

'It didn't occur to me before, but you and Mona are very similar. Physically, I mean. Isn't she, Richard?'

179

He nodded. 'When Iris came by for the first time last week, I thought of that, but I didn't want to say anything because it was kind of creepy.'

They had Iris's full attention now. 'Why?'

'We always thought that Mona resembled my mother. I'd brushed it off as a coincidence, but I guess there aren't any coincidences in things like that.' Tracy slid off the bench and began gathering the plates and silverware. 'I suppose I didn't want to think that my brother might be a little loony. But now that I've seen you, the second woman I've met who Todd was in love with, it seems like he picked women who looked like our mother. Excuse me.' She pushed open the sliding glass door with her foot and took the dirty dishes inside the house.

Iris was so surprised by the revelation that she forgot to ask if she could help clear the table. Then she was glad to find herself alone with Richard. 'What do you think? Do you think Todd was loony?'

Richard took a deep breath and folded his arms across his chest. 'Let's put it this way. If someone told me Todd had done something cruel and selfish, it wouldn't surprise me.'

'Robbery, murder?'

He thought it over. 'That's pretty strong, but could be. For all his charm and jokes and everything, there was something about Todd, something cold. Tracy never saw it. She thought the sun rose and set in her brother. It was as if a part of him was shut off. I think he was aware that he had a piece missing and he did a good job covering it up.'

'Is this based on a gut feeling, or did you see something that made you feel this way?'

He turned to look inside the house behind him, twisting this way and that, trying to locate his wife. 'Let me tell you a story about Todd. My wife doesn't know this.'

'I won't say anything,' Iris promised.

'When I coached Todd in high school, he had a buddy on the football team, a guy named Rocky. That's what everyone called him. Todd, Mike Edgerton, and Rocky hung around together. Todd had his eye on this car that the guy who ran a deli in town had for sale. A sixty-nine Ford Cougar. It was real cherry.'

'The one he drove cross-country in after he left Cal-State Fresno.'

'Tracy told you about that. That's the same model car, but not the one I'm talking about. Anyway, Todd didn't have the money but he wanted that car. He wanted it big time. He got a part-time job bagging groceries to earn money and asked the guy who ran the deli to please hold the car for him. The guy said he'd see what he could do. If someone made him a good offer, he'd have to sell it. He was a jerk that way. One day, Todd sees his friend Rocky tooling around town in this Cougar. Rocky got his father to buy it for him. It was the kind of thing where Rocky didn't know he wanted that car until Todd wanted it. I don't think Rocky thought much about it. In his mind, the best man had won. About a week after he bought the car, he's coming out of the corner market and three guys jump him, beat the hell out of him, and steal his car. When the police find it a week later, it's been completely stripped. Rocky's dad hadn't had it insured yet, so it was a total loss. No one could pin it on Todd, but I heard from a reliable source that Todd had paid those guys to mess up Rocky and the car.'

'Rocky must have heard the rumors too.'

'He did but then he started to have his doubts. Then everyone had their doubts and before long no one believed that Todd had had anything to do with it.'

'Why?'

'Because Todd started a fund-raising campaign to earn enough money to have Rocky's Cougar fixed. Car washes, bake sales, you name it. Todd was a hero.'

'He was covering his behind.'

'Maybe, but what happened after that was the strangest part of the whole thing for me. During the next two years that Rocky and Todd were in high school, Todd acted like nothing had changed between the two of them. They were as tight as ever. Now, that takes a cold-hearted son of a bitch to pull off something like that, huh? I never saw Todd the same way after that.'

Neither of them said anything for a while, their silence giving the story weight.

Iris could have added another chapter to Todd's saga, but she didn't. She changed the subject. 'Do you know whether Mike Edgerton smokes?'

'Like a smokestack,' Richard chuckled. 'He started in high school. I used to catch him sneaking cigarettes. He's tried to stop a hundred times. I smoked for twenty years, so I know how hard it is to stop. The best Mike could do was switch from Marlboros to some low-tar, low-nicotine phoney cigarettes.'

'Do you know what brand?'

Tracy stuck her head through the opening in the sliding glass door. 'Iris, would you like some ice cream? We have chocolate and strawberry.'

'Thanks. A tiny bit of each, please.'

'Honey, do you still have that pack of cigarettes that Mike left here the last time he and Mona came over?'

Tracy gave her husband a sharp look. 'Why?'

He smiled. 'They're not for me. Iris was asking what kind of cigarettes Mike smoked.'

'I think I've got them somewhere.' She disappeared inside the house.

'Can I ask why you want to know, Iris? Sounds like something the police would ask.'

Iris knew that saying she just wanted to know on a whim would sound lame and probably make him suspicious. So far neither of them had asked why she had insisted Tracy was someone else when she'd first come to their front door. A lie was the most efficient response. 'The police found cigarette butts in the Edgertons' house and asked if we knew whether Mike smoked.'

181

Tracy returned carrying a tray which she put on the picnic table. Between the three bowls of ice cream was a pack of True cigarettes. 'I found them.'

'Great,' Richard said. 'Now you can tell the police detective.'

'Tell him what?' Tracy busily distributed the ice cream.

'When he asked us about whether Mike smoked because they'd found cigarette butts in the house,' Iris said.

Tracy winced. 'He did?' She raised and dropped her shoulders. 'I've been so jumbled up, I couldn't tell you half the things that happened today.'

Iris smiled meekly. She didn't like to lie. She wasn't proud of having successfully pulled it off.

Iris was running barefoot down a narrow street, its cobblestones slick beneath her bare feet. She peered through the glass front window of Le Café des Quatre Vents on which Madame Mouche had written the day's specialties with a black crayon. The small room was crowded and filled with smoke. Todd was standing at the bar, laughing and putting his arms round the shoulders of the men and touching the hair and kissing the cheeks of the women. When Iris opened the door and walked inside, everyone turned to stare at her. She looked down at herself and realized she was wearing only a slip. Then Todd held his hand out to her. She walked toward him and everyone returned to what they were doing, no one paying attention to her any more. She no longer cared that she was undressed. She reached to touch his cheek and scratched the stiff bristles of his beard with her fingernails. 'You grew a beard,' she told him. He smiled as he stroked his facial hair. 'It's cold in Moscow. You need all the fur you can get.'

Iris looked round. They were no longer in the café but on the steps of the Metropolis Hotel in Moscow. He pulled her down to sit on the steps next to him and kissed her passionately. He pulled her on top of him, leaning back until they were lying across the steps. People walked by as if they weren't there. There was the sound of rapid gunfire. Iris gasped and sat up. People were running in all directions without any purpose or destination. She raised her hand and saw that it had blood on it. She turned to Todd who was lying still against the steps. He was oozing blood from tiny holes that covered his face and body. She recoiled in horror. Above his eyebrow, splitting it in half, she saw a white scar. At the sound of her name, she jolted awake and found herself in her own bed. She heard her name again and turned to see Todd standing by her bed, cleanshaven and whole. He leaned over her, his outstretched hands reaching for her neck.

Iris awakened with a start, her heart pounding. She pressed herself against the headboard, scanning the darkness for the intruder but saw no one. She gathered her nerve and went through the house, flipping on lights and checking doors and windows. Todd Fillinger was only in her nightmares.

182

Chapter 26

Iris pulled open the heavy glass door on which was marked in simple brass letters: McKinney Alitzer Financial Services. The suite's décor was subdued but not staid, colorful but not frivolous, making a statement to employees and clients alike that this was a place that was serious about money.

Iris knew all about money, from not having it, to figuring out how she could get it, to busting her butt to earn it, to raking it in hand over fist, to having more than she'd ever thought she'd see in ten lifetimes, to wondering if it was all worth it. There was one thing about money that she would never discount: money was power. Without it, one was always beholden to someone else. That truth alone propelled her, kept her going year after year, swatting down ambitious interlopers who would knock her from her position. So she kept on, earning a lot, saving as much as possible, investing conservatively here and aggressively there, counting her pennies, no longer a wild spendthrift like she was when she first starting pulling down real dough, now preferring to see her money growing in her portfolio than decorating her back, keeping her thumb securely on the pulse of her wealth, fretting over any irregularity, and working until the day she had enough money. Problem was, she didn't know how much was enough.

She energetically walked through the suite with a slightly haughty attitude that she used to fake but no longer had to, letting her employees know that she was the boss. She was. And as much as they might sometimes hate her for the control she had over their working hours, they knew that without her firm hand, the office would flounder like a ship without a rudder. In return for doing what she demanded of them, she looked after their interests in every way she could, lavishing on them all the bonuses and perks that she could. She might be leaving for bigger and better things. She still hadn't made up her mind about the regional manager position.

'Morning, Louise,' Iris said to her assistant who was at work in her alcove.

Louise looked up from her computer with the same slightly harassed demeanor that she manifested regardless of the time of day. 'Good morning, Iris. How are you feeling today?'

The question took Iris aback then she remembered she'd called in sick with the flu the day before. 'Much better, thank you.'

She walked into her office, hung her suit jacket behind the door, put her purse in the top drawer of her filing cabinet, and her briefcase on the credenza behind her desk. Louise brought in a mug of hot coffee, a gesture that used to embarrass Iris but that Louise insisted on and that Iris had come not only to accept but to expect. Yet another small but subtle shift in Iris's transformation from hard scrabble junior investment counselor cold-calling for new clients to the queen of the roost. The mantle of authority which had chafed awkwardly at first now felt comfortable and correct.

She sorted through her mail and phone messages which would take her half the day to follow up on. As she prioritized them, she couldn't shake the image of a man, his body sprawled across worn marble steps, his face and body torn with dozens of bullet holes, his clothing and skin covered in blood that was an astonishing deep red hue – a color that would have been beautiful in other circumstances. Apart from the gore and the horror of the scene, the one detail she couldn't shake was the man's left eyebrow and the scar that split it in two. Had she seen it in reality or was her dream the product of the power of suggestion? She'd turned it over and over in her mind during the long, dark early-morning hours that she'd lain awake after she'd had the nightmare. Her memory of seeing the scar seemed real. At best it was another piece of circumstantial evidence.

There was a bright rat-a-tat-tat on her door. She looked up to see Lisa Roman, the investment counselor who had asked for her own assistant last week. Iris had forgotten all about it. Lisa had waited a respectable amount of time before broaching the subject again. Iris reflected on her own struggles trying to get the attention of the revolving door of different branch managers who had passed through the office.

'Come in, Lisa. Have a seat.'

'Hi, Iris. I was hoping to catch you this morning to see if you've had a chance to think over my request for my own assistant.' She crossed her legs at the ankles and tucked them underneath the chair. Her mannerisms were slightly stiff and formal, as were her words, which seemed carefully prepared.

Iris suspected the young investment counselor had thought about every last detail, probably including her selection of the sedate pearl-gray suit with a conservative hemline. She saw a younger version of herself in Lisa, although she had been much more brash and rough around the edges.

'If you've had a chance to review my sales figures for the past six months, you'll see that they've exceeded everyone else's at my level.'

'How much do you think your sales would increase with an assistant?'

This caught Lisa off guard. 'Umm . . . Forty per cent.'

'You've got a full-time assistant. But at the end of six months, I expect a forty per cent increase in your production.'

Lisa's eyes brightened. Iris knew what she was thinking. She was glad she'd won but was wondering what she'd got herself into. 'Thanks so much, Iris. You've made the right decision.' She bumped into Liz Martini as she left the room, her carefully manicured composure now rattled to pieces and her expression of gratitude deteriorating into gushing. 'Thanks again, Iris. Thanks, Liz. I mean, sorry.'

'What was that all about?' Liz plopped into one of the chairs facing Iris's desk and crossed her legs, hiking her already short skirt well up her narrow thighs. No demure ankle-crossing for Liz. She didn't need to make an impression on Iris. Liz's sales figures spoke more loudly than anything she could do or say. That was another thing about money.

'She's getting her own sales assistant.'

'You're being magnanimous today.'

'It's good to be king.'

Liz tossed the folded newspaper she was carrying on Iris's desk. On the front page was a color photo of the Greentree restaurant with a coroner's van and many police officers in front. Curious onlookers stood behind police tape that blocked off both ends of the street. A body with a sheet tucked securely round it was being wheeled out of the restaurant on a gurney. Iris picked up the paper and handed it back to Liz.

'Rita Winslow and Fernando Peru,' Liz read from the article. 'Weren't those the people who were involved in your . . .' She was mindful of the open door and the over-eager ears in the suite. 'Russian business deal?'

Iris stood, opened the filing cabinet and took a few dollars from her purse. 'Come with me downstairs. I have the urge for a gooey, chocolate chip muffin.'

They left the suite and got in the elevator which was empty. It was not quite 8:00 a.m. and people were rushing to get to their desks on time upstairs, not descending to the lobby.

The elevator doors closed and Iris spilled the beans. 'Todd Fillinger is alive.'

'What?'

'Well, I think he is. I'm almost certain of it. The evidence is circumstantial, but it all fits together and it's the only thing that makes sense. He had his former best friend, a guy named Mike Edgerton, murdered in his place. Todd grew a beard and lost weight so he'd resemble Mike. Close enough anyway. Todd counted on there being so much blood and terror that I wouldn't look too closely at the man who was gunned down on the hotel steps. He must have instructed the assassins to make sure to shoot Mike in the face. It worked like a charm. If it hadn't been for Rita Winslow's jealous rage over Fernando Peru, I would never have found out. That damned Weems.'

'Who's Weems?'

'Oh, man.' Iris rolled her eyes. 'I haven't even told you about that yet. I thought it would all be over by now, but it's not. I've got to talk this through with somebody. I feel like I'm losing my mind.'

185

Liz put her hands on her slender hips. 'You've completely lost me. Let's start from the beginning. Todd Fillinger wasn't murdered but he made it look like he was?'

'Todd needed to drop out big time. He not only had to, he wanted to. Being Todd Fillinger wasn't working out for him and never had. I think the whole thing got rolling when Todd got into trouble with a powerful drug dealer in France, a guy named Enrico Lazare. He must have stolen money from Lazare or something because Lazare came gunning for Todd in Paris, in this café where Todd used to hang out. Todd escaped, but one of the café's owners was shot and killed. Todd fled for London where he lived with his buddy Fernando Peru in the house of Peru's wealthy benefactor, Rita Winslow.'

The elevator opened onto the busy lobby. The worker bees rushed into the car before Iris and Liz had a chance to exit. Liz planted her feet outside the door and firmly held it open, ignoring the unhappy faces who pointedly stared at their wristwatches, and waited until Iris squeezed out from where she had been pushed into the corner.

'Some people,' Iris complained after she'd made her way through the crowd and into the lobby. She started walking toward the coffee shop but quickly changed direction when Liz took hold of her upper arm and started walking toward the building exit. Liz was surprisingly strong for someone who appeared so undernourished.

'Let's sit outside,' Liz ordered. 'I want to hear the rest of this.'

They sat on the cement wall of a raised flowerbed with organically curved lines that broke up the stark façade of the black granite building.

Iris continued her tale. 'Todd stayed in London for two years then left again, first for Prague then to Moscow. At some point, Lazare tracked him down and gave him an ultimatum. Either that or Todd got a tip that Lazare was closing in. Todd had to disappear again and he was getting tired of running. Then he had a bit of luck. He stumbled across the Tsarina's Fox and he got an idea. What better way to disappear than to have everyone believe you've been murdered? If you can settle old scores at the same time, get back at people whom you trusted who did you dirty, better still.'

'What grudge did Todd have against Mike Edgerton?'

'Mike stole Mona, Todd's first true love, from him when they were all in college.'

'And then there's you, ol' leave-'em-at-the-altar Iris.'

'And there's me.'

'Why didn't—'

Iris put her hand out, stopping Liz from going on. She whispered, 'Don't look directly at him, but there's a man sitting on the other side of the plaza who was in the lobby when we got off the elevator.'

Liz casually combed her hair with her fingers and scanned the plaza. 'The one with glasses and the newspaper?'

'That's him. He's been watching us. I think he followed us out here.'

'Iris, you're being paranoid.'

'Let's find out. Let's go into the coffee shop and see if he follows.'

They stood and began walking back inside the building. Liz held the door open for Iris, casting a glance back at the man as she did so.

'He's still there, Iris.'

In the small coffee shop, they found a seat at a corner table. Iris intentionally sat so she could watch the door.

'To finish my earlier question, why didn't Todd just steal the fox once he found it? Why involve Winslow and Peru and the rest of it?'

'He needed Winslow's money to get him started.'

'How did he convince Mike Edgerton to come to Moscow and pretend he was Todd?'

'Mike had been unemployed for months. He and Mona were strapped for cash. He most likely got Mike to Russia with the same ruse he used on me. Somehow Todd got Mike to stand on the steps of the Metropolis Hotel dressed in his clothes and wearing his jewelry. I can't imagine how he convinced Mike to do that, but Todd was nothing if not persuasive. I assume the Russian authorities took fingerprints of Mike's body. Todd probably paid them to falsify their reports. Mona suddenly had a lot of cash in her last days. She showed up at her workplace wearing expensive clothes and told a co-worker that her life was about to take a dramatic change.'

'Sounds like a recipe for disaster.'

'Mona's dead. She was found strangled. Todd couldn't risk leaving her around. He probably planned on killing her after he got back to the States. Ironically, poor Mike is their top suspect.'

Liz gave her a look that said she couldn't believe what she was hearing. 'Where's Enrico Lazare? How did he get involved in the fox?'

'I don't think he is. After Todd was so-called murdered, he needed an interim identity while he sold the fox. What better than to pose as a notorious criminal, someone known for his ruthlessness? That piece worked too. Roger Weems never doubted that Lazare was the mastermind behind the fox theft and Todd's murder.'

'Who is this Weems?'

'An FBI agent who's having me followed. Don't turn around. Our bespectacled friend is back.'

'Where is he?'

'About three tables away, facing us. Now he's opening his newspaper. He's dressed in a suit, but he looks kind of shabby. Weems could have at least sent someone who looks like a businessman.'

'What's the point of having you followed?'

'Weems is trying to harass me. If he seriously wanted to watch my comings and goings, I don't think he'd be so obvious about it. He wants me to see this guy. Prick.'

Liz leaned on her elbows closer to Iris. 'Tell me about Weems.'

'Let me back up again.' Iris filled her in on her meeting with Rita Winslow at the Peninsula Hotel, her being apprehended by Weems afterward, the failed plot to buy the fox from Lazare and Dean Palmer, the pleated paper napkin she found in the hotel room, her visit with Tracy Beale, the discovery of Mike and Mona Edgerton, the visit with detective Russ Proctor, and the scar above Mike Edgerton's eye.

Liz chewed on her long acrylic thumbnail as she listened. 'Why don't you tell Weems your theory about Todd Fillinger? At least the FBI will know who they're looking for. Weems suspects you know more than you're telling anyway. You'll get him off your back.'

Iris stubbornly set her jaw. 'I don't have a compelling desire to help Roger Weems. He lied to me.' She jerked her head to indicate the man sitting behind them. 'Now he's started harassing me. Winslow and Peru are dead because of him. He's as amoral as any of the crooks involved in this thing. I refuse to help him.'

'Your only other option is to let Todd Fillinger walk away scot-free with millions of dollars when he sells that fox, which you know he will do eventually, after having murdered two people and used you to smuggle stolen art. And I'm wondering whether he didn't murder Lazare too or one of his men. If his issue with Lazare was just owed money, seems that a guy like Todd could have weaseled a couple of hundred thousand out of somebody. His friend Rita Winslow, for example. I bet you fun money and peanuts that Todd was into Lazare for something much more serious than money.' Liz crossed her legs and waggled her foot clad in an unbusiness-like, high-heeled sandal. 'Has anyone seen Lazare lately?'

'Weems says he's not seen around much.' Iris ran her finger along her string of pearls. 'The FBI doesn't even have a good picture of him. He runs his empire from this castle-like compound in Corsica. There are rumors that he's had plastic surgery lately.'

'A man without a face. Todd couldn't have picked anyone better to impersonate.' The intensity of Liz's foot-waggling increased. She abruptly stopped. 'Call Weems.'

Iris drew back one side of her mouth, indicating she didn't agree with Liz's prescription.

'Why not?'

'Todd has so many layers of people between him and the fox that Weems will never get to him. And Weems doesn't care. All he ever wanted was the fox. I'm the only one who wants Todd Fillinger.'

'Why? Revenge?'

'Justice.'

'Indeed.'

'You look like you don't believe me.'

Liz delicately untangled her cluster of gold and diamond bracelets with her long fingernails. 'Do me the courtesy of admitting that there's a scintilla of revenge in this.'

'OK, fine.'

'You said you want Todd. What does that mean?'

'I don't want him to think he got away with it, that's all.'

'What are you going to do?'

Iris drummed her fingers against the table. 'I'm going to buy an *objet d'art*. A small, jeweled statuette of a fox.'

'If Todd finds out you're on to him, he might try to kill you.'

'There's that possibility, but I think I can outfox him.'

Iris purchased a chocolate chip muffin and she and Liz had eaten the gooey top off it before the elevator reached the twelfth floor. They left the man with the glasses standing in the lobby. Iris blew him a kiss just as the elevator doors were closing.

Back in her office again, Iris dumped everything out of her purse and felt each inch of the lining. There were no bugs.

She returned all of her phone messages as quickly as she could and went through most of her mail with model efficiency, dispatching each item in such a way that it passed through her hands only once. She'd been distracted from her job responsibilities lately, but she needed to keep up appearances. Fortunately, her nutty boss Sam Eastman darkened her doorstep only occasionally and her day-to-day activities were not closely scrutinized by anyone. It was good to be king.

She picked up her office telephone to make a call then hesitated and returned the receiver to its cradle. She didn't think Weems would go so far as to bug her phone, much less her office phone, but she couldn't be too careful. She walked across the suite to Liz's office.

Liz was on a call on her telephone headset, rapidly jotting notes on a yellow pad and muttering, 'Uh-huh.' She gestured for Iris to come in.

Iris started talking, knowing that the headset blocked out background noise, preventing the person on the other end of Liz's line from hearing her. 'Let me borrow your cellular phone.'

Liz dug around in the huge leather handbag that she kept stashed on the floor under her desk and handed Iris the instrument without question. 'Yes, darling. I *completely* understand how you feel, but you'll only lose money if you sell the stock. It's just a blip. The price will come back up, sweetie.'

Back in her office, Iris dialed directory assistance for San Francisco. 'The Bay City Diner please.'

The operator said, 'Here's your number,' and a recorded voice spat digits at her, changing pitch and tone in a manner that unsuccessfully mimicked normal speech.

Iris dialed the number.

'Bay City Diner,' a woman answered.

'I'd like to leave a message for Douglas Melba. This is Margo Hill. I need him to call me as soon as possible at this number.' She gave the number of Liz's cellular phone.

189

Melba called back within fifteen minutes. 'Is this Margo Hill?'

'Mr Melba, my name is Iris Thorne. Margo Hill was an invention of the FBI and you know it.'

'Yeah, I figured that out when those two apes slapped handcuffs on me last night. I let Weems think that I didn't know you were part of his scam just to see what he would do next. So is this his next brilliant move?'

'I'm not working for Weems any longer.'

Melba snorted. 'And you expect me to believe that.'

'I do.'

'You're wasting my time. What I should do is come down there and knock your teeth out.'

Iris spent a moment considering his comment but carried on in spite of it. 'Mr Melba, I have a business proposition for you. It's worth five thousand dollars in cash. No cops. No FBI. Just you and me.'

There was silence on the other end of the line. Melba finally said, 'Why should I trust you?'

'Five thousand dollars, Mr Melba, in your pocket. Just hear me out.'

Melba didn't hang up.

Chapter 27

At 2:30 p.m., the end of the McKinney Alitzer workday, Liz Martini drove her Silver Shadow through the garage, passing Iris's red Triumph TR6 parked in her reserved spot. At the exit, she slid her key card into the slot. The gate lifted and she turned right onto Flower Street. From there it was a short drive to the Harbor Freeway. Today she took it southbound instead of her usual trip north to the junction with the 101 through the San Fernando Valley on her long trek to her house in the Malibu Colony.

'The coast is clear, Iris.'

Iris climbed onto the back seat from where she had been crouched on the floor and rubbed her knees.

'How are you going to get home tonight?' Liz said with concern.

'I've reserved a rental car at the airport. Can you pick me up on your way into the office tomorrow?'

'No problem. Did you get the cash?'

'I went down the back stairs and out the side door to the bank. You should have seen my shadow's face when I came walking in the front door of the building.' She chuckled. 'I asked him if he'd missed me and his face got beet red.'

'Five thousand dollars is a lot of money to throw away, Iris.'

'I'm not throwing it away.'

'I hope you know what you're doing.'

'I hope I know what I'm doing too.'

The posh Redwood Room in the Clift Hotel was a place where the only thing that had changed over the years was the menu. Steak tartare had been replaced by the more fashionable tuna tartare. The tall redwood-paneled room, overseen by obsequious waiters, had been the meeting spot for San Francisco's well-heeled for decades.

Douglas Melba started complaining as soon as he came in the door when the maitre d' forced a jacket and tie on him before he was allowed to enter. Melba disdainfully punched his flabby arms through the jacket sleeves and draped the tie round the neck of his knit shirt, to the amusement of Iris, who was sitting in a corner banquette, enjoying an outrageously overpriced glass of Chardonnay.

Melba walked brusquely toward her, his arms constrained by the tight jacket, pulled out the chair opposite and sat with his knees spread, his ample thighs not permitting any other posture. He smelt of cigarette smoke. 'I hate this fucking place. They charge an arm and a leg so you can hobnob with the city swells and be waited on by faggots.'

The comment was overheard by the waiter who didn't bat an eyelid but politely asked if the gentleman would like to order a cocktail.

'Gimme a Stoly rocks.' Melba drew his hands across his remaining dark hair, which had deeply receded into an interesting line, revealing a smattering of freckles across his head. Freckles also covered his chubby cheeks. When he smiled or grimaced, both of which he did frequently, revealing teeth crammed willy-nilly into his mouth, his freckled cheeks became as round as apples. With his thickly lashed eyes, he looked like a cherub gone bad. 'You look better as a blonde.'

Iris didn't know if the comment was intended to be a compliment but decided it was best to take it as one. 'Thank you.'

'Why did you come to the Greentree in disguise?' He answered his own question. 'Palmer and Lazare know you and you were trying to get them busted. What's your angle on this? Why were you working for Weems? You know because of that little event in Pasadena, my business is ruined. Everyone thinks I've got the hex on me or something.'

Iris couldn't have cared less. She kept her feelings to herself and waited for him to finish.

'Plus I didn't get shit from that deal. Palmer wouldn't even pay for my time or air fare. What do you think of that?' He drew back his freckled lips.

'I'm prepared to give you five thousand dollars right now.'

'I don't do business with cops or informants. I have principles.'

'I told you on the phone, I don't work for Weems anymore. I stupidly got involved with the fox, I don't want to go into details about how. Roger Weems threatened to arrest me and ruin my reputation unless I helped him. In my business, reputation is everything.' She reached inside her purse, pulled out an engraved silver case, slid out a business card with her thumb, and tossed it to him.

Melba picked up the card, read it, and tapped it against the table. 'Got any stock tips?'

'Sure. Don't forget that I nearly got shot last night. Weems lied to me and used me. He's no friend of mine.'

'I still don't believe you.' Melba flicked the card with his thumb. 'I want to make sure you're not wired.'

Iris upended her purse on the table, attracting curious glances from people at surrounding tables and a reproving look from the waiter as her belongings spilled across the pressed white linen tablecloth and a lipstick rolled onto the carpet. Melba squeezed the empty leather purse.

Iris slid from the banquette, took off her suit jacket and tossed it to Melba. As he searched her jacket, she stood with her back to him, legs akimbo. 'Go ahead.' She ignored the stares of the other people in proximity who with curiosity and disapproval were openly watching Melba pat Iris down with his ham fists. An older woman with a frozen hairstyle crooked her finger at the waiter who leaned over so she could speak in his ear.

Melba dropped his hands and Iris picked up her jacket, put it on, then slid into the banquette. She was gathering her belongings into her purse when the waiter came over.

'Is there anything wrong, any sort of a problem here?'

A smirk stretched Melba's thick freckled lips and he opened his mouth to speak but Iris jumped in first. 'Everything's just fine. I'd like another glass of wine please. Another drink, Mr Melba?'

Melba made a lazy gesture toward his empty glass and the waiter hurried off. Iris smiled pleasantly at the older woman who'd obviously complained and she quickly looked away.

Melba placed his palms on the table. 'So what do you want?'

'I have a buyer for the fox.'

'Here we go again.'

'I have many wealthy clients, Mr Melba. Some of them collect art. I made a discreet telephone call to one of them and told this individual that I might be able to negotiate a deal for the Tsarina's Fox. My client is very interested.'

'I'll contact Palmer and see what I can do.'

'Not good enough, Mr Melba. I want to contact Palmer directly.'

Melba pointed a stubby finger at Iris. 'You're not cutting me out of this deal. You're not the only one who almost got shot because of that damn fox.'

'I don't have any choice. You're tainted goods. The FBI is watching every move you make. You know they've tapped your office phone. I know for a fact they're going to put a bug in your home phone. Why do you think they let you go so easily? They hope you'll lead them to the fox. I can't risk that. I'm your last best chance to make any money from this deal.'

'If the FBI is watching me right now, they're watching you too.'

'That's my problem.'

'I'm not going to be cut out of the loop.'

'I can't use you, Mr Melba. That's final.'

Melba drew circles on the table top with the pads of his fingertips. 'So what's the deal?'

Iris picked up a small manila envelope from the banquette and placed it on the table. She kept her fingers on it like a chess piece move she was still evaluating. 'Five thousand dollars to put me in touch with Dean Palmer or Enrico Lazare.'

Melba eyed the envelope. 'All I have is the number of an answering service Enrico Lazare uses in Fresno. When I call I say I want to leave a message for Lazare. I give my name and number and Dean Palmer calls me back within twenty-four hours.'

193

Iris was still touching the envelope. 'You've never spoken to Lazare?'

'Never.'

'You don't know where Palmer is calling from?'

'No, but I think it's a public phone in a restaurant or something. I always hear people in the background and plates and things, like a diner or something.'

'Do you have the answering service number on you?'

He raised his hips to reach into his rear pants pocket. With difficulty he fished out a tiny black telephone book, licked his thumb and used it to turn the pages.

In her purse, Iris found another business card and a pen. Melba jotted down the number in an unusually flowery hand with loops and long tails.

Iris slipped the strap of her purse over her shoulder, tucked the manila envelope under her arm and left with the phone number.

She returned a few minutes later and tossed the envelope on the table in front of Melba. He eagerly picked it up and stuck his big hand inside, pulling the wad of bills out just far enough so he could thumb through them. The more he counted, the wider his close-mouthed smile stretched. After he'd finished, he let out a satisfied sigh as if he'd consumed a good meal, folded the envelope in half and distractedly shoved it in one of the pockets of the jacket. He pushed back his chair and stood. 'Thanks for the drinks.'

Iris extended her hand, catching him off guard. His relations with women didn't appear to include business deals. He clasped her hand with his moist palm.

'Thanks for meeting with me, Mr Melba.'

She watched as he quickly left the bar, only to have the maître d' chase after him to retrieve the borrowed jacket, hanging it in a closet after stripping it off Melba. Iris counted not quite to ten before Melba scurried back and demanded the jacket he'd been wearing. He safely retrieved the envelope containing the money and left.

It was just short of 10:00 p.m. when Iris drove the rental car into her driveway. A minivan she didn't recognize was parked across the street one house up from hers, right where Weems had parked when he had been watching her.

'Pay attention, boys,' she muttered to herself. 'You just might see something.'

She pulled her mail from the brass box next to her front door and went inside her house. It was a welcome sight. She immediately checked her phone messages on the answering machine she kept in her home office, holding her breath as she played back the two that were there, hoping she hadn't missed Palmer's call. They were both from Garland, the second one left an hour ago. He was worried about her and wanted her to call as soon as she got in, regardless of the hour.

She looked at her watch. From a public telephone in the Clift Hotel she'd left a message with Lazare's answering service for Palmer to call her at home at 10:00 p.m. She had call-waiting, but didn't want to awkwardly interrupt her talk with Garland if Palmer called. She'd have to call Garland later. He'd definitely try to stop her if he knew what she was up to. It was best if she kept it from him. He wouldn't understand. She didn't quite understand herself why she was doing it.

She pulled off her pumps with a groan and dangled them from her fingers as she walked into her bedroom and put them away on her shoe rack next to many other similar pairs in different colors. She closed the blinds over her windows, feeling slightly creepy at the thought that Weems or his people could be standing outside in the darkness watching her. She took off her jacket and began to unbutton her blouse when she saw something that unnerved her more than a Peeping Tom. The receiver on the telephone next to her bed was in the cradle backward, the end with the cord turned toward the top. She never hung up the phone that way.

She picked up the receiver, put it to her ear, and heard the loud, dead sound of the dial tone. There was no indication that the bug Weems had planted was there. She could have easily removed it from that phone and the others in her house, but there would be plenty of time for that later. She set the receiver back in the cradle the right way, suppressing the anger that welled inside her. As much as she resented the violation of her privacy, she had hoped that Weems would do something like this. She had played right into his hand and now he was playing into hers. She took off the rest of her clothes, brusquely wadding them for the dry cleaners, and put on her old terrycloth bathrobe.

It was 10:15 and she was starting to wonder whether she'd thrown away $5,000 for nothing. Then all the phones in her house rang in a chorus of different tones. She rushed to her bedroom and smiled when she saw the location and phone number displayed on her Caller ID device. The call was from Furnace Creek, California.

'Iris Thorne.'

'Hi, Iris, it's Dean Palmer.'

'Hi, Dean,' she said, trying to sound warm.

'Is this on the up and up?'

'Look, Dean. The FBI forced me to pose as Margo Hill. This agent, Roger Weems, threatened to arrest me if I didn't. You know me. I'm no FBI informant. I'm a stockbroker. I'm through with the FBI. This is between you and me now.'

'How did the FBI catch up with you?'

'Fernando Peru was an informant. He was passing on everything that happened with the fox to Roger Weems. Weems is an asshole. A real piece of work.' She poured it on for Weems's benefit through her bugged telephone line.

195

'If Peru was a rat, that explains a lot. What's your angle now?'

'I have a client who's willing to pay top dollar for the fox.'

'No bull?'

'No bull.'

'Why bother? Like you said, you're a stockbroker, not a stolen art fence.'

'Money,' she replied simply. 'When I heard about the cut Melba was getting by just hooking you up with a buyer, I thought to myself, I can do that.'

Palmer hesitated. 'I don't know, Iris. I have to talk to my partner. You were working for the FBI. I don't think he's going to go for it.'

'I explained how that happened. Look, I've got a client with lots of money. You need to unload this fox, the sooner the better. Things are hot for you now. You may not get another chance like this. The next deal you do will probably be with the FBI.' If there was one thing she excelled at, it was closing a sale.

'I'm ready for something to happen with this fox. I've got a lot invested to be sitting like a prisoner out here. And we've got a little power trip going on too, which is starting to get under my skin.'

'Think about it. Call me at this number.' She gave him Liz Martini's cellular phone number. 'If I don't hear from you by tomorrow, the deal's off.'

'That's not much time, Iris.'

'This has to be done pronto or not at all. I'm not going to wait around until the FBI gets wind of it.'

'Well, they won't hear about it from me or my partner. He's covered all our tracks. No one will ever find us.' Palmer blew out a puff of air as if he couldn't begin to tell her about it.

Iris looked at the Furnace Creek telephone number displayed on her Caller ID, confirming her belief in the importance of staying abreast of new technology. She glanced at the photocopy of the shots Todd had done of the Furnace Creek city marker with the donkeys standing in the shade of the shadow cast by the sign. 'Hey, who was the woman who picked up the urn at LAX?'

'Kathleen, my fiancée. She's a good gal. Puts up with a lot of crap.'

'Dean, you can make yourself a rich man with one phone call.'

'It's sounding sweeter by the moment.'

'Call me tomorrow.'

She hung up and called Garland, trying to sound as chipper as possible as she told him the truth, but not the whole truth. It didn't quite seem like lying that way, but it was a lie and it was getting too easy for her. She wondered whether rubbing elbows with thieves and liars was having a permanent adverse effect on her. She trusted it would go away as soon as she closed the deal for the fox.

She threw on some clothes, climbed into the rental car and drove to an all-night coffee shop on Pacific Coast Highway in Santa Monica. The van followed her.

It wasn't late enough for the real parade of weirdos through the coffee shop to begin. A few lonely souls hunkered over cups of coffee at the counter. Iris took a booth by the window so that her shadow in the van could keep an eye on her. She ordered a tuna salad sandwich on wheat toast and splurged on a chocolate shake. It was the first real meal she'd had since lunch that afternoon although she'd downed two saucers of hot, salted mixed nuts at the Redwood Room.

When she was midway through her sandwich, she got up and made her way through the restaurant to the ladies' room. Looking out of the corner of her eye through the big windows, she didn't see anyone leave the van to follow her. She was glad to see that the pay telephone near the restroom was unoccupied and functioning.

Chapter 28

Roger Weems entered the conference room in the Department of Justice office full of energy and good cheer. He looked dapper in a lightweight wool suit that fitted his athletic physique well but its dark color with his black hair gave him a sinister aura. Maybe Iris found this to be so only because she knew the man's true character.

'Iris Thorne!' he exclaimed. 'I was so pleased to receive your telephone call. What good news, what good news.' He was as effusive as a Pentecostal preacher at an Easter Sunday service. He pulled out a chair next to where Iris was sitting, sweeping it in a semicircle before planting himself down. He propped his elbows on his knees, steepled his hands and gazed at her over his fingertips, demonstrating that she had his full attention. 'What's on your mind?'

Iris knew darn well that he had listened to her telephone conversation with Dean Palmer. She didn't know whether he'd been shadowing Douglas Melba even though Melba had bought her line about that, probably because it made him feel important to think the FBI was following him. He could use it to impress a few of his cronies and maybe some dim-witted women, until he wore it out.

She set down the bogus Tsarina's Fox she'd been looking at while she'd waited for Weems to show up. She turned it so that the fake ruby eyes were looking at her as the fox slinked away. 'I got in touch with Dean Palmer.'

Weems leaned back and regarded Iris with surprise. 'How did you manage that?'

'I contacted Douglas Melba through the Bay City Diner. He gave me a number for an answering service that Lazare uses. I left a message there and Palmer called me back.'

'My, my, my, Iris. You are resourceful.'

'Did you know about the answering service?'

'Hell, of course we knew about it. It's a dead end. Registered to a post office box that's registered to some nonexistent address. What possessed you to do all this?'

'I've set up a buy for the fox. I told Palmer that I have a wealthy client, an art collector, who's willing to pay big money for it.'

'And he went for it even though he knows you were working for the FBI?'

Iris demurely clasped her hands in her lap. 'Well, I sort of ran you down to him. You're not any friend of mine and all that.'

He grinned, his small, square teeth gleaming. 'That's all right. Whatever it takes to get the job done. What did Palmer say?'

'He went for it. The way he talked, the situation between him and Lazare is starting to crumble. He wants to sell the fox and get his dough out fast.'

'When does this go down?'

'Tomorrow.'

Weems raised his eyebrows. 'Short notice. Well, I guess there's no time like the present. You've worked out the details with Palmer?'

'Yep. Public place, middle of the day.' She knew that Weems had heard her entire conversation with Palmer and was well aware of the arrangements she'd made to exchange the money and the fox.

Weems spread his arms. 'Maybe you should have considered a career in the FBI.'

She smiled blandly.

'Why are you going to all this trouble, Iris? I thought you wanted to put this whole incident behind you.'

'For the same reason I helped you in the first place. I want Todd Fillinger's murderer.'

'It's an honorable motive.'

'And I want you out of my life.'

The simpering grin faded from Weems's face. 'Now, Iris, I'm just trying to do my job.'

Iris privately considered the history of horrors committed with that as a justification. 'I suppose you are.'

It was late morning by the time Iris arrived at her office, and business was in full swing. The market had been on a roller-coaster ride for two weeks, hitting new highs then plunging hundreds of points when profit-takers took their money off the table, then soaring again as investors rushed in to snap up bargains. These cyclical periods had been so frequent lately that neither the bulls nor the bears paid much attention to them. During them, McKinney Alitzer's clients put in lots of calls to their brokers and Iris's staff conducted few transactions but held many hands. It came with the territory.

Iris's boss, Sam Eastman, was leaning over her desk when she came in. Louise had stepped away from her alcove so wasn't able to warn her.

'Sam, what a surprise,' Iris said truthfully. She wondered if he was here to tell her that he was retiring. Jim Hailey had told her that no one in the company at large would know that Sam had been forced into retirement. They'd let him leave with dignity. She was glad. Even though she and Sam had been adversaries, there was something sad about his departure. All things considered, he'd been an occasionally irritating but generally benign presence in her life. Unfortunately, he'd be remembered for his final accomplishment, the holy desk, which he was examining when she came in.

'I can't find it.' Bewildered, Sam traced his finger along the wood grain in Iris's desk where the obscure image of the Virgin Mary had been.

'Louise had the desk refinished.' Iris hung her jacket behind her door and stashed her purse in the top drawer of her filing cabinet.

'Huh.' His face dropped with disappointment. He recovered quickly and began rubbing his palms together in a gesture intended to suggest that he was about to impart exciting news. People who work together for years become as predictable to one another as old married couples.

'Well, Iris, I'm retiring. I know Jim Hailey's already broken the news to you, but I still wanted to tell you personally.'

'Jim did tell me. Congratulations, Sam.'

He put on his broad salesman's smile but his eyes seemed sad. 'My youngest is graduating from college this year and Janet and I thought it was time to enjoy life for a change.'

'It's wonderful. How many years have you been with McKinney Alitzer?'

'Twenty-five,' he said momentously.

'That's quite an accomplishment.'

He sat across from her, his arms stiff against the arms of the chair. 'I know Hailey's offered you the regional manager job. I told him I didn't know a better person to fill it.'

'Thanks, Sam. I'm touched,' she said sincerely.

'Well, I know we haven't always seen eye to eye, Iris. But I think you know how much I respect you and the job you've done here. Have you made your decision?'

She shook her head. 'I have to decide by the end of the week.'

'If you'll allow an old guy to give you a piece of advice, make certain it's what you really want to do. I've made a couple of career decisions based on what other people thought was the right thing for me. Let me tell you, it doesn't pay in the end.'

It suddenly occurred to Iris that Sam's bizarre behavior through the years was due to the fact that he hated his job. He'd felt forced into it. That's why he continually shot himself in the foot. He wanted to sabotage his career.

'Iris, I'm telling you this because I'm not convinced you want the job. I've known you a long time. If you really wanted the job, you would have decided by now. If the decision is taking too long to make, there's something amiss. There's no shame in being happy with where you are.'

He slapped his knees and pushed himself up. 'I hope I haven't spoken out of turn.'

'Not at all. I appreciate your candor.' She stood as well and held her hand out. He took it between both of his. 'Thanks for the advice, Sam.'

He patted the back of her hand then turned and left.

Iris was still standing, looking at the empty doorway, when Liz's cellular phone rang. It could have been Liz's hairdresser or manicurist or her dogs' hairdresser or manicurist or one of Liz's innumerable friends. She hoped the call wasn't for Liz.

She walked to her door and tipped it closed then picked up the ringing telephone. 'Iris Thorne.'

'It's Dean Palmer.'

'Dean.' She suppressed a sigh of relief. 'So glad you called. I've met with my buyer and the deal is good. Five million.'

'Five? That's great. That's more than we'd hoped for. The same arrangements we made last night?'

'Almost. My buyer wants a small change. Here's the deal . . .'

Chapter 29

Union Station in downtown Los Angeles, at noon on a weekday, was virtually empty. A brand-new light train system was being constructed and several lines had been completed, but Angelenos still preferred their cars. The sparse number of train travelers pleased Roger Weems, who sat on the last of several rows of massive wood benches, pretending to read a newspaper.

At the far end of the bench facing Weems, an aluminum briefcase full of money was standing on the ground next to the feet of a female FBI agent who was posing as the representative of the buyer of the Tsarina's Fox. Other undercover agents were nearby. Iris had told Weems she would not participate in the exchange this time. She had set the deal up and that was as far as she was going to take him. That was fine with him.

The aluminum briefcase contained hundred-dollar bills in banded stacks. Palmer would arrive with the fox and ask to see the money. The agent would quickly show it to him, then demand the fox. As soon as he handed the statuette over, Weems would arrest him. The female agent could easily arrest Palmer, but Weems had made it clear that this was his moment.

High noon, the arranged time for the deal to take place, came and went. Weems noisily turned a page of his newspaper and looked at his watch, even though a prominent clock high on the wall facing him displayed the correct time. Minutes ticked by. A homeless man attempted to sit next to Weems and there was a small altercation as Weems tried unsuccessfully to get him to move. A twenty dollar bill finally did the trick.

A man and a woman entered the station, looking around as if they weren't certain where they were going. They were thin and ragged and their clothes needed laundering.

Weems had seen Palmer only in photographs, and the man with sunken cheeks and jaundiced skin wandering through the station looked like a caricature of those photos. There were small sores on Palmer's hands. He looked like a junkie and the woman with him didn't look much better.

Weems carefully folded the paper into quarters. The FBI agent sitting with the briefcase caught the signal and turned to see Palmer and the woman scanning the benches with a hint of panic in their eyes.

Finally, Palmer spotted the aluminum briefcase. He tugged his partner's arm. She couldn't disguise her excitement and clasped Palmer's hand between both of hers. They scurried to the briefcase. Palmer asked the FBI agent, 'Is that it?'

'Dean Palmer?' she asked him.

'Yes. Is that it?' he sharply repeated.

'Just take it and let's get out of here,' his partner hissed.

'Kathleen, I have to check it out.' Palmer sat on the bench next to the agent. 'Well?'

'Go ahead.'

Palmer grabbed the briefacase handle, picked it up, and set it on the bench next to him. Kathleen wrung her hands and looked nervously around. 'Hurry up. Let's go.'

Palmer snapped the clasps and opened the case. He sucked in a breath when he saw the money then quickly ran his hands over it.

'Let's go,' Kathleen said urgently, dancing from foot to foot.

'I'm supposed to count it,' Palmer reminded her.

When he picked up a bundle of notes, the agent firmly grabbed his wrist. 'Wait a second. Not until I see the statuette.'

Palmer looked bewildered. 'What do you mean?'

Weems could no longer maintain his cover and openly watched the exchange.

'The statuette. The fox,' the agent whispered.

'It's not here,' Palmer said. He closed the briefcase and stood, holding it by the handle.

Kathleen could contain herself no longer. 'Let's get out of here!' She grabbed the briefcase. Surprised by its weight, she let it go and the bottom hit the ground, jerking her arm with it. She lifted it again and quickly made her way toward the exit.

'Hold it right there. Put your hands up.' Weems pulled his gun on Palmer, his booming voice attracting the attention of the few people within earshot. They scattered at the sight of the gun.

Palmer raised his hands above his head but Kathleen kept moving, ignoring the several men who approached her with guns drawn.

'Hold it! Ma'am, put the briefcase down.'

She kept walking toward the exit, not looking left or right.

'Kathleen!' Palmer shouted. 'Stop! It's not worth it!'

An agent grabbed her from behind and another wrenched the briefcase from her hand. They forced her against the station's glass doors, kicked her legs apart and searched her, finding a handgun in her large purse. She began sobbing hysterically and collapsed to the ground when handcuffs were snapped round her wrists, only to be roughly dragged to a standing position by two agents. Her feet barely touched the ground as they moved her near Palmer.

An agent patted Palmer down, finding a small caliber handgun.

Weems stood close to Palmer, his hands on his hips, his head cocked with his ear toward him as if he wanted to be certain to catch every word. 'What do you mean, the fox is not here?'

'It's not here,' Palmer said. 'That wasn't how the deal was supposed to go down.'

Weems winced and silently mouthed Palmer's words. He removed his hands from his hips, grabbed Palmer's bony shoulders and started shaking them. 'Where is it! Where the hell is it?'

Kathleen screamed, 'Don't hurt him!' and began sobbing again. Her knees bent and she crumpled to the ground. An agent pushed her to a bench where she folded into a heap.

Another agent pulled Weems off Palmer. Weems shook the agent's hands off him, then wheeled round, taking agitated steps, breathing deeply, his mouth working with unvoiced words. With barely maintained composure, he returned to Palmer and asked in a tight voice, 'Where is the fox?'

Palmer shrugged as if the answer was obvious. 'Zabriskie Point.'

Weems looked at the other agents with exasperation. 'Zabriskie . . .'

'It's in Death Valley,' one of them offered.

'Death Valley? That's three hundred miles from here. Get me a plane,' Weems ordered. '*Now*.'

Chapter 30

The Triumph TR6 looked like a bright drop of blood against the dun-colored desert sand. Iris turned off highway 127 and onto 178 which cut west then straight north through the heart of Death Valley. The thermometer she kept in her glove compartment indicated the temperature was 111 degrees. At a little past noon, the hottest part of the day was still to come.

The heat seemed to make the rippled, wind-swept low hills undulate, their smooth organic forms shifting suggestively as she drove past. The black asphalt shimmered, as if she was driving on air. Holding the steering wheel with her elbows, she opened the jug of water and took a miserly sip from it. She now realized that she should have brought more than one with her. She'd been in the desert for two hours and already water had become a precious commodity.

There was no one else on the road. Death Valley's two cities, Furnace Creek and Stovepipe Wells, had tiny year-round populations. The hotels and tourist attractions were mostly closed for the summer. Curiously, Death Valley in the height of summer was a favorite destination for European visitors who had nothing so vast, bare, and hot on their continent.

Iris entered the valley, framed by the Amargosa Mountains on the east and the Panamint Mountains to the west. The ground grew a white crust of salt. The valley's walls were marked with the multicolored hues of minerals exposed by the endless leeching effects of wind and sand. The painted hills were pale in the bright midday sun, but would come alive when the sun began its descent. Like a flower that only bloomed at night, the desert slept during the day. The white midday sky was as forbidding as the blackest night elsewhere.

Iris drove alone through this quiet world, like a bold and foolish intruder who mistook the plain, bland openness of the land for harmlessness. But the dangers presented by the desert were simply more subtle and insidious.

She headed up the valley wall until she reached Zabriskie Point, a jagged ridge that overlooked the entire valley. Benches were set around the perimeter next to steel railings framed with Plexiglas. Plastic-encased maps described the history of the spot and the landmarks visible from the point, which could be viewed through coin-operated telescopes positioned around the edge.

Iris parked the Triumph, grabbed a baseball cap and pulled it down low on her forehead. She stepped out into the heat that was only slightly worse than the temperature inside the car. Reaching back inside, she picked up a long-sleeved shirt which she put on to protect her bare arms from the sun. The Triumph's engine made small pinging noises after the long drive.

She slowly looked round, not seeing anyone else. She walked to one of the lookout points, her shoes loud against the sand, the dry air seeming to amplify sound, and leaned against the Plexiglas and steel barrier. A light wind whistled in her ears and sent loose sand whirling into the air. The valley stretched to her right and left as far as she could see, melting into a blur of sand and white sky.

Behind the jagged point were boulders and scrubby pine trees. She abruptly turned at a noise, real or imagined, behind a massive rock near where she'd parked. After standing motionlessly for a long while, her ears sifting through the unfamiliar sounds of the canyon made by the wind flowing across the barren land, she faced the steel railing, leaned against it, and waited.

Time passed. She touched the moisture that had formed on her upper lip and around the back of her neck. It quickly evaporated in the heat. She was daydreaming when she saw something moving on the valley floor. Finding a quarter in her pocket, she dropped it into the big telescope, the heart-shaped head sporting two thick eye-like lenses. The barrier inside the lenses dropped away and she turned the telescope toward the highway, swinging it too far in either direction until she finally got a bead on a car. A small motor inside the scope whirred as it counted off the time purchased for a quarter.

It was a sports utility vehicle in a dark color. It made the turn to ascend to the point, moving out of Iris's view. She walked away from the telescope and toward the road, hearing the telescope snap closed behind her.

Before long, the car came into view and drove onto the point. It was dark green and brand-new, still bearing the dealer's license plates. It turned a semicircle on the parking lot, scattering sand. When the engine was cut off, the slow whistling of the wind again took over.

Iris straightened her sunglasses, tugged the bill of her cap, and walked toward the car.

Todd Fillinger looked tanned and healthy for a dead man. He'd shaved the beard he'd grown and regained the weight he'd lost to better resemble his buddy, Mike Edgerton, and again had the physique of the football player he once was. In his hand he carried something wrapped in red velvet. Iris guessed it was the Tsarina's Fox. A handgun was jammed inside the waistband of his jeans. He wasn't happy to see her.

'Where's Palmer? Why didn't he call me?'

'The FBI probably has him by now.'

'Just as well. At least he's out of my hair. And I still have the fox, or do I?' He looked around. 'Where's your cavalry?'

She shrugged.

'Pretty ballsy, Iris. Pretty ballsy.' He pointed his index finger at her. 'I always liked that about you.' He walked to the railing and leaned against it. 'So what's this meeting for? Did you bring the money yourself?'

'There's no money.'

'No money, no foxy, Iris.' He held up the velvet-encased object and twisted his hand at her. 'So what's the point of this meeting, then? You don't even seem surprised to see me. Weren't you expecting Enrico Lazare?'

'I figured out what you did.'

'Really? How?'

'Pieced it together.'

Todd bent his neck back and forth as if it was stiff and he was only marginally interested in what she had to say.

'I know all about Mike and Mona Edgerton.'

'Mike and Mona,' Todd slowly repeated. 'Two of the dumbest people on earth.' He shuddered theatrically. 'Scary, isn't it?'

Iris remembered that about him. The broad gestures, almost as if he was playing to an audience. She licked her dry lips. 'I saw your sister. Met your brother-in-law, your niece, and your nephew.'

'You've been a busy girl. That's one thing about Iris Thorne, boy oh boy, never lets any grass grow under her feet.'

Undeterred by his sarcasm, she went on, determined to say what she had come all this way to tell him. 'They were very sad to hear about your murder. Your sister cried a great deal about the two of you. Told me a lot about how you grew up, your life, what happened to your parents. I know the whole story. Why didn't you just tell me the truth, Todd?'

He raised his hands and his shoulders. 'Because it was ugly. Why live an ugly reality when you can create a beautiful fantasy?'

'How did you get Mike Edgerton to go to Moscow and pretend he was you?'

Todd smiled broadly and chuckled quietly as if relishing the memory. 'Getting him over there was easy. Money talks. Once I got him to Moscow, I told him I was trying to throw some guys off my track while I went to pick up some money. Could he dress like me and stand on the hotel steps? I met him around the corner from the hotel and gave him my coat and jewelry. I wanted to make sure he wore my ring and watch on the slight chance you'd notice.' He flicked his hand dismissively. 'No brainer.'

'Why were you on the run? Was Lazare after you?'

'After me?' He threw his head back and laughed. 'That was the least of my problems. He'd been after me for years, ever since Paris. I owed him money. He made a bigger deal about it than it was worth. One night, I saw him in a club in Moscow. He went there on business and didn't even know I was living there. Wouldn't you know, the idiot wanted to start it up again. I got him to meet me on the outskirts of town and killed him.' He shrugged as if it couldn't have been avoided.

'I hid the body. Did a damn good job of it, too. But I knew I was in deep this time. Then this baby turned up,' he held up the velvet-shrouded fox, 'and I saw a way out but good. I figured Todd Fillinger had run out of luck. His future looked bleak. Time to leave him behind.'

He walked over to her, peeling away the red velvet that concealed the fox. 'Want to see it?'

The solid gold was cold and heavy in her hands. The blue diamonds set in rows covering the statuette's back and sides broke the bright sunlight into a kaleidoscope of rainbow colors. The rubies in its eyes were deep red. The statuette was the same size and shape as Weems's imitation and depicted a fox crouching with its tail low between its haunches, looking back over its shoulder, slinking away. The tongue lolled from an upturned mouth that suggested a satisfied smile from having got away with some misdeed.

Iris turned it over and over in her hands, mesmerized by the brilliant jewels which grew warmer from the desert sun and her touch.

He watched her face to see her reaction. 'Is it as beautiful as you thought it would be?'

She blinked back tears that welled in her eyes, thinking of Winslow, Peru, the Edgertons, and God only knows how many other people through the decades who had died because of the fox. 'More.'

He plucked it from her then slid his hand over hers, squeezing them gently. 'It's good to see you again.' He stared deeply into her eyes, moving his hand to her face, caressing the line of her jaw. He raised her chin and gently kissed her lips. He slowly pulled back. 'Do you want to come with me?'

She rested her hand against his cheek and looked into his soft brown eyes. 'Todd, you had everything going for you.'

'Yeah,' he agreed, his voice thick. 'I guess you're not coming with me.'

She shook her head.

He rested his hand on the gun in his waistband. 'Then I have to kill you.' He rapidly blinked at her, his face contorted. 'I wish you hadn't come here. Why did you?'

Her breathing grew shallow as she eyed the gun. She slowly stepped away from him. 'I wanted you to know that you hadn't gotten away with it.'

He raised his eyebrows and sighed with great sadness, then grabbed the butt of the gun. A voice startled them.

'Please place your weapon on the ground in front of you and clasp your hands behind your head.'

They turned to see Konstantin Markov walk into the clearing from behind a large boulder. Beads of perspiration dotted his bald head. Damp circles had formed in the armpits of his white dress shirt which was tightly tucked into black slacks. Thick black hair curled through the opening underneath his partially unbuttoned shirt. He extended a hand

210

toward Todd then gestured at the ground. 'Mr Fillinger, your weapon, please.'

Todd snarled at Iris, still clutching the butt of his gun. 'Markov? You called Markov?'

'Mr Fillinger, I'd advise against making any sudden movements,' Markov warned in his careful English. 'Place your weapon on the ground in front of you, please.'

Todd pulled out his gun and aimed it toward Iris who screamed and dropped to her knees. A loud cracking noise exploded from the boulders behind the point. Todd wrenched his body backward. The fox flew from his grasp and scuttled across the sand, the velvet lightly landing like a butterfly near his feet. The echo of the gunshot reverberated down the canyon, over and over, long after the gun that fired it was quiet. Blood oozed from the back of Todd's head. It didn't spread far across the sand before it was absorbed by the thirsty earth.

Iris pulled her hands away from her face to see Markov gently blowing sand off the fox. He reached down to pick up its velvet wrapper. He slapped the cloth against his thigh, trying to knock the sand from it.

Markov's sharpshooter stood over Todd, his high-powered rifle slung over his shoulder. He prodded Todd with his foot, but it was unnecessary. The single bullet had struck Todd squarely between the eyes. Markov said a few words to his gunman in Russian, and the young shooter walked away from the body and into the boulders and pine trees behind the point.

'I am sorry, Miss Thorne,' Markov apologized. 'We had hoped that it wouldn't turn out like this, but as you witnessed for yourself, Mr Fillinger gave us no other choice.'

She cringed from the body, her face ashen.

Markov held up his prize, admiring the fox in the sun. His delicately outlined, upturned lips curved a bit more and he uttered a small sound of pleasure, then quickly wrapped the red velvet round the fox.

'I'm very sorry to leave you here like this, but we must make our departure.' He held his hand toward her and when she raised hers, he gently held her fingers and pulled the back of her hand to his lips. 'If there is anything I can ever do for you at any time, please do not hesitate to contact me.' He took a step back and with his hands held by his sides, he quickly bowed toward her. He turned on the heel of his well-polished shoes and walked across the point, disappearing behind the rocks and scrubby trees.

Iris returned to her car, trying to avoid looking at Todd's body. She gagged once, tried to stifle another one, couldn't, and vomited. Dizzy, she leaned against the hot steel of the car. Finally managing to pull open the door, she sat behind the steering wheel and took a drink of water that was hot in the plastic bottle, swished it in her mouth, and spat it on the ground. She drank some after that, then splashed water on her face and neck. The drops that ran into her mouth were salty. She held her head in her hands and breathed deeply.

She heard an engine kick over followed by the whoop, whoop of helicopter blades, slowly increasing in velocity. She climbed from the car, still unsteady on her feet, and watched as the helicopter swooped low and traveled over the canyon. While she was watching it grow smaller and smaller, several cars pulled onto the point, their tires skidding on the sand as the drivers carelessly screeched to a stop.

People spilled from the cars and busily scattered this way and that with much shouting and confusion. Roger Weems wasted no time. He marched over to her and angrily pointed at the body as if it was a toy mislaid by a careless child. 'Iris, who in God's green earth is that?'

'Todd Fillinger.' She drank another swig of water.

'Todd . . .' He quickly turned his head from side to side as he tried to process the information. 'What did you say?' Then another issue took precedence. 'Where's my fox?'

Iris slowly screwed the plastic top back on the water bottle then pointed to the helicopter which was now a small dot at the end of the canyon. 'Todd was robbed by Konstantin Markov.'

'*Who?*'

'Markov. The head of security for Nikolai Kosyakov, the man Todd stole the fox from who owns the Club Ukrainiya.'

'*Markov?* How the hell . . .' He gave her a bilious look. 'What are you trying to pull here? I have a feeling I've been set up and I don't like it.'

'That makes two of us.'

Epilogue

Iris opened the glass doors of the McKinney Alitzer suite and gave a cheery hello to the receptionist and everyone else she passed on her way to her office. The junior investment counselors were working away in the bull pen, the senior people were wheeling and dealing in their private offices, and Liz Martini, the stockbroker diva, was late, as usual.

'Morning, Louise.'

'Good morning, Iris.'

Iris had barely finished hanging her jacket behind the door and stowing her purse in the filing cabinet when Louise placed a fresh cup of hot coffee in her mug on her desk.

'Thank you,' Iris muttered as she looked through her phone messages.

Louise lingered in the doorway and Iris expectantly looked up at her. 'I thought it was a lovely retirement party for Sam.'

'It was very nice. I know he was touched that so many people came.'

Louise smiled fondly at Iris. 'He was touched by your speech.'

'We've had our differences, Sam and I, but I'm glad we managed to resolve them.'

'Iris, I'm not only speaking for myself when I tell you that I'm glad you didn't take the regional manager position, for purely selfish reasons, of course. We're all glad you decided to put up with us at least a little bit longer.'

Iris blinked back tears. 'Come on, Louise! Don't make me cry so early in the morning. I have the rest of the day to get through.' She pulled a tissue from the box in her desk drawer. 'Who would have thought? The girl who never met a promotion she didn't like or a pay rise she couldn't live without.'

'When does the new guy start?'

'Next week. He's supposed to be a pistol.'

'Guess we'll have to be on our best behavior for a while anyway.'

Iris gave her a careless wave. 'We're gold. No, make that platinum.'

Louise started to leave then returned to Iris's doorway. 'Oh, Tracy Beale called. They're going to scatter her brother Todd's ashes two weeks from Saturday and would like you to attend if you can.'

'Did she say where?'

'Death Valley.'

213

Iris twisted her shoulders as a chill went down her spine.

'She said it was one of Todd's favorite places and somehow it seemed appropriate.'

Iris smiled sadly. 'I think Todd would have liked it.'

'How does the family feel about this situation with Todd? Are they mad at you?'

'Shocked, dismayed, sad, but not mad. Tracy's pleased that I tried to preserve Todd's memory for her, but on the other hand she's glad he didn't get away with murder.' She rested her chin in her hand and gazed across the room. 'Markov wasn't supposed to shoot him.'

'From the way you described it, it was either Todd or you.'

Liz's assistant pushed past Louise and into Iris's office. 'Excuse me, Iris, but I must speak with you.' He sneezed violently several times and his eyes were watering. 'She's brought in those damn dogs again.'

Liz pushed in behind him, cradling Thelma and Louise under each arm. The assistant yelped and jogged across the room away from them.

Liz darted a brightly enameled fingernail at Iris. 'Iris, if Mr Sensitive can't handle me bringing in my dogs once in a while—'

'Once in a while!' the assistant exclaimed.

Louise quietly slipped back to her desk, leaving Iris to begin another workday.

Iris reclined in a lounge chair in her backyard. It was late Friday afternoon. Scattered clouds were moving across the sky and watching them created the illusion that she was the one who was moving, as if she was lying on a raft in the middle of the ocean. A shadow fell across her eyes, followed by the face of Garland. He kissed her sweetly on the lips.

'Hello,' she said. 'I didn't expect you until later.'

'I caught an earlier flight. I rang the doorbell and when you didn't answer, I let myself in with the key you gave me. I hope it's all right.'

'I wouldn't have given you a key if I didn't expect you to use it.'

He brushed a strand of hair from her face. 'She turns down a job promotion, gives a smelly, sweaty man the key to her inner sanctum. Where's the Iris Thorne I knew?'

'She's still here. She just stopped running. It was a good, long run but now it's nice to relax, take a deep breath.'

He rubbed his thumb across her fingers. 'I brought in your mail. The rest of it looked like bills and junk, but you got a postcard.'

Iris propped herself up on an elbow and looked at the colorful picture postcard of Istanbul. The message had been written with a blue fountain pen in small and precise handwriting:

Miss Thorne,
I mail you this card from Istanbul, but do not attempt to contact me here as I am simply passing through. I considered that you might

214

appreciate news of the Tsarina's Fox since you have been so intimately involved with this notorious and, some would say, cursed statuette. After I left Death Valley, I did not return to the employ of Nikolai Kosyakov but quickly made my way to the home of a very wealthy individual who had contacted me in Moscow regarding possible purchase of the fox. The fox was safely delivered to this individual who was very happy to obtain it and for which I was paid handsomely. I now start a new life. I want to express to you again my sorrow for how things turned out with your friend Mr Fillinger, but I acted with your safety in mind.

I wish you well, Miss Thorne. You are a woman of bravery and integrity, qualities which are dear to my heart.

Konstantin Markov

'How about that?' Iris said.

'That's information your Roger Weems might like to have.'

'I bet he would.' Iris sat up and tore the postcard in half then quarters, continuing to tear it until it was in small pieces. 'But it's over. All over.'

He sat next to her. 'Except for us.'

'That's only just beginning.'